Cottonwood Saints

University of New Mexico Press ■ Albuquerque

Cottonwood
Saints

A NOVEL

Gene Guerin

© 2005 by Gene Guerin
All rights reserved. Published 2005
Printed in the United States of America
09 08 07 06 05   1 2 3 4 5

LIBRARY OF CONGRESS CATALOGING-IN-PUBLICATION DATA

Guerin, Gene, 1938–
Cottonwood saints / Gene Guerin.
p. cm.
ISBN 0-8263-3724-4 (pbk. : alk. paper)
1. Women—New Mexico—Fiction.
2. Las Vegas (N.M.)—Fiction.
3. Mothers and sons—Fiction.
4. Rural families—Fiction. I. Title.
PS3607.U46C68 2005
813'.6—dc22

2005015318

DESIGN AND COMPOSITION: *Mina Yamashita*

For

Margaret Ortega Guerin

Part One

Margarita Juana

Chapter One

I am Michael Galván.

I am a defrocked priest.

I say this now to get it out of the way. I have no interest in saving this revelation for later melodramatic effect, for this story is neither about religion nor religious crisis, at least not in the usual sense. To attach some exaggerated weight to my clerical failures, and there were many, would serve no purpose except to sidetrack from this narrative.

Just know this. I have an enemy that I love. She is full of promises unkept. Yet, I continue to pursue her, hoping. She is both comforting and cruel. She manipulates. She nurtures. She is New Mexico. She is a land that oftentimes seems more phantasmagoria than place.

Los santos know this place for what she is. That is why these religious images, carved from cottonwood by long-dead artisans, are all so sad—the melancholy Virgin Mother, the fiercely armed St. Michael, the brooding St. Anthony, all coated with gesso and painted in vivid comic-book colors, with lacquer-black hair, large, dark, almond-shaped eyes, pink skin and thin, serious, red lips; the Christ figures with vermilion blood streaming from open sores on knees, elbows, torsos, and thorn-encrusted heads; and, La Muerte, a skeletal, unpainted crone in raw wood with no adornment save strands of stringy human hair attached to its grinning skull, seated with droll dignity atop a wooden cart drawn by who knows what invisible nightmares.

Perhaps I make too much of this New Mexico.

Only the cottonwood saints know for sure.

1913

On a warm day in June, not one of the cruel days but one that spoke of early summer promise, a female baby was born in a lumber camp wedged into a canyon at the eight-thousand-foot elevation of the Pecos Wilderness in the Sangre de Cristo mountain range. She was born to Leopoldo Zamora and Tamar Pacheco, their first viable offspring after two stillbirths.

Tamar delivered her on a crude, wood-framed bed in a long, narrow one-room house. A previous owner had thrown together the shelter with lumber milled on site from the massive ponderosa pines that blocked out the sun for great stretches up and down the steeply sloping canyon walls.

The shaper of the canyon was a small, unruly stream spawned from snow melt higher up. The river, for that is the designation New Mexicans give to any trickle of moisture that has a current and can sustain vegetation, rushed headlong over boulders and fallen tree carcasses to cut a deep, narrow passage through high banks thickly carpeted with dead pine needles. The water was always cold, always noisy.

The sounds at the birthing were scatter-shot, undisciplined. Outside there was the uneven putt-a-putt of an old gas engine straining to move the wide, flopping canvas belt that turned a large circular blade. There was the screech of the double-pointed saw teeth that bit and churned the seasoned logs into planks. Chipmunks chattered to each other to warn of a high circling hawk.

Inside, Tamar forced short pantings and grunts through her clenched teeth and flared nostrils.

Overall, the woman in labor was of a plain sort. Her face was broad. By the bump on its bridge her nose might qualify as Roman except that it lost its classic look as it spread out into thick, pulpy nostrils. Her eyes were brown, running to yellow. Her bones were large and her hands, even at twenty, already showed arthritic swellings at the knuckles from too many days doing laundry in frigid waters. She now used these hands to grip the sides of the bed while she dug her heels, red and raw, into the coarse flannel sheeting.

Tamar's husband, Leopoldo, was not present at the birth. He had left early that morning with a pair of draft horses in harness to bring in a giant of a tree that he and one of the mill hands had felled and trimmed the previous day.

Even had Leopoldo remained, his wife would not have permitted him in the room with her. Instead, when her water broke, Tamar summoned Don Kiko, the camp cook, to attend her.

Don Kiko's boast to her when she called for him in her desperation was that he had delivered many calves and foals and had even performed a caesarean on a ewe with a breached lambkin. "I sewed

up her belly with an umbrella spoke and a piece of string. She
bounced right up and began to eat some sweet clover. She was fine,"
he added quickly to assure Tamar of his competence.

"*Ándale*, Doña Tamar, *ándale*," Don Kiko now urged. "I can see
the top of the head. Many black hairs. Now is the time. Get the business done."

So glazed were Tamar's eyes that it was impossible to tell whether
they were filled with pain, anxiety, or sheer hatred for Don Kiko and
all men.

He struggled to gain purchase of the back of the baby's head.
"*Otra vez*. Try again. There. I have it. Give it to me now."

With one final push, Tamar evacuated her belly. Suddenly Don
Kiko's hands held a confusion of blood, a small amount of greenish-
brown, watery feces, clots of mucus, and a solid lump of baby.
Quickly he reached for the towel he had draped, for modesty's sake,
over Tamar's splayed thighs and with the same motion pulled her cotton nightshirt down over her lower torso. He balanced the slimy newborn in one hand and arranged the towel over the other. Then he
deftly transferred the tiny bundle of flesh and began to wipe it.

"*Una mujercita*. And so small. This one may not live."

He glanced at Tamar for some reaction but all he saw were her
half-closed bobcat eyes.

Back to the work at hand.

First the umbilical cord, gnarly, opaline, and obscenely thick.
Such a fat conduit of nutrients and oxygen for such a small and fragile creature. No matter. In all likelihood they would be ready to bury
la pobrecita by the time Leopoldo returned home.

Don Kiko tied off the cord with a short length of cotton twine,
snipped it, and set the newborn adrift from its mother.

His mind went on to other things. What were the protocols?
Should they wait for Leopoldo in case they had to baptize the baby
without the priest? Who should give the name, the father being
absent and the mother incapacitated? Who was the family saint?
Whose feast was being celebrated on the Church calendar that day?
If the child died, who would say the prayers? Would Leopoldo even
want to be here for the burial? Would it not be better for him not to
see the daughter he would never know?

Don Kiko looked at the baby, now face down in repose on Tamar's stomach. He sensed, more than saw, a slight movement, a quiver, a spasm. But it was making no sounds. Of course. Unlike calves, foals, and lambs, human infants sometimes needed a reminder that they were now part of this world.

He grasped the baby by her feet, dangled her away from him, and directed a sharp slap to her soft, wrinkled, conical butt cheeks. There was an immediate response, a not-too-loud but quite definite yelp from the vicinity of the small head. He righted the child and looked into her face. The features were screwed up into a tight mask, then the mouth opened, and Don Kiko heard a wail loud as any he had heard from his barnyard progeny.

He held the baby up to the face of the exhausted woman.

"*¿No ves*, Doña Tamar? Not more than three pounds I would guess. But she wants to live. *¿Quién sabe?* It is in God's hands."

Don Kiko was beside himself with excitement. He had waited for several hours in the shadow of the house, so that he would not have to speak with any of the mill hands. It seemed only proper that the father of the child be the first to hear the news. Finally, when he saw the giant pair of gray horses turn down the bend beyond the house, he rushed up the slope. "Leopoldo, Leopoldo. You have a daughter. Very small and very puny. She may not live, but who knows? I've seen stranger things happen. Perhaps we should pray for a miracle. *¿Quién sabe?* Who can say what would be better? Doña Tamar is resting but she is fine. She says she will be up for supper."

At this moment Leopoldo had other things on his mind.

The horses were in a mighty struggle to drag the massive log over one last rise and they were losing ground. Behind them a clean straight trench of dark earth marked the sparse meadow grass where they had passed with such ease. But now the earth was roiled with gouges from hooves and from the log, which had decided to dig in like a stubborn child.

Leopoldo reached up with his forearm to wipe the sweat dripping into his eyes. "Not now."

Had he heard anything Don Kiko had told him?

Leopoldo's eyes were narrowed with the effort it took to keep

the giant brace in line. His chin ran brown with tobacco juice from
a forgotten wad in his left cheek. His heels dredged the loamy soil
and he muttered half syllables unintelligible to any living thing
except the horses.

Gravity was beginning to win the battle. The log slid slowly, laterally
down the embankment toward an arroyo that ran alongside the rise.

Don Kiko at last appreciated how irrelevant the news of the baby
girl was at this moment. She was born. She might live. She could die.
And there was nothing these two men and this team of horses could
do about it.

Jumping to the high ground above the team, he picked up small
rocks and pinecones to throw against the wide flank of the lead,
uphill horse.

"¡Ándale! ¡Ándale!"

For a painful instant, the top horse slipped sideways. Its hind
hooves scooped out generous clumps of dirt. At last, the animal stiffened its legs and the sliding slowed, then stopped. The downhill
horse, smaller and younger, now had time to recover.

Leopoldo clucked and shook the reins and both horses began to
pull again as a team. The log lurched, then moved across a small
swale. Finally, amid curses and coaxings, they reached level ground
and came to a stop.

Sweat ran freely down Leopoldo's face and neck from underneath
his battered felt fedora. He exhaled loudly, unraveled the reins from
around his gloved hands and tossed them unto the log. Off came the
gloves and out came a dirty blue-patterned rag from his back pocket.
He removed the hat and slowly mopped the perspiration from the
crown of his head along the back of the neck and over his face,
streaking the tobacco juice across one cheek.

Don Kiko lobbed a final pinecone in the general direction of the
horses and beamed at his *patrón*.

"We did it. *Gracias a Tatita Dios.*"

Leopoldo slapped his gloves sharply against the log. "What were
you thinking? Running up like that? Screaming like a crazy man? I
could have lost the horses."

The slap at the log might as well have been across Don Kiko's
face.

"But I helped."

"Helped what? I didn't need help until you came with all your yelling!"

Don Kiko stood up slowly, and with whatever dignity the slippery slope allowed. Straightened to his full five foot three, he spat out his words.

"You have a daughter. She will probably die."

With that he stuck his hands in the rear pockets of his overalls and walked down the incline into the meadow. He fully expected Leopoldo to call him back. If he did, he would pay no mind. Let Leopoldo beg for news of a most difficult birth.

But Leopoldo did not call to him. He was not so much as thinking of Don Kiko. So it had happened. The child had come early. So much for his promise to Tamar to get her to her aunt's house before her time. A little girl. If she were to die like the other two, let it be now, before he knew her.

He picked up the reins and made a clicking noise with his tongue. The horses lifted their heads from their desultory grazing and pricked their ears. So soon? Never mind. They were ready.

The team leaned forward. Their shoulders stiffened and rippled with effort.

For a moment the horses swayed side to side and strained the harnesses to their snapping point. Slowly they broke the inertia of the log, gained momentum, and moved down the hollow toward the blue smoke of the sawmill and home.

With the help of the men running the saw, Leopoldo turned the log out onto a wooden trestle. He unhitched and unharnessed the horses, watered them, fixed their feed bags around their soft, cottony snouts, and wiped them down with a piece of burlap. Some final pats to their haunches and he started toward the house.

He could see Don Kiko, who stood in wait several feet from the doorway paying ceremonious attention to a fingernail.

Stupid little man.

Leopoldo made to pass him in silence. They had nothing more to say to each other.

"Aren't you even going to wash yourself?" With that parting shot,

Don Kiko strolled away, now thoroughly involved in his manicure.

Leopoldo stopped and looked at his own hands, rough and scratched, with dirt crammed into cracks and under fingernails. He turned and walked to the side of the house.

The former owner had sunk an open steel drum into the ground nearly up to its flanged lip. This created a small cistern, into which flowed a tiny rivulet from an underwater spring that broke to the surface just above the house. The overflow spilled out the far edge to continue its journey to the river beyond.

To one side of the drum lay a weathered section of planking. On it sat a rusting coffee can lid that held a cracked piece of yellow lye soap.

Leopoldo knelt on the plank, cupped his hands, and filled his mouth with water. The water was so cold it electrified his teeth. He swirled it gingerly around until he could feel the grit of the mountain and the scum from his tobacco wad wash loosely around his tongue. He spat to the side and took more water, this time to drink. Then he rolled up his sleeves and picked up the plug of soap.

He scrubbed away at his neck, face, and hands and ignored the burning of the oily suds on his skin. When he was done with the lathering he leaned over and plunged his arms up to the elbows into the perfect circle of icy water. He splashed his face several times until he was reasonably sure he was properly rinsed. Finally, he stood and pulled out the blue rag to dry himself.

The milky film he had created on the surface of the water swirled in the drum, then began to wash over the side and into the downhill stream. For a moment he followed the soapy residue as it moved away.

It was time.

Don Kiko was nowhere to be seen. Good.

When he stepped inside from the glaring sunlight, Leopoldo was momentarily blinded. He knew where the bed was so instinctively he moved in that direction. Off to his right, in a corner, he heard the sound of splashing water. He turned and saw Tamar.

She did not sense him.

She stood in a shallow basin. Her nightshirt was hitched up and gathered into a cloth belt to expose her narrow thighs. She poured water from a ceramic pitcher down the insides of her legs and rubbed the skin with her free hand. The strokes were hard, impatient.

Leopoldo took the moment to study his *esposa*. It was not love that he felt. Perhaps loyalty, even admiration, but certainly not affection. She seemed all right. A little pale and puffy faced but nothing more. She had prevailed, and more, she was up and about.

He looked away before he spoke so that she would not be embarrassed when he made his presence known.

"Don Kiko says we have a little girl."

Tamar shot her head upward in surprise then quickly, to conceal her nakedness, jerked closed a blanket draped over a cord that was stretched between two nails.

Leopoldo heard the pitcher replaced on the washstand. Then the water rippled as Tamar stepped out of the basin.

"Yes," she said from behind the privacy of the blanket, "another daughter."

Well, not strictly speaking, he could argue. They had no other daughters, only two vaguely remembered dead babies.

Leopoldo took it on himself to approach the bed. At first he could see nothing that indicated a living thing. But there, between two pillows, was a small bundle. He reached down and pulled back a loose corner of the swaddling cloth. What he saw was a tiny head plastered with dank, dark hair, the cheeks and forehead dusted with soft, reddish down.

He could tell nothing from what he saw. Did she resemble one of them? Did she even resemble a person he knew or might want to know? He could not tell.

He heard the swish of the blanket rubbing on the cord.

With the basin at arm's length, the barefoot Tamar padded across the gray planking. Her wet feet left darkish prints where she stepped. At the open door she tossed the water from the basin to one side of the stoop.

"Very small," he said.

Back in the room, Tamar set the basin on the washstand and took a towel hanging on a nail. She let herself down heavily on the bed, her back to her husband, and began to dry her ankles and feet. She still had not looked at him.

"And you?" he asked.

"We must take her to Mora. She needs to be baptized."

Leopoldo reached out to touch Tamar's shoulder but thought

better of it. Instead he stooped to replace the flap over the baby's head. He rested his hand on the covered lump for a moment, then stood straight and walked to the door.

"I'll go load the wagon. You have a name?"

"Margarita Juana, like the other two."

"Margarita Juana. Pray God it brings her better luck than it brought her sisters."

They left the camp before daybreak. The only transport available to them was a high-riding wheeled platform, somewhat resembling a giant buckboard, which Leopoldo used to haul lumber from the mill into town.

He and Don Kiko, mollified by now, had spent the entire night loading the wagon with freshly lumbered planks.

There were two very practical reasons for doing this. The first was monetary. Why take a long and arduous trip down the canyon and into town without some financial return? The other reason had to do with safety and comfort. The wagon was designed to carry heavy loads. Its springs were massive and impossible to flex without several tons of lumber pressing down on them. To ride without a load was courting disaster. One medium-sized bump would be enough to send the wagon bouncing high into the air. Passengers could go flying off their lofty perch onto the hard, unforgiving road or into the boulder-studded river.

The couple did not speak, partly because of the noise from the iron-clad wheels against the hard pan of the road and from the loudly creaking wagon, but mainly because there was not much they knew to say to each other.

Tamar held a cardboard shoebox on her lap. She had warmed a bucket of bran and spread the seed husks to about a three-inch depth in the bottom of the box. Over this she placed several plies of flannel and into this warm nest she transferred the infant. Thus insulated and secure, the baby lay quiet.

Stopping only occasionally to rest and to feed and water the horses, it took them until midmorning the next day to reach Mora. Tamar's milk was slow in coming but, conveniently, the baby did not have much of an appetite.

Their specific destination was the hacienda of Tamar's Uncle

Delfino and Aunt Adela Arellanes. They were blessed with all manner of riches: land, livestock, and a general mercantile store. But the greatest treasure of all had eluded them. They had no children. Custom thus dictated that they take in a child from their extended family. Tamar had been their surrogate daughter since birth. Tamar's mother, Adela's younger sister, was rich in children but little else.

When Tía Adela heard the rumbling and creaking of the lumber cart coming up the narrow lane to their large, territorial-style house she was not surprised. She had been expecting them for several weeks. It had been decided on an earlier visit that Tamar would deliver her baby there, under the ministrations of Nasha, the indentured Indian servant. She walked out to the courtyard and waited. Look at them— like two gypsies, wagon and all.

She had never fully embraced the marriage between Tamar and Leopoldo but usually managed to keep her counsel to herself. Leopoldo, to give him his due, was a hard worker and handsome to boot. He had the reddish blond hair and blue eyes that marked him as someone with European breeding in a land where the blood lines between Spanish and Indian had long been blurred in converging streams of dark and light. Also, to be frank, and Adela prided herself on her honesty, Tamar, despite a generous dowry, had not attracted much male attention, being plain and with a tendency to surliness.

Leopoldo said that he hailed from California. He came to Mora, as he put it to Don Delfino, "to look for opportunities."

Tamar was instantly smitten. She was unaware of, or chose to ignore, what everyone in Mora was saying behind her back: "She has money and the Californian needs money."

After their marriage, Leopoldo invested some of Tamar's dowry in a saloon. Unfortunately, his clientele consisted in the main of those who had already run up hefty tabs at the other drinking establishments along Mora's single commercial street.

"This is one pump you can't prime," Delfino warned him.

The enterprise failed within eight months.

Next there was the flourmill. It burned to the ground a month after he opened it. It was widely believed, but never proven, that a rival mill owner was responsible.

With the little that was left of the dowry, Leopoldo purchased the timber rights to a stand of ponderosa pine. With the lease came a gas run-saw and the one-room long house where he and Tamar lived.

The wagon squealed to a stop and Adela stepped forward. She could see from the look in Tamar's eyes that it was too late for hot water, clean linen, and Nasha's attentions.

Standing on tiptoes, she received the shoebox from Tamar's hands.

Tamar immediately began to whine. "I couldn't help it. She was early."

Leopoldo had by now climbed down from his side and was around to help his wife from her seat. Tamar came down slowly at first, then all in a rush, falling from weakness and fatigue into her husband's arms.

Adela tilted her head back and spoke to the heavens. "Nasha, ¿Dónde estás? Come out here now!"

The Indian, who had been standing in the shadows of the open doorway, trotted out into the courtyard, her head down, her hands tucked inside the bodice of a large calico apron, her feet bare. Nasha owned one pair of shoes, which she diligently stored beginning in the first week of May, not to be resurrected until the first week of November.

"Sí, sí, estoy aquí, madrecita."

"Help Tamar! Don't you see what's happened? She's already had the baby." To Tamar, "Can you walk?" To Nasha, "Put her to bed. Then fix her some tea and broth."

With each order Nasha nodded. "Sí, sí, Tía Adela. Right now. Sí, sí."

Aunt Adela then addressed the issue of the shoebox.

"Is this the best you could do for a coffin? Couldn't you even spare a little of your precious lumber for a poor innocent who should have been born here in our house instead of in a mountain shack?"

"But," Leopoldo stammered, "she's alive."

Adela pulled the blanket back and thrust a finger in the baby's mouth. There was a weak sucking response. "¡Por Dios Santo! She does live."

The procession quickly made its way into the cool of the house and through to the large kitchen in back. Adela laid the box on the table and pulled up the small infant, covers, flannel bedding, and all. Grains of bran cascaded onto the checkered red-and-white oilcloth that covered the table.

"We must get her to the church at once to baptize her."

"That's why we came," Tamar said.

"You go to bed right now. Nasha, what did I tell you?"

Nasha, always busy, had been brushing the bran from the table into her cupped hand. She dropped the grain into the box and took Tamar by the arm.

"*Venga, mi angelita*. Nasha will make you feel better."

They entered the bedroom and Nasha shut the door.

Adela looked at the child in her arms and then at the father.

"You had to wait, didn't you?"

Leopoldo was now slumped into a straight-backed chair by the stove. He had closed his eyes and his head was already rolling back.

Adela prodded his boot with her foot.

"Sleep later. Have some coffee. It's hot. I'll send for Delfino. We will be the godparents. Do you have a name?"

"Margarita Juana. Tamar chose it."

"*¿Otra?* She's stubborn enough, that wife of yours."

So the baby was baptized Margarita Juana, ending the string of misfortunes that had accrued to the name. For, unlike her predecessors, she survived. And, in fact, she ended up surviving them all.

It was a turn of good fortune that redounded to me since, in due time, she was to be my mother.

Chapter Two

1913–1917

By the time my mother, Margarita Juana, was a week old, her throne was secure in the household of Delfino and Adela Arellanes. And Nasha, the Indian, was her adoring handmaid.

A gentle conspiracy soon sprang up between the *dueña* and the bondservant. A lumber camp was no place for an infant, especially a girl. Especially Margarita. Tamar's milk, or rather the lack of it, gave them their edge.

That which had been a mere trickle to begin with soured and stopped entirely within two days of Margarita's birth. This gave rise to a steady parade of wet nurses through the Arellanes kitchen and into Nasha's bedroom where the crib had been set up.

There had been five wet nurses in all. The ever-vigilant Nasha dismissed three of them for cause, at least as defined by her. One was not very clean. Another had the evil eye about her. A third already had too many sucklings up and down the valley clamoring for her tits. A fourth came once, took fright at Nasha's impertinence, and never returned.

For a month after Margarita's delivery, Tamar was too debilitated to return to the hardships of the wilderness. However, she was a strong and healthy twenty-year-old who was soon up, taking solid nourishment, and making herself a general nuisance around the house of her foster parents.

She tried to revert to a girlhood when Adela refused her nothing and Nasha was there to see to her every need. Her aunt and the Indian, however, no longer shared this conceit and told her through both words and actions that she had permanently and irrevocably ceded her role as reigning deity of the house to her own infant daughter.

And lest there be any discussion on the matter, Nasha made it plain that Margarita was hers.

From the moment Adela carried the baby into her house in the shoebox bassinet, Nasha had taken over her care. Whenever Tamar made some effort to practice her sluggish maternal instincts, Nasha was at her shoulder scolding and correcting her.

"Don't hold her like that."

"Don't gather the diaper like that, it will surely rub her and cause a rash."

"Leave her alone. I just put her down for a nap."

And so began the separation of mother from child. Even had Tamar wanted, she could not bond with Margarita, so isolated did Nasha keep her from the baby. Finally, she stopped trying altogether and gave the exclusive care of Margarita over to the Indian. After that, and then only with continual prodding from Adela, Tamar would hold her daughter for a few minutes every evening after the dishes had been washed and put away. Nasha hovered as always and Tamar would, as soon as decency permitted, resign the delicate bundle to the nanny and go to bed.

The only one who did not know about Tamar's recovery was her husband.

Every two weeks, when Leopoldo came down from the mountains with a load of lumber, he would dutifully stop at the Arellaneses' to check on the progress of his wife and child.

His arrival on the ponderous wagon was unmistakable. Now empty of its load, its deafening clatter warned Tamar that he was on his way long before he made the turn up the lane to the house. This gave her ample time to take to her bed, often fully clothed and coifed. She would pull the heavy comforter over her head to speak to him in muffled tones from a script that grew stale through many repetitions.

"Make sure the door is closed. I cannot bear the light. The outer door too. I cannot bear the drafts."

"They are closed, Tamar."

"Did you bring a load down?"

"Yes."

"Did they try to cheat you again?"

"I watched them unload."

"I need some money. The baby needs food and clothes."

Leopoldo had just been with the baby and understood full well that it lacked for nothing. But he never argued. Instead he would pull a small bundle of paper currency from the bib pocket of his blue coveralls and peel off a few bills.

"Is this enough?"

"Whatever you can manage for your wife and child. Put it on the corner of the bed."

This he did. Sometimes, before he left, he added a bill to the little pile. Sometimes he took back a coin or two if he felt unreasonably put upon.

"*¿Te sientes mejor?* Tía Adela tells me you are feeling better."

"Some days, yes . . ."

Tamar let the sentence trail off. For every good day there had to be a bad day, and if he did not know that, she had no words nor the patience to explain it to him.

"When will you be strong enough to travel?"

"I will not leave my baby. She needs me."

This was a complete fabrication. The baby had not needed her from almost that first moment when Don Kiko severed the cord between them.

"Besides," Tamar lied from under the covers, "I am still not right. I am not eating well. I sleep very little. And the baby fusses all the time."

The scene played itself out for four months. Then one day Leopoldo left the wagon at the blacksmith's for some repairs. It was a pleasant morning and his muscles were stiff from the long trip down the canyon. A leisurely two-mile stroll to the Arellanes house was just the thing to help him stretch out. He knocked at the kitchen door and entered without being asked.

There sat Tamar at the table. She wore a white cotton cloth around her neck to cover her bodice. Her chin glistened with grease as she gnawed on a savory rib from a roasted kid goat. The plate in front of her looked like a mastodon burial ground, piled high with bones stripped clean of their meat. Her mouth went slack at the unheralded sight of her husband.

Leopoldo pulled out a chair opposite her at the table and sat down.

"*Qué bueno.* You're feeling stronger."

Tamar yanked the cloth from her neck and dropped it over the accusing heap of bones.

"I was a little hungry this morning."

"Good."

Adela and Nasha's only reaction to Tamar's "sudden" return to health was a rolling of their eyes. But they were positively glowing in their enthusiasm when Leopoldo announced that Tamar would be returning to the camp the next morning. Adela loved her foster daughter but had grown tired of her idleness and lack of purpose. Besides, for better or worse, a woman's place was by her husband. Nasha had her own agenda and it was currently sleeping like a little angel in her bedroom.

Every day, in the quiet of the afternoon, after the wet nurse had left, Nasha went into her room and retrieved from underneath the baby's mattress a beaded leather purse with a drawstring. Its contents, more precious to her than the rarest of gemstones, was the roasted bran that had provided Margarita with a warm and protecting nest on her journey down the mountain.

Careful as an apothecary, Nasha measured out a tiny amount of the grain into a small saucepan of boiling water. Once the watery gruel was cooked, she strained it through a piece of muslin into a whisper-light china cup. Behind the closed door to her room, she folded Margarita into her arms and sat on the bed. Then she took a piece of clean linen, dipped a corner into the bran water, and put it to the baby's mouth.

As Margarita contentedly sucked on the soggy rag, Nasha rocked back and forth and softly crooned lullabies in Spanish and in Tiwa, the barely remembered tongue of her infancy.

> "*Hati pam'one*, Precious little blossom,
> *Tcakwil 'a'eye*, Come to me.
> *'Amaxutcetci*, Let me hold you."

It would take about an hour for Margarita to finish the contents of the cup and Nasha received more than one thump on the back from Adela's broom for neglecting her regular duties. But Nasha did not stop the feedings, not until that magical bran that gave Margarita her life force was completely used up, and was now part of her forever.

There was no question but that when Tamar and Leopoldo left, Margarita would stay behind. Leopoldo could see no purpose at all for a female infant in a lumber camp. Tamar was past caring one way or another. All agreed that the baby would thrive best if left in Mora. Adela welcomed the distraction of a new life in the house. And, as for Nasha, she had already decided to curse with baleful purpose anyone who attempted to take Margarita from her.

The infant offered no opinion but it was clear that she preferred Nasha's strong, wiry arms and warm bosom.

Nasha came from the Indian pueblo of Picurís, which lay across the mountains to the west about thirty-five miles from Mora. When Nasha was five years old her father gave her to Doña Prisca Pacheco, Adela's mother, part of a settlement over some missing sheep.

A group of Picurís shepherds were summering their flocks on grazing land that abutted Doña Prisca's vast holdings. One day a fold of twenty-five sheep on nearby pastureland simply vanished. The shepherds swore that they knew nothing about it. But, in a gesture of goodwill, they offered Doña Prisca a fine ram and ewe, which, they told her, would eventually bring many more sheep than the paltry twenty-five she was missing. They would also, again for goodwill's sake, give her a young girl, the fifth daughter of one of the shepherds, to be of whatever service the grand lady should require.

Doña Prisca was shrewd and knew that this was the only arrangement she could expect.

"Better something," she said to her husband, Vidal, "than nothing. And who knows what mischief they would do if I insisted on the twenty-five sheep?"

The ram humped tree stumps rather than sheep and a mountain lion dragged away the ewe. But Nasha's worth, by the time it was all over, exceeded that of ten thousand sheep.

When Adela took in Tamar, Doña Prisca made a gift of the Indian to help with the child's rearing. Now, twenty years later, Nasha was ready to take up the education of Tamar's daughter.

For the next several years, Margarita grew in wisdom and knowledge and in fear of nothing. With Nasha as a champion how could there ever be anything to fear?

In her fourth year of life, Margarita's education began in earnest. By now, she and Nasha were inseparable. What a pair they made! The Indian at four foot eleven inches, barefoot except in winter, in a simple cotton dress meant for a child of twelve, and wearing her ever-present apron that hung to her ankles. The little girl, in petticoats and fresh gingham jumpers, with long ringlets of auburn hair rippling down to well below her shoulders.

Margarita seldom let Nasha out of her sight, which suited the Indian perfectly. Even while Nasha was attending to her rounds of household duties, the little girl was there, her brown eyes serious and wide, to absorb every fascinating detail of sweeping, dusting, scrubbing, washing, ironing, and cooking.

For the tiny autocrat, life was full and generous.

The Arellaneses belonged to the top echelon of Mora society. They owned fifty thousand acres of land, great numbers of livestock to graze it, and a general store from which Delfino managed the post office, thus allowing him to keep his finger on the pulse of the local body politic. He also sat for several terms as probate judge.

Mora's early history was sanguineous. Because of the constant threat from Comanche raids, the settlers were forced to build their houses close together and to go fully armed while clearing their fields. Often, even these precautions were not enough and marauders wiped out more than one family.

By the last decade of the century, Mora had become a flourishing business center boasting a succession of lumber and flour mills, hotels, mercantile stores, and many saloons. It was a wide-open town that attracted the misbegottens and outlaws from other communities across the territory. With money came the usual noxious side effects—gunfights, murders, rapes, extortion, terrorism, and swift vigilante justice.

Even the parish priests were not safe. One pastor was the victim of poisoned wine, which he drank from a golden chalice during the celebration of Mass. It was widely speculated that the good father had pressed his luck by challenging the corrupt elements of Mora during one of his Sunday sermons.

By 1917, Mora's unruly years were mostly behind. With a few

exceptions, the people of the valley were content to let the seasons be the shapers of their lives.

On the first morning of the planting season in the fourth year of Margarita's reign, Adela and Nasha packed a hamper of provisions, and with the child between them, walked into the fields. There, under a cottonwood, they built a small fire and began to heat up a tin bucket full of coffee. While they waited for the brew to boil they sat and watched the tillers in the distance. How grand they looked with reins draped over their necks. How skillfully they maneuvered the horse-drawn plows to turn over the chocolate earth in long, evenly spaced rows. The heady, rich aroma of the soil intoxicated the women with its freshness and promise.

When the coffee was ready Adela sent Margarita to announce the collation. She pushed her short legs through the moist, soft earth, stumbling and recovering, sometimes falling, but never defeated. "*Muchachos*. My aunt says to come. You have to come now," she chanted.

Adela and Nasha covered their mouths to hide their laughter as more than once the child tumbled face first into a mushy furrow, picked herself up, sputtering and spitting and wiped the sweet, pure loam from her mouth.

But even in this rare moment of lightness between the two women, Nasha's breast tightened while she watched Margarita dwindle into the growing distance between them.

The men finally saw her and whoaed the horses to a stop. They greeted the child, their voices drifting across the greening valley. Margarita ran the last few yards to them and one of the men accepted her with open arms to be carried in regal splendor on a strong, sure shoulder.

Nasha handed each of the men a tin cup to fill with a steaming liquid so black and thick it could have been brewed from the very ground they were working. From the hamper came freshly baked *moyetes*, sweet rolls pungent with anise seed. The men blew on their coffee and slowly sipped it. When they bit into the soft buns, they turned away lest they be embarrassed while they chewed and dropped crumbs on their denim overalls.

They talked about the progress of the planting, discussed a plow that needed a new blade and a horse that was showing its age since last spring. They even teased Margarita, but not too much, since Nasha's reputation as a formidable palace guard was already well established.

After they finished eating, the men returned to their plowing. The women packed up and started home. Adela carried the hamper and Nasha pulled the exhausted and protesting child along with a firm but gentle hand, for Margarita had expended all her energies on the long solo cruise across the swells and wavelets of this dark brown sea.

Spring was also cleaning time. Women threw doors and windows open at the first sign of mild weather and set themselves to dusting, beating carpets, scrubbing floors, and washing windows.

That year, for the first time, Adela allowed Margarita to go with Nasha to the river to launder the heavy cotton ticking that covered all mattresses and pillows in the Arellanes house.

Nasha piled the empty sacks, flaccid like the skins of some exotic gray-and-blue-striped creatures, into a washtub in the back of a two-wheeled cart. Then she hitched up the pet billy goat and perched Margarita on the top of the load to be transported to the river like Cleopatra on her barge.

The laundering of the bed covers was a community affair. By custom, on the first sunny day of the second week after Easter all the servant girls from the grander houses met at the bank of the river.

Some of the girls had been there since daybreak to prepare the water and the soap. They set several footed, black iron kettles on wide flat stones and filled them from the river. Others foraged for pieces of dry wood and kindling to pile underneath and up the sides of the giant pots.

"*¿Quién tiene fósforos?*"

Immediately, from half a dozen apron pockets, came boxes or loose handfuls of thick kitchen matches. The girls ran to the kettles, jostling, pushing and giggling, striking matches on the sides of the kettles only to have them blown out by the person next to them. Finally, somehow, from this chaos came fire.

As they waited for the rest of the laundry party to arrive, the girls traded old gossip while they crushed the dried roots of the amole plant between flat stones. They would be mixing the mash with a small amount of water to create a sudsy pulp for soap.

Each household brought its own washtub and washboard. Once the water was hot, the women scooped out pails of it for their individual tubs and washed the bedding by rubbing it with the amole soap and scraping it vigorously across the frets of their washboards.

Nasha kept a sharp eye out for the little girl. "Stay away from the kettles, Margarita. You could hurt yourself."

The older girls reinforced the admonition by regaling her with the story of a careless child who had stumbled head first into the boiling water just the Easter before.

"Her name was Margarucha, and she looked like you. With a few potatoes and carrots and an onion or two, we had a fine stew," one of the girls pretended to recall. For effect she rubbed her belly and licked her lips while the others snickered behind cupped hands.

Once they had cleaned the ticking, the women lifted it out of the washtubs in heavy, sodden masses to drop into the river. While a girl held tightly to one corner, the brisk current unfurled the piece of bedding until it was a long streamer, dunking and bobbing in the water.

At one point the fast-moving water ripped a mattress cover from the hands of a careless girl. This hapless one ran along the bank and prayed that the cloth would snag so she could hoist her skirts and wade in after it. All this time she could hear the jeers and laughter at her back.

Margarita especially enjoyed the clusters of white suds that sloughed off the cloths and floated down the river. They were a much grander armada than the few paper boats she and Nasha launched on days when they came to the river by themselves. These suds were thousands of boats, crashing together and merging and forming and reforming again and again, wondrous ships with delicate bubbles for sails that quickly passed out of sight and on to worlds she was anxious to know. How wonderful to sail far from the valley! She abruptly broke her reverie when she could not picture Nasha standing on the deck alongside her. Then she ran and wrapped herself in Nasha's skirts.

"What's the matter, *hijita*, did you miss your Nasha?"

"No!"

Margarita pushed herself away, angry that she could be so trans-parent.

The month of May was most welcome in Mora since it ushered in the first real opportunity to socialize after the long days of late winter and the household bustle of early spring. Pious women with time to spare, in other words Adela and the other Mora dueñas, would gather each afternoon to recite the rosary. When the hosting of the devotions fell to Adela, she relegated Nasha and Margarita to the kitchen.

"Now, remember, you are to sit here quietly and say your rosaries with us. When we're done, you can serve the *biscochos* and the tea."

Nasha sat dutifully and closed her eyes. When the prayers started in the other room, she began to mumble to herself.

These mutterings, it soon became obvious to Margarita, bore no resemblance to the singsong phrases put forth by the ladies beyond the door.

"Shhh!"

The startled Indian popped open her eyes to see the child shaking a finger at her. Nasha grabbed at the finger and did some shaking of her own.

"You mind your own prayers, and I'll mind mine."

Margarita was sure that with all this carrying on Adela would be storming into the kitchen to scold them both. As for the Indian's blas-phemy of pretending to say her Hail Marys while actually indulging in some pagan chant. . . . Well! Her nanny was stiff necked and unre-pentant and would probably end up in Hell. Best to plead with the Heavenly Father to spare her when His lightning struck Nasha dead. She lifted her eyes heavenward with this fervent prayer.

Within a few minutes, Margarita began to nod. Finally, she suc-cumbed entirely to the numbing cadence of the incessant *Dios Te Salves* floating through the house and dropped her head to the cradle of her arms.

She slept so soundly that she did not feel the touch that settled gently on her head nor the warm kiss on her neck from the lips of the blaspheming Indian. These *cariños* were as sanctifying as any from the heart of God.

June was the time to harvest the season's first crop of herbs. Early one Wednesday morning, Nasha packed a lunch of hard-boiled eggs, cold beef ribs, and chokecherry jelly sandwiches and headed out with Margarita in tow. Their destination was a meadow by the river.

First, the Indian picked the blossoms of the *rosa de castilla*. These she would later separate and dry for tea to combat high fevers, blisters, and sore throats. She made note of the *oshá* plant, the evil- and strong-smelling staple of everyone's medicine chest, a cure-all that was particularly efficacious for toothaches and infections. These she would harvest in the fall. Finally, she harvested mint for general use as a tea and for ailments of the stomach, kidneys, and intestines.

While Nasha carefully searched for the choicest of the plants, Margarita, who had grown tired of the botanical lessons the Indian was trying to impart, began to rip at any and all greenery that struck her fancy.

At the end of the day, Nasha carefully separated the little girl's random harvest from her own. She saved the weeds until the child had moved on to other distractions and it was safe to discard them.

For the next two days, Nasha devoted her time to the herbs, washing them and setting them out in the sun to dry before bundling and hanging them by nails driven into the roof beams in the *dispensa*, just off the kitchen. From there their pungency reached like invisible tendrils to permeate every room of the house.

"Where are the ones I picked?" Margarita asked.

"Oh, *angelita mía*, they were so special that your Aunt Adela decided to give them to the priest."

Margarita tilted her head and gave the Indian a very odd look. She had lately come to realize what she had long suspected: Nasha, like most grownups, did not always tell her the truth.

Fall was butchering time. Roasts for corning in brine. Beef strips for jerky. But the real affair was the butchering of the hogs. Early on the morning of *la matanza*, hired hands prepared a large kettle of boiling water next to the sty. Soon neighbors and friends gathered for the refreshments, the camaraderie, and the largesse that the day would afford them.

Margarita stopped her aunt, who was rushing by her into the house.

"Will they have to kill the pigs?"

"Of course, child."

"How?"

"With a gun. And then they will slit the throat."

Adela brushed Margarita into the house with her extended apron. "Get in the house. There is nothing for a *mujercita* to see." And off the aunt went in search of a pot to catch the blood, which would soon gush from the pigs' gullets.

It took Delfino but one clean shot into each hog's brain to do the job. A deep, long, almost languid swipe of his razor-sharp knife across their throats was enough to open the floodgates of red.

All the while, Adela, like some Aztec priestess, waited patiently for her pot of blood. She would pour the dark red soup into a greased frying pan to cook until it browned and contracted into loose brown curds. With some onion, salt, pepper, oregano, and a sprinkling of seeds from a dried chile pod, the mixture would go quite well with Delfino's eggs the next morning.

Once the men hoisted the carcasses onto wooden trestles, the butcher set about his work. First he gutted the hogs, and Nasha reverently carried the livers, kidneys, and other internal organs into Adela's kitchen for processing.

In the meantime, others of the assembly scurried to form a bucket brigade for boiling water. This softened the hogs' tough, wiry bristles enough for one of the farmhands to shave them with the same finely edged knife that had done the honors on their gullets.

"I'm next. But don't shave me too close, I'm going to a dance tonight!" someone shouted and rubbed his chin.

"And here's your *novia*," the pig barber yelled back, holding up the hog's snout. "How about a kiss?"

Once the carcasses were free of bristles, the butcher stepped in to quarter them and peel away their outer layer of fat. Here, the assembly line broke off in two directions. Some carried slabs of fat into the kitchen, where Adela hacked them into manageable chunks and dropped them into a large copper pot to render into lard. She also accepted the two massive heads and scooped out the brains and eyeballs for headcheese. The heads themselves were now placed in giant roasting pans, sprinkled with salt, smothered in sage, and placed in the oven.

The butcher prepared the better part of the meat for the smoke-house. There, hams and bacon would hang from large hooks embedded into the vigas, a veritable portière of pork that Delfino would have to bob and weave through every time he entered the shed.

Nasha spread-eagled a short tripod with a small iron kettle over a bed of charcoal. Into the kettle the Indian tossed small cubes of pork fat edged with hints of meat. The pork sizzled and spat and fried crisp in its own grease until Nasha spooned out the *chicharrones* onto freshly grilled tortillas held up to her like beggars' bowls by eager gourmands.

A dash of salt and a dab of green chile on the cracklings, a mason jar of cold cider, and a spontaneous musicale courtesy of a wheezing accordion—the *matanza* was into its last act. All the occasion lacked was a patron saint. This was soon remedied when one of the party hoisted some cider laced with *mula*, a locally favored corn distillation, and proposed a toast to the holy martyrs, *los santos marranos*, the Holy Swine.

The threshers came later that month. Adela and Nasha prepared meals. These were served on long makeshift tables in the courtyard of the house. There were biscuits and tortillas, pots of beans and chile stew, great rump roasts of beef and smaller ones of mutton, corn on the cob, green beans with tender bits of onion, stewed apples, and a wide sheet of yellow cake with white icing.

These men were itinerants who, with their families, moved with the harvest. Nasha looked on all of them, children included, with slit-eyed mistrust. She did not allow Margarita to speak to them and made the little girl understand that they were different and not to be befriended since no good could ever come of it.

"They are not like Juan and Livorio," Nasha pointed out, referring to the familiar and friendly hands who worked the estate year round.

In response, the little girl jutted out her lower lip and pushed the Indian away in annoyance.

After all the grains were winnowed and bagged, it was time to take them to the mill. The procession down the main street of Mora was a spectacle to behold. In front, seated in a black-canopied surrey with brass fittings, rode Doña Adela at the reins with Margarita next to her and Nasha wrapped tightly in a shawl in back. Behind them rolled four buckboards, each driven by a farmhand, carrying sack upon sack of wheat, barley, and corn.

Once Adela had struck her agreement with the mill owner, the two women and the little girl climbed back into the buggy and retraced their route until they reached Delfino's store.

A sign stretched across its entire length, proclaiming proudly, "Arellanes General Mercantile—Est. 1891."

With Margarita still at her side and Nasha trailing at a decorous distance, Adela sailed into the store.

Several customers in the store were quick to greet the eminent señora. "*Buenos días le dé Dios.* May God give thee good days, Doña Adela."

To each Adela extended a gracious *buenos días* and inquired after a spouse, a child, or an ailing grandparent. She took the time to chat about this or that, but was always on course to the rear of the store. There Delfino sat at a battered rolltop desk with pigeonholes crammed with yellowing papers.

"I'm here for some cloth so I can start my sewing."

Delfino smiled as if this were a wonderfully unexpected visit, although Adela had been warning him for a week of her intentions. He kissed his wife on the cheek and bent over to smother Margarita in a hug. Then he pointed to the shelf behind him.

"There you are, *vida mía.*"

"Is that all you have?"

It seemed to Margarita that there were bolts of cloth sufficient to clothe every person in the world with prints and calicos. In reality, Delfino's inventory was sparse and Adela never tired of complaining about his taste in fabrics for women's clothing.

"What can I do with this?"

Adela pulled out a tight bolt of a floral-patterned material and unfurled it down the length of the counter.

"It's ugly. It was ugly last year when you couldn't sell it. It's ugly this year and you won't sell it again. Perhaps," she conceded, sighing, "I can use it for aprons, or undergarments that no one will see. I'll take seven yards. But why did you buy anything so ugly?"

Adela picked over and chose her fabrics and Delfino cut, rolled, and bound them in twine. It was time for Margarita to be fitted for her winter shoes.

She dreaded the ordeal. New shoes meant angry blisters and the discarding of her old, battered friends with soles so thin by now that she could feel every pebble she stepped on.

By late October the attic was piled high with sacks of corn that had been removed from the cob, cooked, and set out on large squares of canvas to dry in the sun. There were also wicker baskets straining with their loads of squash, plums, peaches, and apples. Cabbage, red beets, pumpkins found room next to onions and rutabagas in the root cellar. The shelves in the dispensa creaked and bowed with jars of capulín, plum, and apple jellies sealed with thick caps of paraffin.

Now it was time to prepare the *chicos*.

One cool morning, Nasha built a wood fire in the beehive-shaped mud *horno* that sat outside the kitchen door. After the fire had completely consumed the wood, the Indian raked out the ashes and stacked the inside of the hot oven with ears of corn. She then sprinkled the stack liberally with water and sealed the door of the oven, a seal not to be broken until the next day.

As the corn steamed, its aroma billowed through the small opening at the top of the horno and sent out a delicious perfume. That night passed in delectable anguish for the entire household, especially Delfino, as all of them dreamed of endless topaz rows of corn and awoke intermittently with a ravenous appetite for maize.

In the morning, Nasha removed the steamed ears from the horno, peeled their husks back, and braided them together to form many dozens of clusters. These she hung to dry on the portal under the autumn sun.

A week later the Indian shucked the chicos from the cob and stored them in sacks in the dispensa next to the dry beans and peas. The kernels would provide a crisp corn flavor to many a pot of beans over the next twelve months.

Winter in Mora was always quiet and, in spite of rumblings of a war in Europe, this one was no exception. Adela sewed and trimmed and burned an endless store of candles before the wooden image of San Isidro, patron of farmers. Nasha cooked, did the laundry and house-cleaning, and made sure that the dispensa was free from dirt and vermin. Margarita was bored.

Nasha tried to entertain her as best she could but the child was growing too old to be satisfied with the simple amusements the nanny had to offer. Even an invitation to set the brooding hens, which seemed somewhat promising to Margarita when described to her, grew quickly tiresome and she soon wandered back to the house.

The community Christmas party was the biggest social event of the winter and one that Margarita began to anticipate from the middle of November, when she was told that she was now old enough to attend.

The immediate preparations began the morning of the party, a morning that had dawned as if made to order for the occasion, with an overnight storm that had left a good two feet of snow on the ground.

Nasha rose earlier than usual to prepare the dough for the biscochitos, a traditional holiday shortbread made with flour, lard, anise, and a jigger of sweet wine, white being preferred since red muddied the color of the cookies. She rolled the dough flat and cut it into precise one-and-a-half-inch squares. On these she made four parallel cuts to create five fingers, which she separated and curled so that they resembled the crowns of the Three Kings. Finally, she dipped the cookies in cinnamon sugar, spread them out on wide baking sheets, and slipped them into the oven to bake to a golden brown.

The rest of Nasha's day consisted of pressing Adela's fine dark green brocade gown with black lace and silver buttons. Next she worked on Margarita's burgundy velvet dress and starched and pressed its round white linen collar with its delicately crocheted edges.

Soon it was time for Margarita's afternoon nap, always a struggle of wills between Nasha and the little girl. On this occasion especially the child kept calling for her nanny.

"Is it time yet?"

"No, my angel."

"How could you know? Ask my Tía. It's her clock."

By three Margarita had won the battle, and she was permitted to return to the kitchen, where the task of washing her, curling her hair, and dressing her began. Margarita was particularly delighted when, after she was dressed, Adela took a thin sheet of tissue coated with perfumed talc from a packet not unlike the ones that held cigarette paper and gently powdered her face. The final touches were rouge for her cheeks and a daub of red for her pursed lips.

Delfino produced a small square of folded brown paper from his pocket. "So beautiful a little queen needs something special for tonight."

Margarita unfolded the paper with quivering fingers and found a small cameo locket on a thin gold chain. "Put it on me. Please put it on," she begged Nasha.

Then she paraded around the kitchen and pumped her small chest to its fullest to display the pendant.

At the last glow of day, it was time to go. As Nasha helped her into her coat Margarita looked the nanny over with a critical eye. "Aren't you going to change your dress?"

"Why, my angel?"

"For the party."

"Oh, *hijita*, I'm not going with you."

"Then I won't go."

"Oh, but you must. How else can you tell me about it?"

"But why?"

Nasha smiled and brushed at a piece of lint on Margarita's coat. How could she explain that such grand doings were not for people like her? Not because she was an Indian. Indians of substance were always treated with respect in Mora. But everyone knew that Nasha was little more than a slave.

"You are growing up, my angel. From now on there will be many things you will do without me. It is the way it should be. Now, let me put on your hat so you can show me how pretty you look."

Nasha carefully fitted the fur-trimmed bonnet over Margarita's meticulously curled tresses and wiped at a tear.

It seemed to Margarita that the whole world was at the schoolhouse. She had never in her life seen so many people in one place, even at Sunday Mass.

A trio with accordion, guitar, and violin supplied a constant stream of loud, pounding polkas and reels. The musicians showed off a particularly eclectic repertoire of the songs popular at the time—the lilting rhythms of *Jesusita en Chihuahua*, the bombast of *Under The Double Eagle*, and the raucous syncopation of *By The Sea*.

There were children everywhere, darting through the crowd. Little girls jumped up and down to the tempo of the music. Little boys pushed and shoved at each other with the early stirrings of machismo.

Margarita felt shy and lost in a great sea of legs and gowns that milled around the floor. The children around her seemed as foreign and threatening as the urchins that Nasha had warned her against when the migrant threshers and their families had visited them.

In a household so full of things to learn, she had been provided with few of the social skills needed to survive with her peers. Her world had always been peopled with adults. She did not understand the improvisational nature of the games nor the small cruelties that passed for amusement among those her age.

In one corner of the room she spied the Christmas tree, decorated with paper garlands and popcorn balls and with a large irregularly snipped tin star perched crookedly at its top. Across the room were two long tables loaded with refreshments and, as a centerpiece, the single most beautiful object Margarita had ever seen. It was a cut crystal punch bowl filled to the brim with a sparkling red liquid.

Despite her shyness she was drawn again and again to the punch bowl, where she placed her small hand on its side to feel its regular pattern of hard ridges against the soft pads of her fingertips. She also delighted in the way the illumination from the many oil lamps around the hall shone through the liquid in the bowl. It created shimmering rubies on the tablecloth and on her white arms as she turned them this way and that to catch the reflections.

She eventually tired of this game, however, and sought out her aunt.

Adela was sitting near the stove with four other doyennes and trying to gossip over the noise. She absently put one arm around Margarita while she continued her spirited conversation. Finally, however, she grew annoyed with her niece, who had begun to pick at the lace on her cuff. One thing that Adela could not abide was a clingy child.

"Don't hang on my sleeve like that. Look at all the children over there having such a good time. Go play with them. Why did we bring you if you spend all your time with me? You can do that at home."

Margarita separated herself slowly from the warmth and comfort of her aunt's velvet sleeve and moved reluctantly to stand at the edge of the children's circle.

A little girl whom she did not know stuck her tongue out at her and Margarita was too stung to respond.

How she wished that Nasha had been allowed to come with them.

The musicians embarked on a furious *Over the Waves*, and Margarita felt a presence behind her. Suddenly she was whisked up and around and she was in her Uncle Delfino's arms, spinning and dipping across the floor.

"*¡El juez! ¡El juez!* The judge!" she heard someone shouting, and dancers moved off the floor to give Delfino and his tiny partner more room. Around the floor they danced to the three-quarter time of the music, now joined by the rhythmic clapping of the people who circled them.

When the music ended, and a grandly puffing Delfino bent to place Margarita back on the floor, he whispered in her ear, "Now, my princess, we must bow."

Together they bent deeply from their waists. As Margarita straightened she caught sight of a sullen little face at the edge of the crowd. It was the girl who had stuck her tongue out at her. In the spirit of the season and in the flush of her triumph, Margarita Juana almost resisted the temptation to retaliate in kind.

Almost.

Chapter Three

1918–1920

Slave or not, Nasha was the ever-nurturing, ever-protecting guardian spirit to Margarita Juana.

There was the time when Margarita was five that she was shocked into wakefulness late one night by loud noises coming from the kitchen. They were men's voices, angry and competing.

Nasha was by her side even before the child called.

"Did they wake you, my angel?"

"Who is out there? Why are they shouting?" Margarita whimpered in half sleep.

"It's nothing. Your uncle is talking to some men about business. Go to sleep now. Let me sing to you."

The sound of Nasha's voice, barely above a whisper, was enough. In a moment the child was fast asleep again.

In the kitchen Delfino was seated at the table. Before him stood a man, two burly youths, and a boy. The boy's nose was running blood and there was an ugly swelling of his left eye. His good eye was open wide in fear and confusion. On either side, the young men held tightly to his arms.

"He is as good as dead," shouted the older man as he pushed the butt of his rifle against the back of the frightened youth. "No one steals from Arsenio Montenegro. No one. Especially not a worm like this one."

"Tell your sons to let him go, Don Arsenio. Then we can talk," Delfino politely suggested.

"Don Delfino, we are here for justice and you are the judge."

Delfino raised his voice for the first time. "And justice I shall give you, but only if you obey the law. Let him go."

The father nodded at his two sons, who released their hold on the boy with a shove.

"That's better. Now then, you claim that Lito took your horse."

"I claim nothing. I know it."

"How do you know it?"

"My sons saw him when it was getting dark. He was sneaking by our pasture. This morning the horse was gone. We looked for this *hijo de puta* all day. We finally caught him walking down from the *crestón*. He hid the horse up there somewhere. There is no doubt."

"And your proof?"

"He came up to me last week and told me he wanted to buy it. I laughed at him. Where would he get the money to buy a horse?"

Lito Castillo, a distant cousin of Delfino's by marriage, was, for lack of a better description, Mora's resident idiot, a bastard son who lived with his mother. In the minds of the townspeople, Lito had been cursed with dimwittedness because of her salacious habits. Through seventeen years the boy had learned few practical skills and was so sadly lacking in common sense that people regularly had to rescue him from the ordinary perils of life in the valley, dangers that he was incapable of appreciating.

Delfino turned his attention to the boy. "Well, Lito, it looks like Don Arsenio and his sons have not been very gentle with you. Would you like to press charges?"

This went completely over the half-wit's head but created havoc among his three captors.

"He ran. We told him we wanted to talk to him and he ran. Why did he run if he had nothing to hide?"

"Don Arsenio, we all run from the Montenegros. You know that." This grim reply came from one of the few men in Mora who had never run from this trio of bullies.

"We fight, others run."

"And you fight so much. Now, Lito, did you do such a foolish thing? Did you take Don Arsenio's horse for a ride? Did he throw you off and make you walk home? Is he running around the *campaña* right now?"

"He didn't go for a ride. He took the horse to keep it."

"And what was he going to do with it? Where was he going to stable it? Where could he go with it that everyone in Mora would not see him?"

"Who knows how idiots think?"

"Well," said Delfino, "it appears that this is nothing we can settle tonight."

"You refuse us justice?"

"This is my judgment. We will wait. If the horse is in the mountains it will be back in a day or so."

The elder Montenegro took a step forward.

"We will wait," continued Delfino, "until I can talk to Lito under better circumstances."

"It is not enough. In this valley no one takes what belongs to me."

Two days later, a group of children on their way to the fields found Lito. Someone had looped a belt around his neck and hooked it securely over a fence post. The crows had already pecked out his eyes and part of his tongue.

As soon as he heard the news, Delfino went looking for the Montenegros. No one knew where they were.

A week later he saw them riding into town.

"We've been away. We went up to Black Lake last Friday to see my uncle."

"It wouldn't take much time to dispose of a poor *inocentócman* like Lito," Delfino pointed out. "In fact, someone, especially with two strong helpers, could do it easily on their way out of town."

Arsenio Montenegro's smile was cold. "Proof, Don Delfino— sometimes proof is so hard to find. Even when you wait."

The horse never returned. There were rumors that the two sons had incurred a gambling debt and that they had used the horse to pay it off. But, again, as with so many curious things that happened in the valley, there was no proof.

With so few other diversions to occupy them, the people of Mora amused themselves by visiting each other. They would meet on the street, or in church, or at a place of business.

"How have you been?"

"How are you? It's been so long."

"You must come and see us."

They set a date and early on the morning of the day agreed upon, the visiting family would travel to the home of their hosts and not take their leave until late in the evening after supper.

A favorite visit for Delfino and Adela Arellanes was the small ranch of Don Florencio and Doña Clara Santillanes, four miles east of town. It was a call they made twice a year, when, by long-standing practice, Delfino delivered sacks of beans and other necessities to the elderly couple. By this time in her life, Margarita was accustomed to short separations from Nasha and had already visited the Santillaneses several times.

Don Florencio was a pioneer of the valley, having settled his small homestead in the 1840s. Delfino relished the opportunity to sit and talk with the old man about the history of the area, in particular the role the Arellanes family had played in it. Adela would bring her sewing basket. She sat and crocheted while Doña Clara, whose eyes were useless except to distinguish between light and dark, asked her about everything in Mora, about weather, and children, about aches and pains, about who had died and who had been married or, best of all, disgraced.

Don Florencio was a hunchback, badly deformed. When he was a child an older brother had pushed him from a hay wagon onto a large stone and he had broken his back. His spine had knit so poorly that he spent the rest of his life lifting his head and bending it sideways like a nearsighted tortoise to see where he was going.

The seven-year-old Margarita was morbidly fascinated by the strange old couple.

Doña Clara would take the little girl's face in her hands and, as if willing her eyes to see through the pearly clouds that covered them, would go on about how big and lovely Margarita had grown.

The old woman was blind, this Margarita knew to be so. How then could she see that the child was beautiful? It was a source of great puzzlement. When she returned home from one of their visits and shared her confusion with Nasha, the Indian only laughed.

"But everyone in the world knows how pretty you are."

The response was so glib that Margarita stuck her tongue out at the Indian and stormed away.

Don Florencio was also terrible and wonderful in his deformity. Here he was, a grown man, an adult, older even than Uncle Delfino, but when Margarita stood by him and he twisted his head around to speak to her, they talked at eye level. She wanted badly to touch his hump but Adela had admonished her time and again never to touch anything when they went to people's houses for visits.

Here again, Nasha was of no help. She told Margarita that it was rare good luck for anyone who rubbed the hump of a hunchback.

The Santillanes house was long and narrow, five rooms built one at a time over the years, connecting in a row, with a step up or down between each. The floors, dark brown ponds dotted by islets of rugs and sheepskins, were of dirt, hardened with cow's blood. Years of sweeping had given them the luster of baked tile.

While the adults sat in the kitchen at one end of the house, Margarita ran back and forth through all five rooms. She never tired of examining the mementos, knickknacks, and pictures that the old couple had accumulated during a lifetime on the frontier. There were religious icons painted on tin and set in rough frames, Indian pottery, colorful glass bottles, and sepia-toned photographs of people she did not know, except for one in a gilded oval frame.

In it Don Florencio was much younger. His hair and mustache were dark. He leaned over the arm of the chair in which his young wife sat so that his black frock coat stuck out in the back like a beetle's hard shell. In the picture, Doña Clara's eyes were alert and seeing and they seemed to follow Margarita wherever she moved around the room.

The room farthest from the kitchen, the bedroom, was by far the most interesting in the house. The bed was a *camalta*, a high thick-mattressed barge of carved dark wood. Margarita delighted in climbing on the bed, threats from Adela notwithstanding, to inspect the headboard with its complex carving of a large horn of plenty. There were perfectly arranged bunches of grapes and apples, and fruits that she had never seen. Leafy vines swirled and intertwined. She never tired of running her fingers along the maze of branches, always finding her way to the heart of the carving where she would rub round the smooth clusters of grapes and sensuously cup the larger fruits in her small hands.

As entertaining as her odyssey through the highways of the carving was, it could not compete with the rapture inspired by the round crystal ball with a castle inside. Don Florencio had shown her how, if she turned the ball upside down then righted it, the scene became a wondrous fantasyland of softly falling snow.

As many times as she dared during each visit, Margarita sauntered toward the bedroom, her hands clasped behind her, with an occasional look back through the series of open doors at the adults four rooms away. Once in the bedroom she moved directly to the dresser. There the crystal sat on its black onyx base. She would carefully pick up the ball and look at the scene in all its pristine clarity before gently turning it over to set off a tiny blizzard. Then she would hold the ball away from her to watch with rapture what she, the mistress of the storm, had wrought.

Her obsession with the globe finally led to a disaster she never revealed to anyone, not even Nasha, who knew all her secrets. She was playing with the crystal when her aunt called. "Margarita, come and wash your hands, the food is hot."

Margarita had been lost in a snowy day by a fairy tale castle, and Adela's voice startled her. On tiptoes, she stretched out to return the crystal but did not set it squarely on its stand. In horror she watched the crystal slip off and roll to the back of the dresser.

Try as she might, she could not reach it. She needed something to stand on. There was a chair by the bed but it was much too large for her to move. Then her eyes caught sight of something to one side of the dresser, a large porcelain chamber pot with a lid on it. Off came her shoes. Up she stepped onto the pot and scooted onto the dresser. There, she reclaimed the crystal and put it carefully back onto its stand.

"Margarita, do you hear me?"

She shimmied off the dresser, her stomach hard to its edge, her feet inches from the top of the chamber pot.

"Margarita?"

"*Aquí voy*. I'm coming."

Her feet did not hit the chamber pot evenly. One foot rocked the container and she flailed blindly for some added stability Her other foot touched then pushed the pot over. By this time she was too far down to reclaim her perch. Still, she did manage to launch herself to one side.

She stood frozen, certain that the noise had aroused everyone in the kitchen. As it happened, Don Florencio had just made a very clever remark and Delfino's laugh, an ursine bark of prodigious volume, swept through the house, overriding every other sound.

Then she looked down and realized that she was still doomed.

The round, jolly chamber pot was now on its side, rocking back and forth. Alas, it was not empty. In fact, it had been quite full. And now its sorry, unspeakable contents were slowly spreading across the floor.

"Margarita, I will not call you again."

Margarita did nothing about the spill. What could she do? She reached down for her shoes, which had been spared the deluge, and ran out of the bedroom.

In the parlor she came into direct contact with the photograph and Doña Clara's eyes, the ones that could see, the ones that were looking at her now, the ones that followed her as she tiptoed to the kitchen.

"Where were you? Why did you take your shoes off? Have you been dancing on the bed?"

Doña Clara turned her head in the direction of the little girl. "*Deja la niña*. Let her be. There is nothing she can harm. Come, child, sit by Clara. We haven't visited yet and I must know everything."

Margarita walked slowly around the table to the chair Doña Clara had pulled out for her. She gazed intently into those milky orbs behind which the old lady hid her soul. She must know everything? Did she know everything? Had the picture told her?

But the old lady was as kind and solicitous as ever. She gently urged food on her. She asked her about her days in such a big house with no one but Adela and Nasha to keep her company.

"But why do you keep moving to the other side of the chair, my child? Scoot over so that Clara can feel you next to her."

The meal proceeded without incident even though Margarita insisted on answering all of Doña Clara's questions in monosyllabic whispers, which somewhat dampened the general good spirits of the table.

Adela gave her niece a scathing look. "She must be tired. I can't get her to stop talking most of the time."

Doña Clara suddenly raised her head and set her sightless eyes on the rooms beyond.

"What do I smell?"

"What, *mi vida*, what is it?" Don Florencio asked.

"That smell."

The hunchback turned his head to the side and sniffed. "I can't smell anything, *vieja*, just the smoke from the stove and the delicious food."

"It is something and it smells," she insisted.

Don Florencio looked apologetically at his guests. "Ever since *mi esposita linda* went blind her ears and her nose have become miraculous in their keenness. She can hear a hawk swoop. She can smell rain while it's still in the mountains two days away."

"Don't be a fool, old man. I smell something. Something bad."

"Perhaps the wind from the back of the house. Perhaps the door to the commode has blown open. Or, perhaps, Don Delfino's horses are getting restless out front."

"Perhaps." The old woman went silent.

Through all of this, Margarita sat as still as a defendant in her uncle's court.

Finally, Doña Clara could restrain herself no longer. "Surely someone can smell that besides me. It's coming from in there."

She indicated the direction with a thrust of her lower lip.

Don Florencio rose from the table. "I smell nothing, *mi linda*, but I will make sure, if it makes you happy."

He sidled into the next room and into the gloaming of the late afternoon.

Margarita began a slow slide down her chair until only the top of her head could be seen over the edge of the table.

"Sit up, child," Adela snapped at her, more to break the awkwardness of the moment than to correct her niece, who, in any case, was paying not the slightest heed to her.

"Ah, yes, my little bird, I think I can smell something now." Don Florencio's voice grew fainter as he shuffled from room to room. "It is stronger here. Yes, I can definitely smell something."

From under the table, Margarita could see the old man, in his perpetual turtle crouch. He moved through the house, declaiming all the while, "Worse. Worse. Much worse now."

Finally, he entered the far bedroom.

After a lifetime, Margarita saw Don Florencio framed far away in the bedroom door. He closed it behind him and began his long trek back.

All eyes, including Doña Clara's useless ones, were turned to him.

"Yes?" demanded the old lady.

Don Florencio made no effort to turn his head to the side as was his habit when he spoke. Rather he addressed the floor. "You were right, Clara. There was a smell."

Margarita closed her eyes.

"And I was right. The door to the commode did swing out and the window in the bedroom was open. Nothing more."

On the road back to Mora, with Margarita a subdued bundle between them, Delfino rambled on about this and that.

"Shhh. Margarita is trying to sleep."

They rode in silence for another a mile.

"You know," Delfino finally said, "I think I was starting to smell something too."

Later that summer, Margarita found her first very best friend. Her name was Tina, the nine-year-old daughter of Francisco Jaramillo, an elder of the pueblo of Picurís.

Delfino and Francisco had been friends for sixteen years, a relationship that had begun as a business transaction over some tableland that Delfino needed to winter a herd of cattle. The acreage in question was one of the pueblo's few remaining assets. After some delicate negotiations with Francisco as his patron before the tribal leaders, Delfino secured rights to the land on an annual-lease basis.

Every August tenth, on the pueblo's feast day of San Lorenzo, Delfino would visit Picurís to renew both the agreement and his friendship with Francisco. Adela usually accompanied him while Margarita stayed at home with Nasha. This particular year, however, the aunt, who had begun to fail mysteriously a few months before and would never feel better again, begged off the trip across the mountains.

Margarita, on the other hand, had been lobbying for weeks to be allowed to go. She kept at it until her uncle was vanquished. Her aunt would not be so easy to bend.

"She's too young. She'll get in the way. It's not proper."

"She's seven years old," Delfino countered. "It's time she saw something of the world. She can play with Francisco's little girl. Besides, it will give you some peace and quiet around here."

And so it was decided.

Margarita jumped and screeched when she heard the news.

"Be still, child," Adela scolded her. "If that's the way you're going to act on the trip, you'll disgrace the entire family."

For her part, Nasha slipped into a deep melancholy. The three-day trip would be the longest separation yet from her angel. This was reason enough for her to be sad. But it was even more than that. For most of her life she had harbored a deep resentment against the tribe that had tossed her off so easily. The name *Picurís* had become anathema to her. To realize that her Margarita would soon be walking on ground that had been denied her by her own blood was more than she could bear. Since she was powerless to strike out, she folded herself up into a hard little shell.

Nasha grew even more remote as she helped Margarita pack for the trip.

"I want that dress. No, no, not that one, the other one, the green one."

Margarita pointed to her finest, the one reserved for feast days, the one Adela would never have allowed her to take across the mountains to an Indian pueblo. However, Adela had no energy and spent most of her day in her darkened bedroom fingering her rosary beads and sleeping. So the packing was left to Nasha, who, unfocused and inattentive, stuffed whatever the child asked for into a canvas bag.

"I wish you could go, Nasha. You could show me where you used to live when you were a little girl."

"I would have nothing to show you. I lived in the mountains most of the time."

"But you could meet your family again. Don't you want to see your family?"

"That is not my family. I belong to Doña Prisca, who gave me to your Tía Adela. I cost twenty-five sheep. Those Picurís made a good bargain. They were satisfied. Why would they want to see me?"

Delfino and Margarita left on a Monday with a buckboard loaded with two sacks of potatoes and one of wheat flour, a small tribute that Francisco had never asked for but had come to appreciate.

The trip to the pueblo stopped being a wonderful adventure for Margarita about two hours out of Mora on their ascent into the monotony of the pine wilderness.

The seat of the wagon grew harder, the midsummer sun grew hotter, and the long, ever-climbing road bumpier and dustier. Margarita fell into fitful dozes. Her head rocked rhythmically on her uncle's lap until some sudden shock would bring her bolt upright. She would be confused for a moment, then she would remember where she was and wish for her home and Nasha.

The travelers marked the halfway point of their trip at a rustic fishing compound, nothing more than a row of one-room log cabins set up along the banks of a rushing stream. The accommodations, at fifty cents a night, were there for the convenience of the hardy anglers from Taos and vicinity who looked to escape even farther from civilization. Each little house sat on wooden blocks about three feet off the ground. The interiors were devoid of furnishings except for sleeping pallets hinged to the walls and supported by rough, uneven pieces of unplaned lumber.

Their room was ripe with the musky smell of the creatures that found shelter in the roof and under the floor. Margarita opened her mouth to complain about the stench but thought better of it. Delfino, unlike Adela, would be no ally in such situations.

They ate a supper of bread and ham and retired. Margarita's layer of quilts did little to soften the unyielding wood of the raised platform. The next morning, the water from the nearby stream was too cold for Margarita to do much more than sprinkle her face and hands. Her hair was a nest of snarls, which snagged painfully as she gingerly moved a brush through her flattened curls. She missed Nasha's gentle touch.

After the better part of another wearisome day on the mountain road, they began their descent into the Río Grande Valley, finally to enter Picurís. For Margarita, the sight of the sad little adobe village was yet one more disappointment on a trip already strewn with shattered expectations.

The Picurís of its glory days was no more. The tiered apartments, stacked up to match those of Taos in their geometric grandeur, were now sad mounds of dried mud. The few families that still lived there had built individual flat-roofed dwellings away from the seven-hundred-year-old kiva at the center of the pueblo. It was as if the present generation were ashamed to presume cohabitation with its illustrious ancestors.

Delfino and Margarita pulled up to a three-room adobe bungalow, where Francisco and Celestina Jaramillo were waiting to greet them.

Francisco smiled and spread out his arms in welcome. Celestina stood a step behind, one arm wrapped tightly around their infant son to pin him to the saddle of her hip. The baby squirmed against the wide silver and turquoise bracelet that dug sharply into its middle. Celestina put her free hand to her mouth to cover a shy smile while little Tomás grunted, complained, and pushed his plump brown hands against his mother's wrist in a futile attempt to rearrange his situation.

Francisco reached up and helped Margarita to the ground. "Tina will be happy to see you."

The whereabouts of his daughter was a subject that Francisco did not think to address and one that Margarita did not know how to pursue. For now, she contented herself with playing with the baby on a blanket spread out in the sun while the men and Celestina unloaded the wagon.

Delfino and Margarita had arrived just in time for supper. The men took some of the sheepskins from a corner and spread them on the floor. On a bare spot between the skins Celestina deposited a plate of roasted mutton, and another with fat ears of corn, gray and greasy after being steamed in the horno outside. Next to these she placed a shallow wicker basket containing two rounds of freshly baked bread.

Francisco let himself down effortlessly to the floor and his legs crossed in front of him. Delfino showed none of his host's easy grace. He went heavily to his knees and after some effort to untangle the toes of his boots from the sheepskin that had gathered behind him, sat clumsily with his legs bent beneath him and to one side.

Margarita could not believe her eyes. Here was the most important man in Mora, a merchant, a judge, a man of means who always insisted on the most comfortable chair in his house, sitting on the floor.

Delfino patted a spot on the sheepskin by his side and Margarita knelt down by him, so close that he had to nudge her over to free his right arm. Once settled, she modestly spread her dress, the fine green one she had put on that morning, over her knees.

Celestina passed tin cups of steaming coffee to the men and laid one with water by Margarita's side. Then she sat across from them and placed the baby, Tomás, in the hollow formed by her crossed legs.

Francisco spread an upturned palm over the food. "Please, my friend," he said to Delfino. With this simple benediction, the men helped themselves to the meat and corn and began to eat.

Delfino offered Margarita a small piece of his meat, which was dangling from the bone by a strand of gristle. She shook her head and he did not force the issue.

Margarita looked across to where the mother and her baby were sitting.

Celestina was chewing on a piece of meat. This she removed with a greasy finger and inserted it into the hungry mouth of the infant. Tomás happily accepted the morsel and kicked at the air and smiled as he ate, with saliva and meat juices dribbling down his chin and onto his smooth, brown, naked chest.

Margarita cringed. She could never ever take food from someone else's mouth.

But then, the baby looked happy. He was fat and healthy. It must be all right.

This conclusion put Margarita in a mood to eat. She reached out for a piece of meat and an ear of corn and soon she was eating with the same abandon as Delfino.

What would Adela say when she saw the greasy evidence of the feast down the front of the green dress?

Toward the end of the meal Margarita glanced up to the open door. The light from the evening sun streamed in with an intensity that made her eyes hurt. Into this blinding pool stepped a figure.

It's Nasha. She came after all.

But as the figure stepped farther into the room it was not Nasha. It was a little girl, a year or two older than she—the elusive Tina. The girl sat down by her mother and placed a tiny cloth bundle, not much larger than her fist, at her side.

Tina shot a quick look at Margarita from beneath dark silken lashes, took a small piece of meat and some bread, and slowly began to chew. Her full attention was on a spot on the floor just in front of her.

When the meal was over, the men stood, wiped their hands and faces with handkerchiefs they pulled from their back pockets, strolled to the door and, with no word to anyone, were gone. Celestina handed the baby to Tina and began to remove the empty plates of food.

Tina busied herself with amusing Tomás. He stood unsteadily in front of her, his thick, well-formed little legs bowed out as he curled his hands around his sister's extended fingers. He raised one foot and then the other, walking in place with short wobbly steps. His large, perfectly round head with its shock of soft, black, spiky hair bounced up and down with each jolt as he pounded his chubby feet into the shaggy sheepskin. His body could not keep up with the driving pistons of his legs and he teetered, lost his balance, and fell back on his rump. Startled, he was ready to cry until Tina clapped her hands and buried her face in his belly, noisily blowing into it until he howled with delight.

Margarita laughed and Tina looked at her and also laughed. Thus encouraged, she and her baby brother repeated the performance several times until Tomás tired and began to fuss for his mother.

Celestina sat down by Tina and Tomás lunged at her. His toes caught in the tall wool and he pitched forward into the ample bosom of his mother. Celestina laughed and hugged him tightly for a moment before she rearranged him in her arms. From within her blouse she brought forth a lustrous brown globe with a purplish stub of a nipple. When he saw this, the eyes of the infant grew wide then closed into small, cunning slits. With the desperation of the true addict, he took his mother into his mouth and began to suck frantically. Soon enough he reached the level of comfort that allowed him to relax and establish a slower, deeper rhythm for himself. Celestina placed her cheek on the top of the baby's head and son and mother were immediately adrift in each other.

With her small bundle in hand, Tina stood and went to the door. Margarita sensed that she should follow.

Behind the house four poles stuck up from the ground, forming a square held in place by a few slats of horizontal fencing and crowned by a piece of corrugated tin. At one time it had been a goat pen, but now it was abandoned.

A worn board lay on the ground along the back of the pen. On it, separated into neat piles, were shards of pottery, bits of blue, red, and amber glass, and smooth pebbles, black, mottled pinks, and grays striated with white. Next to them was a worn cardboard carton full almost to the top with even more of these colored bits.

Tina sat down cross-legged. From her little bundle she extracted several bits of red and green glass and two black, egg-shaped pebbles and added them to the rest.

Then Tina began to create. Her fingers moved quickly and surely, plucking a glass shard, a clay bit, or a pebble from one of the piles and setting it on the plank.

Margarita stood and watched, mesmerized by the shifting shapes and colors that eventually yielded a pattern of exquisite symmetry and beauty, arcane symbols to which Tina alone held the key.

Satisfied, Tina brushed the design off the plank and into the carton. "Did you bring a doll?" These were the first words Margarita had heard her speak.

Margarita shook her head.

Tina reached into a corner of the pen and pulled out a roll of ragged blanketing. Wrapped in it were two dolls made from ears of corn.

Tina handed one of the dolls to Margarita. "This is Lupe."

And so they played until darkness covered the pueblo.

That night they slept together in the bed of Delfino's wagon.

The next day, El Día de San Lorenzo, was a day of great celebration. The girls spent most of their time in the large dirt courtyard in front of the church where the ceremonies for the feast were unfolding.

The featured attraction was the Corn Dance, an ancient ritual of song, drama, poetry, and movement. It was a prayerful quadruplet evolved over the centuries to plead with the powers of heaven for rain, for a bountiful harvest, and for the general welfare of the supplicants.

Margarita stared in fear and wonder as the Koshares pranced into the circle of spectators. The bodies of these dancers were painted in black and white or ochre, some striped, some speckled, some made up in solid colors. They danced. They raised small clouds of dust that dissipated high above the assemblage, mostly native but with a sprinkling of the Anglo tourists who were beginning to discover the Land of Enchantment. To the beat of drums and the chants of the singers, the Koshares acted out the entire cycle of the corn, from planting to harvesting. It was a passionate reminder to the spirits of how things had been and an equally persuasive argument for how things should be.

There were also jumping contests, wrestling matches, and footraces. Young men in breechcloths competed over the dusty roads leading into the square for the honor of being declared the swiftest member of the tribe. And there was the pole climber. This young man shinnied up a tall pole to retrieve a bag of seed as if snatching it from the sky, a fetish that recalled the bounty that the heavenly spirits sometimes dangled teasingly just out of reach.

When the two girls finally tired of the nonstop ceremonies, they returned to the playpen behind the Jaramillo house.

Margarita had never felt so much at one with anyone except Nasha. How alike the two Indians were! Birdlike and compact. The way they kept their arms folded when they walked. The tilt of their heads when they considered a question. The same patience, the same kindness, the same quiet strength. The same intuitive feeling for what it took to enrich the lives of those they touched.

After the evening's meal, Delfino announced that they would leave for Mora at first light.

The two girls walked to the plaza and around the old kiva, then back to the lean-to behind the house. Margarita helped Tina sort her box of bits and then they lingered for a while over the dolls.

Their evening ended in a sacrament of their own making.

Tina reached into the pocket of her skirt and drew out a small bowl with a flanged lip. It was not a cracked or chipped discard, but a perfect three-quarter globe with a raised pattern of corn leaves circling its middle. It had been fired many years before into a bronzed glaze with golden flecks of mica, in the fashion of the Picurís potters. Tina sat the vessel gently on the ground between them. From a hollowed-out gourd she filled the bowl with water. Then she drank from it and held it out. After Margarita had drunk, Tina took back the bowl and slowly tipped it so that what remained of the water splattered to the ground between them.

"My grandmother made it for me," she said and put the bowl back in her pocket.

At five o'clock the next morning a half-awake Margarita sat alone in the house with her breakfast, a cup of warm milk and a piece of bread that dripped honey tasting of apple orchards. She ate alone. Tina was not there when she awoke and she had not seen her around the house.

"Probably looking for pebbles," Celestina said.

Margarita was standing with the adults by the wagon when she finally saw her friend by the corner of the house, the makeshift bag loosely at her side. Then she turned and disappeared. When Margarita reached her, Tina was already absorbed in arranging her collection of colored bits into yet another runic design.

"We have to go now."

"Yes. I know."

"Come some time and see me in Mora."

"Maybe."

They were silent then, neither old enough to understand how this moment should be handled. Finally, Tina stood up and turned to Margarita. Her appearance from the day before had changed radically. Her eyes burned red and there were heavy dark splotches beneath them. Her face was bathed in perspiration despite the morning chill that still hung over the pueblo.

"Here," she said with an unnatural hoarseness and held out the small, delicate bowl from which they had shared their communion the evening before.

"But, I can't."

Tina insisted and thrust the bowl into Margarita's hands. "Here."

Margarita placed the bowl carefully on the ground and reached behind her neck to unclasp the small golden-chained cameo that Delfino had given her three Christmases before.

"Have this," she said. "But no one must know. It has to be our secret."

"Margarita, it's time to go." Delfino's voice had the insistence of a traveler anxious to set out.

Margarita placed the bowl in the wide pocket of her dress and walked back down the incline. When she reached the corner of the house she turned to wave. Tina was gone.

The night of Margarita's return to Mora, she had a dream, the first of a sort she would have at other times in her life, a dream that caused her to awaken trembling, sobbing, and gasping for breath.

She and Nasha were at the river for the annual laundry of the bedding. They were alone. Nasha stood at a cauldron of boiling water, stirring its contents with a sturdy stick. The steam from the boiling water rose like a thick veil, obscuring her features, making her almost as anonymous as the Koshare dancers in their face paints. The Indian fished a long white cloth out of the cauldron and held it out to Margarita.

"Take it to the river."

Margarita reached for the steaming, dripping sheet and was surprised to discover that it was neither hot to the touch nor heavy with water. In fact, as she walked to the river, the cloth became so weightless that it began to billow and swirl in the air above her. Suddenly it was ripped from her hands and flew high overhead, blocking the sun and casting a fluttering shadow over her. She turned to Nasha, who must certainly be very angry with her for being so careless. The cauldron stood cold and black, the coals beneath it gray with old ash. The Indian was gone. Margarita turned back to the river in time to see the sheet alight on the surface of the water. There it rested, stationary, seemingly impervious to the currents that swept by it. Suddenly, it began to twist onto itself, at first slowly, then faster and faster until it became a writhing, churning tangle of white. Just as suddenly, the mass of white slowed in its spin and as it came out of one last revolution it was no longer a twisted cloth but the figure of Nasha. She lay face up with her arms crossed over her bosom. It was a very young and smooth-skinned Nasha, a very Tina-like Nasha, dressed in a native costume. A beaded band of white leather around her head. A bone-colored buckskin tunic and skirt. A pair of delicately worked moccasins of soft rabbit fur.

Margarita laughed with delight to see how beautiful her Nasha looked and called to her. But this Nasha, with eyes that looked as if they had been lacquered on her face like a wooden santo, took no notice. She floated on top of the water for a few moments longer before she began slowly to sink and as she sank the river rushed over her and through her and her form became less and less defined. Then it was no *longer Nasha. It was an elongated cluster of white tufts that began to pull apart and to float down the river like an armada of soapsuds.*

For the first time, Margarita knew the terror of separation.

The next morning Margarita rose in a foul mood. She snapped at Nasha for pulling at her hair while brushing it. She threw a tantrum when Adela tried to force one more bite of breakfast on her. She threw the cat off her lap as it jumped up to cradle in her arms.

"Leave that one alone," Adela said to Delfino when he reached over to pat Margarita on the head. "She should have stayed in Picurís."

As soon as she could, Margarita sneaked into her bedroom and from underneath her pillow she retrieved the bowl Tina had given her. She tucked it into the folds of her pinafore and went outside to hide from Nasha. How she resented Nasha's abandonment of her in the dream.

All day she tried to relive Picurís.

First she gathered as many colored pebbles and bits of glass as she could find and spread them out on the wooden bench just outside the barn. But try as she might, she could not manipulate them with anything approaching the skill of her friend. Her patterns were crude and uninteresting and ultimately without meaning.

Next she went to the stables where she took an ear of corn from the crib and tried to fashion a doll from it. The results were totally unsatisfying and she flung the half-made toy as far as she could onto the roof of the tack shed.

Her only comfort came from the little bowl. She drank water from it several times during the day, and thoughts of sharing the cup with Tina cooled her agitation even though the water burned her throat. But then her memory of Tina began to cloud so that by the end of the day she found it difficult to recall what her friend looked like. She thought of Nasha, a template to recapture Tina's face. But she could see nothing of Tina, only Nasha's wrinkled brown face with streaks of gray running through her tightly bunched hair, and for one frightening moment, even this became indistinct as if seen through a steamy mist.

By the time she was called in for her weekly bath she was no longer thinking of Tina and Picurís. Her head was aching too much to think and she winced each time she tried to swallow. She came in the house and went to her room to undress. Her actions were automatic, but she did remember to replace the bowl beneath her pillow before she came out to the kitchen wrapped in a blanket and ready for her bath.

Even in the warm water of the large galvanized tub, which had been set up on the floor by the stove, Margarita shivered uncontrollably.

Nasha looked into her eyes, which were now half closed and rheumy.

"What is the matter, my angel? Why do you tremble so? Mama Adela, look at this child. She feels so hot. And her eyes are so red."

Adela dipped her hand into the tub and then touched Margarita's forehead.

"Is it a fever or is the water too warm? I knew that trip was a bad idea. She probably caught a cold or worse."

"She was fine when we got home last night," argued Delfino. "Who knows about children? Give her some supper and put her to bed. She'll be fine in the morning."

During supper, Margarita grew more and more listless. Finally she pushed away the plate of untouched chicken stew.

"If you won't eat, my angel, drink this tea. And here is something you like."

Nasha presented the little girl with a saucer of two glistening halves of stewed tomato on which she had sprinkled a heaping spoonful of sugar.

This was a treat Margarita had never been known to refuse. But now she managed to eat only one of the tomato sections and dawdled over the second.

"*No más.*"

Margarita pushed her chair away from the table and allowed Nasha to take her to her room.

The rest of Margarita's night was a fragmented confusion. She knew that she was very cold and that Nasha piled several blankets over her. She felt nauseous and suddenly sat bolt upright in bed to vomit a torrent of stringy red clots over her nightgown and the bedclothes. She became hysterical, thinking it was blood. But Nasha was there, quick to reassure her that it was only bits of stewed tomato.

It was while Nasha was changing the bed that she discovered the bowl.

"Where did you get this, my angel?"

"It's mine. Tina gave it to me. Don't tell Tía Adela. Please don't tell her. It's mine. Let me have it."

Margarita snatched the bowl from the Indian and held it tightly.

"I won't tell. I promise. Now come back to bed. It's fresh and clean. Just try to sleep."

By the next morning Margarita's condition was worse.

Nasha tried every remedy in the dispensa for throat ailments but her teas and compresses were powerless against the fever.

Finally Adela summoned the local *curandera*.

Even as the medicine woman was preparing her own batch of potions, Delfino was already at the mercantile to use one of the town's only telephones.

Late that afternoon, a doctor arrived from Las Vegas.

His examination was thorough. Then he took out an evil-looking hypodermic syringe from an oblong stainless steel box.

"I am going to give her an inoculation," he informed Adela and Delfino. "Then I will scrape her throat to relieve some of the congestion. It won't be pleasant for her. Someone will have to hold her so she won't struggle."

"But what ails the child?" Adela asked.

"I'm almost certain it's diphtheria. If I'm right, I want to start the treatment immediately."

"Will she be all right?" Delfino could scarcely dare ask the question.

The doctor responded with a shrug and dug into his satchel.

Margarita was so delirious with fever that she offered little resistance to the shot or to the metal spatula that scraped against her tender throat.

"Now, for the rest of you," said the doctor. "You will also need inoculations. Then quarantine for at least three days. No one comes into the house. No one leaves. Understand?"

Afterward, when all the doctoring was done and Margarita was settled once again in her bed with Nasha by her side to daub at her sweat-soaked temples with a wet cloth, the doctor spoke in whispers with Delfino and Adela.

"Now we wait. This is the first diphtheria I've seen in the valley. There have been a few cases reported around Taos and in a couple of the pueblos."

"The pueblos," groaned Adela. "My little baby, we have killed her."

Delfino felt the room spinning for a moment and had to catch the edges of the table to steady himself.

"I took Margarita to Picurís. We just got back. But no one seemed sick while we were there."

"It happens quickly. Two to three days from exposure to full presentation. The family where you stayed, were there any children?"

"Two. A little girl and a baby."

"They need to see a doctor right away. Take me to your telephone."

At Delfino's store, the doctor called the clinic that sat at a crossroads not two miles from Picurís.

While the doctor talked, Delfino fashioned a crude sign from butcher paper and hung it in the window of the store. *CLOSED THIS WEEK.*

"The nurse will call me back in an hour. I'll wait here. You'd better see to Adela. She's not very strong herself."

Back at the house, Delfino began an incessant pacing that took him from the sitting room through the kitchen and to the doorway of Margarita's room. He would move as far as the door frame and lean in but could not bring himself to enter the room.

The hour stretched into two and then three and finally the doctor returned.

Delfino was at the front door to greet him and escort him back into the kitchen. "You talked to the nurse? Did they see Francisco and his family?"

The doctor sat down heavily at the table.

"Yes, I talked with them. The children, both the little girl and the baby, died this morning. The mother is very sick too. There's little hope for her."

Adela crossed herself. "*Jesusito, qué tragedia.*"

Delfino walked to the window and stared out at the sun. By now it was moving behind the crest of mountains to the west. The valley was already plunging slowly into a violet haze.

"I send you the sun, my good friend Francisco," he thought. "Will you curse it? I know I would."

That night, Delfino drew up a chair next to Margarita's bed to begin his vigil. He ordered Nasha to bed, but when it came to the welfare of her angel, she obeyed no one. So she took a blanket, wrapped herself in it, and squatted out of sight in a dark corner of the sickroom.

Through the night, Margarita thrashed about and tossed her bedclothes violently from her. This would startle the nodding Delfino into wakefulness and he would readjust her covers, feel her forehead, and resume his watch. What he did not know was that at those times when the child's restlessness was not pronounced enough to waken him, Nasha was up and at her side.

By dawn the fever had broken.

Nasha rose, folded her blanket neatly, and put it back in her room. In the kitchen, she rekindled the fire in the stove and set up the coffee pot for brewing.

Delfino awoke to the metallic ring of the iron burner plate rattling into place, checked on his niece, who was now in a deep and restful sleep, and came out to join the Indian.

"She is better."

"Yes."

"*Gracias a Dios.*"

"Yes."

Delfino took a cup of coffee and stepped out on the back stoop. He could hear the barking of a faraway dog and the sharp sounds of iron-rimmed wagon wheels crunching over the road on the upper side of the valley. The sun was not yet up but the sky to the east was already awash in pink and magenta, against which the mountain ridges stood out like sharply cut stencils.

He thought of Picurís, and Francisco sitting on the floor of his cold and empty house, naked and covered from the top of his head with ashes. The coffee was suddenly bitter. He tossed what remained from the cup on the ground, wheeled and reentered the kitchen. Through the door of Margarita's bedroom, he saw Nasha seated in a chair cradling the blanket-wrapped child. At any other time the scene might have played as comedy. The tiny woman was all but engulfed under the weight of the seven-year-old and the bulky coverlet.

Delfino walked over to them and placed his hand on his niece's head. His eyes wandered to the bed, and there, half hidden in the twisted sheets, he saw a small, round shape.

"What is this?" He lifted the small bowl from its nest of sweat-dampened sheets.

"It is Margarita's."

Delfino was by no means a student of pottery but he had eaten more than one bowl of beans cooked in the distinctive pots of the Taos and Picurís pueblos. There was no tastier bean anywhere, it was said.

"But it is Picurís."

"Her friend gave it to her."

"What is it for?"

"It is a drinking bowl."

Delfino turned the bowl in his hands and looked inside it. Although it was empty his eyes saw contagion. Tina had drunk from this bowl and she was dead. Margarita had probably drunk from it and she had almost died.

He began to tremble uncontrollably and then, as if to cast the demon from him, he raised his arm and sent the bowl sailing across the room. It struck the hard stuccoed wall and shattered in a shower of pottery dust and jagged pieces of clay shell. He stood there, panting, then stumbled from the room.

A few days later, when Margarita was again alert and ready to begin the reign of terror that would mark her long convalescence, she asked Nasha about the bowl.

"It was broken by accident when you were sick. But here." She handed Margarita the beaded leather purse that had at one time held the magical bran that had sustained the child in the first days of her infancy.

The little girl drew open the pouch and poured a small stream of pinkish brown powder with golden specks into her hand.

"I ground the pieces up in the *metate*," explained the Indian. "It is now a very strong medicine. Keep it under your pillow and the sickness will never harm you again."

A few weeks later, when Delfino felt she had recovered enough to take the news, he told Margarita about Tina's death.

He had expected her to cry, to beg for explanations. Instead she looked away to the window and said nothing.

After her uncle left her she continued to stare at the clouds that drifted by. Perhaps in one of these she might see the face of her friend. But it did not happen since she could she not remember what Tina looked like at all. Eventually, she turned her head and closed her eyes and fell asleep.

Margarita kept the purse with its powdery relic for a few years. During one of the many moves she and her family made, it was lost.

Death was no stranger to the people of the Mora Valley. A portion of them died early, from disease, from childbirth, from accidents, and from murders. The rest somehow managed to reach a reasonably old age.

Margarita grew up knowing about death. She often accompanied Adela to rosaries and funerals, never afraid but always in wonderment of the antics of the mourners. The women ripped at their clothing and flung themselves on cadavers in open coffins. The men hung back and looked pointedly at the ground, many of them still drunk from the long night they had kept in vigil with the corpse. The women were quick to recover from their grief. They washed their faces and brushed their hair and set about attending to the stream of visitors who came to their houses. The men reclaimed their funereal right to drink, so that by the end of the day they were in turn maudlin and combative until they were escorted home none too steadily by wives and children.

Tina's death was the first that Margarita truly had to assimilate on a personal level. The next opportunity came the following Easter. Unlike Tina's death, which had created a vague emptiness in her, this one left her feeling indecently satisfied and almost wickedly elated.

With her flagging health Adela was less and less able to perform any but the lightest duties. Delfino hired a neighbor woman to come in and help Nasha with the running of the household.

The woman, a spinster, had a nephew named Porfirio who lived with her. Porfirio walked with a pronounced limp, having been kicked by a mule in France, where he had served two short weeks as a private with the American Expeditionary Forces.

Margarita hated Porfirio. To begin with, he was physically reprehensible. He was only twenty-two but already he was slightly bent over and his face, a crisscross of scars and pockmarks from chicken pox and acne, was lined and leathery. His two front teeth were discolored a darkish yellow and protruded almost perpendicular from his mouth so that his lips were parted in a perpetual leer. His breath smelled of stale tobacco and sweet wine that had soured in the steamy orifice behind those jutting teeth.

His physical appearance was certainly enough to repulse a fastidious seven-year-old, but it was nothing compared to his piggish behavior.

With a small government pension, Porfirio allowed himself to be comfortably and unabashedly unemployable. His only commitment in life was to fetch his aunt from her job at the end of the day to protect her from the snapping dogs who came out in the evening while their masters were at supper.

Porfirio's visits were a part of the day that Margarita grew to loathe.

It began innocently enough, at least in the minds of the adults in the house. Porfirio would enter the kitchen, where his aunt was helping to prepare the evening meal. The instant he spied Margarita, he would begin his teasing.

"And how is my little bride this evening?" His tongue mopped across the edges of his overbite. "Porfirio loves you so much that he is waiting for you to grow up so he can marry you."

His aunt would laugh and gently chide him. "Do not annoy the child so, *mi corazón*. She is too young to understand. See how bashful you have made her?"

But it was rage not embarrassment that caused Margarita to flush deeply and leave the room.

At first, Porfirio was content with words. Then he began to advance his remarks in a physical way. He started to pat her cheek whenever he saw her. This soon escalated to running his hand down the back of her head and lingering for a fraction too long on the softness of her neck. Next he took to kissing her forehead, his foul breath raising the bile in Margarita's throat so that she had to turn and bury her head in the crook of her arm to settle the nausea.

Porfirio's assault on Margarita was so subtle and so long in building that it went unnoticed by everyone, even Nasha. The problem was compounded by the fact that Delfino had gradually brought Porfirio into the family circle.

At first when he came for his aunt, Delfino offered him a cup of coffee and a chair by the door. Eventually he invited Porfirio to sit at the table to keep him company. "Talk to me, Porfirio, about your travels."

Delfino had been out of New Mexico only once in his life, when he and Adela traveled to St. Louis for the Louisiana Purchase Exposition of 1904. There he had been exposed to such wonders as ice cream cones and automobiles—steel, chrome, rubber, and leather miracles propelled by steam, electricity, or gasoline. Both the confection and the conveyance had become obsessions with him.

From this trip, Delfino had also acquired a hunger for knowledge. He became a reader of history and geography. He began to fill a notebook of odd facts about foreign lands—the height of the Eiffel Tower, the number of stones in the Great Pyramid of Giza. He had even begun to pencil in a possible itinerary, a Grand Tour for Adela and himself when Margarita was married and out of the house.

Porfirio became one more resource to help Delfino flesh out his catalogue of dreams. And, lie as he might about his personal accomplishments abroad—he was forever assuring everyone that his medal for valor would arrive in the mail any day—Porfirio proved a surprisingly adept and engrossing raconteur. His descriptions of the sights and sounds he had encountered in the Port of New York, across the Atlantic Ocean, and during his abbreviated stay in France were so rich in detail that even Margarita found herself listening.

But, for Margarita, Porfirio's storytelling skills could not long overshadow his basic repulsiveness and she soon quit the supper table altogether. She preferred to eat with Nasha after her uncle and his minstrel had left the kitchen. She also began to absent herself from the house in anticipation of Porfirio's arrival. For several weeks Margarita caught only glimpses of Porfirio from afar as he limped laboriously up the lane and later, when he and his aunt returned to their own house to a chorus of barking dogs.

It was one afternoon in early April. Margarita was bouncing a ball against the front wall of the open barn. She was so fixed on her game that she did not sense a shadow behind her.

"And how is my little bride?"

Startled, she jumped back and the ball bounced by her into Porfirio's hands.

He tossed the colored sphere from hand to hand. "I have not seen you for a long time. Are you trying to hide from Porfirio? You've hurt my feelings, you know."

"I don't care." Margarita was more angry with herself for her lack of vigilance than with the mouthings of this creature before her.

"Now, that is no way to talk to a friend of your uncle."

"Give me my ball."

"Your ball? This ball? Here. Catch it."

With an underhand toss he arched the ball high over Margarita's head and into the gloom of the barn behind her.

"Stupid."

It took a few moments for her eyes to adjust to the semi-darkness inside the door.

Where did it go? Probably to the very back. What a horrible, ugly man.

She reached the back wall and began to look around in the straw spread thick on the floor.

"Did you find it?"

This she had not expected. Rather than continuing toward the house to join her uncle, Porfirio had followed her into the barn and now stood no more than five feet from her.

"Let me help you."

"No! Go away!"

"Don't be foolish, now. It's my fault. Let me look."

For a minute they raked through the hay with their feet. Margarita made sure she maintained some distance between them.

"Here it is," Porfirio said brightly and held out the ball for Margarita to see.

Margarita reached a hand out. "Give it to me."

"Of course, of course." With one hand he held the rubber sphere in front of her face. The other hand went to her head and he spread his fingers so that they were all but enveloped in the abundance of her hair.

"Such a pretty girl. Such soft hair."

Porfirio's hand slipped to her shoulder and under the wide scoop of her dress collar to the bareness of her back. His eyes were glazing over and his tongue darted across his jutting teeth.

"So soft," he slurred to himself.

It was then that Margarita remembered something important. The ugly knot at the side of Porfirio's knee. The one that he constantly bragged on and displayed. In his tellings, it was not a mule's kick but a shell fragment that had done the damage.

"It always hurts," he would say, whenever he had a willing audience. "It hurts so much that I can hardly bear to touch it." But touch it he would, gingerly placing a finger on the spot only to recoil and hiss in pain.

Now Margarita remembered the knot. With all the force she could muster she let go with a prodigious swing of her foot. The kick caught Porfirio unawares, but more importantly it landed true on its target.

At least in the matter of the severity of his wound, Porfirio had told the truth. The slightest touch to the knot could be excruciating. In an instant he was on the floor of the barn, writhing in the straw, clutching at his leg and shrieking to the rafters.

Margarita stood there but for a moment in awe of the calamity she had wrought. Then she picked up the ball, which had rolled to her feet, and ran out of the barn.

She did not mention anything of what had happened to her uncle nor especially to Nasha. In the first place, she was not sure what had happened. Porfirio had touched her, it was true, but he had also touched her in the presence of others and nothing had ever been made of it. In the second place, she knew that whatever had happened would never happen again. This made her smile.

A week later word came that Porfirio was dead of pneumonia.

He belonged to the Brotherhood of the Penitentes, a religious confraternity of self-flagellants, who saved their most extreme and violent penances for Holy Week. During that time, in honor of the sufferings of Christ, they would sequester themselves in a small chapel in the mountains to pray and to endure the pain of knotted cords and leather quirts on bare skin.

During this particular Holy Week, the Brotherhood elected Porfirio to carry the large cross up to their chapel. Fortified by his favorite brand of cheap wine, he scourged himself until the blood flowed down his thin back. Then he carried the rough cross for a mile up the side of the mountain. After this, exhausted and weak, he caught a chill, then a cold, then pneumonia, then he died.

On the night the corpse lay in state at home, Delfino and Margarita attended the rosary.

Porfirio's aunt was inconsolable and repeatedly interrupted the flow of prayers with cries of grief and despair.

"*Mi vida. Mi hijo. Mi corazón.*"

The body lay in a mean coffin of raw, unplaned lumber. Resin still dripped like amber teardrops from almond-shaped knots in the wood. They had covered the lower part of Porfirio's body was a black cloth onto which a neighbor woman had crudely appliquéd a large white cross unevenly cut from one of the dead man's shirts.

Porfirio was dressed in his soldier's uniform, the breast devoid of any medals or ribbons. How his aunt had hoped that his mythical medal for valor might arrive before the burial. His face was bloated and purple and the flesh at his neck bulged over the tight collar of his brown woolen tunic. His mouth was now and forever set in that toothy leer.

Amid the crying and swept up in the moment by the soulful dirges of Porfirio's Penitente comrades, the rest of the assembly stood or sat in grim and silent respect. Among them however, there was one for whom the moment was one of unmitigated jubilation.

"Now, go find someone else to marry," Margarita whispered to the coffin.

Looking up she almost convinced herself that the eyes of the carved cottonwood Christ hanging on the wall behind the coffin actually blinked.

Chapter Four

1920–1921

After the birth of my mother, Tamar next gave Leopoldo two sons in succession, Eugenio and Gerónimo, easy deliveries both.

Nasha, with no investment in these wrinkled and pink males, left Tamar alone. After each birth and convalescence, mother and child returned to the lumber camp.

Margarita Juana had little contact with her mother even on the occasions, five or six times a year, when Tamar, Leopoldo, and their sons came to Mora together. There was hardly ever any exchange between daughter and mother.

Leopoldo, a more frequent visitor at the Arellanes house because of his deliveries to the Mora lumber mills, often sat Margarita on his lap to talk to her and offer her a nickel, or perhaps just a penny if he were feeling put upon.

Before the births of the two boys Tamar confined herself to her bedroom. Afterward she busied herself with nursing and attending to her babies. Unlike with Margarita, her breasts were swollen and hard with milk. Although she still did not demonstrate the natural affection one might expect from a mother, she performed her duties toward her sons ably enough.

Sometimes when Tamar sat in the Arellanes kitchen she watched Margarita chat with Adela or help Nasha with some chore. The little girl was often aware that those cat eyes were on her, eyes that were alive, not painted on like the eyes of the *santos* or in a photograph like Doña Clara's. What Tamar actually thought of her firstborn was anyone's guess. She made no inquiries and her perfunctory "hellos" when she arrived and "goodbyes" when she left bracketed weeks of not speaking directly to the child at all.

Adela and Nasha did not press the point, and while all the social niceties were maintained—Margarita always referred to Adela as *Tía* and to Tamar as *Mamá*—there was never any doubt in the little girl's mind who her real mother was.

Margarita's indifference to her mother blossomed into virulent dislike on the occasion of the baptism of Gerónimo, the second son. It started innocently enough. Margarita was dressed in her Sunday best, which included a pair of high-top shoes with tassels. While she sat on the back stoop, waiting for the adults to get ready, Eugenio came out of the kitchen and plopped down awkwardly beside her.

Eugenio was an oddity to Margarita. He was her brother, born two and a half years after her, but in the context of her life in Mora, the word *brother* had little meaning. She had often heard Adela talking about her own brothers, but these were grown men and the little girl could make no connection between them and this runny-nosed, large-headed, barrel-chested creature with his father's sandy red hair.

In boredom, Margarita began to tap her feet together. This set the tassels on her shoes to dancing. Eugenio grunted in amusement and came instantly to life. He pointed at his sister's shoes and grinned stupidly back at the open kitchen door, hoping that there was someone watching to share his delight.

Soon the children were engaged in a little game. He would reach for one of the tassels and she, waiting until the last delicious moment, would shake her feet vigorously to elude the grasp of his fat little fingers. Eugenio was dull and even less coordinated than most children his age. He had, however, the determination of a shoat pursing its mother's teat.

The game progressed until Margarita's cockiness led to her downfall. Eugenio had worked his left hand underneath her foot while he poised his right hand above. When she jerked her foot away this time, he clamped both his hands together. He had her foot and with it the shoe with its tassel.

He grinned widely.

"Let go," Margarita said.

Eugenio looked at the tassel, then at her, and then his grin began giving way to a smirk.

"I said, let go."

But Eugenio was not about to give up the trophy he had worked so hard to hold.

"Let go." Margarita gave the boy such a shove that he went rolling off the stoop and down to the ground. There he sat, stunned, but tightly in his hand he held the prize, one of the tassels.

"You little pig. You tore my shoe." She pounced on Eugenio and began to pry his fist open. His defense was to roll up in a ball with both hands tucked tightly inside, like a woolly caterpillar fending off a magpie.

She began to pound on his back. "*Dámela.* Give it to me now!"

This was no longer part of the game. Eugenio began to wail loudly.

In an instant Tamar was out the door and in the yard separating the two. Adela was right behind her.

"*¿Qué pasa aquí?*" Tamar screamed, and pulled Margarita off of her brother.

The little girl stood defiantly, panting with rage and exertion. "He tore my shoe."

Tamar looked down at her son, his face streaked dirty from dust and tears, his nose running even more than usual. He still gripped the tassel in one pudgy paw.

"*¿Esta mugre?* This piece of junk?" Tamar plucked the tassel from Eugenio's grasp and flung it at her daughter.

"I don't want it anymore. He's ruined it."

Margarita threw the tassel to the ground. Eugenio snatched it up and sat in absolute contentment.

"Who do you think you are?" Tamar set her jaws so squarely that her face looked twice as broad as usual. Then she reached for one of Margarita's thick pigtails and began to pull.

"Enough," Adela shouted. "Let her go!"

But Tamar had been waiting too long for this moment.

"You are the most rotten, horrible little girl I have ever met." She jerked down on the braid, forcing her daughter to bend over to ease the tension on her scalp.

Margarita began to cry, as much to encourage Adela's intervention as in anger and pain.

Adela tried to loosen Tamar's vise on the braid but with no success. Looking around, the aunt took a broom that was leaning against the wall by the door and began to lay it across Tamar's back. The more she struck, the harder the other woman pulled, and the louder Margarita cried. Finally, broom straw lay scattered everywhere, on the ground, on Eugenio, on Tamar's back, and in her hair.

With one last, vindictive wrench, Tamar let go of the pigtail, scooped up Eugenio, and stormed back into the house.

The baptism was an awkward affair. Adela and Tamar would not even look at each other. Embarrassed and uncomfortable, Delfino and Leopoldo stood self-consciously by their spouses. The baby Gerónimo's godparents, Tamar's sister and her husband, were adrift in neutral territory, virtually ignored by everyone.

Tamar and Leopoldo climbed onto their wagon immediately after the ceremony at the church and left for the mountains. The rest of the party returned to the house to eat cake and fruit compote in near silence.

Tamar did not return to Mora to visit again.

The next time she saw Adela was at the older woman's deathbed.

"Why did you stop being my mother?" was all she could think of to say.

That summer, shortly after Margarita's eighth birthday, Tía Adela began to die in earnest.

For more than a year she had felt poorly. Her strength and her appetite walked out the door hand in hand like two former friends now allied against her. The usual home remedies had no effect and by the time a doctor came, the cancer had a grip on her that no treatment could pry loose.

Her illness suspended the Arellanes household in a limbo-like state where not much was done other than what was absolutely necessary. Nasha kept the house clean and cooked as before, but the long-range projects that so involved Adela's fine hand—stocking the dispensa, sewing, refurbishing the house and its furnishings—were put on indefinite hold.

The time came when decisions had to be made regarding Adela's last days. Doña Prisca, who regularly came the thirteen miles from Guadalupita to Mora to sit with her daughter, made the final determination.

"I shall take Adela back to my house, where she was born," she advised Delfino. "She'll be comfortable there and it will be easier for me to see to her needs."

"What about Margarita? Should I have Tamar and Leopoldo come for her?"

"A lumber camp is no place for her. She needs her schooling. Besides, Adela would miss her too much. She will come to Guadalupita with me. Keep Nasha here to cook and clean for you."

Margarita was unaware of how her fate, for the span of that conversation between Doña Prisca and Delfino, had teetered in the balance. How close she came to a permanent reunion with her natural mother. How unthinkable that would have been.

What everyone had anticipated would be Adela's long and lingering decline lasted less than a month.

Delfino made the trip to Guadalupita three times a week to sit with his wife. After his first visit Adela made a request of him.

"The next time you come, bring a notary."

"A notary? *¿Por qué, Adelita?*"

"You know perfectly well. The land, the cattle for Margarita."

It had always been her intention to give Margarita a piece of land and a small herd of cattle as a dowry. It was Adela's property, left to her years ago by a favorite aunt. Now that she knew she would not live to see Margarita's betrothal she was determined to leave a document of entitlement signed in her own hand and notarized.

"*Bueno*," said Delfino. "Next time."

But the next time and all the subsequent times Delfino came alone, always with an excuse.

"He was out of town."

"I came at the last moment and didn't have time to look for him."

"I talked to him and he says he'll come next week."

Toward the end, chagrined and defensive, Delfino snapped at her. "I know what you want, Adela. Even if the notary doesn't come, I give my word it shall be as you wish."

Adela was too weak to argue. Still her very last words before she slipped into her final coma were to her husband. "*¿Dónde está el notario?*"

After Adela's funeral, Doña Prisca declared to Delfino that Margarita would now permanently live in Guadalupita and Nasha would return to Prisca's service. "It's time I got my use out of her."

Delfino came to see Margarita three or four times after Adela's burial. Eventually, though, he stopped visiting altogether.

Word got back to Doña Prisca that the widower had shucked off his mourning and was sporting a very loose leg. He became both an absentee merchant and farmer. He was more and more indulging in his passion for travel and was leaving the day-to-day operation of his holdings in the hands of thieves and incompetents.

A year after Adela's death he took a trip to Denver and returned with two acquisitions, an automobile and a new wife. In between he had taken his bride on a honeymoon to San Francisco, where they had stayed at the St. Francis Hotel, dined at all the finer eateries, and filled trunks with clothing and household knickknacks that had no practical use back in the Mora Valley. Delfino subsidized the trip through the sale of a parcel of land and a herd of cattle that had once been the property of his first wife, Adela.

On their return, Delfino and Soledea, his bride, were the sensation of the valley. Everyone wanted to meet the new dueña of the Arellanes estate. Delfino obliged them with a fete the likes of which had never been seen before in those parts.

He engaged a caterer from Las Vegas and, taste whetted by the exotic seafood of the coast, he also arranged for the delivery of a barrel of shrimp from Galveston and a case of crab from Seattle. There were silver settings, fine china and crystal, damask tablecloths and napery, and even an ice sculpture representing a swan. Unfortunately, its neck snapped off somewhere during the thirty-mile transport from Las Vegas and by the time the caterer repaired and placed it on the table it more resembled a large duck than a graceful trumpeter.

To everyone's surprise, Soledea was a delight. She was only twenty-one years old, a full and willowy two inches taller than Delfino, with mountains of light brown hair. Her charm was infectious, fortified by a slight separation of her front teeth and a daubing of small brown freckles across the bridge of her nose, imperfections that made her even more endearing.

Every man in the valley fell instantly in love with her. Most of the women, far from feeling any resentment or jealousy, immediately took to her as if she were a younger sister or even, in some cases, the ideal of how they saw themselves in their dreams. When they drove from Mora to Guadalupita in their sparkling yellow and silver 1921 Overland Tour Car, built, as Delfino proclaimed to anyone who would listen, by the Willys-Overland Motor Company of Toledo, Ohio, they turned every head along the way. When they entered the village, they created a hysteria among the passels of dogs who had grown up nipping at horses' ankles and ramming their snouts into slow-turning wooden buckboard spokes. Now the pack was thrown into a confusion of hair and snapping teeth, unsure how to contend with this new thing that caused them to swallow smoke and gas fumes and frustrated their attempts to nip at its blur of silver rims and rubber tires. By the time Delfino and Soledea reached the house of Doña Prisca only one dog remained in pursuit, the leader of the pack. The mixed hound sniffed cautiously at one of the rear wheels now at rest, lifted its leg, and pronounced its judgment on this outrageous contraption.

Doña Prisca was prepared to do a little sniffing of her own by way of a haughty dismissal of Delfino and the evidence of his dotage. But the charms of Soledea were too powerful even for the old woman to withstand. Within minutes of their meeting, Doña Prisca folded Soledea's arm into hers and escorted her to the house as if the young bride were on a state visit.

"Start the tea," she said to Nasha. "And bring out the good service."

Margarita was also enchanted. Never had anyone made her feel so alive and vibrant. While Doña Prisca directed her house servants in the preparation of the parlor for company, Soledea invited the little girl to show her around. While they walked through the formal rooms, those that had not yet been closed off, and out to the courtyard and orchards that fronted the U-shaped hacienda, Soledea asked every question and made every comment that would make any little girl feel grown-up and important.

"How do you keep your hair so soft and beautiful? The well water is so harsh on mine."

It was all due to Doña Prisca's store of roots and unguents, Margarita explained. "I'll give you some if you want."

"Do you read yet? What am I thinking? Of course you do. I love to read. I still remember my favorite books from when I was your age. I must get them for you."

Yes, she read quite well. Her literacy in Spanish came from her aunt's devotional books. Her proficiency with English came from textbooks and magazines, as well as children's works from the meager shelves of what had passed for a public library in Mora.

"Do you like to travel? Delfino and I will have to take you to Denver with us sometime."

Margarita grew pensive. How long had it been since Picurís? She described the visit to the pueblo, her friendship with Tina, her own subsequent illness, and the death of her friend.

To all of it Soledea listened with undiluted attention. When Margarita was finished the young woman hugged her tightly and brushed a tear from her own eye.

By the end of the afternoon, Margarita felt that, although no one could ever replace her dear Tía Adela, Soledea was a most acceptable substitute. She could imagine herself sharing life in Mora with her uncle's new wife. For there had never been a doubt in Margarita's mind that Delfino would eventually bring her and Nasha back to the home where they belonged.

Maybe they'd take her today, her and Nasha, in their wonderful car. Maybe she should go tell Nasha to pack their bags.

However, there was no hint that the child's desires were part of Delfino's plans.

Soledea took Margarita aside before she and Delfino climbed into the open coach of the stately automobile. "I shall be your friend, if you'd like me to."

This did nothing but confuse the issue for the little girl while fanning her hopes. But Soledea's pledge, as vague as it was, was all she had to cling to as she watched the road car disappear in the distance to the renewed accompaniment of barking dogs.

Over the next three months, during two subsequent visits by the couple, nothing was said about Margarita's future.

Despite the good impression that Soledea had made on Doña Prisca, the old woman was still unbending in her assessment of the state of Delfino's sanity. Reports from Mora only served to confirm her worst suspicions.

Finally, Doña Prisca received word that Delfino was selling what remained of his assets in Mora and moving to Denver so that Soledea could be closer to her family.

A scheduled farewell visit to Guadalupita never materialized. Doña Prisca surmised quite correctly that Delfino was not man enough to face her and answer for the dissolution of the estate that Adela had helped him build up so carefully over the years.

As for Margarita, she understood that her seven years of delight in Mora were over. Now all she had left was her precious Nasha.

Chapter Five

1921–1922

Life for my mother and for the bondservant, Nasha, underwent a radical change in the hacienda of Great-Grandmother Doña Prisca Pacheco.

It was a house run formally, in the old style, with two live-in servants, Indian slaves like Nasha. Behind the manor, in a one-story building that once housed thirty, five permanent hands now resided.

The estate had come to Doña Prisca through her husband, Don Vidal Pacheco. He had died before Margarita was born when he fell off a hayrack and broke his neck. The Pacheco homestead in Guadalupita had been established during the Taos Rebellion of 1847, when Vidal's father, Gregoire, escaped from Taos with his family and six bags filled with silver and gold.

The fact that Doña Prisca still held the land of her husband's family was a miracle of benign neglect. By 1921, most of the major Hispanic landholders were gone, casualties of the land-grabbing frenzy that followed the Civil War.

The 1870s marked the organized settlement of New Mexico by the Yankees. There were newly arrived farmers and ranchers from the East, vying for the grasslands of the northern plateau. There were miners after the rich mineral deposits around Raton Pass. The railroad was pushing its way through from Colorado. With these entrepreneurs came the inevitable flood of investors, speculators, and lawyers, all hungry to cash in without regard for the people who preceded them.

Their greatest obstacle was the old Spanish land grants, which had been passed on from generation to generation since the time of the viceroys. In 1891, the Congress of the United States set up the Court of Private Land Claims to review all deeds and petitions. By 1903, the court's job was finished. Few were surprised that about 80 percent of the holdings established by Spanish and Mexican land grants ended up in the hands of Anglo lawyers and new settlers. One lawyer, in fact, who came to New Mexico with little more than the clothes on his back, found himself richer by over a million acres within a year.

Other lands, specifically the *ejidos*, once held in common by Hispanic villages, were swallowed up by the Department of the Interior and the United States Forest Service. To continue to use this land, these same Hispanics who had taken their rights for granted for over two hundred years now had to compete head to head for usufruct with large-scale Anglo ranchers. They never had a chance.

The Pachecos were spared, for although they were prosperous and their holdings were significant, they were small potatoes in the grand scheme of western expansion. There were no minerals in the area worth mining. There was not enough open range to support many thousands of cattle. The weather was capricious. And timber stands in the area were much more accessible through other routes. Thus, in the absence of easy opportunities, no one came to covet what the Pachecos owned.

After her husband was killed by his fall from the hayloft, Prisca forged on with remarkable persistence and acumen. From her quiet domestic existence she made an agile adjustment to the world of business. She became a woman who made decisions. She determined, for example, that she could operate almost as efficiently by using seasonal laborers, so she kept only seven of the twenty resident hands whom Vidal had employed. She built a press to produce barrels of cloudy, tawny apple cider for marketing in Las Vegas and Taos. Finally, Doña Prisca closed the small and marginally profitable lumber operation, preferring to lease the timber rights to others more willing to worry about milling, transporting, and marketing.

In spite of her enterprise, Prisca was eventually caught in a slow but inexorable erosion of her situation. She was fighting to survive in an agrarian world while the rest of the country was firmly entrenched in the mechanical. People from the valley were moving on with no one to replace them. Las Vegas, her main link to the markets beyond Mora, and once a fast and sleek clipper ship on the sea of commerce, was now ragged of sail and becalmed. Its banks closed, its rail yards moved south, and its rows of Victorian houses sagged with the weight of their boarded-up windows.

Eventually, the hacienda, which boasted twenty-one rooms, including two dining salons, two parlors, a sewing room, and an attached carriage house, began to leak. At first, Prisca worked diligently to keep ahead of the problem. But finally she realized the futility of it all. So she began to shut down the house, room by room, beginning at the extremities. She felt like a diabetic watching her own body cut from her piece by piece.

By the time Margarita and Nasha came to live with her, Doña Prisca had already closed up nine of the rooms. Lately, however, she had run across a dull white circle on the floor at the far end of the formal sitting room. When Prisca followed its path up to the massive vigas that stretched across the ceiling, she saw a spongy, swollen discoloration symptomatic of one more leak. She knew it was the beginning of the slow decay and eventual amputation of yet another of her lovely rooms.

The major difference for Margarita between living in Mora and Guadalupita was her transformation from a happy princess to a china doll. Each school morning Nasha fed and dressed her. Under Doña Prisca's supervision the Indian combed her hair with a pomade made from chicken fat rendered in a double boiler and beaten with a dash of perfume until it was a fluffy white. The little girl brushed her teeth with another of Prisca's recipes, a powder made from eggshell with a pinch of alum. It was not that commercial products were unavailable to them in Guadalupita. But Prisca was well known for her thrift. Besides, given a choice, she always preferred to hold on to the old ways.

A farmhand then took Margarita by carriage to the one-room schoolhouse that stood among the cottonwoods lining the banks of a creek, the same that tumbled past her father's sawmill fifteen miles up the canyon. After school, Doña Prisca sat her down in the *sala grande*. At the room's main table, a massive affair with carved legs, she was expected to continue her studies for another hour. Instead, she fidgeted on the plush wine-colored cushion of a heavy chair and whiled her time away gazing at the column of dust motes caught by the light angling through the large central window.

There were no challenges to Margarita in the simple cipher and reading exercises of the village school. When she asked Doña Prisca if she could page through some of the books sitting on the shelf in the

sala, the old woman took a surprisingly atavistic posture, considering
her own struggles to emerge from a traditional woman's role.

"You only need to learn what is taught you in school. Once you are married, you won't have time for books."

On the days when Margarita did not have to go to school, her sense of confinement was even keener. She was not allowed to climb trees. She was not permitted to ride horses nor to play in the hayloft as she had in Mora.

The crowning affront was that Doña Prisca never allowed her out of the house unless she wore a large, floppy sunbonnet and a long-sleeved dress to shield her skin. Doña Prisca was a firm believer that fair, unfreckled skin was a young woman's greatest asset.

When Margarita, her courage rising with her dander, pointed out that Doña Prisca's own skin was now very brown and leathery, the old woman laughed, not a common occurrence in that house.

"When I was your age, I was never allowed outside. When your great-grandfather Vidal asked me to marry him, he said it was my smooth and milky skin that turned his head."

"But now?" The old woman looked at her veined, liver-spotted hands. "Anyway it was all so very long ago." And then the gentleness that had crept into her voice with the laughter dissipated.

On days when she was permitted outside, Margarita sat by the well in the courtyard and played with her dolls or hosted tea parties that no one ever came to.

Nasha was no longer Margarita's to cater to her every whim.

"You're too old to need a nurse," Doña Prisca had informed the girl early on. "And besides, Nasha still owes me many hours of work for those twenty-five sheep I lost."

When Margarita needed to fill her little teapot with water it was easy enough to go into the kitchen. But it was even easier to coax Nasha into drawing fresh, cool water from the well. After that it was a simple thing to entice the Indian to sit down with her and have a drink from a tiny cup and eat imaginary biscochitos. These occasions, however, usually ended badly, with the bleat of Doña Prisca's voice from the *portal*.

"Nasha, do you have so much time to spend doing nothing? Then why is there always so much work undone at the end of the day?"

Nasha would scurry off in a direction away from the voice, if at all possible. If she walked by Doña Prisca she was sure to have one of her braids yanked or feel the hollow thump of a fist on her back.

Doña Prisca ran a strictly regulated enterprise with all duties well defined. There were five full-time hands who took care of the farm and the herds. Two others worked around the compound.

One of these two, Don José Argüello, was a general handyman. His charge was general maintenance. He could fix anything except, to Doña Prisca's consternation, a leaky roof. At sixty-nine, he argued, he was no longer spry enough to climb and edge across the steep pitch of corrugated tin.

Margarita fancied him her Santa Claus. He certainly looked the part, with his long white beard and his open, friendly face. He even carved wooden toys for her in his spare time. Her favorite by far was one that the old man called a *roon-roon*, a piece of notched wood attached to a long piece of string. When Don José twirled it over his head, it blurred and produced a sound, "roooon, roooon," that reverberated across the open fields. The faster he spun it, the louder the noise.

The other house hand, Toribio Martínez, was hardly so congenial. His duties were to help Doña Prisca tend to the orchards and to take care of the milk cows, the hogs, the chickens, and the turkeys. He undertook these chores with a surliness that often crossed into open animosity.

No one liked Toribio, including the cows, who instinctively shied away from him every time he approached them with stool and pail. More than once he had lost a bucket of milk when a cow, spooked by his rough and careless handling of a tender teat, kicked the container over.

Margarita avoided all contact with Toribio. She recognized in him the same coarse temperament as she remembered in Porfirio, the brutish cripple who had taken liberties with her the year before. She watched from afar as Doña Prisca talked to Toribio to give him his day's instructions or to berate him for yet another substandard performance.

Toribio never looked his mistress in the eye. Rather, he preferred to bow his head, and turn his face to one side whenever he whined his excuses. Once Doña Prisca's back was turned, Toribio would find his courage. He stared defiantly after her, screwed his face into a mask, and mockingly mouthed her words back to her. He always ended his pantomime by clutching at his genitals and spitting in the direction of Doña Prisca's retreating figure.

Toribio's career on the Pacheco estate came to an abrupt end one hot September morning.

Since her rising at daybreak, Doña Prisca had occupied herself with rearranging the shelves in the dispensa. At midmorning she happened to glance out the kitchen window. It was one of Toribio's early-morning duties to let the chickens out as soon as he had finished milking the cows. But the chickens were nowhere to be seen.

When Doña Prisca went out to the henhouse she found the door still propped shut. Throwing open the shed she saw what at first seemed a shapeless, ghostly white heap. Closer inspection revealed the horrible truth. Her chickens were piled high on the floor or prostrate on the roosting shelves.

She began picking up chickens and tossing them outside. Some squawked to consciousness and fluttered clumsily to the ground. Others sailed lifelessly through the air and lay where they fell with sickening thumps. The job was simply too much for one person, so Doña Prisca ran back to the house.

"*Muchachas*, bring water in whatever you can find. The chickens are dying from the heat!"

Margarita ran after them and stood behind the high wire fence as the four women scurried around the pen, splashing water on anything that moved.

Of one hundred and forty-two chickens, they were able to save sixty-two. The others were dead from heat prostration or had suffocated under the weight of their fallen coopmates.

Once the grim inventory was over, the women proceeded to work on the surviving birds, dipping them into the water and trying to force some of the liquid down their gullets.

Toribio chose this moment to walk in from the orchard.

"*Vagamundo*. You have killed my chickens!" Prisca screamed at him while she madly fluffed up the feathers of her favorite rooster with cool water. "What were you thinking, leaving them inside on a hot day like this?"

"But I thought it was going to rain."

Prisca stabbed her finger into the clear, cobalt sky. "Rain? Do you see rain? This cannot be! Take your things and leave. And don't expect any money. See what you have cost me!"

Toribio once again tried to plead his case, but Doña Prisca was not in a listening mood. She wheeled and reentered the coop and a moment later another shower of dead chickens flew out the coop door.

Toribio looked around but neither Margarita nor the Indians dared to meet his poisonous glare. He stomped off to the bunkhouse but just before he entered he turned and performed his usual dance of defiance. He wagged his head, moved his mouth, clutched his crouch, and then added something extra. He began to hop back and forth from one leg to the other. In spite of her fear, Margarita had to laugh, for he looked like someone who needed very much to relieve himself.

Late that night, Margarita awakened to shouts coming from outside her window. Her bedroom wall was a sheet of dancing patterns of orange. From the kitchen door she saw a wild scene illuminated by a fire roaring in full fury. Doña Prisca, the Indians, Don José, and the other hands were racing back and forth from a horse trough by the barn. They were all swinging buckets, which they dipped into the water and carried over to throw on the conflagration that had by now totally engulfed the chicken shed.

Dawn's light allowed them to assess the damage. Nineteen more chickens were dead, among them the rooster that Doña Prisca had worked so hard to revive the day before. The poultry shed was in ashes. To one side of the kitchen door they found a coffee can that smelled of kerosene. There was a large, oily streak across the back wall where the fuel had been splashed. Whether the arsonist had been frightened off before he could fire the house or had simply had a change of heart they could not tell.

When Doña Prisca made inquiries in the village about Toribio's whereabouts, none claimed to know. He was never seen in the valley again.

Chapter Six

Filiberto Pacheco made quite an entrance.

It was evening and Doña Prisca and Margarita were seated at the kitchen table finishing their supper. The door flew open with a frightful bang and an apparition stood before them. His face was a mask of bruises and dried blood. His clothes were torn and muddied and his hair was plastered tightly to his skull. Filiberto's appearance was so unsettling that it took even his mother an instant to recognize him.

When she recovered her wits, she sprang from the table to her son's side. "*Dios del cielo*, what has happened to you?"

He staggered to the table with Doña Prisca's help and sank heavily into a chair.

"*Tengo sed*," he rasped through cracked, swollen lips.

"Nasha, some water. Quickly, girl, quickly," ordered the old woman. "And a basin. Hand me those towels."

While Doña Prisca carefully removed some of the grime and dried blood from his face, Filiberto gave a terse account of what had befallen him.

"My horse. It kicked me in the face. It lost a shoe and I was trying to fix it when I got kicked. When I came to, the brute was gone. I've been walking since yesterday."

"Well," Doña Prisca announced as she pressed gently on his cheekbones and around his jaw, "you were lucky. Nothing broken that I can tell, except for your nose. You will have a nice scar on your upper lip, though."

Filiberto Pacheco was the youngest child of Don Vidal and Doña Prisca, their only son, whom they had spoiled shamelessly from birth. He was still unmarried at the age of forty-six. There was a reason for this.

If the chicken killer and arsonist, Toribio, could be described as mean spirited, Filiberto Pacheco had honed his malevolence into a veritable art form. It was as if he had chosen to devote the entire store of his energy to one purpose, to be calculatingly cruel to as many creatures as had the ill fortune to meet up with him. Only Doña Prisca was spared his bile, for reasons more self-serving than filial.

He did not drink. He did not chew tobacco. He did not gamble. And, as far as anyone knew, he had never kept a woman. Aside from his temperament, his only real vice was a certain vanity about his appearance. Not that he cared what others thought of him. Rather, he had set a certain standard for himself, for both the interior and exterior man, and he worked diligently to live up to it.

He was handsome in a toxic way. From his grandfather, Gregoire, he had inherited a long, fine Gallic nose and light complexion. His dark and sleepy eyes were from his grandmother. He kept his shiny, dark-brown hair swept slickly to the back and he cultivated an extravagant mustache that formed a rich, silky arch across his upper lip and down to the jaw line on either side. He preferred black, from boots to hat, which matched the shadowy cast to his lower face even when he was freshly shaved. He stood, at six feet one inch, a giant among the men of Guadalupita. Many women would have loved him had there not been so much to fear.

His favorite horse was a dapple gray, a stallion with a long, bluish mane that whipped at his face as he pushed the animal hard and fast at every opportunity.

People in their homes always knew it was Filiberto going by just from the pounding drive of his horse's hooves on the hard-panned dirt roads just outside of their windows.

"It's Filiberto," they would say, "on his devil horse."

Parents were known to frighten their children into being good just by rhythmically slapping their palms in imitation of a horse at full gallop. "Listen. Hear that? It is Filiberto looking for bad little children to carry away to the mountains."

Filiberto had no idea he had been dubbed the bogeyman of Guadalupita. Had he known, he likely would have accepted the logic of the choice and smiled in a self-satisfied way.

Margarita knew less of Filiberto than anyone else in the village.

She had seen him not more than twice in her life, each time a fleeting opportunity. He had never spoken to her. He did not attend the funeral of his sister Adela. He was elsewhere when the little girl and Nasha came to live in Guadalupita.

From conversations she picked up between Doña Prisca and the ranch hands, Margarita knew that Filiberto was in a place called Cherry Vale, fifty miles to the east of them. It was ideal cattle country at the intersection of the Canadian and Mora rivers where the Great Plains began their eight-hundred-mile stretch from the base of the Rockies to the Mississippi Valley.

At Filiberto's insistence, Doña Prisca had advanced him a herd of fifty cattle to try his luck at homesteading. She was encouraged, if suspicious, by his sudden appetite for real work. She also welcomed the opportunity to get her son away since things always went so much more smoothly when he was not around.

During the next few days, as Filiberto recovered from his injuries he let it be known to his mother in a roundabout way that Cherry Vale had been a failure.

His excuse was *los gabachos*, as Anglos were locally known. "They kept me from the grass and water and finally made me sell out."

This pricked Doña Prisca's ears. "You sold my cattle? You had no right."

"They were mine to use as I saw fit. Anyway, I couldn't drive them back here. They would have died on the trail. And every day I waited *esos desgraciados* cut the offer by ten percent."

"So where is the money?"

Filiberto looked directly into her eyes, as he always did, she knew, when he lied to her. "I lost it somewhere along the way. I don't remember. I had to walk so far and I kept fainting.

Doña Prisca summoned one of her hands and told him to ride back to Cherry Vale and find out what had really happened. "Talk to the people there. Ask them about the cattle. And keep your eyes open for Filiberto's horse."

On his return, the hand reported to Doña Prisca that Filiberto had indeed been forced to sell the cattle to one of the big ranches. But then his story took a different track. Filiberto had failed, according to the foreman at the ranch where the cattle had been left, because, in the end, he could find no one to work for him. Those he hired he pushed mercilessly even while he tried to cheat them out of their pay. Within a month his reputation as an employer was so tarnished that no one would have anything to do with him. At last, in desperation, he came to the rancher to sell the herd. He had taken the first offer tendered.

"A little below the market value," the hand noted, "but fair enough considering he was in such a hurry to leave."

As for Filiberto's horse, the hand had found it along the trail. It was dead, still tethered to a fence post and with a gunnysack tied over its head.

"I couldn't get too close to it since it was already rotting," he said.

"And the saddle and bridle?" Prisca asked.

"Gone. Probably somebody came by and took them." The man stood to leave, then hesitated. "There is one more thing, a piece of fence post. It had dried blood on it and bits of hair, blue, like the horse's mane. The gunny sack around the horse's head was almost all blood."

Doña Prisca never spoke of Cherry Vale to Filiberto. But she knew her son, and knowing him, knew his story. He had kept the money from the sale of the cattle. He had stolen from her before and so this was no surprise to her. As for the horse, she had seen how he mistreated animals. She surmised that he had hooded the horse to calm it. The horse had probably kicked wildly about and smashed Filiberto in the face while he dug impatiently into its tender hoof. So he had gone into one of his rages and struck the horse repeatedly with the fence pole until it fell. He had kept beating it long after it had died. Doña Prisca knew it in her soul as surely as if she had been there to witness it.

With the return of Filiberto, Nasha stopped sleeping in the room she shared with the other two Indian servants. Instead she would drag out a thin mat every night and spread it on the kitchen floor by the door to the backyard. Her explanation to Doña Prisca was that she could no longer sleep in the same room with Beta and Hannah because they were Taos and she was Picurís. The other two Indians were constantly ragging her for coming from such humble origins while they could claim, even though they had been purchased like her, the grandeur that was still Taos. However it was not her roommates but the presence of Filiberto in the house that caused her to seek the open spaces of the kitchen where she could not be cornered and defenseless.

There was a violent history between Nasha and Filiberto that culminated when she was fourteen and he a young buck of eighteen. Up to that time she had weathered abuse of every form from him. If he was in one of his rages and Vidal and Prisca were not around to intervene he would rush at her and throw her down, raining kicks and blows on her body that left her stiff and hobbling for days after.

"What is the matter with you, girl?" Doña Prisca would snap impatiently. "You're walking around like an old woman."

Nasha never told because she knew she could never escape Filiberto.

One day, ten months before she was mercifully delivered into the household of Delfino and Adela to care for the infant Tamar, Doña Prisca called her to a special chore.

"One of the hens has been nesting in the barn. She's to be locked in the yard until I can break her of the habit. But I'm sure she's left some eggs. Go look for them."

In the dimness of the barn, Nasha began carefully to search, first in the loft and then in the hidden recesses below. She shuffled her feet cautiously to avoid stepping into a nestful of eggs.

She turned when she heard the clopping of horse hooves on the wooden floor.

"*¿Qué quieres aquí?*"

Filiberto was leading his mount into the coolness of a stall.

She felt a sudden constriction in her chest and even though she opened her mouth to answer him no word came out.

The young man, already tall and robust, uncinched the saddle and swung it easily with one hand to drape it over the side railing. He began to fold the blanket, slowly, deliberately into smaller and smaller squares before he dropped it on a tack box. Finally he spoke again. There was now annoyance in his voice. "I said, what are you doing here? Looking for something to steal? There is nothing here for you."

"*Huevos,*" she finally managed to say. The word came out like a whimper.

"What?" The quirt looped around his wrist swung slowly by his side as he moved out of the stall and toward her.

"Did they send you to spy on me?"

"Your mother sent me to look for eggs."

He was standing not two feet from her when he laughed. "Oh. Eggs. *La indita quiere huevos.* Why didn't you say so? I can show you eggs."

She looked at his empty hands.

"*¿Qué pasa?* Don't you believe me? Look here."

He slowly uncoupled a wide, silver buckle and the two ends of his belt fell away. He undid the buttons on his pants and pushed the flaps open. Taking her wrist roughly he plunged her hand into his crotch.

"Here are two nice eggs for you, and a sausage, too."

In one furious motion, he spun her around and sent her sprawling face first against a large wooden crate. Then he threw her skirts up over her shoulders, ripped at her undergarments, and took her from the rear.

She did not struggle or cry out. Instead she collapsed heavily against the box and felt pain. There was a sharp cutting pain as the edge of the crate pressed unyieldingly into her pelvis. There was a blunt, throbbing pain as she was entered, she knew not with what, between her thin quivering thighs. She felt spittle and sweat and tears on her cheeks and neck. She was enveloped in sounds, the snorting and stomping of the horse in the stall behind her, the bleating of a goat beyond the planking of the back wall of the barn. And there were grunts and curses from Filiberto and the banging and scraping of the crate as it bounced and slid across the floor.

When she returned to the kitchen, Doña Prisca was in a grand snit.

"Where have you been? How long does it take to find a few eggs? And where are they? What a useless girl you are!"

Nasha could only look at her and spread her hands out in supplication, her mouth open and moving but silent. Then she wrapped her arms around her small frail body and shook.

Doña Prisca was much too involved in her own agitation to notice. "Look at you. Your face is filthy. Go wash. And then come with me."

Doña Prisca marched Nasha back to the barn, leading her none too gently by one of her braids. As hard as they looked they found no eggs. But Nasha only pretended to look. For in the half-lit barn everything she saw, every shape, every form seemed to be rising up and closing in on her to press her down to the earth so she could relive the pain.

Seven months later the fetus in Nasha aborted itself. None but she knew about it. She wrapped it carefully in a piece of burlap and hid the sorry little bundle in a place she thought no one would ever discover.

This is why, twenty-eight years later, Nasha left her bedroom to come to the kitchen to sleep by the door. Here at least there was an openness she could use to her advantage for escape should Filiberto ever approach her again. But he never so much as spoke to her.

Doña Prisca had abandoned the master bedroom with its high cherrywood bed and matching furniture on the day her husband died. This room was now kept solely for the memories it held. At times she would sit there in the dark and wonder why she was still alive. Now she slept in a back bedroom, stark and melancholy and functionally furnished. There were two beds here and Margarita slept in one of them.

On the occasional night when Margarita awoke in a start from an unpleasant dream and could hear the even, shallow breathing of the old woman asleep, she would sneak from her bed and quietly make her way to the kitchen to curl up with Nasha on the small mat next to the door. It was the only way she could think to rekindle the warmth and affection that had been buried on the day of Aunt Adela's funeral.

Nasha would welcome her and run her fingers gently through Margarita's hair. "My angel," she would say and whisper the refrain from so long ago, repeating it again and again until the little girl was asleep. "*Hati pam'one*, precious little blossom, *tcakwil 'a'eye*, come to me. *'Amaxutcetci*, Let me hold you."

Doña Prisca had finally had enough. It was the white stain on the floor of the sitting room that did it. Where once the old woman might have looked at the pale blemish as one more step toward the inevitable collapse of the Pacheco estate, now she decided to take a stand.

"Why should it be?" she thought. "Why must it all crumble and die? I can stop it. I will stop it! I owe it to the family. I owe it to Vidal."

She called in Don José Argüello. "We have a new leak."

"But, Doña Prisca, I'm too old to climb the roof."

"Don't you think I know that? I have no intention of sending you up there."

"But then how can we fix it?"

"From the inside, of course."

"From inside?"

"Through the attic, you old *simplón*. We'll take a lantern into the attic and find the leak and patch it there."

"But how do we find it?"

Doña Prisca clicked her tongue with impatience. "We will mark the place of the stain. Then we will go into the attic and find the spot on the ceiling that is right above the stain. Then we will follow it to the hole in the roof."

So the old woman and the old man carefully triangulated the position of the stain on the floor and climbed the narrow steps up to the trap door leading to the attic. Taking the key ring from her waist, Doña Prisca unhinged the padlock and stood aside as Don José pushed the door up and over, letting it drop into the attic space with a rafter-rattling crash.

The attic had not been opened in years, not since she had placed Vidal's personal belongings into a chest and a younger, stronger Don José had hoisted it up and set it beneath the roof timbers. This done, she had ordered him to install a sturdy hasp and staple to which she could attach a padlock.

The two climbed up and stood in the attic, allowing their old eyes to become accustomed to the semi-dark. They were at one corner of the bottom stroke of the U that defined the shape of the house. Before them at one end of the attic space there was a small window that filtered in a weak, broken shaft of sunlight. Its panes were curtained with a lace of dirt on the outside and grease on the inside, residue from many years of smoky fireplaces and cookstoves. Behind them, the attic went for a distance of about seventy feet above the sala grande. From there the building angled around to disappear in darkness down the other arm of the house. There was a pattern of planks laid across the exposed vigas to step on, a long-ago trail blazed through a wilderness of dust and cobwebs.

"It needs an airing out." Don José pulled out a large, soiled handkerchief from his back pocket and planted a loud sneeze into it.

"Yes. It's been closed up a long time. When we're done with the leak, I want you to take Don Vidal's chest back down. Maybe there's something in it you can use. We'll probably have to burn most everything. Who knows what's been nesting in there."

She turned to the trap door, leaned down, and called out, "Beta, Hannah, Nasha, come here."

When Beta's moon face appeared at the foot of the stairs, Doña Prisca gave her instructions. "Get some brooms, some soapy water, and some rags, lots of rags. We're going to clean this attic out." Turning back to Don José, she extended an arm in the direction of the faraway window. "Over there."

Don José lit the kerosene lamp he was holding and began to pace off the attic, stepping carefully from plank to plank, moving one or two of the boards about when he needed to stray off the beaten path.

"Here," he declared at last, pointing down triumphantly. "This should be right over the stain." He brought the lantern low and raked it down the channel between the joists. Then he stopped. "What's this?"

He could not tell what it was, only that a bundle was enveloped in several layers of moldering burlap. Poking his finger at it, he pushed away a frayed flap. "*Dios mío.*"

"What is it? What did you find?"

"*Dios mío*," he repeated and crossed himself quickly with his left hand as his right hand raised the lantern high enough for Doña Prisca to see over his shoulder.

What greeted the old woman were the small, dark, burgundy-colored remains of an infant in a perfect state of mummification, its arms and legs drawn up under its chin as if it were still resting in its mother's womb.

When Nasha had hidden her secret between the attic joists almost three decades ago she had been too frightened to consider those effects that spring from the natural course of things. As the aborted fetus had decomposed, its juices had seeped out of the sacking and eaten away at the wood beneath. There was not enough of the infant to cause much corrosion, just enough to rot a small hole almost all the way through the space between two of the juniper poles that lay at an angle between the vigas. Once the roof above sprung a leak, it was only a matter of time. The waters from the heavens had seeped through the earthly remains of the stillborn child of Filiberto and the little Indian slave, found the chink, and dripped onto the dark, polished floor below.

"We're ready, Doña Prisca." It was Beta. "Just Hannah and me. We can't find Nasha. She's never around when there's work to be done."

The old woman wheeled in the direction of the voice. Beta's large, almost perfectly round head had poked through the opening in the ceiling, and was now rotating owl-like to survey this mysterious region shut off for so many years. Beta finally spotted Doña Prisca and Don José. They stood frozen like a quaint study in chiaroscuro created by the casual illumination from the window behind and the lamp in front. The Indian opened her mouth to speak. She never got out a word.

"Get out of here!" Doña Prisca screamed. "Leave us alone."

"It's Nasha's fault," whispered Beta to Hannah as they retreated into the kitchen. She could not appreciate how right she was.

Doña Prisca stepped down from the attic onto the top stair. She bit off her words to the trailing Don José and walked resolutely out of the room. "Close it. Lock it."

That night, after Margarita was in bed and the house was quiet, Doña Prisca came to the kitchen and stood above Nasha laying on her mat by the side of the stove. "I was in the attic today. We found. . . ." Doña Prisca's resolve cracked for a moment and she hesitated, then began again, her voice now hard and strong and deadly calm. "We found a baby. A dead baby. A baby that has been dead a long, long time."

Nasha came to her knees and bowed her head to her mistress.

"What do you know about this?"

Nasha began to cry then, at first softly but building into spasms that jerked her body mercilessly.

"You are a devil," the old woman hissed. "You are the daughter of hell."

Reaching into the kindling box by the stove, Doña Prisca drew out a dried and gnarled piece of root from a cedar tree and began to strike the Indian, not furiously, but with hard, measured strokes, steady and constant like a metronome, until Nasha slid into a heap on the floor.

Doña Prisca was so spent that after she struck the last blow she did not have the strength to pull back the club. She simply released it where it lay across the Indian's back. It balanced there for a moment then rolled off onto the floor.

Doña Prisca heard an exhalation from the heap in front of her. Not a groan. A name.

"Filiberto."

Nasha lay on the floor for a long time after Doña Prisca left until she felt strong enough to crawl to the door. Once she had it open, she wedged her body out onto the back stoop, missed the first step, and went rolling off onto the ground below. There she lay for another while. Finally she rose unsteadily to her feet, fell over, rose again, and stumbled off into the night.

Doña Prisca sat in the dark in her husband's bedroom until she heard a rooster crow. With a struggle she rose from the chair and walked out of the room, gently closing the door behind her.

When she walked into Filiberto's room his eyes, dark and cold, were already open. "Get up. We have work to do."

They buried the bundle among the brambles that grew along an arroyo some hundred yards from the house. To his question about the baby, Doña Prisca answered with one word. "Nasha."

When Filiberto had finished refilling the tiny hole, he turned to leave.

"Can you not even stay a moment? One small prayer for your own child?"

He hesitated only a beat, threw the shovel over one shoulder, and walked away, leaving Prisca to mourn alone.

Margarita awoke that morning in a start. Rousing herself was something she was not used to doing, since, for as long as she could remember, her first sensation of each day was of the cool, callused hand of Nasha on her cheek.

Beta and Hannah raised their shoulders and turned down their mouths when she asked them where Nasha was. Over the child's head, they looked at each other and stifled a giggle.

Doña Prisca snapped at the little girl when the question was raised to her. "Never mind. None of it concerns little girls. Get yourself ready for school. You're old enough, God knows. It's time everyone here looked to themselves."

After a week of waiting, Margarita knew that Nasha was gone for good. Doña Prisca told Beta and Hannah to go through Nasha's things, keep what they wanted, and discard the rest. Margarita felt a heaviness that she had not experienced since Tía Adela had deserted her.

In two weeks it was as if there had never been a Nasha. No one spoke of her and there was no trace of her left in the house. Margarita did not understand what had happened but she also realized that there was no one in that dark house willing to explain it all to her. She cried in private for many weeks after. Eventually those tears washed away the last vestiges of her childhood.

Doña Prisca no longer nagged her about her studies. The embroidery hoop with its meticulous stitching over which the child had labored so painstakingly under Doña Prisca's tutelage lay untouched in the sewing room. She was given chores to do both inside and outside the house. She no longer was forced to wear a bonnet and spend her time in the shade of the trees around the old well. All Doña Prisca would say was, "It won't be so easy for you when you get back to the sawmill. Tamar won't have you sitting around. You'll have two small brothers and a sister to look after."

This was the first time that Margarita had ever faced the inevitability of life after Mora and Guadalupita. But why should Doña Prisca talk of a future that included Tamar? Her place was here until she was called to live with her Uncle Delfino and the delightful Soledea.

"I won't live forever," Doña Prisca reminded her.

What Margarita did not know was that Doña Prisca, in the predawn in her husband's room before they buried the infant, had determined to herself to grow old quickly and make an end to it. She began to walk with a pronounced stoop. She grew more and more detached, less inclined to monitor the work of the estate. Beta and Hannah quickly took advantage of the old woman's loss of interest and began to perform their duties in a slap-dash manner. Doña Prisca handed over the daily details of running the estate to Filiberto and consummated the transfer of authority by giving him the key to the trunk in the sala grande.

"It has all the papers," she explained. "Deeds, bills of sale, crop and stock tally books." The key to the padlock that sealed the attic door she had long since removed from her belt and thrown down the well.

She slept longer now, retiring shortly after sunset, not to rise until well after daybreak. One day, she decided not to leave her bed at all, complaining of vague aches and a lack of energy. The curandera came, made a sweeping diagnosis that included old age, the weather, and the will of God, and left behind a foul weed that was to be made into tea and consumed four times a day.

Although Doña Prisca ignored the prescription, she considered the curandera's visit important if only because it marked, with some ceremony, the start of her own death watch. She ate less and less. Eventually she was reduced to the indignity of being fed spoonfuls of broth by either Beta or Hannah. She lay passive, waiting to be draped with a towel to catch the dribblings off her chin.

Beta, the older of the two Indian house slaves, became the de facto mistress of the manor.

Margarita became a servant to the slave. Her duties were increased to fill her day and she no longer had time for school. Beta particularly relished her new role as the child's caretaker. With Nasha gone and Doña Prisca incapacitated Beta now made it as unpleasant as she could for the child. "You've had it your own way long enough. And don't think you can go running to your grandma. She's too sick to worry about you."

In the final week of Doña Prisca's life, Beta consigned Margarita to the gloom of the sickroom to watch over the old woman. "Sit with her. At least you can do that, you're so useless for other things."

So Margarita sat, passive, confounded and very afraid, in the bedroom she had shared for the last two years with Doña Prisca. Occasionally the old woman would stir and Margarita would offer her a sip of water or wipe away with a damp cloth the crusty deposits from the old woman's mouth, nose, and eyes.

On Doña Prisca's last day on earth, the priest was called in from Mora to administer Extreme Unction. Everyone in the house, with the exception of Filiberto, gathered kneeling around the deathbed to recite, at the priest's direction, the prayers for the dying.

After everyone had left, Margarita again sat alone and allowed her eyes to wander from Prisca's bed to her own, covered with a heavy white spread she had never been permitted to sit on. There was the handmade chest that Doña Prisca used for her clothes, clothes, the little girl thought, that would never be worn again. She glanced over to a small footlocker on the floor by the end of her bed where she kept her own belongings. Where would the chest go? Where would she go? She looked at the tall-backed rocking chair and the small stool next to it and thought of the many times Doña Prisca had sat and rocked and made her sit erect next to her as she read from a worn and ragged book of devotions. Finally, her gaze fell on the wooden statue of the Virgin in a niche carved into the thick adobe wall. She found no solace in the shiny black eyes.

"Filiberto."

Doña Prisca had opened her eyes. "Filiberto," she repeated.

Margarita ran out of the room in search of Beta.

"She wants Filiberto."

"Well, go find him."

Margarita found him retooling a bridle in the carriage house.

"Grandma wants you."

He continued to work on the leather for a minute. Finally, he put down the rein and with considerable passion drove the awl he was using deep into the wooden workbench. He strode out of the carriage house, across the inner courtyard, onto the porch that swept around the entire length of the house, and into his mother's room.

"What do you want?"

Doña Prisca looked up to her son with a gaze suddenly so sharp and focused that it would have astounded those who had grown accustomed to her disoriented starings. "I've already sent money to your sister. Everything here, it is yours."

"I know."

"Everything. Yours. Even the stain in the *sala*. May God help you."

With that, Doña Prisca closed her eyes and willed the last wisp of breath from her lungs.

Two days after Prisca's funeral, Margarita Juana sat atop the footlocker that held all her earthly goods. It had been loaded onto the back of her father's wagon to be transported with her up the tortuous boulder-strewn road to the lumber camp. It was her first return on the road she had traveled in a shoebox nine years before.

That night, Filiberto gathered up all Doña Prisca's personal belongings, including the bedclothes in which she had died, and piled them high in the backyard. He soaked the mound liberally with coal oil and set it on fire. As the flames whipped and tore in the wind of the cool fall night, Beta and Hannah hid behind the curtains of the kitchen window to spy. What they saw was a man in black, face lit brightly by the blaze. He was smiling.

While the fire burned, the two Indians packed up their meager belongings, took some food and a water skin, walked defiantly out the front doors of the great hacienda as if it were their right, and began their long walk home to Taos.

Within six months, all the hands except Don José had abandoned Filiberto, cursing him for his cruelty and larceny as they rode off. Don José was gone in a year, moving to Pecos to live out the remainder of his days with his daughter and carrying to his grave the secret of the bundle in the attic.

Filiberto stayed on the land for many years after, selling off stock, equipment, real estate, and furniture as needed, watching the house fall, room by room, around him. At the end he lived in the only room left standing, the one with the white stain on the floor.

Filiberto lived until he was eighty-five years old. When he was seventy-nine the county took over what was left of the Pacheco legacy for back taxes. The authorities, at a loss as to what to do with the old man, sent him to a nursing home in Las Cruces.

On a blazing late July afternoon in 1959, an attendant wheeled him out into a back courtyard of the facility and promptly forgot about him. His absence was not noted until suppertime. When they found him he was dead of sunstroke, his face a mass of blisters oozing gelatin that ran down to the tips of his still luxuriant mustache to drip onto his faded black shirt.

Chapter Seven

1922–1925

From the age of nine to the age of twelve, Margarita Juana had occasion to cry every day. The general cause of her misery was her exile to the lumber camp of her father, Leopoldo. The immediate instrument of her pain and sorrow was her mother, Tamar.

Among Tamar's more unattractive qualities was her ability to hold a grudge. Her resentment of her daughter had festered since the infant Margarita had managed to unseat her as the favorite of her foster parents and Nasha, the bondservant. Tamar's rancor grew with every visit to Mora where her own stock plummeted while that of her daughter climbed to heights that even she had never claimed.

Now it was her turn.

Tamar's vendetta began almost immediately after Doña Prisca's funeral, on their way up the canyon. The adults with the infant, Agapita, sat in front. In the wagon bed, Margarita and her two younger brothers, Eugenio and Gerónimo, held on for dear life. After one particularly violent jolt, which sent the girl crashing sideways to knock her face against the side of the wagon, Margarita began to cry. Tamar turned her head to see her daughter sitting awkwardly astride a pile of rough bark, sticky with resin. Across Margarita's forehead there was a red line along which an angry ridge was starting to rise.

"¿*No ves?*" Tamar said to her husband. "She's crying already. What a spoiled child we're bringing to live with us! Well, I know how to fix that." Tamar made sure that her voice carried to Margarita even above the clanking and clattering of the wagon.

And so it began, the persecution, the river of tears.

Margarita cried because Tamar hit her at least once every day. In fact, Tamar's swats at her eldest daughter became such a daily routine that the men who worked for Leopoldo began to call her Doña Mano Suelta, "Madam Loose Hand."

Margarita also cried because Tamar found ways to make tongue-lashings even more painful than actual blows.

"You are lazy!"

"You are stupid!"

"You are ill-bred!"

Although Margarita soon learned to twist and turn her body to misdirect the blows, she never found an adequate defense against that tongue.

Finally, and most especially, Margarita cried because she was lonely.

Aside from Leopoldo, there was no one in the camp who showed her the least attention. The men were too busy during the day and too tired at night to be friendly. During the week they slept in cabins along the river. By noon on Friday they were on the road to their homes and families up the canyon and down to Guadalupita, not to return until Sunday evening.

At night she could hear laughter and accordion music from the direction of the cabins, but that was alien territory, nothing more than a bitter reminder to her that there was still joy in the world outside.

And so Margarita wept every day and fell asleep with wet eyes every night from the blows, from the scoldings, from the loneliness, from self-pity. But these were only surface tears. The deep tears, the ones she felt for Adela, Delfino, Prisca, and especially Nasha, did not flow. Rather, they created a pool that lapped gently up against the walls of the subterranean grotto where her childhood had gone to hide.

Margarita's list of daily chores was unvarying. Rouse and dress herself and the children. Serve breakfast. Wash the dishes. Pick up the house. Make several trips to an underground spring that emptied into the river and tote water in tin lard pails back to the house. Tend to the chickens. Prepare and deliver a midmorning collation to the workers. Help prepare the lunch. Serve the lumber crew. Wash the dishes. Put Agapita down for a nap. Replenish the reservoir on the side of the stove so that there would be enough hot water for the evening's needs. Tend to the small vegetable patch by the side of the house. Prepare the supper. Wash the dishes. Wash, feed, and put the children to bed.

Added to these daily duties were laundry days, sewing and mending days, days to scrub floors and shake out and air the rugs and bed clothes, and days to scrub the privy that squatted a demure twenty paces behind the house.

All of these activities were supervised by the yellow-eyed Tamar. Naturally, her daughter's best efforts never met her expectations, although she herself had never been more than an indifferent house-keeper.

"You chipped another plate, you clumsy thing!"

"Why is the water from the spring so cloudy? Did you scrape the pail against the bottom again?"

"Why is Agapita crying? Where are the boys?"

One morning, after a night of thunder and lightning that had kept Margarita's head buried in her sister's thin and unyielding back, she went to the spring.

As usual, Tamar had a parting shot.

"It rained last night. Don't you be bringing any muddy water back to me."

Near the spring Margarita sensed a strangeness about her. Why did the place seem so different? Then she saw the river, bloated and over its sides with waters that careened out of control through the rocky gorge just above the camp. This mountain stream of playful effervescence now roared and spat and clawed at the grasses and wildflowers that lay flattened on both its banks. It was a muddy maelstrom of branches, pinecones, and large pieces of driftwood crashing against boulders. Sprays of water kicked high, misted, and created layer upon layer of rainbow fragments against the slashes of sun that found passage between the trees.

Margarita was completely disoriented. A bush that had marked the location of the spring's mouth was gone. And where was the spring itself? Was it possible that this mighty rush of water had swept the tiny rivulet away? What would she do? What would Tamar say if she returned to the house with empty pails?

She leaned far over the bank where she estimated the spring had once gurgled forth. Nothing. She craned her neck out a little farther. Then she felt her feet slip and her legs were suddenly high above her head as she flipped into the roiling flood.

The river slapped a gag across Margarita's mouth and dared her to scream. Her arms flew out to beat at the current. Her feet stabbed downward in a desperate search for something solid. She fought to

bring her head above the surface but each time another wave whipped
over her and another blast of water shot up her nose, into her mouth
and down her throat. Her arms and legs began to grow heavy. There
was a sharp cutting pain against the palms of her hands and she realized that she was still holding on to the pails by their wire handles.
When she finally opened her hands and released the tins she was
already at the far edge of her reserves. One weak and final flailing of
her arms and she gave herself up to the river. It immediately pinned
her to its gritty bed and ripped at her clothes while it groped her body.

With her total capitulation came blessed relief from the panic
that had stoked her efforts. Now she had time to think.

There was Nasha. How many times they had played by the river!
The gathering of happy girls once again sang, joked, laughed, did
laundry, and spread wide expanses of cloth across mulberry bushes
to dry. And there was her river dream. Would she now twist and
whirl until the current spun a cocoon around her from which she
would metamorphose into a beautiful Indian princess? Would the
water now flow around her and over her and through her to eventually break her into tufts of white that would float down the river and
beyond?

Warm, peaceful, and contented for the first time since the death
of her Aunt Adela, she wondered no more. She gave herself fully to
the water and its numbing embrace.

At a bend the river widened and lost its potency.

Margarita bumped up against a half-submerged log and after a
moment the narcotic caress of the river gave way to harsh sunlight on
her face and the slimy feel of the wood. She lay across the log for a
moment then felt a violent eruption inside her. She retched long and
convulsively, spewing water and dirt from her nose and mouth and
finally pieces of tortilla and white and yellow bits of egg, which had
been her breakfast.

Finally Margarita was able to stand. She found herself in a mere
foot of slowly eddying water not five paces from the bank. Her feet
sank deeply and made sucking sounds in the viscous clay. Once she
reached the bank she collapsed. Then she vomited again.

Turning toward the house, she could see the gray smoke from the
kitchen flue lifting and mingling with the blue exhaust from the diesel

engine that churned nearby in its incessant struggle to move the belt that spun the mighty saw.

Tamar was at the kitchen table with her back to the door when Margarita walked in. She was peeling a large pile of potatoes and dropping them into a large pot of water.

"Where have you been? Here you have me doing your work. Don't I have enough to worry about?" With this she plopped a newly pared potato into the water with enough force to send a spray over the sides of the pot and onto the table.

Margarita stood soaked and shivering. Her hair lay in streaks across her face like oily raven feathers. Her head jerked up and down as she worked her breath with short, sharp pants.

Tamar turned to look at her and her narrow eyes slitted even more. "Did you fall in the river after I told you about the rain? And where's the water?"

Tamar looked down to Margarita's feet. A circlet of water was starting to form around them from the steady dripping off the hem of the girl's dress.

"Look at the mess you're making. And your shoes! Where are your shoes?"

For the first time since Margarita came up from the water she had some sense of her situation. She looked down and saw that she was barefoot. She could not remember where she had lost the shoes. Was it when the river was violating her or afterward, after it discarded her and she stepped from the streambed into the suction of the mud?

Furious almost to blindness, Tamar rose from the table. She began to pummel the girl with the thing most handy to her, one of the large, brown, gnarly potatoes. The rage had been stoked in her for a full decade. Again and again she brought the fat, dusty root down on the head, back, and shoulders of the defenseless girl. The skin of the potato broke and its white meat began to pulp and shred and spray milky juices across the kitchen floor. When Tamar finally stopped, her arm was weary and her fingertips were bruised where they had curled unprotected around her weapon.

"Now clean this mess up. And then go back to the river, find my pails and get me my water."

While the overriding causes of Margarita Juana's unhappiness for two years in the lumber camp were her mother's abuse and her own deep hole of loneliness, the undercurrent to all her wretchedness was fear.

The canyon was dark and moody. The house was a dreary string of cells with no peace or privacy. The sounds of the mill were shrill and abrasive. And when they went quiet they were immediately supplanted by the monotonous rush of the river, by the wind moaning through the tall pines, by the howl of the coyote, the hiss of the bobcat, the raucous cries of crows and hawks circling high above, and by the other sounds, those thumps, creaks, and growls emanating from deep in the perpetual twilight of the great pine forest.

Her fears were somewhat allayed during those times once a month when Leopoldo delivered a load of timber to Las Vegas. Mora as a commercial center was no more. Tamar would always accompany her husband. She wanted to be sure she was there to take charge of the money before he had the chance to spend it on friends and liquor. The trip also afforded her a break from the camp and offered her the diversion of shopping for the necessities as well as for an occasional luxury—a bar of Ivory soap, a box of raisins, a loaf of store-bought bread.

Were it not for the nights, Margarita might have found passing enjoyment from her days in the camp without her mother. The daily regimen of chores was greatly eased since most of the work crew took the opportunity to go home to their families. The children presented no particular problem. The boys had grown accustomed to entertaining themselves. They sometimes fished the stream for cutthroat trout but mainly spent their time romping across and tumbling down the two-story mountain of sawdust that flanked the mill. Agapita was a quiet child who was content to let Margarita lead her around by the hand when she went for water, fed the chickens, or visited the small patch of garden to the side of the house to pull out deep orange carrots or lavender-capped turnips, which they ate raw for their lunches.

During these times, Margarita talked to her little sister as an intimate in words that went completely over the little girl's head.

"When my Uncle Delfino and my Tía Soledea come from Denver for me, Agapita, I will ask if you can come and visit us. We'll go to the zoo and see monkeys and elephants. We'll eat ice cream—Uncle Delfino loves ice cream. We'll buy beautiful new clothes and play with dolls that have eyes that open and close. We'll play until they call us in to sit with them in the parlor and have tea and *biscochitos*. And every night before we go to bed they'll give us big hugs and tell us to sleep tight."

Her loneliness turned Margarita Juana into a dreamer. It was something new for a girl who had always relied on what she could see, feel, smell, taste, and touch. Before, she had always left the arcane and the mystical for Nasha to deal with.

"You have crossed your comb and brush," the Indian might say to her, quickly separating the offending objects. "The hens will not lay eggs tomorrow."

Or, "You have spilled your milk in the shape of the sun. It will rain for three days."

Margarita would rise the next morning to brilliant sunlight or to the smell of an egg frying in the kitchen and rush out to confront her nanny. But, when pressed, Nasha would only look grave, with no hint of drollery, and ask: "Do you know every hen in the world? Have you stuck your nose into every chicken coop in Mora?"

Or, "I sprinkled salt on your milk spill and took the curse away so the sun would shine."

With Nasha around, Margarita had little need for a fantasy life. But Nasha was gone.

In her reveries, Margarita transported herself back to that world where sometimes hens did not lay eggs or the sun did not shine, because Margarita Juana, the supreme ruler of the universe, had been careless, casual, or capricious.

It was this way for almost two years. The spitefulness of Tamar, the endless cycle of chores, the fears of the known and the unknown, the dreams she could share with no one, and the tears.

All of this changed on a day in early June just before Margarita reached her thirteenth year, when Leopoldo and Tamar returned to the camp from Las Vegas.

Margarita was standing with Agapita in front of the house and spreading corn for the chickens.

Eugenio and Gerónimo were frolicking atop the huge mountain of sawdust, nervous fleas on the back of an old yellow dog.

The air was suddenly alive with the chug of a motor far down the canyon.

It soon grew loud enough to interrupt the boys' roughhousing, and they began to shout and point. Eugenio started running down the sawdust pile, slipped onto his backside, and slid down the rest of the way. Gerónimo was trying to catch up but succeeded only in tripping over his own stubby feet and tumbled head over heels past his surprised brother. Then the two jumped to their feet and ran down the dirt road that followed the river as it curved out of sight.

From a cloud of blue smoke billowing around the turn there emerged a coughing, complaining motorized conveyance. It was not at all like the sleek and beautiful chrome-and-leather chariot that had so excited Margarita when she saw it drive up to Doña Prisca's home with Delfino and Soledea sitting regally in it. This contraption was another thing altogether, a fuming, belching, grinding mimicry of a real automobile. Behind it rolled an open-bed trailer on which Eugenio and Gerónimo were now riding. And behind that, hitched to a ring on the trailer, trotted the two draft grays.

At the wheel of the car was an ashen, bug-eyed Leopoldo. Next to him sat Tamar, a decidedly green Tamar, not Eris, the Goddess of Discord, but a Tamar who was pasty faced and tight around the lips, a Tamar who had been vomiting with hourly regularity all the way from Las Vegas, a Tamar who was biliously and gloriously car-sick.

Leopoldo pulled the vehicle in front of the house and sent chickens squawking in every direction.

The mill workers had been relaxing in their cabins, swigging from an earthen jug of mula and playing cards. Now they trotted out as steadily as their condition would allow.

Leopoldo looked straight ahead. He had pulled down his hat so far on his head that its brim bent the tops of his ears forward. His fingers were locked onto the steering wheel as if he feared that to let go would cause him to lose touch with the earth's gravity and go spiraling helplessly into space.

Tamar was gasping as she rolled off her seat to lean heavily against the frame of the car.

"*Nunca más. Nunca, nunca más.*" She pushed herself away from the car and stumbled up to the house. On the way in she completely ignored her children, except to beg Margarita for a cool, wet cloth. The request was in a tone of voice she had never used on her oldest child—meek and most unwaspish.

Leopoldo finally pried his fingers from the wheel, stepped down from the cab, and made directly for the cistern. There he fell to his knees, yanked off his hat with both hands, clutched at either side of the iron rim, and plunged his entire head into the icy water. He came up after a good twenty seconds, snorted and flicked his head vigorously from side to side, spraying water all about him like an old bear who had just missed a trout in a stream. Then he let out a whoop that echoed through the camp and up and down the canyon and sent several crows clattering from branches into unscheduled flight.

"I've done it!" he bellowed. "She didn't want me to, but I went and did it anyway! We now have a modern operation!"

He climbed up on the trailer and like a candidate out on the hustings, addressed his audience. All five of his workers were now assembled before him, as were his two sons, the draft horses still hitched to the trailer, and nine chickens who were trying to peck around legs and rubber tires for their rudely interrupted feast of corn.

"'No,' she said. 'You can't do it,' she told me. 'I won't have it,' she said. And here we are!" Leopoldo pointed dramatically at the car.

The "she" in question was by now stretched spread-eagle on her bed, a cool, moist cloth across her brow.

"Be a good girl, Margarita, and keep the children away from Mamá for a while."

"Sí, Mamá," an amazed Margarita answered.

"And bring me *el basín*. You did clean it with boiling water like I told you to?" This last Tamar tried to deliver with some of her old vinegar but the fight was clearly out of her.

"Go now. And close the door." And Tamar rolled over on her side to stick her face in the chamber pot to throw up.

Margarita retreated quietly, unsure why but somehow feeling newly empowered.

Outside, Leopoldo was already well launched into his oration.

"Now we can keep the horses here and use them for what God intended, to bring logs down from the mountain. That trip to Vegas was getting to be too much for them."

"What is this thing?" one of the more forward of the crew asked, emboldened by the moonshine. "I've never seen a car like this."

"What do you mean, what is it? Have you never seen an automobile before?"

"But what kind of automobile? It's different."

"A Ford. A Model T."

"But my cousin owns a Model T, and it doesn't look anything like this!"

"Well, she had a little accident. They had to use parts of a Chevrolet to fix the cab. And the hood, it's from a Mercedes-Benz." He stretched out and savored the words as he said them. "She's not pretty, but she will make life a lot easier for us. I can haul more wood, I can deliver more loads, more often."

"You mean more work," one of the men muttered.

"More money," Leopoldo rebutted. "I tell you," and the candidate wound down his speech, "it's a new day."

Leopoldo was not much of a prophet and an even worse businessman. The purchase of the Ford and the trailer had strapped him financially and so he was not able to take on any new workers. This meant he could not expect an increase in production. In fact, it slackened off as the men groused about the patrón who spent money foolishly and had none left for them.

Chapter Eight

The introduction of the Model T occasioned no dawning of a new day for anyone in the camp except my mother. The homely hybrid was no Cinderella's carriage but it was just as effective in carrying the little princess into a new life.

Relations between Margarita and her mother were now markedly different. It helped that Margarita had seen Tamar with her head half submerged in a chamber pot. But there was much more to it than that.

The new order of things began that evening.

At the supper table, Tamar, who was now recovered sufficiently to take food with the family, began to harangue Leopoldo. "I will make that trip to Las Vegas with you one more time, and one more time only."

"*Sí, mi vida.*"

"Do not '*sí, mi vida*' me," she snapped, "I'm serious."

"*No, mi vida. Sí, mi vida.*"

"We are moving to Las Vegas in September."

"But the sawmill."

"You will keep your precious sawmill, for all the good it's done us. Why should I have to stay up here with you? Enough is enough. I will take the children to Las Vegas so they can go to school instead of running loose around the mountains like wild animals."

Up to now the education of the two boys had been a catch-as-catch-can proposition—a winter in a rented house in Mora when the snows had been too high for lumbering, and last spring in Guadalupita when the boys were left with a cousin while Margarita stayed at the camp to help Tamar.

"You will find a house for us on one of your trips," Tamar continued. "Then when you come down with your loads you will stay with us instead of running off with your no-good friends to drink all our money away."

"Yes, my life."

"And besides, I don't want to go through another pregnancy up here. It's not right. It's not decent. I need women around me." In this off-hand way did Tamar inform Leopoldo that another child would soon be born to them. "When we leave here in August that is the last time I make this trip, God help me. But don't think that gives you a free rein for the rest of the summer. Margarita will go with you when you deliver the loads. You will give her the money, all of it, and you will take her to the store to buy what we need."

Leopoldo was now fully attentive. "But . . ."

"I do not want to hear it. No telling where we'd be right now if I had left everything to you."

"But Margarita's just a child. What does she know about such things?"

"Margarita is smart. Margarita knows how to get things done."

Margarita, who was seated at one end of the table cutting Agapita's meat into small pieces, looked up. This was the first time that Tamar had ever spoken of her in any but the most derogatory of terms.

Leopoldo now stared at his daughter intently. His jaw was set. Whatever went through his mind, whatever assessments he made or conclusions he drew were consummated in an instant. His mouth relaxed and there was a twinkle in his eyes.

"Well, *hija*," he said, "it looks like you have one more person to look after."

The next morning, when Margarita fetched the water pails to make her first of several daily trips to the spring, she heard her father's voice from outside the door.

"Margarita, come out here."

Leopoldo was standing by the open hood of the car.

"Come down here. I need to show you something."

"Mamá needs me to go for the water."

Leopoldo turned to the sawdust pile where the boys were rollicking. "Eugenio, get down here!"

Eugenio, with Gerónimo as always dogging three paces behind, rolled down the hill, righted himself, and approached his father. He performed a little jig in an effort to shake out through his pant legs the itchy sawdust that had worked its way into his overalls. This left a ragged yellow trail behind him all the way to his father.

"What?" he asked when he finally arrived at the car.

"Go get water for your mother."

"But Margarita does that."

"Now you do it. Margarita has more important things to do. Go on. Get the pails from her."

Tamar had come to the door during this exchange to stand next to her daughter. "What is all the shouting about?"

Margarita dared not look at her mother. "Daddy wants Eugenio to go get the water. He needs me for something else."

If ever there was an opportunity for Tamar to regain the upper hand this was it. Instead, she looked at her eldest son, who was himself waiting for the lines to be drawn. "Well, don't just stand there with your mouth moving like a billy goat. Get the water." Then, almost as an afterthought, she reverted to the old Tamar. "And don't drag the pail along the bottom of the spring. I don't want to see muddy water."

Margarita set the pails down and walked away from them like a prisoner just released from a ball and chain. She could hear Eugenio behind her scolding his little brother. "Well, pick them up! They won't bite, you know."

Standing by itself without the impressive length and mass of the trailer, the Model T looked positively scrawny and forlorn, like a sheep after a shearing.

Leopoldo poked around the innards of the car. "So you're smart, are you?"

"I used to be smart in school."

"Well this isn't school. Your mother says you can get things done. Can you?"

"I don't know."

"If you're going with me you have to know something about this car." Leopoldo extracted his head from the bowels of the Model T and pointed the wrench at her. "Can you put a patch on an inner tube?"

"No."

"Do you know how to use a jack?"

"No."

"Do you know where the gas goes?"

Margarita pointed unsurely at the radiator cap.

"No. That's where the water to cool the engine goes."

"Oh."

"Do you know how to start the motor?"

Margarita dropped her head. This was not going well at all.

"Your mother says you're smart. But I think that you're not so smart that your old *tata* can't teach you a thing or two."

And so Margarita's education began.

On that first morning she learned how to mend a punctured inner tube by scraping at the smooth, black stretch of rubber to roughen it up so it could take the adhesive and the patch.

She learned the importance of keeping the radiator full and how to fill it.

"If you don't," Leopoldo cautioned, "the engine will overheat and be ruined."

She learned the location of the gas tank, lying across the middle of the car directly under the stained and torn bench seat.

"It's a ten-gallon tank," Leopoldo informed her, "which means we have to carry an extra can of gas in the back in case we need it."

When Tamar interrupted the lesson, it was with a certain deference. "She has to come in. It's almost time to feed the men. I can't get the food ready by myself."

"That's enough for now," Leopoldo told Margarita. "We'll do some more this afternoon."

That afternoon, Margarita's life of rural insularity was forever breached as she plunged headlong into the twentieth century aboard a coughing, sputtering, and complaining Model T.

When this day finally ended it was the first full twenty-four hours in three years that Margarita's mother had neither scolded nor struck her. And it was the first time she had gone through an entire day without crying. That night when she went to bed she paid no mind to the sounds that emanated from the darkness beyond the walls of the house.

The next day Margarita rushed through her morning chores and bounded out the door to the klaxon call of the car. "Oogah, oogah!"

Father and daughter sat in the cab of the Model T.

"First, we have to start the engine. Do you remember what to do?"

"Pull the brake lever back and put the car in neutral gear, then turn on the switch."

Leopoldo pulled the brake lever toward himself until it clicked into place.

"Now we switch on the engine," he said, reaching over and turning on the ignition switch. "Then we go around to the front."

Leopoldo inserted a large iron crank into its socket through a slot in the grille and pushed in until he felt the ratchet engage.

"Now watch. You have to be careful when you crank up the car or you can hurt yourself. When you grip the crank handle don't wrap your thumb around it. If the engine kicks back you could break your hand." Leopoldo then showed her the proper way to grip the crank handle by cupping his entire hand around it with the thumb wrapped on the same side as the other fingers.

"Now I give it a quick jerk."

It took several tries before the engine kicked over. Finally something coughed to life.

"Hurry, hurry. Jump in."

The car chugged and quivered while father and daughter scrambled around and bounced into the wide seat.

"Now, we give the engine a little gas," Leopoldo shouted over the din and pulled the throttle toward himself. "Then push the clutch pedal halfway down so it's in neutral and let the brake lever out." He pushed the brake lever forward. "Press the clutch pedal to the floor and here we go."

The car lurched forward and shuttered violently, jerking Margarita and Leopoldo back and forth. Leopoldo's hands flew wildly around as he tried to balance the spark and throttle levers. Finally, the car reached its own internal comfort level and began to move forward.

"Once you get her going let the clutch all the way up and close the throttle a little bit."

Around and around the clearing they drove, waving at the men working the mill as they went by, scattering chickens and bouncing over gopher holes.

"Now we stop," Leopoldo shouted over the noise of the car. He proceeded to press down the clutch pedal halfway into neutral and stepped on the brake. Once they were at a halt, he pulled back on the brake lever, opened the throttle to accelerate the engine for a moment, and threw off the switch.

"There," he said, as they sat side –by side looking out the front window.

Then with a twinkle in his eye he turned to her. "Shall we do it again?"

They did it again and then again and continued to practice for an hour or so each morning for the rest of the week.

By Saturday, Margarita was driving.

Leopoldo handed her a cushion, "to sit on so you can look over the steering wheel."

He also held out two wooden blocks with straps of cloth tacked to them. "They're not as fancy as the shoes the girls are wearing in Las Vegas but they'll help you reach the foot pedals."

"I don't see why she has to drive," Tamar complained to her husband as they lay in the darkness of their bedroom that night.

"You never know," Leopoldo answered. "Maybe someone has an accident and has to go to the clinic in Mora. If I'm up working in the canyon, who can drive the car? Or maybe I get too sick to drive while we're down in Las Vegas."

"Or too drunk," Tamar snapped back.

"Tamar, this was all your idea."

They lay in silence for a full five minutes until Tamar spoke again, determined, verily preordained, to have the last word. "The girl is to handle the money. And don't you forget that!"

With that, she turned heavily on her side and faced the wall.

Chapter Nine

Margarita's five trips to Las Vegas with her father that summer, while not particularly adventuresome, were anything but uneventful.

The Model T, its trailer stacked high with boards, ground down through the canyon and forded the winding river four times before it reached the valley floor. This leg of the journey was usually good for at least two flat tires. Sometimes Leopoldo had to unhitch the lumber-laden trailer and drive the hobbled car to a patch of dry and level ground before he could jack it up to remove the tire and fix it. Then he had to slowly back up to where they had left the trailer and rehitch it, so they could continue their journey. A flat tire on the trailer was an even more spectacular ordeal.

Typically, it took them two hours to maneuver the rock-and-pothole-infested road until they hit level ground just outside Guadalupita. Into Mora it was twelve more miles. Into Las Vegas it was another thirty.

The radiator had a tendency to boil over every six or seven miles, which forced them to stop to let it cool down. Then Leopoldo refilled the reservoir from a canvas bag, wet and heavy like a bloated pig's bladder. When not in use, the bag, which also provided drinking water for the trip, hung across the front grille of the car, attached to the hood ornament by a small loop of rope. The idea was that the air rushing by the car would keep the canvas bag and its contents cool. However, the Model T never went fast enough either to prove or disprove the theory.

Whenever Margarita drank from the bag, the water was always warm and tasted oily and of car fumes.

Las Vegas, New Mexico, sprang up from its modest beginnings as a pastoral village along the banks of the Gallinas River to become the principal stop on the Santa Fe Trail. It was the only town between Missouri and Santa Fe where a traveler could actually sleep in a bed under a roof. All of this luxury came at a substantial price, of course.

If the Santa Fe Trail made this daughter of the plains forget her shyness, the railroad made a shambles of her modesty. It dressed her in off-the-shoulder velvet and taffeta, powdered and rouged her ample breasts, and added mother-of-pearl buttons to her high-stepping shoes.

The town became a shipping center for the great cattle and sheep ranches of northeastern New Mexico. She was bawdy and bold. Telephone service, newly invented in 1876, was installed in Las Vegas three years later. Las Vegas was one of the first towns in New Mexico to have electric lights, glittering rhinestones to complete her party finery.

Her citizens hustled, merchandised, and caroused. They built elegant hotels, beehive-busy mercantile stores, gigantic warehouses, opulent saloons and gambling houses, perky funeral parlors that hid blue satin petticoats under their widow's weeds, and impressive homes. The late-Victorian architecture of Denver, St. Louis, and points east—Queen Anne, Romanesque, and Italianate—shot up in Las Vegas like a prairie dog colony.

In the last quarter of the nineteenth century no town, not Dodge, not Tombstone, not Deadwood, gave sanctuary to more gamblers, desperadoes, and gunslingers than did Las Vegas, New Mexico. Billy the Kid, Wyatt Earp, Doc Holliday, and Jesse James were in and out depending on who was after them or whom they were after. Bob Ford, "that dirty little coward who shot Mr. Howard and laid poor Jesse in his grave," joined the local constabulary for a time until his tarnished reputation drove him out of town.

By the 1920s the party was over. Las Vegas sat exhausted and slumped on a bar stool, her hair loosed from its ribbons and combs, her cheeks and lips smudged, her dress ripped and soiled, and her strings of bright beads broken and strewn across the sawdust on the floor. Many of her banks closed their doors and the railroad and its shops abandoned her for younger, fresher pickings down the line.

The first stop in Las Vegas was always the lumberyard. There Leopoldo unhitched the trailer so that he and the yard foreman could make an initial tally of the load. When the count was done, Leopoldo took the signed receipt and gave it to Margarita for safekeeping.

"Hold onto this. Sometimes they try to unload some of the lumber overnight without telling me."

After the trailer was secured in the yard they sped at twenty miles an hour to the home of one of Leopoldo's former employees, Atanacio. He had come to Las Vegas to find a less taxing and more profitable way of supporting himself and his young wife, Petra, who was now carrying their first child. After they had finished their supper, Leopoldo and Atanacio sat at the kitchen table long into the evening drinking from a jug of wine while they exchanged news, gossip, and outright lies.

Margarita sat quietly and listened to them until her eyes began to blink and she hid her mouth behind her hands while she yawned. Eventually Petra ushered her into the small sitting room to settle her in on a thin mat spread out on the floor.

The lumberyard opened for business at seven-thirty in the morning. Leopoldo and Margarita were waiting when the gates swung in. While Leopoldo and one of the yardmen busied themselves with unloading and stacking the lumber, Margarita sat to one side, a solemn overseer.

Through the morning, the stack grew taller and taller. The men laid narrow slats between each layer to provide space for air to circulate through the wood to cure it. Eventually the stack would reach a height of nine or ten feet and join row upon row of other stacks, lined up like mausoleums for the hundreds of trees that had fallen.

The unloading could take up to four hours so it was inevitable for Margarita to grow restless and bored. When this happened she walked out of the yard and across the street to the town plaza. There, under the canopy of a massive cottonwood, she sat down and configured her spine to the tree's gray, deeply ridged trunk.

It had been an unusually late spring that year, so the *alamo* was just now opening her pods to release a blizzard of downy moltings. These airy tufts drifted lazily down onto Margarita's head, shoulders, and lap. Occasionally she held out her hand to catch one of the wisps to study and lose herself in its exquisite weightlessness. With whiteness falling all around her, it was as if she had entered the crystal globe in the bedroom of the hunchback, Don Florencio Santillanes, and his blind wife with the keen nose, Doña Clara.

Next she focused her attention on the plaza itself. It was a block square park, enclosed on all four sides by rows of tallish Victorian false fronts interrupted by an occasional low-slung flat-roofed adobe edifice. The queen among these buildings was the Plaza Hotel, three

stories of red brick with white granite and sandstone accents and two
rows of ornately pedimented windows, thirteen to the rank. A tiara-
like cornice topped it all off.

But to Margarita, it was not a hotel. It was the castle in the crystal.

Margarita made sure that she was back at the lumberyard in time for
the final tallying of the load.

While Leopoldo and the yardman stood at one end of the stack
and counted across each row, she sat on the trailer and silently moved
her lips to count along with them. Then, after the tally had been
adjusted for any warped or split boards, Leopoldo took the signed
receipt and walked with his daughter at his side into the business
office where the manager of the lumberyard counted out the money.

A few minutes later they were outside on the sidewalk, the early
afternoon sun so high that their shadows were nothing more than
small dark puddles at their feet. Leopoldo recounted his money, gave
a shrug, and stuffed the wad into the wide bib pocket of his overalls.

Out on the sidewalk he petted Margarita along the back of her
head. "Ready for some shopping?"

The store they walked into belonged to Juan Galván, the oldest son
of a family whose name could be traced back to the Spanish
Conquest. Behind the butcher case labored the twenty-four-year-old
Miguel Galván, Juan's younger brother.

"Just follow the list your mamá gave you," Leopoldo instructed
Margarita. "I'll take care of the big things like the flour and potatoes.
And maybe see what else looks good."

Margarita let the remark pass. She would have to deal with her
father's infamous sweet tooth soon enough.

With her first step down one of the aisles of the Galván Grocery
Store, Margarita was immediately transposed into another time and
place. How familiar it still was! The smells. The sights. The quilt
work of labels on cans and cartons. She could very easily be walking
by the shelves of her Uncle Delfino's mercantile store in Mora while
her Aunt Adela railed at him for buying such ugly bolts of cloth.

She followed her mother's list with the strict adherence a young
bride would give to a recipe. Six cans each of peaches, pears, and fruit

cocktail. Four boxes of kitchen matches. Two yards of cotton wicking for the coal oil lamps. Six clusters of garlic. A tin of black molasses. A small angry bottle of tincture of iodine. Two cans of baking powder. Two bottles of Father John's Elixir and Cough Medicine.

On her third trip back to the counter with an armload of groceries, Margarita almost collided with her father. His arms were stacked high with bags and boxes of every confection and pastry imaginable—cookies, candied fruits, chocolates, nougats, hard candy, and cellophaned packages of frosted sweet rolls.

There between the high shelves father and daughter had a whispered but spirited conversation. The upshot of their discussion was a compromise: a small package of sugar cookies for the trip home, the gum drops for the children, the cookies for Tamar, another box of assorted cookies, which Leopoldo clung to like a stubborn infant at a teat, a package of glazed cinnamon rolls, and a small sack of chocolate drops. These last, Leopoldo insisted, were a little surprise for his dear wife, even though Margarita knew that neither her mother nor anyone else would ever share in them.

"And chewing tobacco," Leopoldo added hastily, just as Juan Galván was about to total up the bill.

When they arrived back at Atanacio's after their shopping and before they stepped down from the Model T, Margarita held her hand out, palm up, to her father.

Leopoldo's eyes widened in innocence. "What?"

"The money."

"What about the money? It's right here." Leopoldo patted his bib pocket. His lips were edged in brown from the chocolate drops he had been dipping into since they left the store.

"Daddy." Margarita stretched out her hand even farther until it was practically under her father's nose.

Leopoldo looked at her for a moment and seeing no break in the resolve of her firmly set mouth, sighed and reached into his front pouch for the wad of currency that rested so close to his heart.

"There. Two hundred and nineteen dollars and forty-six cents." He laid the penny down with a flourish.

"There should be two hundred and thirty-eight dollars," Margarita declared evenly.

"But the groceries. I paid for the groceries. And we got some gas for the car. Don't forget that."

"The man at the lumberyard paid you two hundred and eighty-eight dollars and twenty six cents. The groceries cost forty-seven dollars and fifty cents. The gasoline was two dollars and thirty cents. That leaves two hundred and thirty-eight dollars and forty-six cents."

Leopoldo's eyes widened again, this time not in feigned innocence but from astonishment that a mere twelve-year-old had beaten him at his own game.

"Daddy, do you want me to show you? I wrote it all down."

"Well, that's all I have. You must have figured wrong." He leaned over to her and pulled out the wide breast pocket so she could look in. "See!"

"What about the other pocket?"

"What other pocket?"

"The one in your trousers, on the other side, where you put the money after you paid for the gasoline."

Leopoldo stared at her, assessing his situation, Tamar's termagant voice suddenly ringing in his ears: "If the girl is to go with you, I want her to handle the money. And don't you forget that!"

With as much bluster as he could generate, Leopoldo sank his left hand into his pants pocket and pulled out a wad of wrinkled bills.

"Ten dollars," he snarled at her, dropping the ten spot in her lap. "And, one, two, three, four dollar bills." Then he held up the five to her nose. "This I keep. I promised Atanacio I'd buy him a drink after supper. It's the least we can do for his hospitality."

"*Bueno*. I will tell Mamá that that's the way it has to be."

She smoothed out the slim stack of money on her lap, folded it neatly in two, opened a large change pouch, pushed the bills carefully inside, and snapped the purse shut with a flourish of her own. Then she stepped from the car and walked through the gate, up the front sidewalk of the house, onto the porch, and through the door into the house.

She left a stunned and badly overmatched Leopoldo seated in the car and staring at her backside. "Tamar said you were smart. Too smart if you ask me," he shouted after her.

Margarita did not turn around but she was smiling as she closed the front door behind her.

Chapter Ten

The return leg of all the trips that Leopoldo and Margarita took that summer soon fell into a comfortable pattern.

Once they cleared the traffic of Las Vegas and were on the road out of town, Leopoldo would pull over, put the car in neutral, and exchange seats with his daughter. It was for times like these, as Tamar had rightly suspicioned, that he had taught his daughter to drive.

With Margarita, cushion in place and blocks strapped to her feet, behind the wheel, Leopoldo could lean back, pull his hat over his eyes, and begin the fitful sleep that would help him recuperate from his excesses of the night before.

Margarita drove at a steady twelve miles an hour, her eyes locked onto the ruts in the dirt road before her. When other cars or trucks approached them from either direction, and this did not happen very often, she pulled off to the side until they were safely by. Always she exchanged a wave and a salute of the horn to acknowledge the shared kinship of the open road.

The noise of the horns sometimes caused Leopoldo to start and sit up with a jerk so that his hat tumbled from his face to the floorboards. With a scathing glare at his daughter and at the world in general, he would retrieve his battered fedora, jam it back on his face, and resume his therapy.

On the outskirts of Mora they exchanged seats again so Leopoldo could take them through the town, into Guadalupita, and up the canyon to the lumber camp.

The final accounting was done by Margarita and her mother at the kitchen table. Margarita carefully counted out the money and pushed it across the shiny, slightly gummy oilcloth to Tamar, who sat grimly watching her.

"And this is what's left after we bought groceries and gasoline."

Margarita always found creative ways to bury the missing five dollars that Leopoldo kept back without fail for his nights on the town with Atanacio. To her mind the truth of these five dollars was not worth the effort of a lengthy explanation to her mother, one she would reject anyway.

"Well," Tamar sniffed, "I suppose it's all right. But you let him buy too many sweets after I told you not to."

Margarita did not respond. In the new relationship with her mother, she thought it prudent to allow this now toothless tiger her occasional snarl. Margarita kept her father's secret to herself, never realizing that Tamar had an even bigger secret of her own.

What Tamar was careful to conceal was that there had never been so much money to show from a trip into town. There were always twenty or thirty dollars more on the kitchen table during Margarita's stewardship. Despite all her naggings Tamar had been too lazy or too dull to try to understand Leopoldo's financial dealings with the lumberyard and the grocery store.

As much as Margarita treasured her trips with her father for their release from the drudgeries of camp life, her greatest pleasure lay simply in being alone with him.

Away from the life-sucking dourness of Tamar, Leopoldo was able to expand into his true self. Leopoldo loved life. He loved to pop a chocolate drop into his mouth and let it melt until its woolly, buttery sweetness coated his tongue and palate before it trickled sensuously down his throat. He loved to laugh. Telling a joke or listening to one, his face would begin to flush deeply, rising to full bloom from his neck to spread in all its unabashed rubicundity to the crown of his sparsely thatched head. Then his blue gimlet eyes would lose themselves in the folds of their lids, and with a mighty venting of air through his nostrils and mouth, he would rock back and forth with no sound but a strangled whimper until the laugh came, full and throaty like a diesel engine popping to life.

And most especially, he loved to talk. Name the subject, he had an opinion. State an opinion, he had a rebuttal. It didn't matter, just as long as there was talk.

What Margarita cherished about her time with Leopoldo was his ability to weave a tale. For hours on the road he would regale her with stories about his life and about the people he had met along the way.

Leopoldo had been born in Salinas, California.

Hours later his mother was dead.

His father was Dutch, which explained Leopoldo's fair skin, reddish blond hair, and blue eyes. The Dutchman was a sailor off a cargo ship in San Diego. He had wandered up the coast, found himself in love in Salinas, and settled down with his sweetheart in unmarried bliss. After she died he stayed around for another year but eventually succumbed to the tug of the sea. He left Leopoldo with the dead girl's family, returned to San Diego, and sailed out on the next ship, never to be heard from again.

Eventually, the stigma of Leopoldo's illegitimacy and his mongrel blood became too much for the Zamoras to bear. When he was barely two and a half, they took him to Oakland, to an orphanage that catered to unwanted Mexican children.

"Where is his mother?"

"*Muerta.*"

"And his father?"

"Who knows? Dead too, we can only pray. And may the devil take him!"

The man at the admissions desk looked over Leopoldo's birth certificate. When he saw the indecipherable string of o's, i's, u's, and umlauts in the Dutch sailor's name he blanched. So, even as the grandparents were making a quick exit before some bureaucratic glitch forced them to reclaim the child, the man at the desk was already inserting the word *unknown* in the place on the form where the father's name should have gone. Thus, by default, and in spite of their efforts to be rid of him, Leopoldo was given their name, Zamora.

Leopoldo spent his early years dressed in a dull blue cotton smock identical to those worn by all the orphans regardless of their sex. When he was old enough he walked in a supervised line with the other children to school. The student body was almost exclusively Hispanic, with an Asian thrown in here and there, and the faculty was entirely Anglo, mostly misfits exiled from other parts of the school system and waiting either for rehabilitation or retirement. For seven years Leopoldo was taught little except what seemed to be the core of the school's curriculum—Mexicans are too dumb to learn much of anything.

At fourteen he ran away. A sheriff's deputy found him sleeping on the docks and returned him. At fifteen he ran away again. This time it took. All he owned were the clothes on his back and his name, Leopoldo Zamora.

He returned to the Oakland docks. He was big and strong for his age and found work almost immediately as a stevedore's apprentice. On the advice of a grizzled dockworker of many years who befriended him and offered him a place to stay, he began using the name Leo Logan. The alliteration made it easy to remember.

"They don't like Mexicans on the docks," the old man explained to him. "You're white enough even though you talk like a greaser. Just keep your mouth shut and you'll be all right."

By the time he was eighteen he had risen to a full-fledged long-shoreman.

"I might have stayed there," Leopoldo told Margarita. "Gotten married. Had a family. Never come to New Mexico. Then where would you be?" He laughed and patted his daughter's head.

Margarita was growing impatient. "So how did you get here?"

Working on the docks, Leopoldo admitted, was not something he cared to do the rest of his life. It was hard and it could be very dangerous. One day, while he was working next to another boy about his age, a cargo net had snagged as it was being hoisted a hundred feet above them. A crate of machine parts shifted and toppled out of the net. The load barely missed him but fell on his companion and crushed both his legs.

"That was close enough for me," said Leopoldo to his daughter. "I handed in my time card that day, got my money, packed my clothes, and headed south."

Ironically, the road south brought Leopoldo back to his birthplace, Salinas. The stop meant no more to him than a place to find a job. The job he finally found was on a lettuce farm.

His very un-Mexican appearance gave him certain advantages over his fellow *peones* and he soon climbed the job ladder over more senior pickers. He went from field hand to field foreman to a supervisor in the crating sheds. His appearance also led to his eventual downfall.

Cleotis Bates was a young man two years Leopoldo's elder. He was also the son of the man who owned the lettuce fields.

Under his father's tutelage, Cleotis was learning the business. Mainly, his father taught him that the Mexicans on whose backs they had built the family fortune were lazy, stupid, dishonest, and unreliable. Cleotis caught on quickly.

Cleotis chose one midafternoon to make an appearance down at the warehouses where the field hands were loading several refrigerated cars on a rail spur. On his arm he escorted the lovely Harriet, the daughter of a neighboring lettuce grower. Marriage between these two would virtually corner the lettuce market in the Salinas Valley for their fathers.

Cleotis was of a mind to impress Harriet that morning in prelude to a marriage proposal he would make that evening at a birthday party for his father. Today it would not be enough simply to crack the whip. He needed to show his beloved how masterful he could be.

With much ceremony Cleotis settled Harriet under the shade of an awning at the top landing of a wooden staircase that zigzagged two stories up the outside of the warehouse. They could see Leopoldo below them, holding a clipboard on which he was tallying the crates the workers carried up a wooden ramp and into the rail car.

"I'll be right back," Cleotis told Harriet. "These people."

He took the steps down the staircase two at a time, stopping once to wave at Harriet just to make sure she was watching. When he reached Leopoldo, he tapped him officiously on the back with the riding crop he always carried, one of his several annoying affectations.

The scene that now played out in Cleotis's eyes was not the same as the one interpreted by Harriet two stair flights above.

Cleotis saw himself a study in command and control. He grabbed the clipboard from Leopoldo's hands and pointed at the columns of numbers with great animation. His face reddened and his voice became strident. He moved to the ramp and gesticulated fiercely at the porters. He forced them to stop and wait, the sharp edges of the wooden crates digging painfully into their necks and shoulders. He screamed at them and pointed this way and that, first inside the car and then at the large conveyor belt bringing the crates up from the black maw of the warehouse. For his grand exit he tossed the clipboard to Leopoldo and strode back up the stairs.

But screaming at Mexicans was no way to make an impression on Harriet. She had heard it all before. So her attention wandered to the *dramatis personae*.

There stood Cleotis, the protagonist, short and spindly, dressed in plantation hat, starched khaki shirt, and matching jodhpurs, the thinness of his calves accentuated by the tightness of the pant legs that bound them. When he yelled, his prominent Adam's apple moved up and down, striking the knot of his tie repeatedly, like a small, round bobbin on a fishing line.

Facing him was the supposed antagonist, Leopoldo. Even at five foot ten, he seemed to tower above Cleotis. His hat was pushed back to show his blue eyes. His features were fine and even. His shoulders were broad, and his knotted arms filled out the rolled-up sleeves of his shirt. His shirt was open to the waist and Harriet dabbed the drops of moisture from the top of her lip with a lace handkerchief as she watched the glistening perspiration from Leopoldo's face run down and lose itself in the thicket of his coppery chest hair.

Leopoldo showed no reaction during Cleotis's tirade. It was only when the owner's son was striding triumphantly to the stairway and beginning his climb that Leopoldo looked up and caught Harriet looking back at him. He smiled, his greatest physical asset, saluted her with a finger to his hat brim, and returned to his clipboard.

"These people," Cleotis said when he rejoined Harriet. "You have to tell them everything ten times."

"Who was the one you were talking to? He doesn't look Mexican."

"Who? The big one?"

"Uh-huh."

"That's Leo."

"And who is Leo?"

Cleotis was beginning to feel some irritation. "Don't let his looks fool you. He looks white but he's a Mex, all right."

"No. Really?"

"Yes, he is. Leo Zamora. Leopoldo. White on the outside but he talks like a Mexican, thinks like a Mexican, and smells like a Mexican."

"But he has blue eyes."

"Yeah. How about that? Some kind of albino freak, I guess."

With this revelation, Harriet became immediately and thoroughly disinterested in Leopoldo.

But Cleotis did not know this. What he did know was that Harriet had cast too many looks in Leopoldo's direction as they were talking and when he turned to follow her eyes he saw that Leopoldo was looking back.

Cleotis's voice broke into a falsetto of anger. "You! What do you think you're looking at? Get back to work and keep your eyes where they belong."

"Can we go now?" Harriet was suddenly whiny.

Harriet did not come to the birthday party that evening and unknowingly spared herself Cleotis's proposal.

"Too much sun," her father said. "Came home, said she had a headache, and went right to bed."

Harriet's mother added fuel to the young man's frustration by mentioning that Harriet was talking about going back East to college.

"Out of the clear blue. Practically had a fit over it when I brought up college to her last spring. Now she says she wants to go. Who knows? Out of the clear blue. She say anything to you, Cleotis?"

"No, ma'am. It's news to me."

"Well then I don't know what." The mother ended the conversation with a flick of her lace handkerchief.

Cleotis was in a state and by the time he reached the warehouse late the next afternoon he had had more than twenty-four hours to stew.

He ambushed a passing worker, almost causing the man to drop his crateful of lettuce. "Leopoldo—where is he?"

The man looked at him blankly.

"Leopoldo. Leopoldo Zamora? *¿Dónde está?*" Cleotis sprayed tiny globules of spit into the man's face.

As best he could, the man balanced the crate with one arm as he pointed with the other.

Cleotis set off in double time up the ramp and into the artificial coolness of the boxcar.

Leopoldo was standing on a crate of lettuce to rearrange a row above his head.

Coming up behind him, Cleotis used all the strength he could summon from his scrawny shoulders to whip his riding crop in a wide arc and brought it across the backs of Leopoldo's thighs. "Don't you ever look at a white woman like that again!"

With the crate of lettuce high above his head, Leopoldo was defenseless. He teetered, lost his balance, and came tumbling backward off his perch. He was on his feet immediately, snarling and ready for battle. But his opponent was suddenly indisposed.

Cleotis was half slumped on the floor, his back against a cloudy block of ice. His head hung awkwardly to one side, his bird neck unable to support it. A trickle of blood ran down his cheek from a gash where the falling crate of lettuce had struck him on the side of the head. His eyes were open but glazed over. Snot bubbled from his nose to the rhythm of his shallow breathing.

Leopoldo moved cautiously toward Cleotis and called to him softly, almost gently. "Cleotis? Cleotis?" He picked up the fallen man's hand and let it drop. It fell heavily to the floor of the car with a thump.

"*Dios mío. Lo maté.*"

Cleotis had not been killed. He had simply been knocked silly. In a few days the little man would be up and around, a patch on his head, screaming at every Mexican who dared cross his shadow.

Leopoldo could not know any of this. All he knew was that he must run and hide. More than one dead Mexican had been pulled from the Salinas River after a run-in with his boss. And this was a run-in of the first order.

Leopoldo stuck his head out the boxcar door and saw that the peones were busy at the other end of the loading dock. He slid down to the ground and under the car to the other side, righted himself, and trotted into the fields. He did not stop until he reached an irrigation ditch some three hundred yards away from the rail siding. He jumped in and sloshed along until he reached a culvert that ran under a road. Peeling back the wire mesh, he crawled in, and pulled the wire across the opening behind him.

He didn't know how long he sat shivering in the culvert. Long after the excited noises from the dock and the subsequent search for him had subsided. Long after the sun was down and the chill blew though his hiding place to make his teeth chatter out of control.

At about three the next morning he heard a train whistle and remembered that the lettuce he had been loading was scheduled to be moved out that very day. He left the culvert and scurried on all fours, dropping regularly to lie flat between the high rows of lettuce plants. Eventually he made his way to a spot behind a pump shed some fifty yards from the train. There he waited.

The crunching sounds of metal on metal signaled that the three refrigerator cars were coupled to the end of a long line of other freight cars. Then the train lurched and began to move slowly forward.

Leopoldo made his final dash. He stumbled once, almost going under the wheels, before he pulled himself onto a flat car that was piled high with large squarish forms covered over with tarp. He wriggled his body under the canvas and lay flat to the floor, his face grinding into the creosote-soaked boards.

Two days later Leopoldo was in Las Vegas, New Mexico. When the train pulled out of the station to continue its journey to deliver three boxcars full of Bates lettuce to Chicago housewives, Leopoldo stayed behind. Three weeks later, still acting the fugitive, he found himself in a place as remote as possible from the lush lettuce farms of Salinas.

He was in Mora.

And so ended his story, and Margarita almost afraid to breathe, stared at her father in awe.

"And then what happened?"

Leopoldo looked at her long and soberly. "One night when I was sleeping with your mamá there was a knock on the door. Some men rushed in, put me in irons, took me back to California, tried me for murder, and hanged me until I was dead." With this he stuck his tongue out to one side, rolled his eyes, and made several exaggerated gagging sounds.

Margarita swung hard at his arm. "No, really. Do you know what happened?"

"As a matter of fact, I do. A couple of years later your Uncle Delfino sent me up to San Luis, Colorado, to bring back a wagon of potatoes. I was just standing there and I heard someone call my name. It was one of the farm workers from Salinas."

"Did he call the police when he saw you?" Margarita's eyes were wide and round as she savored the deliciously melodramatic turn of her father's story.

"No, he didn't call the police. But he did tell me that Cleotis had not died. That he was now the new *patrón* and that he was the meanest man in California."

"So you were hiding for no reason at all?"

"Well, I think if he knew where I was, Cleotis would be after me. But he doesn't and he won't. He's too busy making his peons hate him."

"And so you met Mamá and married her."

"And so I met your mother and married her."

They drove quietly for over a mile before Margarita spoke again. "Why?"

"Why what, *hijita*?"

"Why did you marry her?"

Leopoldo pulled out a plug of tobacco, ripped off a chunk with his teeth, and worked it into his mouth until it was a soggy bulge against his right cheek.

"I guess, *hijita*, because it was meant to be."

Margarita slumped in her seat.

What kind of reason was that?

Chapter Eleven

True to her word, Tamar did not repeat the agony of her trip in the Model T until the family moved to Las Vegas for good in late August.

When she finally set herself ponderously into the front seat of the car—pregnancy already smoothing out the folds of her belly—she covered her mouth loosely with a wide shawl in a vain attempt to filter out the fumes from the car. She also carried by her side a yellow tin of Arm and Hammer baking soda. With a spoonful of this in some water as needed, she intended to ward off the nausea that had so undone her in her previous experience with Leopoldo's demon car.

The usual nine-hour trip stretched out to eleven. The tires seemed particularly perverse on this run, and Leopoldo had almost twice as many flats as normal. The children also had their needs. However, the main cause for delay was Tamar. She ended up drinking a prodigious amount of the water in which she mixed her palliatives. The result was that, although her remedy for carsickness was moderately successful—she threw up only five times—they had to stop every mile or two so she could pee.

In Las Vegas they settled in the rented house that Leopoldo had found for them and Tamar took the two boys to register in the public school.

My mother, Margarita Juana, was another case altogether.

"She's twelve years old, almost thirteen, and she needs to make her First Communion," Tamar fumed at Leopoldo one evening. "We have to put her in the Sisters' school."

"But that costs money."

"I'll talk to the sisters. She can work off her tuition."

Two days later, Margarita found herself sitting with Tamar before the principal of Our Lady of Sorrows School. They met in a parlor-like room with an oriental rug on the polished wood floor and half walls of dark wainscoting. Pressed tin, painted a soft ivory, covered the upper walls and the ceiling. The walls were a clutter of religious pictures and misty photographic portraits of stern ecclesiastics framed in gilded splendor.

Margarita listened to her mother's stiff and clumsy conversation with the nun. It seemed that her stock, which had enjoyed a meteoric rise during the summer, was now in definite decline. They were talking about her as if she were not in the room.

The nun tsk-tsked over the patchwork that was the girl's academic record. "She must prepare for First Holy Communion, you say?"

Tamar nodded her head piously.

The nun finally addressed Margarita directly. "You do want to receive Our Lord in the Eucharist, don't you, Margarita?"

Margarita had absolutely no idea what that could possibly mean. She looked at Tamar for help.

Her mother glared at her and sharply bobbed her head to prompt her daughter.

Margarita nodded dumbly.

"Well, we'll have to see about that, won't we?" The nun did not sound optimistic.

The upshot of the meeting with the principal was this: despite Margarita's age she would begin the school year in the third grade, then they would see; she would work off her tuition by staying after school every day to help with the cleaning; and the sisters would consider her candidacy for Holy Communion only if she were able to handle the workload both as a student and a janitor.

From her first day in her new school, Margarita was miserable.

At five foot three she stood a good head and a half taller than the other children in the class. The nun sat her in the very back of the room with the slow students. Actually, Margarita was far advanced over the rest of the class. Her knowledge of reading, arithmetic, and geography far surpassed theirs, and school quickly became a torturous waste of time. In the first few days of school she did hold her hand up several times to answer questions. The nun ignored her in preference for the better-dressed children sitting in front.

Then, one afternoon as she sat gazing out the window the nun finally called on her.

"Margarita, what state do we live in?"

Margarita had not heard the question and was startled into attention when the sister repeated her name, this time loudly and with considerable irritation.

"Margarita?"

The rest of the children turned in their seats and stared.

She flushed deeply, not knowing why she was the sudden center of the class's attention.

"Do you know the answer?"

Not having heard the question, Margarita shook her head.

"Well," sniffed the nun, "I'm sure someone does. Class?"

"New Mexico!" the class answered in raucous chorus.

For the remainder of the afternoon, while the other children buried themselves in art projects, Margarita labored over her tablet, writing the sentence "I live in the state of New Mexico" two hundred times. She gripped the pencil so tightly she could feel a small node rising on the first joint of her middle finger. To make matters worse, her hand became so wet with perspiration that she had to continually wipe it across the front of her dress to keep it from sticking to the paper as she wrote.

When the bell rang to end the school day the nun took the papers from her. As Margarita walked toward the door she heard the nun exclaiming none too quietly to herself, "The girl can't even write decently."

From that day on, Margarita was never called to recite in class and her homework always received a D or an F. Written in a perfect hand at the top of each paper was the cryptic note, "I can't read this! S. M. T."

Sister Mary Thomas was old, that much Margarita knew for sure. Just how old was anybody's guess. It was always difficult to estimate a nun's age. Her back was the model of perfect posture when she sat. When she walked she seemed to glide effortlessly, an illusion advanced by her long black skirt that reached to the floor so that her feet were invisible as they propelled her noiselessly forward. Her starched wimple, tight to the face, pulled her skin and smoothed it out to a fine marble. Her hair was completely covered, so what was beneath her veil, whether dark, gray, or white, no one could see.

Margarita had three telling pieces of evidence, however, to support her theory that Sister Thomas was quite old.

First, the nun had false teeth, a sure sign of someone advanced in years. Sometimes when she talked, more often when she screamed, the teeth would lose their precipitous hold on her gums and begin to squirt out of her mouth. With the practice of years, Sister Thomas would lunge her head forward like a chicken pecking at an ear of corn and clamp down on the dentures before they had a chance to fly completely out of her mouth.

The second reason that Margarita knew that Sister Thomas was old was her need for frequent catnaps during the day. The nun would set the children to some quiet study activity, quiet, that is, until her sibilant purring drifted over the heads of the children bent to their assignments. Most of the time her siestas were light interludes. She usually sprang to wakefulness at the drop of a pencil or the crumpling of a piece of paper. But occasionally, the sleep of the nun was deep and resolute. Then a dozen dropped pencils would not stir her, nor the wadding of an entire ream of paper. The children would look at each other as her soft, almost wistful breathing turned into protean snores and they would begin to giggle and whisper to each other. Two or three of the boys would stand up at their desks to shake their bodies and wave their hands, daring the sleeping nun to catch them at their dance.

The disturbances soon shook the nun into consciousness. When this happened, Margarita had her third and most telling proof of Sister Thomas's dotage.

Sister Thomas would take a yardstick and run down the rows between the desks. She swung the long ruler back and forth in front of her like a farmer with a sickle going through a field of grass. She kept the stick about two feet above desk level and the children knew the drill. They quickly placed their heads in their arms on the desktops as the yardstick whistled harmlessly over them. One or two of the boys always dared their fates, waiting until the last second to duck and raising their heads quickly after she passed, timing their moves to barely avoid the nun's saber strokes.

The first time it happened Margarita was too astonished to react. She did not lay her head down in time and caught the stick across the side of her head. Thereafter she knew what to do with her head, but when the nun reached her she always seemed to dip her arm just enough to catch Margarita on the shoulder or on her back.

When she came home at night, Margarita begged Tamar to let her go to public school with Eugenio and Gerónimo.

"She hates me. She teaches things I already know. She's old and she's evil."

But Tamar would not bend. "God will punish you for calling the sister evil. You are the evil one for having such thoughts. There you are and there you'll stay until you make your First Communion. That should take some of the devil out of you."

Indeed, there was no question that Sister Thomas was now too old to be in a classroom with a bunch of third graders for six hours every day. She was, in point of fact, seventy-seven years old and edging into senile dementia. She was starting to dream strange, terrifying dreams that surrounded her as she lay on the cot in her cramped, cell-like room. They were dreams that now came even before she fell asleep, black illusions that frightened her and made her call out for her mother in the dark.

Nun bashing has always been a time-honored tradition among the alumni of parochial schools. Even nuns talk about the nuns who taught them when they were children. And, yes, there was ample reason for Sister Thomas's students to carry stories home and for their parents to complain to the principal about her. But lost in the moment's cruel truth was the dedicated teacher that Sister Mary Thomas had been for almost six decades.

None of this mattered to Margarita. All she knew was that her situation was as bleak as it had ever been.

One day in late November, Margarita was busy sweeping out the combined seventh and eighth grade classroom. She was trying to be as quiet as possible because the sister who taught the older children was still there, tutoring a student on the mysteries of compound multiplication.

Sister Apolonia stood at the blackboard with the boy. "Just remember your times tables, Carlos. Take one number at a time."

"Yes 'ster."

"Do you think you can do a couple of problems on your own?"

"Yes 'ster."

The nun chalked out two sets of neatly stacked numbers. "Try these. I have to run over to see Sister Basil for a few minutes. If you get done before I come back, just leave everything on the board for me to see."

After the nun left the room, Carlos stood back for a full five minutes, looking at the mocking rows of numbers, no clearer to him now than before. Finally, with a cry of disgust, he picked up the chalk and raced with it across the black board, setting off squeals of agony as chalk met slate. He threw up numbers at random, wanting only to end this ordeal so he could join his friends playing in the street outside the window. When he finished he tossed the chalk on the tray, clapped his hands together to dispel a cloud of white dust, grabbed his coat and books, and raced out the door, slamming it behind him.

In the quiet of the classroom, all that could now be heard was the whisper of the broom. Then this sound also stopped. Margarita was standing at the blackboard and warily eyeing the numbers parading across it. She had propped the broom against the wall and held a stubby finger of chalk in her hand. At a corner of the board she began to recopy one of the multiplication problems. Her touch was so timid and light that it was almost as if she were tracing the numbers with wisps of smoke. Then—for she had been listening as carefully as she could to the nun's instructions to Carlos—she began to calculate the problem. She tried once and unsatisfied with the result, she tried again, erasing her mistakes as she went with the cuff of her sleeve.

"Don't forget to carry the seven."

Margarita was so engrossed in the puzzle of the numbers that she did not hear the nun reenter the room.

Hurriedly eradicating her work with a swipe of her arm, Margarita returned the chalk to the tray.

"Never start what you aren't prepared to finish. Especially a problem in mathematics. And how did our friend Carlos do? Not very well, I see. Now, which one were you working on? Ah, yes, this one."

With the eraser she wiped away the hieroglyphics that the boy had generated and held out the chalk to Margarita. "Let's start this one again."

"I have to finish sweeping."

"Later. But now you have to finish this." The nun pointed at the problem and once again offered the chalk to Margarita.

It took half an hour but at the end the girl had mastered the intricacies of compound multiplication.

"You know your times tables very well. They don't teach that in the third grade, do they?"

Margarita shook her head. "My Daddy taught me so I could help him with the lumber orders."

"And what else do you know?"

Margarita shrugged her shoulders.

"Why don't we find out?"

Over the next six months Margarita attended two schools every day, the one with Sister Thomas and the one with Sister Apolonia.

Sister Thomas's classroom did not change. Margarita continued to receive Ds and Fs. The nun continued to snatch her dentures out of mid air, to sleep, and to run up and down the rows of desks with her yardstick, seeking, however ineffectively, to decapitate her nightmares.

Sister Apolonia's classroom, after the school bell, was where Margarita did her learning. She conquered long division in three days, simple fractions in a week. Sister Apolonia gave her a stack of seventh-grade-level textbooks—World History, English Grammar and Composition, American Literature, and Spelling. These she took home and devoured. The nun also gave her a dog-eared copy of the Baltimore Catechism, which she memorized, word by word, so that when the priest asked her at her examination for Holy Communion, "What is the Holy Eucharist?" she was able to answer loudly, with confidence, "The Holy Eucharist is a sacrament and a sacrifice; in it Our Savior Jesus Christ, body and blood, soul and divinity, under the appearance of bread and wine, is contained, offered, and received."

At the end of the school year, Margarita received two report cards. The one from Sister Thomas bore, in red ink, the legend: "Passed to Fourth Grade (Conditionally)."

As Sister Mary Thomas explained to the principal: "The child did not learn a thing in my class. God knows how she got ready for First Communion. But I simply can't keep her for another year. She's too big. Her breasts are starting to show!"

After school, that final day, Sister Apolonia called Margarita into her classroom and handed her a small envelope. "This is for you."

Margarita opened it carefully and removed a lacy card with a pale blue ribbon worked into the border on one side. The card bore

the image of the Blessed Mother holding the Christ Child. "Thank
you, Sister. It's beautiful."

"Look on the back."

Margarita turned the card over and read what Sister Apolonia had written in her small, neat nun's hand. "Margarita J. Zamora. Promoted to the 8th Grade: Sr. M. Apolonia."

Margarita reread the words several times without really grasping what they meant. Finally, still puzzled, she looked up at the nun.

"It's true. I talked to the principal this morning."

"And it's all right?"

"It's all right."

The next year was an unqualified academic success for Margarita. She received straight As in every subject except penmanship where even the ever-supportive Apolonia could not justify more than a B minus. She did so well that when it was time to name the top eighth grade girl to crown the Virgin during the annual May Devotions, Margarita was the runaway selection.

Sister Thomas was no longer teaching. Over the summer her mental decline had been cataclysmic. Her body gave out at the same time and she was suddenly bent-over and withered. Since she knew no other home than the convent in Las Vegas her superiors elected to leave her there. She spent most of her time in the chapel sleeping in the warm glow of the red sanctuary lamp. Or she walked with slow, jerking steps along the inner porch of the courtyard, lecturing aloud to fifty-seven former classes of invisible students.

"Eyes front. Sit up straight. No talking." These admonitions substituted for the Hail Marys that she counted absently on the beads that slipped through her gnarled fingers.

Sister Thomas had always been in charge of the organization and presentation of the May Coronation. Now the function was in the hands of others. As a courtesy, and because it was one of her more lucid days, she was invited to the sacristy at the church to check out the preparations before the ceremony.

When Margarita appeared at the door, dressed in white, Sister Thomas did not recognize her. "Come over to the window," the nun ordered her, "where the light is better."

Peering into Margarita's face, there was at first no hint of recognition in the old nun's eyes. Then, suddenly, "You're that one. The big-breasted one. Why are you here? You don't even know what state you live in!"

In mid-July of that summer, when Leopoldo was down from the camp to deliver a load of lumber, he received the news.

The owner of the lumberyard handed him his money with a caveat. "This will be the last load I buy from you, Leopoldo. I sold the business to some people from Lubbock. They're taking over next week."

"I can still sell to them?"

"'Fraid not. They have their own mills. And they just signed up with the Forest Service for fifteen thousand acres up near Eagle Nest."

And so, after sixteen years, Leopoldo was out of business.

"But what will we do?" wailed Tamar.

"I'll get work here in Las Vegas. Sell the mill. Something will come up."

"Is there work here?"

"I don't know. I guess I'll find out."

There was no work in Las Vegas, not the kind that paid enough to support the growing Zamora family. The town was already a grim precursor of the Great Depression that would engulf the country four years later.

The sale of the mill went badly. The only bid Leopoldo received was from the same company that had run him out of business. They gave him thirty-five cents on the dollar for his lease and equipment. At least the two draft horses, Leopoldo's beloved twin towers of strength, brought full price at the stock auction.

He kept the Model T with its trailer and used it to haul freight around town. But he was competing against several long-established freight handlers and he had to content himself with the smaller jobs that the others could or would not handle. He became a part-time janitor for several stores. He became a process server for the county but lost that job to a man who was a cousin of the sheriff.

Then in September, as the children were getting ready to begin another year of school, the Zamoras had a visitor, Tamar's brother,

Pacunio. "Come to Denver. There's lots of work there as long as you don't mind being called a Mexican."

Denver.

The name reverberated through Margarita's body like a magical tuning fork.

Denver.

Uncle Delfino and Soledea. The promise, long dormant, flared brighter than ever.

Leopoldo sold the Model T and the trailer and with what little money was left from the sale of the mill and his piddling holdings of livestock purchased a three-year-old Buick four-door, five-passenger sedan, Model 21-47.

On a cool September morning, the Zamoras closed the door to the house in Las Vegas, handed the key over to the landlord, loaded themselves and what property they could carry, and headed north.

Chapter Twelve

1926–1928

The happiest time that Margarita Juana was ever to spend with her family, and in particular with her mother, was the week of preparation for their exodus from New Mexico to Colorado.

Even though the Zamoras' move north was dictated by financial problems, Margarita, going on fourteen, was at a point in her life when any change dripped fat with possibilities. She was moving to Denver, a city twenty times larger than the one she was leaving. There would be new opportunities. And, more importantly, there was a chance for a reunion with her Uncle Delfino and his princess bride, Soledea. Denver, the girl believed with all her heart, held her future.

It was also during this week that Margarita came as close as she ever would to understanding her mother.

The closer the date for their departure from Las Vegas loomed, the higher Tamar's spirits rose. She and Leopoldo sold off many of their furnishings and it seemed that for every bed, table, or chair that passed out the door with its new owner, another mooring line was cast from Tamar's soul. At the end, when she stood in the middle of an empty house, surrounded by piles of clothing and a few household essentials ready for packing, she looked almost buoyant. It was as if her wide, beltless cotton dress might suddenly billow and lift her up, unfettered and happy at last to drift away from her family and the burden they imposed.

While she and Margarita sat to fold and bundle clothes, Tamar initiated the first real conversation she had ever had with her daughter. She spoke of her own youth, the time before she was married to Leopoldo, during her turn in the house of Uncle Delfino and Aunt Adela when Nasha, the Indian bondservant, was at her beck and call.

"You think that Tío and Tía were yours alone? You were only with them for seven years. I lived in their house for twenty," boasted Tamar. "The clothes they bought for me! The trips we took! Every week it was from Mora here to Las Vegas. Every month, in good weather, it was to Santa Fe or Albuquerque. We would eat in restaurants and sleep on

soft beds in hotels. Tía Adela hated spending the money. She always
wanted to stay with relatives or drop in on friends for meals. 'After all,
they're always welcome to our house,' she'd say. But Tío would not
hear of it. I can still hear him. 'That's no way to travel. Why go somewhere new and exciting just to see the same people, stay in the same
houses, and eat the same food?' Our best trip was to Denver."

"Denver? In Colorado?"

"That's the only one I know."

"When did you go there?"

"I was seventeen. Two years before I married your daddy."

With mention of the marriage, Margarita sensed a melancholy
change in her mother's face. With a gentle prodding she led Tamar
back to happier times. "So you know all about Denver?"

"Well, I can't say I know it," responded Tamar after a beat, her
tone softening again. "It's a very big city."

"We stayed at the Albany Hotel," she continued brightly, back
again in happier times. "It was beautiful. The floors were polished
like glass. They had everything there. We could eat every meal in our
room if we wanted to. We had our own bathroom and we could take
baths and use all the hot water we wanted. And the towels were soft
and as big as bed sheets. In the morning we would go downstairs for
breakfast and when we came back to the room it was like we were
walking into it for the first time. The beds were made. Everything was
put up and clean. The only way I was sure it was our room was to
open the closet and see our clothes hanging there.

"And then we would go out and walk up and down the side-
walks. There were so many people. So many stores. Places to eat.
And such tall buildings. We went to this place and stood in line for
two hours and paid a dime apiece just to go up in the elevator. When
we reached the top, Tío Delfino walked right up to the window to
look out. Me and Tía Adela stayed back because we were afraid of
falling. But we could see just fine from where we were. There were
mountains far away and flat lands all around us, with thousands of
trees and houses and hundreds of streets that went everywhere.

"And we went shopping. We went to big department stores, a
hundred times bigger than anything in Vegas. Daniels & Fisher and
Joslin's. Mostly we just looked. But Tío bought me a new dress in one

store and shoes to match in another. And he made Tía try on about a million hats before she found one she liked. And he bought himself a new suit and a walking cane. It was all very nice. My *Tío* took care of everything. *Muy bonito todo.*" Tamar's voice had become wistful, a smooth hum that ended finally in a protracted sigh.

She cleared her throat. "Maybe it can be that way again. At least a little bit. Maybe your daddy will find a good job. And you too. Something to do after school. Maybe we can save enough money to buy a house. And sometimes maybe we can buy something in a department store. Or walk into the Albany Hotel and have breakfast and sit in their soft chairs to watch all the people walk in and out."

The family's route to Denver was a direct shot over Raton Pass, across the border into Colorado, through Trinidad, Walsenberg, Pueblo, and Colorado Springs.

There were four in the front seat of the three-year-old Model 21-47 Buick, the adults and the two youngest children, the toddler Alfonso on Tamar's lap and Agapita squeezed between her mother and father. The older children, Eugenio, eleven, Gerónimo, nine, and Margarita fought for territory in the back.

In the very first minutes of the 350-mile trip Margarita realized that she had made a huge mistake. As the eldest, she had asserted her right and settled herself directly behind her father, who was driving. The rules of ascendancy also held for her two brothers. Eugenio, as the second in line, took the other window seat, leaving Gerónimo to squirm uncomfortably in the space between.

Margarita's first inkling that she had not chosen her seat wisely came when Leopoldo reached into his jacket pocket and pulled out a small, evil-looking ingot of densely compacted chewing tobacco. With a violent jerk of his jaw, he tore off a sizable chunk of the plug and settled in behind the wheel to enjoy a chew.

When her father leaned toward the window and spat, the wad, its outward trajectory no match for the wind rushing by the open window, shot back into the car. Margarita sensed rather than saw the splattering mass of wetness on the back of the seat not five inches from her face.

She snatched up a rag lying on the floor and wiped away the vileness. Then she turned to see whether either of her brothers had taken notice.

Eugenio, sitting squarely and solemnly, stared out his window.
Gerónimo was busy poking his finger into a hole in the upholstery between his legs.

"Are you all right, Gerónimo?"

Gerónimo looked at her through eyes squinted with suspicion.

"Would you like to sit by the window so you can look out?"

He hesitated, then nodded.

"I'll trade you places."

Gerónimo tilted his head to get a better view of his sister.

"I mean it," she said. "I'm not teasing. Come on," she commanded, then put her hands under his arms and pulled him over her as she shimmied underneath him to take the center seat. "There, isn't that better?"

Gerónimo ignored the question. He drew his legs up underneath him and, like a dog molding itself to its space, began to twist and grind his torso into the softness of the seat cushion. Finally satisfied, he turned his attention to the view. It was at that exact moment that Leopoldo again leaned toward the open driver's-side window and let fly with another missile. This salvo took the same darting arc of the first, but with far more lethal effect.

"Aiieee!" Gerónimo screamed.

Tamar whipped her head back, ready to skewer with her eyes the children behind her. She was not a person who would tolerate any kind of monkey business in the back seat of a car. What she saw and what made her glare melt away with amusement was the sight of her second son. His eyes were wide, his mouth was open in astonishment, and the entire side of his face was a brown study in tobacco juice.

Tamar, like most people soured on life, found her small pleasures in the misfortunes of others. The sight of someone stumbling or bumping themselves invariably sent her into paroxysms of laughter. She loved going to the local movie house, not to see the romances or melodramas, but to watch people crash into walls or have flowerpots fall on their heads. Once, in fact, she had laughed so hard at a particularly cruel piece of slapstick that she could not hold in her pee and had to sit in her seat soggy and miserable for the rest of the picture. Now, the sight of her second-eldest son, stunned and splattered, triggered in Tamar a most unmaternal urge to cackle.

"Daddy!" Margarita shouted at Leopoldo, poking him sharply on the shoulder. "You're spitting all over us."

She quickly busied herself with the rag, wiping Gerónimo's face with exaggerated solicitude, distracting her little brother from the obvious conclusion that he had been set up for ambush by the very angel of mercy who now attended to him.

An arrangement was quickly worked out between the front and the back seats. Leopoldo promised to be more careful and to lean out the window as far as he could whenever he felt a need to expectorate. Also, when he was ready to discharge, he was to shout in a loud voice, "Spit!" This gave Margarita time to drape the rag over Gerónimo's face to protect him from any vagrant spray.

It was three in the afternoon by the time they reached the summit of Raton Pass. Colorado lay like a green and brown carpet before them.

"We'll never get there," Tamar complained loudly.

"Don't worry," Leopoldo assured her. "We'll make up the time now. It's downhill all the way to Trinidad."

For what seemed an eternity, they hung precariously on the lip of the hill, then pitched forward like a rollercoaster car.

The Buick started slowly down but then began rolling faster and faster as it picked up momentum. By the time they had traveled a mile, the car was a runaway behemoth. Leopoldo bent forward, his fingers tightly wound around the top arch of the steering wheel, his tobacco a forgotten clump in his cheek, his mouth set and his eyes trained on the snaking asphalt in front of him. Down, down they plunged. The car threw up clouds of dust as its wheels bit into the narrow shoulders of the many hair-pin turns. It screeched and zigzagged across the road as Leopoldo over-compensated. Three times they just narrowly missed a head-on collision with other vehicles climbing the pass from the other direction.

Leopoldo's passengers were bug-eyed, speechless, and scared out of their wits for the entire thirteen-mile descent.

Close to the bottom of the pass, the road gentled out and Leopoldo began to slow down the car. Mushy from overheating, the brakes took some time to catch. Finally, the Buick stopped with a jolt that threw everyone forward. This caused Tamar to crack her head on the dashboard. If this had happened to anyone else, Tamar might have laughed out loud. But now her look dared anyone to take pleasure from her pain.

They all sat silent for a full minute.

"Good time. We really made good time," Leopoldo finally observed weakly and sparked the motor to life for the limp into town.

They spent the night in Trinidad, at the house of a former worker from Leopoldo's sawmill. This man had come to Colorado to escape the drudgery and dangers of lumbering. Now he worked in the deep, dark coal mines that honeycombed the hills around the town. Where once he had dreamt of falling onto the giant sawblade to be cut in half he now awoke from nightmares in which he was buried alive.

Tamar maintained her mellow mood for long stretches of the two-hundred-mile trip into Denver. On occasion she leveled quick bursts of anger at one of the family, but clearly her heart was not in it. Soon she would relax and allow the passing landscape to flow over her like a warm purifying ablution that flushed out the miseries she had so assiduously stuffed into the gullies of her soul for the last sixteen years.

From the back seat Margarita studied the profile of this woman who had never been more than a dour presence in her life. Tamar had tucked her coarse hair, now streaked with gray, into a careless bun. Her face showed the wear of dashed hopes. It was a face that had succumbed early to poverty, to the bearing of seven children, two of them dead and under the ground, to season upon season in the confinement of a rude cabin among the tall ponderosas, to living in other people's houses and eating from other people's tables, to forfeiting the future save for that inevitable triad—growing tired, growing old, and dying.

Then Margarita had a most unexpected epiphany. The Tamar of years past, before her marriage, must have been very like Margarita herself. She had lived in the same fine house, been coddled by the same Nasha, been loved and cherished by the same Adela and Delfino. She saw Tamar, the child, clambering onto Delfino's lap to play with his flowing mustache or being rocked to sleep by the warmth of the kitchen stove with her head on Nasha's shoulder. She searched for some reason to love, perhaps even to like, her mother but the best she could come up with was pity.

And what of herself? Would she eventually look that tired, that isolated, that bitter? What was there to stop the fate of the mother visiting itself on the daughter?

Quite simply, she would not permit it to be.

Chapter Thirteen

They arrived in Denver close to dusk. Driving up Broadway, they passed the state capitol with its dome sheathed in pure gold leaf. Leopoldo skillfully worked his way around tram cars and delivery trucks. Tamar's eyes still shone with the glitter of downtown Denver fifteen blocks behind them. Finally, they pulled up at their new home.

Were it not for the grime and exhaustion, Margarita might have doubted her memory of the long trip they had just endured. It was as if they had never left their old neighborhood in Las Vegas. The houses were just as ramshackle, the front yards filled with weeds and rusting tin cans. The children playing on front porches or running into the street had the same brown faces and spoke the same singsong Spanglish. Even the canine population seemed to have been imported from their old home grounds to greet them. There were monstrously fat bitches waddling on too-short legs and dragging their teats in the dust, and thin, arched-back scavengers nosing around garbage cans and baring their teeth to anyone approaching them.

The house, which had been rented for them by Tamar's brother, Pacunio, was as large as the one they had just left. However, even without looking inside, Margarita could tell that it was in far worse condition. A lumpy pillow had been stuffed into a window frame in the front door where the glass had been punched out. The outer clapboard walls were chipped and peeling so that the gray wood dominated over patches of yellow paint. The porch railing was missing several posts, giving the house the gapped-tooth look of an old crone grinning a welcome to them. Two rusting chains that had once held a porch swing swayed loosely from the overhang.

Margarita turned to look at her mother. The spark was gone from Tamar's eyes and her jaw was reset with its customary ferocity. Margarita understood immediately. Tamar had been betrayed. The daughter sensed that this betrayal would be the last that her mother would allow. Tamar would never again tolerate even the slightest wedge of hope to intrude on her soul.

As she stepped up on the porch and through the front door, Tamar irreversibly crossed the threshold from weariness into old age. After that, all that remained was the dying.

Tamar's brother, Pacunio, who had lured the family to Denver with promises of work and prosperity, met the Zamoras with discouraging words. "You came too late, the planting's done. You'll have to wait for the harvest now."

Leopoldo and his brother-in-law sat at the kitchen table late at night after the rest of the family had gone to bed. A kerosene lamp burned sluggishly between them. They drank beer and a little whiskey and they talked in loud whispers.

"But I didn't come to be a picker. I can do things. *Tengo familia.* I need to earn good money."

"It's not that easy to find work nowadays."

"You said there was work here. Plenty of it."

"There is. There is. It's just that things are different here. It's not New Mexico, you know."

"No, I don't know. You tell me."

"*Esta gente . . .*"

"Yes? What about these people?"

"There are lots of jobs, but, well, you know how people are."

Leopoldo banged his Coors down hard on the table. A small geyser of foam and beer rushed up the long neck of the bottle and splashed across the table.

"*¡Mal parido!* Say what you have to say."

"Mexicans, no one will hire Mexicans."

"I'm not a Mexican. I was born in California." Even as he said it, Leopoldo knew that this was an old argument that had never worked. It was Oakland and Salinas all over again.

"*Tu nombre es Zamora.* You speak Spanish. To them that makes you a Mexican. They don't care where you were born."

After Pacunio had left, Leopoldo went outside and sat on the front stoop. He thought of his time on the docks where the Irish long-shoreman had befriended him and advised him to change his name to Leo Logan. "It worked once," he concluded. "Change my name and change my luck."

At five-thirty the next morning, Leopoldo poked roughly at Margarita's back as she lay in sound sleep.

"Margarita. *Levántate.* I need you."

The girl stumbled into the kitchen after her father.

"I poured you some coffee. Wake up now. You have to help me."

"With what?"

"With this." He placed a newspaper in front of her. It was folded neatly to the help-wanted ads. "Help me look for work."

"Why don't you do it yourself? You can read."

"But sometimes I can't understand what it says. Read."

She yawned, rubbed her eyes, took a sip of the bitter coffee, wrapped her bare feet around the chair legs, and began to read. "Help wanted, shoe salesman . . ."

"No, no. Try the next one. . . ."

"Help wanted, experienced cook . . ."

"No. Keep going."

Finally, they struck gold. There in a box that separated it from the other advertisements was the notice:

MECHANICS WANTED
Experience required.
The Denver Tramway Company is accepting applications
to fill numerous vacancies in its motor shops. Please apply in
person at the tramway shops, Broadway and West Alaska
Streets, 7 o'clock A.M. to 5 o'clock P.M., Mon. thru Fri.

"That's it." Leopoldo took the paper from his daughter and carefully drew a square around the ad. "Now you can go back to bed."

At seven o'clock sharp Leopoldo stood outside the gates of the southside Denver Tramway Company shops. A steady stream of workers swinging lunch pails was already walking into the yards to begin the morning shift. He noticed a guard shack to one side. In it sat a uniformed man behind a sliding glass panel, drinking from a tin cup of steaming coffee. Leopoldo tapped on the window and the man looked up with impeccable disinterest, not even bothering to push open the window.

Leopoldo pointed to the ad, which he carried with him. The man wordlessly gestured him to the end of the building.

A minute later, Leopoldo was standing in front of the shop manager.

"Name?"

"Leo Chené."

The man eyed Leopoldo suspiciously.

"Chené. Chené." He mulled over the name. "What kind of name is that?"

"French."

Leopoldo spoke through clenched teeth and as softly as possible, trying to disguise his accent and hoping that what came out of his mouth had at least a passing Gallic flavor.

"Where are you from, Chené?"

"Canada."

"Speaka da English?"

Leopoldo nodded.

"Have you worked on motors before?"

Leopoldo nodded again.

"What kind?"

"Diesel. Gas. Cars. Trucks. Sawmills."

The man stared into Leopoldo's blue eyes for one last clue as to who this man was.

"Canada, huh? They got motors in Canada? OK, Chené, we'll try it for one day. Go down to the car barn and talk to Gus. Tell him I sent you. He'll tell me if you're going to work out. You got all that, Chené?"

Leopoldo nodded, muttered his thanks, and left before there were any more questions.

He was very good with all things mechanical, as Gus was soon to discover. The next morning Leopoldo was again at the gate at seven. This time he ignored the guard, who was only too willing to return the favor, and walked straight into the yard with the rest of the shift.

"Gus says you're OK, Chené. The job's yours."

The supervisor handed him a pencil and a form and Leopoldo began to write slowly in a large, juvenile hand. He tripped himself up almost immediately. As he began to write his name he unthinkingly put down "Leopoldo" and then began to form the Z in Zamora. Realizing his mistake, he furiously tried to erase the accusing zigzag, but in his haste succeeded only in ripping a hole in the paper.

"Well, I hope you can fix motors better than you can write." The man gave Leopoldo a new form and took the torn one from him. Before he crumpled it up he glanced at what had already been written on it.

"Leopold?" the supervisor misread the scribbling. "Ain't that German? I thought you said you was a Frenchie." He wadded up the paper and tossed it on the floor under his desk.

This time Leopoldo was very, very careful. "Leo Chené," he wrote.

"OK. Forty-eight cents an hour. If you join the union it's fifty-two cents. Not worth it if you ask me."

Not a week after they had arrived in Denver, Leopoldo left the house without his lunch pail and Margarita was dispatched to the shops by her mother to deliver it to him.

"And don't forget, his name is Leo Chené."

"But I don't know where to go."

She thrust the pail into the girl's arms.

"Don't be such a baby. Take a bus and ask the driver."

Margarita did not move.

"Well?"

"I need twelve cents."

"Twelve cents! Do I look like a bank? Tell the driver that your father works for the company."

It was Monday, Memorial Day. With no seniority, Leopoldo had been assigned to work the long holiday weekend. The streets were all but empty as Margarita stood at the curb and rehearsed her lines. When a bus pulled up and its doors opened, she saw that the man behind the wheel was thin, watery-eyed, and unfriendly.

"Well," he barked at her, "are you getting on?"

She shook her head and walked away, trying to pretend that she had not been waiting for a bus at all and it was his own fault if he had presumed otherwise.

"If you don't want a bus don't stand at the bus stop." The driver closed the door with an angry slap and peeled away, leaving Margarita in a cloud of exhaust.

A second bus rambled up ten minutes later. Margarita could see the driver's face through the dusty front windshield and despite the glare from the glass she had a distinct impression that she knew the face. The man wore a short, white beard and seemed to bear an uncanny resemblance to Don José Argüello, Doña Prisca's handyman who had carved so many wonderful wooden things for her. In the unobstructed frame of the open door, the driver did not really look much like Don José, but his smile was no less warm.

"Need a ride?"

"I have to take my daddy's lunch to him. He fixes buses at the shop on South Broadway. His name is Leo Chené," she quickly added.

"Well, I can't say I've ever had the pleasure but I'm going right by the barn. Hop in."

"I don't have any money."

"Your dad needs his lunch?"

She nodded.

"Let's get it to him."

Margarita scrambled into the bus and sat two rows behind the driver.

As the bus pulled into the sparse traffic, a passenger across the aisle from Margarita leaned forward and spoke loudly to the driver over the din of the motor. "Hey! How come she don't have to pay?"

The bus driver glanced up to the rearview mirror.

The passenger spoke again, this time even more loudly, and pointed at Margarita. "I say how come she don't have to pay?"

"Professional courtesy," shouted the driver over his shoulder.

The man snorted, slumped back into his seat, folded his arms, and stared out his window.

A mile and a half down Broadway, the bus came to a stop directly in front of the tramway shops. "Here we are, little lady. Just ask the guard at the gate. He'll tell you where your pappy is."

Margarita stepped to the sidewalk, turned back to the driver, and smiled.

"If you want a ride back," the man said, "be across the street in fifteen minutes."

Leopoldo was grateful for his lunch and kissed Margarita on the cheek before sending her on her way. "Go straight home. And don't talk to anyone."

After a five-minute wait at the stop, Margarita saw her friend's bus approaching on its return run. The vehicle was now almost full. When she stepped up beside him, the driver winked and motioned her to a seat with a tilt of his head.

The passengers were in a holiday mood, many of them with picnic baskets and dressed for the first outing of the summer. More and more of them pushed their way on at every stop, so that by the time they arrived at Denver's main intersection, Broadway and Colfax Avenue, the bus was fairly bursting with humanity.

At this point on its north-south route, Broadway opened up into Civic Center, a commons of some three square blocks. The park was flanked by a columned memorial gateway to the north and a curved Greek portico to the south. On a steep bluff to the east perched the state capitol with its dome of pure gold leaf.

Here most of the passengers disembarked. All were primed for a Memorial Day of patriotic speeches, recitations, band concerts, games, and refreshments.

Margarita could see vendors setting up their tents and children running and playing across the huge expanse dotted by trees, fountains, and monuments. She was sorely tempted to join them.

Three blocks later she reached her stop.

"Did your pappy get his lunch?" asked the bus driver as she walked up the aisle past him to the door.

She nodded shyly.

"Good. And I hope he appreciates what a nice daughter he has."

Margarita flushed red. "Thank you."

As she started the walk home she heard snatches of cheering and hooting bouncing off the buildings behind her. There was a crowd of people lining an intersection some two blocks away. Curiosity overcame caution and she turned in that direction.

It was a parade. Her first week in Denver and already she'd get to see a parade.

A parade indeed. The next day's edition of the *Rocky Mountain News* had this to say about it:

Klansmen Parade Thru City Streets
Members of the Knights of the Ku Klux Klan from all parts of
the state of Colorado gathered at the Cotton mills thruout

yesterday for the first state meeting of the organization since the factional fight in the organization several months ago. The meeting followed a parade thru the downtown section of the city of the hooded members, augmented by Ladies of the Ku Klux Klan, who were also attired in their regalia and who were led by their state kleagle and an imperial representative.

This was the first public parade ever staged by the order in Denver and was marked by its quietness and freedom from trouble of any kind.

The article concluded with an airy description of how the Klan ended its busy day.

. . . the klansmen, in automobiles went to various parts of the city, where they carried out the ceremony of burning the cross. Crosses were erected and set aflame at the city limits on the Denver–Colorado Springs Road, on Poverty Hill, at Alameda Avenue and Federal Boulevard, at Sherman Street and East Colfax Avenue, on Inspiration Point, at West Fifty-third Avenue and Federal Boulevard, at the York Street railroad subway, and at East Colfax Avenue and the city limits. . . .

Standing to the back, Margarita could see very little, mostly some sharp points of white, a sea of them, bobbing up and down as they made their way up the street. She pushed her way forward until she stood directly behind the first line of spectators. What she had first perceived as a zigzag of slender, snowy peaks was in actuality a mass of sharply spiked conical hoods like bayonets stabbing at the sky. The wearers of the tall hoods had also draped themselves in long white robes, many bearing an insignia above the left breast, a red circle encompassing a black and white cross. Some of the marchers wore masks with roundish eyeholes. These hung stiffly from the fronts of the hoods like starched visors. Others in the procession wore no masks, their own uniformly grim and pinched faces quite enough to render them anonymous, men, women, and the children alike. A few carried flags, some American, others from the old Confederacy.

The spectators seemed unsure of how to deal with this strangely somber procession. Most of the people were silent. A very few cheered enthusiastically and waved small flags of their own. There was also a smattering of boos and shouts of "Go home! We don't need you here."

This was not to say that none in the crowd were up to engaging in a little holiday sport. Four young men on the opposite curb from Margarita were at that instant hatching a little diversion, a harmless game of Dare-Double-Dare. One of the young men, egged on by his friends, darted out on the street, touched a marcher on his billowing sleeve, and quickly retreated to the hoots and hardy backslaps of his friends. Not to be outdone, another boy ran out on the street, jumped straight up, and flicked his hand across the peak of a hood. Emboldened, a third youth charged out. He started to swipe at another hood and then in a moment of youthful high spirits grabbed at it and pulled it off the wearer's head.

Two burly men dressed completely in black sprang forward from the edge of the parade to cut off the boy's flight. They caught him between them, planted their hands on his shoulders, and forced him to a kneeling position on the pavement. Then, as one of the men pulled the boy's head back by the hair and delivered a hard knee to a kidney, the other ripped the hood from his hands.

The crowd, both the cheerers and the jeerers, fell silent. All that could be heard then was the swish, swish, clop, clop of the white-robed marchers.

The crowd parted and the friends of the young man bore him away. At that moment Margarita saw a tall man at the back edge of the sidewalk. The sight was enough to make her gasp. It was her Uncle Delfino. At least she thought it was. But before she could confirm her sighting, the crowd pushed in again and the man was immediately hidden from her view.

Margarita started to cross the street against the current of the marchers. Three steps and she was engulfed in a tidal wave of white. She bumped squarely into one Klansman, was spun around and ran headlong into another. The force of this unrelenting tide of marchers carried her along. She put out her arms to part a way through the robes but was swallowed up again in a swell of sweating whiteness.

She felt it nearly impossible to breathe. It was almost like falling once again into the swollen, mindless river at the sawmill to be swept away and choked into submission. Margarita started to go down. A strong, rough arm encircled her waist. Her feet left the ground and she kicked ineffectively at the air. Then suddenly she was in the open and being deposited at the opposite curb.

She looked up and saw that it was one of the burly Klan guards.

"Don't make trouble, girl," was all he said before he jogged away to resume his post by the marchers.

By the time Margarita was able to work her way to the sidewalk behind the spectators the parade had passed by. People were dispersing in all directions. She looked at them all, but none of them bore any likeness to Delfino Arellanes.

Chapter Fourteen

During their time in Denver, the Zamoras made several attempts to locate Don Delfino and his bride, Soledea. In every instance, however, the search was fruitless.

He lives across the river, they heard. He sold his house and lives beyond the mountains in Grand Junction. He's in Pueblo. He's in Cheyenne. He moved out of state. He's traveling in Spain.

For Margarita Juana, her uncle remained ever elusive with his ever-elusive promises.

When it came time to enroll in school, Margarita found herself in a similar situation to her transfer from Mora to the parochial school in Las Vegas. No one she spoke to in the Denver school system was willing to accept this countrified girl on her questionable academic merits.

"Yes, I can see you have a diploma from the eighth grade, but where is your report card?"

Tamar had long since disposed of it, the string of A's nothing but grist for the fine-grinding mill of her envy.

Only because she had kept the diploma among her personal belongings had Margarita saved it from the stove in her mother's kitchen.

"Yes, I know you're fourteen and should be in the ninth grade but there's simply nothing we can do about it," said a secretary at the school office.

What was not said was that she must repeat the eighth grade only in small part because she was unproved. By far the overriding factor that kept her from moving up were the six prominent letters inscribed so carefully in black Old English script on her diploma: Z-A-M-O-R-A. She was Mexican, and Mexicans were seldom given the benefit of the doubt.

To Margarita's dismay, she found that most of her schoolbooks were at a sixth-grade level. There was practically nothing in the entire stack of her texts that she did not already know. Her teacher proved even worse than Sister Mary Thomas, not because she was abusive but because she treated all her students with calculated indifference.

Margarita looked among the other teachers for someone she could approach and talk to, but none showed the slightest interest in expanding their responsibilities beyond those of their own students. For the entire year she was unable to find a new Sister Apolonia, a dedicated teacher who would be willing to lead her beyond the walls of Mrs. Hampton's classroom.

At home, Tamar was day by day more irascible. Margarita had been unable to find an after-school job within walking distance of her house. In response, or retaliation, Tamar piled on the chores with even more of a vengeance. Among these duties the care of the younger children was now completely Margarita's. Except for school, she was never allowed out of the house without the two youngest, Agapita and Alfonso, in tow.

Up and down the streets she would walk, sometimes impatiently taking the toddlers by the hand and leading them hastily along, other times allowing them to dawdle and even sit down on the sidewalk when they tired. In their neighborhood there was really no place to take them except the local schoolyard, which was usually full of children. Predictably, the older ones monopolized the playground. Margarita would have to wait in line with Agapita and Alfonso for their turn at the swings, the merry-go-round, the slide, and the teeter-totter.

One place with no waiting lines was the neighborhood church, Sacred Heart. It was a cool and quiet refuge from her fire-spitting mother.

Margarita seldom prayed while she was there. She had lost the habit when she left the house of Doña Prisca. Although the Zamoras, minus Leopoldo, were weekly Mass attendees and there were several religious images on their walls, Catholicism was not central to their lives. Having the children baptized and confirmed, seeing that they made their First Holy Communion and confessed their sins once a year was all that Tamar could deal with.

Leopoldo would have settled for even less. He had gone through long stretches of his life when the Church had done nothing for him.

Even while she sat quietly with her brother and sister in a back pew, Margarita did not think much about the sacred. She enjoyed the smells, the patterns of light from the stained-glass windows and the flickering vigil candles, the glossy-skinned, glassy-eyed statuary, the delicately yellowing altar lace, the oily, dark wood of the pews. It was all so restful, so undemanding. She guarded these moments so jealously that when the back door groaned open to usher in other visitors, she felt a violation of her private world. The intruders were usually old women in black shawls who shuffled in to light votive candles or to rattle rosary beads against the back of a pew. Margarita resented them, one and all.

An old French priest, the pastor of the parish, also made regular appearances. His comings were always heralded by a loud, raucous clearing of phlegm from his smoker's throat.

Margarita's presence in the church with Agapita and Alfonso was a constant irritant to the priest. No child prayed that much, he thought, unless she were the sainted Bernadette of Lourdes. But this seemed highly unlikely, considering that this was a barrio in north-central Denver and not a bucolic French village at the foot of the Pyrenees, very much like his own place of birth. These children could be up to nothing but mischief.

So every time he found Margarita and her two charges in church he made a show of padding around to inspect the candle stands for anything disturbed or missing. He checked all the confessionals to make sure the doors were closed and that there were not even more little urchins hiding in them. He also made a great to-do about leaving. He stomped loudly out the door to the sanctuary and closed it with great flourish, making sure that it stayed ajar. Then he stood behind it and peered out to spy on them.

If Margarita thought to pray it was that she would soon find her Uncle Delfino. That would mean final and complete liberation from her chains.

Among the several visitors who occasionally broke into Margarita's reverie as she sat in the pews of Sacred Heart Church was Miss Constance Plover.

Miss Plover, a pious spinster, had come to the parish from the offices of the archdiocese to set up a catechetical program for the children of the migrant workers. During the week she frequently popped

into the church to thank God for small successes or, as was more
often the case, to wrestle with Him over large failures. During these
visits she sometimes saw a young lady with two small children. And
once or twice, when she was entering or leaving the church, she ran
into Margarita, who was always polite and deferential.

On a certain day in late July of the second year of Margarita's
stay in Denver, Miss Plover stopped at the diocesan offices to pick up
some materials for her work. By this happenstance, it was she who
picked up the phone when it rang.

"Hello," said the voice on the other side. "My name is Standard,
Dr. Maurice Standard. I have a medical practice near Washington
Park. I have a problem, actually more of a proposition, I'd like to dis-
cuss with someone in your office."

"Perhaps I can help."

"We have a daughter, a two-year-old. Marcia, my wife, isn't very
strong, and needs help with her. We're looking for a live-in, someone
young."

Yes, we have arranged such placements in the past, Miss Plover
informed him.

"We're Jewish. I don't know if that makes a difference."

"No, it does not. Although we must be certain that there is an
opportunity to go to Mass Sundays and to attend religious classes."

"Oh, yes. We're very keen on religion," replied the doctor. "In
fact we would prefer a religious-minded girl, someone honest and
loving."

Miss Plover took the doctor's name and telephone number and
told him she would see what she could do.

She had no name, but Miss Plover remembered the face of the girl
that she frequently saw minding the two small children.

She inquired of the old pastor when next she saw him at the rectory.

"Ah yes. That girl. I don't know what she's up to, in the church
all the time with those two little imps."

"Do you know her name?"

"I see them at Mass every Sunday, the mother and the children.
But never the father."

"How could I find out where they live? I might have a position
for the girl."

As with most questions about daily parish life, the priest directed Miss Plover to the secretary.

"Ask Panchita."

Panchita knew the family.

"Zamora. From New Mexico."

A riffling through the parish census cards gave Miss Plover her information: Zamora, Leopoldo/M. Tamar—Margarita, Eugenio, Gerónimo, Agapita, Alfonso. 2761 Larimer Street.

"That's just a block down the street from us," Panchita volunteered.

At that instant, the priest poked his head around the corner of the office.

"Are they using their envelopes?"

Panchita noted a half-dozen donations of fifteen cents over a period of twenty months. "A few times, Father."

The priest shook a finger at Miss Plover. "When you talk to them, tell them that they have to be contributors to the parish."

"Yes, Father, I'll mention it to them."

"If the church finds them work they should be grateful enough to give something back."

"Yes, Father. It would seem so."

Five minutes later, Miss Plover stepped up onto the warped boards of the Zamoras' front porch and knocked on the door. She heard a pounding of feet, a squeal and a thump, and the door was jerked open by a laughing, snorting Eugenio. Gerónimo lay at his feet kicking furiously at him.

For all his mad rush to get to the door, knocking Gerónimo down in the process, Eugenio had no idea what to do next.

Miss Plover smiled at the graceless gnome. "Hello. Does the Zamora family live here?"

Eugenio nodded. Gerónimo scrambled to his feet and ran off shouting into the gloom of the house. "Mamá! Mamá! *Una mujer. Una gringa.*"

From another room, Miss Plover could hear the alto of an angry female voice. She knew very little Spanish other than what she had studied in books but she understood very well from the tone that the woman who was speaking was not pleased that the boys had opened their door to a stranger.

Tamar's rough hand seized Eugenio and pulled him out of the way.

"Yes?" Tamar's eyes showed suspicion and not a little fear. Gringos never meant good news.

"Mrs. Zamora? Tamar Zamora?"

"Who are you?"

"My name is Miss Plover. I'm from Sacred Heart. I was wondering if I could talk with you about your daughter, Margarita?"

"She's not here. She went to the store."

"Oh. Well, if I could just come in for a moment, there's something I'd like to discuss with you."

"Why? What has she done?"

"Oh, no. Nothing, nothing at all. I mean, there's no trouble of any kind. I've seen her around the parish taking care of two small children. There's a job that's come up and I thought of her."

"A job?" Tamar's eyes lost some of their coldness.

"Could I come in? Without your permission, there's no point in discussing the matter with Margarita."

Tamar stepped back to allow Miss Plover to pass into a high-ceilinged front room, orderly but meanly furnished.

"Oh, it's so nice and cool in here. And so neat and clean."

"We know what a broom looks like."

"Oh, certainly. Does Margarita help around the house?"

"All of us do our part." Tamar motioned Miss Plover to a fat couch covered with a threadbare peach-colored bedspread.

"¡Quítense de aquí!" Tamar screamed at the two boys, who were lingering at the entry to the kitchen.

They quickly scooted behind the doorway. From there they could still crane their necks around the jamb to spy over the back of their mother's head.

"This job for Margarita, what is it?"

"A doctor. He needs someone to help care for his two-year-old daughter."

"Margarita can do that."

"The doctor. He says that he needs someone to live with them, someone who can be there all the time. Would that be a problem?"

"Where's the mother?"

"Apparently she not very strong."

Tamar sniffed. She had no truck with a mother who was overwhelmed with one child while she had to deal with five and another on the way.

"And how much would this doctor pay?"

"We didn't talk about that but, based on my experience with such things, I'm sure they'd take care of all her living expenses. And then I would imagine they'd offer her ten or fifteen dollars a week."

"Margarita helps me with the house and the children."

"I certainly understand."

Shrewdness quickly gave way to panic. "But I still have those two in there." Tamar indicated the doorway behind her with a quick swipe of her hand.

By the time Margarita returned from the grocery store with Agapita and Alfonso, her future had all but been settled for her.

"I'll talk to the doctor in the morning and then I'll get back to you," said the lady as Margarita escorted her to the front walk. "I know it will be hard for you to leave home."

On that point Margarita kept her own counsel.

Unexpected resistance came from Leopoldo. "*¿Estás loca?* She's not some goat or chicken you can just turn over to anyone who says they want her."

"But it's with the church. They wouldn't let her go somewhere bad."

"She's our daughter and that has nothing to do with the church."

Finally they reached a compromise. Leopoldo would go with Margarita to meet the doctor and his wife. "And if I see anything I don't like, I'll bring her home. I don't care how much they pay."

The next Sunday afternoon, Leopoldo wrestled on the dark suit in which he had been married and Margarita put on her best dress. They climbed into a southbound bus and, after two transfers, found themselves at the other end of the city.

This was middle-class Denver, elm-lined, geometrically configured blocks of stolid brick bungalows with front lawns studded with rose bushes and spirea.

For all of Leopoldo's bravado with Tamar, he was instantly struck dumb as they were ushered into Dr. and Mrs. Standard's home. This was due in equal measures to his life-long struggle with English, his lack of refinement, his awe of anyone holding a medical degree, and his instant infatuation with the young mother, Marcia.

Like a little bird. Like a pretty little bird.

Even had he not been rendered nearly incoherent by the exalted presence of his hosts, he would soon enough have been thoroughly distracted by the complexities of the refreshments offered them. There he sat, his rump making a prodigious indentation on the edge of a sofa cushion, holding a dewy glass of lemonade while balancing a napkin and a plate with a large wedge of chocolate cake on his knee. As those around him spoke of children, school, duties, expectations, and recompense, he sat stiffly with the fork sticking straight up, like an ax imbedded in a tree stump, in the middle of his half-eaten cake. It was only through a briefing by his daughter on the way home that he was able to muster a terse report for Tamar.

"They are very nice people. They don't have big heads. The doctor is very friendly. The mother is like a delicate little bird." He was proud of the phrase to the point of practicing it to himself on the bus.

Tamar was unmoved. "And what good is a bird when what her child needs is a mother?"

"And the baby? She's a baby, and that's all I have to say about that."

"So. Is Margarita going?"

"She's going."

"How much will they pay?"

"They'll take care of whatever she needs to live with them, clothes, things for school."

"And the money? How much money?"

"They offered ten dollars a week. I argued for fourteen. We agreed on twelve," he lied. In truth, they had mentioned twelve dollars to Margarita and nothing further had been negotiated.

"Twelve? The church lady said they might pay up to fifteen."

"Twelve is better than ten, isn't it?"

"How do we get it?"

"They'll mail a check to us every two weeks."

"A check? What do we know about checks? Why don't they just give us the money?"

The intangible, metaphysical nature of a check, that extra step that required an intervention by a faceless bank before the money was in her hands, was an irritation to Tamar. It was one more of life's little crosses to add to a list she diligently compiled.

"They said they'd pay by check. *Y es todo.*"

But that was not all. Not exactly.

More than once, as Leopoldo lay on his back under the dismantled chassis of a bus, or in the forced lull of his commute to and from work, he thought of the fair Mrs. Standard. These were not lustful thoughts but full of admiration and respect. She was so small and fragile, so beautiful, so cool and serene. Warmth radiated from her lustrous dark eyes and from the softness of her hand when he had shaken it. Here was exquisiteness not available to men such as himself.

Chapter Fifteen

In her new home my mother had her own room, with her own bed to sleep in, her own closet and dresser to store her belongings, her own chair to sit in, her own table lamp to read by, and her own window to look out of. Even in her halcyon days in Mora she had always shared a room with Nasha. In Guadalupita she had slept in the same room with Doña Prisca. And of course once she returned to her family at the sawmill and afterward, there was no such thing as privacy or proprietorship.

Her duties in her new home were practically nonexistent compared to her workload at the house on Larimer Street.

The cooking, the housecleaning, and the laundry were all seen to by a dark, squat, pleasant Italian woman, Mrs. Carpio, who came in daily except Saturdays and Sundays.

As it turned out, the position that Margarita had been hired to fill was not so much to be a nanny to Leah but an older sister.

Marcia Standard doted on her daughter. She spent as much time with her as her poor health, vestiges of a pulmonary ailment that had brought her and her husband west from New Jersey to Colorado, would allow. It was only when she tired that she reluctantly gave her baby up to Margarita.

By the end of the first week with Margarita, Leah regarded her parents with maddening indifference whenever they left for an evening out.

That fall when Margarita enrolled at South High School she felt herself an alien in alien surroundings. There were schedules to learn and bells to respond to. There were long-standing cliques among the students, closed circles that she could never breach. She even felt isolated by her name, which was universally mispronounced by teachers and students alike. Zamora came out of the Anglo mouths as SAM-a-ruh and the unwieldy Margarita soon gave way to the all-American Margie. For many weeks she thought she was the only Hispanic in the entire school.

Only later did she learn that the girl sitting next to her in history who called herself Sally Martin was actually Sadie Martínez.

She did not shine in her classes. The gaps in her education, particularly in Latin, biology, and rhetoric, caught up with her. Her grades were always adequate but nothing that set her apart as the rustic prodigy she had proved herself at the parochial school in Las Vegas.

If her formal education had settled into an unspectacular routine, Margarita's life with the Standards more than made up for it.

Dr. Standard spent long hours with his practice. This left Mrs. Standard to fill the days, as much as her health allowed, with things that would advance the education of her daughter.

Exposure to the best that Denver had to offer created an impressive syllabus for Margarita. Alongside Mrs. Standard she pushed Leah's stroller through the art galleries of the Natural History Museum to view the first collection of oil paintings she had ever seen. There were sprawling Remingtons with their herds of dust-raising buffalo with Indian horsemen in hot pursuit. There were quiet country scenes with waterwheels that reminded her of the grain mills of Mora. And there were portraits of steely-eyed captains of industry and their unsmiling, high-necked wives.

She attended her first symphony, a matinee at the city auditorium. The orchestra drove itself to raving delirium with runs of rippling chords. In a seeming panic of flight, the violinists sawed furiously while the timpani and cymbals waited in ambush to pounce on them and bring the music to a crashing halt. Margarita sat open mouthed through it all.

She ate for the first time in a four-star restaurant where the maitre d' spread a wide menu before her like the wings of a huge ivory bird, and waiters in white coats and gloves attended their every need.

She attended her first professionally produced theatrical performance. The offering was *The Rose of Picardy*, a light musical comedy set in a French village during the First World War. As reports in the local paper announced:

Written especially for Miss Gladys George, the popular local leading woman and said to give her one of the best characters she has ever had to play, "The Rose of Picardy" will have its first presentation on any Colorado stage at the Denham Theater this week and should prove just about the most interesting event of the season.

Mrs. Standard showed Margarita the tickets. "Just you and me. We'll have an early supper at the Brown. Then we'll go to the play and afterward drop in somewhere for some ice cream. But first we have to take you shopping."

Marcia Standard displayed a resolute passion for Margarita's coming out. After visits to at least six emporia, she and Margarita finally settled on a burgundy-colored sleeveless silk shift cut daringly above the knee. They also chose oxblood-tinted shoes with Cuban heels and large stiff bows on the fronts. They finished off the ensemble with a black bolero jacket of faux Persian lamb and a matching beaded clutch bag.

"You're positively stunning," Mrs. Standard gushed as Margarita stood for inspection.

Not since Nasha dressed, powdered, and rouged her in preparation for the Christmas party twelve years before had Margarita felt so special.

There is no record that *The Rose of Picardy* ever had a run, however short, on Broadway. The play is set in a small French village, in the house where the heroine, Marie Rose, lives alone. A squad of American doughboys fresh from the trenches is billeted in the house for some much-needed rest and rejuvenation. Then, as the program notes put it, "the fun begins."

Margarita identified immediately with the heroine, a slight figure in a peasant dress, with a lilting French accent and a pure if thin soprano voice. This was the redoubtable Miss Gladys George, at thirty-seven too old for the part. But to Margarita's star-struck eyes, she was, under heavy makeup and soft lighting, a beautiful ingénue.

The leading man was a pretty actor with an engaging smile and a mischievous shock of unruly blond hair. As he strode the boards, tunic unbuttoned to display an undershirt stretched tightly across his chest, Margarita thought that she had never seen a creature more beautiful. Her only other memory of a man in uniform was Porfirio, that rodent-faced misery who had accosted her in her Uncle Delfino's barn and had paid the price by ending up in a pine box, purple, swollen, and quite dead from pneumonia.

The scene in which Marie Rose and her corporal finally embraced was a moment of revelation for Margarita. She watched Miss George's heaving breasts and felt her own quiver, then rise and fall in vicarious ecstasy.

The final curtain fell solemnly on a scene filled with tearful good-byes, promises to return, and the call of the bugle.

Margarita wept quietly. She had passed the course on incurable romanticism with flying colors.

Margarita's brush with Denver's high life had left her conscious of fashion and of her own plainness. With encouragement from Mrs. Standard, she took a critical look at her wardrobe, selected those pieces that presented possibilities, then cut, nipped, tucked, and hemmed them into a style more reflective of her newly minted sophistication.

She began wearing these creations to school, where, together with her new hairstyle and makeup, she caused a minor sensation. The girls stared at her in shock and secret envy. The boys stared at her in adolescent lust. She became someone with a reputation. Since her notoriety was built solely on her appearance, her classmates constructed a dark history for her.

The girls huddled in corridors and whispered to each other as she walked by.

"I hear she's really a woman. Almost twenty!"

"She was married once. I swear to God it's true. Her husband was thrown in prison because she's still a minor."

"She goes into the gym after school and waits for boys."

"She smokes."

"She drinks."

The boys met in the locker room and boosted their stock at her expense:

"She winked at me in math class."

"She wrote me a note. I'd show it to you but I lost it."

"She rubbed up to me in the hall."

"She let me see under her dress."

"She let me touch her . . . there."

The only thing said about Margarita that bore any semblance to the truth was, "What can you expect? She's a Mexican." Although none of the other charges against her could be substantiated, this one was enough to damn her without trial.

A mother overheard her daughter on the telephone exchanging lies about Margarita. Feeding off this gossip, the mother talked to other parents. One of these wrote a scathing letter to the superintendent of schools decrying the decline in morals of youth in general and of the student population of South High in particular. A concerned father took it on himself to drop in on the principal.

"My daughter is here for an education. She shouldn't have to put up with immoral behavior in the classroom. What are you teaching these children?"

Hard on a telephone call of inquiry from the superintendent's secretary, this visit was enough for the principal to summon Margarita to his office.

The principal pointed Margarita to a chair and settled himself down behind his desk. "Margie, there have been reports about you. Not good reports, I'm sorry to say."

Margarita stared at him dumbly.

He cleared his throat. "Apparently, some unfortunate changes about you have been noted."

"Changes?"

Margarita did a quick mental inventory of her conduct in school. She was still shy and spoke to her teachers only when spoken to. She belonged to no group of friends. She did her work neatly and accurately and turned it in on time. She caused no problems in the classroom, none, at least, that she was aware of.

The principal coughed. "Yes. I've received several complaints about you. The way you're dressed. The hair. The cosmetics. You do know that there's a rule about an excessive use of makeup, don't you?"

If pressed, even the principal would have had to admit that there were other girls in the school who used much more makeup than Margarita and who dressed much more daringly. However, it was only she who had prompted such an outcry. She might not be the trollop that everyone was suggesting, but something about her was stirring the waters and he did not need the aggravation.

Margarita looked down at her dress, a loose cotton smock that she had shortened and hitched at the waist with a wide belt. She self-consciously brushed her hand across her cheek to erase the tinge of rouge, which, in any case, was now overwhelmed by the blush of her shame. She noticed the bright red enamel on her fingernails and quickly shoved her hands beneath the pile of books on her lap.

"But I didn't mean anything."

"Well, perhaps not. However. That does not solve our little problem, does it?"

She shook her head and dropped her eyes.

"No. Of course it doesn't." He picked up a wide card and held it at an angle so Margarita could not see what was on it.

"I've looked over your record. You have no bad marks against you. Your grades are adequate, although I'd like to see some improvement in Latin. This is the first complaint I've had about you, Margie, but it's much too serious to ignore. We concentrate on academic excellence here at South High School. We also see it as our clear duty to form decent, courteous, moral young people. You do see how important that is, don't you?"

Margarita, defenseless, nodded her head.

"Good. Well. I'm glad we had this little chat before things got out of hand. You know what they say, 'A wounded reputation is seldom mended.'"

Margarita sensed that, with this piece of gibberish, the principal was dismissing her. She rose with no understanding of what would now be expected of her other than to recede into the frumpiness from which she had so recently emerged.

She thanked the principal, turned, and walked out of his office. She was unaware of the educator's appreciative ogling of her finely defined rump and well-turned legs.

The Standards' good fortunes now rescued Margarita from further humiliation at school. The doctor's practice and reputation were growing. It was time to move to better surroundings, somewhere closer to the hospitals, something in Denver's fashionable Capitol Hill area with its Victorian mansions filled with tycoons and glitterati.

The move was made to a moderately scaled but handsome

brownstone on Pennsylvania Avenue, three blocks from the home of
Molly Brown. Margarita transferred to East High School. Her reputation did not follow. She sank comfortably into anonymity and did
nothing for the remainder of her school career in Denver to draw any
attention to herself.

This career lasted just seven months more.

On the gray afternoon of October 31, Margarita sat on her bed
putting the finishing touches on a ghost costume for little Leah so they
could tour the block for treats. There was a soft rapping at her door.

Marcia Standard opened the door just wide enough to poke her
head into the room. "Margarita, there's someone here to see you. A
boy named Eugene. He says he's your brother."

And sure enough, there was Eugenio standing, and distinctly out
of place, in an atrium of polished woods and leaded glass.

"Daddy needs you home. Mamá too."

"What happened?"

The little man of fourteen lifted his shoulders and made what little he had of a neck disappear altogether into his cylindrical torso.

Marcia Standard placed a hand on Margarita's shoulder. "Maybe
you'd better go along. Do you need some money for the bus?"

Margarita shook her head. "No. We ride for free."

Eugenio looked at her guiltily. "We have to walk."

Before Margarita could argue the point, Mrs. Standard was
thrusting some coins into her hand. "Here, just in case."

On the way home Eugenio refused any explanation. "I don't
know"; "Something happened"; "It's not my fault," were all she
could get out of him.

As it turned out, the calamity that was now visiting the Zamoras
most certainly was Eugenio's fault.

"We're going back to New Mexico," Leopoldo told his daughter. "If we leave tomorrow we don't have to pay any rent for
November. Take Eugenio and Gerónimo with you and bring all your
things from the doctor's."

Margarita could not understand her father's words. "But why? I
can't! I won't! What happened?"

At that moment, Tamar entered the room. "It's your brother.
That's why."

"What does Eugenio have to do with me?"

"Not only with you, *sonsa*, with all of us."

Tamar dumped a load of clothes on the floor and began to fold them carelessly and with great agitation.

"But what did he do?"

"I kept him home from school to take your father his trousers."

"Trousers? Did Daddy go to work without his pants?"

"Don't be ridiculous. Your father had to go to work with a torn pair of pants. The seat was ripped and I fixed it with a safety pin."

Leopoldo sat pouting. "Everybody at work was laughing at me."

Tamar rolled some shirts into a tight bundle. "What does it matter now, you fool? It's over and you have no work."

At this point, Margarita could only surmise that Leopoldo's temper had flared as it had when he had worked on the lettuce farm in California. Angered at being laughed at, he must have struck out at someone, and now he was a fugitive from the law once more.

"Daddy lost his job?"

"He wouldn't wait for the clean laundry. He made me keep Eugenio home from school to bring him his other pair of pants when they were dry."

"Well, I couldn't go to work with wet pants. I could catch pneumonia."

Tamar crammed some clothes into a pillow case. "Wet pants. Torn pants. Who cares?"

Margarita had to stop this surreal exchange between her parents. "Torn pants? Wet pants? What are you talking about?"

Leopoldo slumped down on the sofa and spoke to the wall. "Eugenio had my pants. When he got to the shops he asked for Leopoldo Zamora. They told him there was no Zamora working there. But he insisted. 'Show me,' the foreman told him. So they walked around until Eugenio pointed at me."

Tamar now lost all patience with her husband's narrative. "So the little cretin confessed everything. Your father's real name, that he was from New Mexico, not Canada. And they fired him on the spot."

"But why do we have to leave?"

"He has no job." Tamar said the words very slowly, relishing the pain they were causing in spite of herself. "There are no jobs in Denver.

It's time to go back where we belong. Can I make it any clearer?"

"Then go without me."

"No, *hijita*," Leopoldo muttered. "That we cannot do. You are our daughter. This is your family. If we go, you must go."

Early the next morning, while Dr. Standard performed an emergency appendectomy at St. Luke's Hospital, Marcia and Leah Standard huddled in an embrace of deep sleep, having wept their goodbyes with Margarita the evening before.

At 2761 Larimer Street, the 1924 Buick and a borrowed Chevrolet Superior were loaded up with all the Zamoras' portable goods.

The family was out of the city by the time first light broke, a sad haze of diffused sun. Margarita sat by Leopoldo in the lead car. Agapita and Alfonso lay fast asleep in the back. Eugenio drove the second car. Next to him, Tamar held the infant Elisandro. Gerónimo was stretched out amid boxes, baskets, and bundles in the rear.

Margarita would not permit herself to look back. Denver meant nothing more to her. She had not found her Uncle Delfino and she had been wickedly enticed into a life that could never really be hers. How she had pretended! But she knew. She was the daughter of a common laborer and his sullen wife. And she wondered for the first time in her life whether she would ever be anything more.

Leopoldo patted his daughter's knee. "You might as well sleep, *hijita*. It's a long trip."

"What will happen in Las Vegas?"

"Who knows. Maybe I can work for the county again."

She turned to the window and rested her head against the back of the seat. She did not close her eyes but watched the hunched-over hills on the outskirts of Denver creep by like thieves sneaking back to their hideouts after a night of mischief.

It was the first day of November 1929.

A week earlier, on October 24, the markets in New York City had crashed. It was as if a giant circus tent had splintered its mast and the canvas had billowed, collapsed, and suffocated all who were beneath it. And the gust from under the tent flaps was certainly strong enough to blow this two-car caravan off the road even on the high plains some two thousand miles away.

Part Two

Two

MIGUEL AND MIGUELITO

Chapter Sixteen

1901–1930

My father, Miguel Galván, seemed always to be the victim of bad timing.

For instance, he was born on January 2, 1901. Thus he was a day late to bask in whatever celebrity was attendant to being a New Year's baby, and more significantly in this case, a New Century baby.

"January 2," he would always say, "is not a good day for a birthday. Christmas and New Year are over. No one wants any more parties. No one wants to give any more presents. Who wants to celebrate anything on January 2?"

I never heard my father complain about anything else.

The Las Vegas, New Mexico, into which Miguel was born was still cashing in on the boom brought on by the coming of the railroad. Just two years previously, Theodore Roosevelt had bellowed into town to celebrate the first of many reunions held there by his Rough Riders. In the valley five miles to the north, a luxury hotel next to a thermal spa was welcoming the rich and famous from around the world. Even the emperor of Japan dipped an imperial toe into the healing waters that bubbled up and spread their sulfurous fumes across the grassy banks of the nearby Gallinas River.

The Galváns had been a fixture in Las Vegas long before Miguel was born. His father, Juan, was one of four brothers from a family that could trace its roots to the sixteenth century when conquistadors, having failed to find either gold or glory, hunkered down to work the land. Not that any of this eminence had done the present group of Galváns much good. By and large, they had settled into the trades. My grandfather, Juan, was a house painter. But, despite their pedestrian fates, they hung with tenacity to the dead, leafless branches of their illustrious family tree.

Thus it was that when Juan returned from Albuquerque with a bride, a López from Atrisco with bloodlines to match those of the Galváns, the family was delighted. This was quickly tempered by the reality that the López clan was as destitute of wealth as the Galváns.

In fact, Francisquita's dowry, which Juan's brothers had coveted from the moment they heard of the union, consisted of nothing more than two bolts of inferior linen, some well-used household items, a trunk half filled with the bride's meager personal belongings, and a small leather pouch containing a dozen ten-dollar gold pieces.

"A hundred and twenty dollars," groused Ernesto, the oldest of the brothers Galván. "Why, that's not even enough to cover the cost of the wedding reception."

But, appearances being everything, the reception went on at the Castañeda Hotel as arranged. The affair boasted the finest in table settings, many sprays of flowers, an eight-piece orchestra, and glistening white silk streamers flowing from the chandelier in the main ballroom. Ernesto was absolutely right. The money from Francisquita's pouch did not cover the cost of the celebration. It was left to the groom to make up the difference, eleven dollars a month for an entire year, until the debt was squared.

In all, Juan and Francisquita had five children, four boys and one girl. Miguel was the fourth child. He was pale, thin, and crowned with a sparse mop of wispy brown hair, so unlike the thick black thatches of his father and siblings.

The Galváns took up residence in a low, flat-roofed, elongated adobe house, stuccoed but never painted. Its battle-ship-gray flanks were a stark, unflattering contrast to the warmth and welcome projected by the neighboring red brick or brown adobe homes.

"Juan, paint your house," Ernesto often chided his younger brother. "*Por Dios*. You're a house painter. What does it say about your work? What will people think?"

Apparently, people thought nothing of it at all. Juan was always busy. Seldom, except on Sundays, was he without a job. Daily he loaded up his two-wheeled cart with ladders, tarps, paint, turpentine, rags, and a variety of brushes. Dressed in white sailcloth coveralls spattered in a thousand different colors from a thousand different jobs, he would be off to cover the walls and ceilings of Las Vegas, New Mexico.

On Sundays the family went to Mass together. Juan's face and hands were raw and red from the scrubbings with paint thinner and lye soap. After Mass there was a noontime dinner followed by visits to or by friends and family that ended when the sun began to diffuse behind the low ridges that fronted the Sangre de Cristo range to the west.

During the week, when time and weather permitted, Juan sat on the front porch to smoke his pipe after the evening meal. Francisquita was always at his side, squinting in the failing light to mend a sock or let out a pair of pants. It was at this time that Miguel discovered a game to play with his father while the other children romped up and down the narrow, unpaved street in front of their house.

"This one," Miguel challenged, pointing at a dried splotch of yellow paint on his father's coveralls.

"That one? Well, let me think." Juan frowned comically and feigned great concentration. "That one is from the courthouse, from Judge Atencio's chambers. The judge complained the whole time. He had to hang his robes outside every night because they smelled like paint and gave him a headache."

"And that one?" Juan put his finger on a splattering of robin's-egg blue.

"Ah, yes, that one. That one gave *me* a headache. Mrs. Dawson, the banker's wife, bought some curtains for her bedroom and wanted walls that matched them perfectly. It took me a whole day of mixing before she was satisfied."

In this way, going from paint blot to paint blot, whenever there was an opportunity and his father felt like it, Miguel learned most of what he knew about his father: his patience, his industry, his good humor, the pride he took in his work.

Miguel never explored the history of a rust-colored smear on the breast of his father's coveralls. Had he asked, his father likely would have dismissed him gruffly, saying that he had tired of this foolish game. Francisquita, however, knew all about such stains. She had tried to remove enough of these dark smudges of blood out of her husband's handkerchiefs.

The small hemorrhages from his nose and mouth finally chased Juan in for a check-up.

After a thorough examination, the doctor sat Juan down. "You don't get enough sun. Your work is too damp. The tissue in your lungs and nose doesn't like all the paint you breathe in. The blood vessels swell and rupture and you bleed. It's as simple as that. You have to find a new line of work, Mr. Galván."

Juan left the office without mentioning the stomach pains, the constipation, the headaches, and the uncharacteristic irritability that he was lately experiencing. Not that it would have mattered by then. Four months after his visit to the doctor Juan took to his bed. Four months after that, at the age of thirty-eight, he was dead from lead poisoning.

Ernesto and his brothers assembled in their deceased brother's kitchen, drank his coffee, and ate his bread and peach preserves. They were a panel of stern-faced auditors who expected Francisquita to justify the hellish year she had just seen her husband and her children through.

"How much money did he leave you?" Ernesto asked the new widow.

She shook her head as she refilled his cup.

"Well, where did he keep his papers, his accounts? Who owes him money?"

"Who could owe him money?" Flavio, the second-oldest brother asked. "He hadn't worked in four months."

By this time, Francisquita had rummaged through the top drawer of a small floor cabinet that stood in a corner by the stove.

"Here," she said and handed Ernesto a small stack of papers, a ledger, and a bankbook. "This is everything Juan kept for his business."

Ernesto attacked the bankbook first. "Forty-six dollars and twenty-five cents. No deposits since last March and then withdrawal, withdrawal, withdrawal. Almost a thousand dollars in withdrawals."

"The doctor. The medicine. Bills," Francisquita tried to explain.

Ernesto sniffed and opened the ledger. There had been no entries since February.

"Matías Márquez still owes him thirteen dollars." He turned the page savagely and stopped halfway down the column. "What's this, now? A Thomas McBride owes Juan a hundred and thirty dollars for painting his house. McBride, McBride." He tossed the name into the ether. "Who is this McBride?"

"He works for the railroad," Flavio volunteered. "Juan painted his house before Christmas. I remember because I saw him there when I delivered a load of coal."

"Well, go see this McBride and tell him that Juan is dead and his widow needs the money."

"He moved out of town last month. I took some boxes to the depot for him. I made sure he paid me right then." Flavio beamed at his own cleverness.

"*Cabrón*," muttered Ernesto, "and more the fool our brother for not getting his money when it was due."

"Maybe here's something." Cándido, the youngest of the brothers, had been rifling through the remaining papers and held up an official-looking packet printed in highly decorative green and black inks.

Ernesto snatched at the document and unfolded it. "It's an insurance policy. Finally we're getting somewhere."

The other two brothers leaned forward in anticipation.

Ernesto flipped through the pages, mumbling to himself until he stopped and spoke aloud. "Ah, here it is. Seven hundred dollars."

He looked at his two brothers. Then all three exhaled slowly, leaned back in their chairs, and scowled at the tabletop.

Finally, Ernesto picked up the bankbook and balanced it in one hand against the weight of the policy in the other. He then brought them together and slammed them down with sudden fury. "Seven hundred and forty-six dollars and twenty-five cents. *Es todo*."

"And don't forget the thirteen dollars that Matías owes," Flavio corrected.

"Of course," Ernesto shot back, "let's not forget the thirteen dollars. Thank you, dear brother. That changes everything."

The three brothers continued to sip their coffee and stare glumly at the papers in front of them. They shook themselves from their doldrums only when someone knocked at the front door.

"That's probably the undertaker. Let's go see what we can work out with him, that money-grabbing old son of a whore. If it's seven hundred and forty-six dollars we have, that's what we have. No sense in trying to spend wishes."

Ernesto led the way out of the kitchen into the front room.

Francisquita could hear them speaking to the mortician in muted tones as she cleared the table and carried the cups and spoons to a basin on the stove.

Outside the window she could see her five children, from the oldest,

Juanito, fourteen, to María, the youngest at six. They were sitting perfectly still beneath a gnarled cottonwood, sent there by their stern Uncle Ernesto while he and the other brothers picked over the bones of their future. She raised her hand to the window, spread her fingers across a pane, and wept.

For the inheritance left to them by Juan, Francisquita and her children received the following:

Embalming services	$ 35
New suit	15
Casket	140
Horse-drawn hearse	35
Mortuary viewing	60
Flowers	15
Burial plot	15
Grave digger	5
One hundred Masses	100
Carved headstone	310
Total	$730

After the funeral, and with great ceremony, Ernesto gave Francisquita what was left of the estate, $16.25. "And the boys and I chipped in a little something for you," he announced piously and handed her an envelope that contained twenty dollars.

Then he called the children of Juan and Francisquita together, sat them down in front of him, and cleared his throat with great ceremony. "You should feel very proud. Your father had one of the finest funerals this town has ever seen, at least since old man Stein died last winter. But now that's all over with and here's what I have to say to you." He passed his eyes from child to child. "From now on you are not children anymore. You boys will have to go to work now to help your mother. There's no work for little girls so María will have to stay in school. I'll talk to the Sisters. Maybe she can help them around the convent in exchange for tuition. There's one other thing. Do not forget for one minute who you are. You are Galváns. That means you do not beg for anything. You do not accept charity. You do not disgrace the family in any way. Is that clear?"

The children, huddled together on the sofa, nodded quietly.

"And remember, you don't have a father to watch over you anymore but you do have three uncles. We'd better not catch you doing mischief or hear anything bad about you around town. Understand?"

After Ernesto put his hat on his head and left, the widow and the five orphans sat in the room long after darkness had crept up the unpainted stucco wall and through the front window into their home.

At the age of nine, my father, Miguel Galván, left school and put on the mantle of adulthood.

All the Galván boys were an enterprising lot. If there was money to be made they made it. They delivered the *Las Vegas Daily Optic* and the Spanish-language weekly, *La Voz del Pueblo*. They carried buckets of gray, soapy water about with them to wash windows, mostly at the saloons up and down Bridge Street. They cleaned chicken coops and ran errands. They swept out stores and public buildings. They shined shoes and washed dishes. And at the end of every day they gathered at their mother's kitchen table, emptied out their pockets, and stacked up the coins to see what they had earned.

Eventually Juanito, the oldest of the boys, thought to provide a more steady source of income for the family by taking up his father's profession. So he pulled out the cart with its supplies and began to take inventory. His plans were quickly scuttled by an uncharacteristically adamant Francisquita.

"I have washed enough blood off of shirts and sheets. You will not be a painter."

Early one afternoon in October, Miguel trotted home with the inside front of his shirt bulging with two dozen apples, payment for helping to mend a woman's fence. He unloaded his haul on the kitchen table, hungrily snatched up an apple, and went looking for his mother.

Francisquita was in the backyard next to the shed where her husband had kept his painting supplies. Beside her was the cart piled high with cans of paint and a wooden box filled with assorted brushes. Miguel could see that she had been crying.

"What are you doing, Mamacita?"

"Your Uncle Ernesto has a man coming over. He offered twenty dollars for everything. I'm getting it ready."

"I'll do it for you."

Francisquita finished folding a small tarpaulin into a neat square and draped it over one of the long handles of the cart. "Don't forget anything."

Miguel pointed at the familiar dappled coveralls. "Even these?"

"Even those."

Miguel finished loading the cart and only then reached for the coveralls. He leaned with his back against the shed, and unrolled the suit against his body like a new skin. The sleeves extended well beyond the span of his little-boy arms, the legs draped over his shoes and trailed off onto the ground.

He found it almost impossible to picture his father now—not the cadaverous mask he had stood in line with the other children to kiss after the priest had left, but the wonderfully handsome man with the jet-black hair, the high, ivory-smooth forehead, the sad, deep-set eyes, and the well-trimmed mustache that floated delicately above a small, determined mouth.

Months later, when Miguel was helping a woman from the wealthy side of town pack some books for storage in her attic, a volume fell open while he emptied some shelves. There, staring at him from the opened pages, was a picture that bore a stunning resemblance to his father. Trembling, he picked up the book and read the legend under the fine-line etching: "Edgar Allan Poe: American Writer and Poet." To the boy, the face of this stranger instantly became the image of his father. From that day on, when Miguel thought of his father he did not see the face of Juan Galván. Rather, it was the intense and forlorn visage of the derelict writer from Baltimore.

But for now, as he held the coveralls to his body, he could recall only the memory of those evenings on the front porch when he and Juan had played their little game.

Now, Miguel took his index finger, pressed hard into one of the spots of paint, and whispered, "This one, tell me about this one, Papá."

He thought he heard his father's gentle tenor voice coming from the rustling leaves of the cottonwood overhead. "That one is from the priest's house. Padre Alberto had been after me for months to paint his study. But I knew he had no intentions of paying me for my work. . . ."

And then the voice faded away and the boy was left clutching tightly at the coveralls.

Chapter Seventeen

It was 1909 when Juan Galván died, and for the next seventy-four years, until he was forced to retire at the age of eighty-three, my father, Miguel, never knew what it was not to work. His industry took him down many paths.

In 1912, the year in which New Mexico entered the Union, the city fathers from both West and East Las Vegas, those twin communities forever fractured by the Gallinas River that separated them, decided to celebrate the historic event in some spectacularly patriotic way. What could be more American than to host a world championship heavyweight fight on the Fourth of July? The people who would pour into Las Vegas to watch the Negro champion, Jack Johnson, take on the latest of the "White Hopes" would fill both public and private coffers. Even the demand from Johnson's camp for a $36,000 guaranteed purse, plus expenses, did not discourage the merchants and politicians. How many people would come to such a spectacle? Ten, twenty thousand? Think of the tickets they would sell, the hotel rooms and saloons they could fill, the goods and personal services they could peddle!

The deal was struck and the press release was circulated.

> Las Vegas, New Mexico, the great city at the foot of the Rocky Mountains, the city that has played host to such luminaries as Presidents Rutherford B. Hayes and Theodore Roosevelt, the Emperor of Japan, and countless others, is proud to announce a heavyweight boxing match for the championship of the world between Mr. Jack Johnson of New York City and Mr. Jim Flynn, the "Fighting Fireman" from Colorado. The match will take place on July 4th, 1912 to celebrate the induction of the great state of New Mexico into the glorious galaxy of our United States.

The hotels in town filled up their reservation books quickly. A good sign. Many fight fans, however, opted for Santa Fe or

Albuquerque, from where they would take special trains into Las Vegas on the day of the match. A bad sign. Still, spirits were high when the two combatants arrived. Having them both in town a full month before the fight started ringing the cash registers.

Jim Flynn, "The Fighting Fireman" from Pueblo, Colorado, arrived first and set up his training camp at the Montezuma Hot Springs Resort. He and his people kept a rather low profile around town and generated precious little passion among the populace. Everyone waited for the real attraction, the fabled Jack Johnson himself.

Most of both townships' inhabitants were at the train depot hours before the champion was scheduled to arrive. The local band was there to stir up spirits, while the two mayors and their staffs elbowed each other for prominence on a bunting-festooned stage built for the occasion.

Miguel had to squeeze and elbow his way through the crowd until his chin met the rough planking of the platform. Then, with everyone else, he waited.

The band went through its repertoire three times. The throng of people buzzed with impatience. The grandees on the platform checked their watches, paced, and gathered to consult with each other.

Finally, with the blast of its mighty whistle, the train rounded the bend and screeched into the station. The band struck up its most rousing piece but no one could hear it over the cheers of the crowd and the complaints of the mighty locomotive as it locked its brakes and spent its steam.

The conductor jumped down and, in practiced manner, placed a portable step in front of the door of the only passenger car. There was a collective holding of breath as an immense shadow came to the doorway. The shadow took on substance when Jack Johnson, the heavyweight champion of the world, stepped down into the high plains sun.

He waved at the crowd and was instantly swarmed over by the dignitaries who fought to be the first at his side. For the longest moment, Miguel could see nothing, and then there was movement from the train as a carpet of bobbing hats made its way to the stage.

The champion was dressed from derby hat to patent leather shoes in an outfit of tawny cream. Combined with the shining mahogany of his broad face, the whiteness of his smile, the brilliance of his gold

tooth, the diamond stickpin on his tie, and the gold knob on his cane,
Jack Johnson was a magnificent confection. And when he finally
spoke, his rich, coffee voice added the final touch. He was the most
delicious mortal Miguel had ever seen.

The town settled into a month of pre-fight hoopla. Flynn came
down from his mountain retreat to pose with the champion and to
engage in the verbal sparring that fed the sportswriters' daily reports
to New York, Philadelphia, and Chicago. Then he retreated to his
camp and left the spotlight to Johnson. The champion was only too
happy to claim it.

He and his people rented a three-story house close to the plaza in
Old Town, to which came a steady stream of visitors—reporters,
photographers, haberdashers, barbers, public servants, caterers, and
promoters of schemes. When not receiving at his home or engaged in
training, Johnson could be seen out and about in the hotels, saloons,
and public venues throughout Old and New Towns. At his side was
his wife, one of the three white women he would eventually marry. If
Las Vegans were shocked at this slap in the face of convention, they
were careful not to show it.

"Hell," a prominent local was heard to say, "if he can bring in
the money he can sleep with a giraffe for all I care."

That June welcomed in a windfall for Miguel and his brothers.
Everyone needed extra help. The sportswriters kept the boys hopping
to the telegraph office with their dispatches and on side trips for
cigars, sandwiches, and clean laundry.

One day, when Miguel entered the Plaza Hotel to see if any of the
scribes seated in the lobby needed something done, the hotel manager
collared him.

"You. What's your name?"

"Miguel."

"You know where Jack Johnson is staying?"

Miguel nodded.

"Come with me." The manager took a stack of folded towels
from a nearby table and thrust them into the boy's arms. "Here.
These are for the Champ. I'll give you a nickel to take them over."

"A nickel?"

The manager looked at his watch. "OK, OK, a dime, you little bandit. But go. They needed these an hour ago."

Miguel set the towels down and held out his hand.

The man glowered at the boy but pulled a handful of coins from his pocket and rammed two nickels into Miguel's upturned hand. "This fight. It's making everyone money hungry." He chose to ignore the fact that he himself had hiked the rates for rooms in his hotel by two hundred percent. "Now go."

As Miguel edged through the front gate of the champion's house he heard a voice.

"And where do you think you're goin', boy?"

Miguel peered from behind the stack of towels and saw a slight Negro of yellow cast standing on the top step of the front porch.

"The hotel sent these towels."

"Abou' time. Follow me."

The little man bounced off the top step of the porch and led the way around the side of the house to the back.

"Put them here," he ordered and indicated a table by the back door.

Miguel did as he was told then waited. Surely he would receive a tip.

"OK, boy, tha's it. You done you're job. Now git goin' and don' be a bother."

"Hey, Little Howard, you get in here," a female voice barked from inside the house. "You finish up these dishes or the Champ's gon' to hear about it from me."

"Comin', honey, comin'," the suddenly nervous Little Howard answered. "Go on now." With one last, malevolent look at Miguel he hurried into the house.

Miguel took time to look around the backyard. It was a large enclosure, hemmed in on three sides by a high wooden fence that had been erected to afford its famous guest some privacy. Most of the area was shaded by three towering trees, beneath which stretched a canopy propped up by tent poles at least twenty feet high. Under the canopy was a raised boxing ring defined by three rows of thick, velvet-covered rope. In the ring Jack Johnson danced and tossed punches at the air. He was shirtless and wore dark tights that accentuated his massive thighs and incongruously thin calves. The perspiration dripped from the perfect globe of his head and washed his upper body with a sheen that made his arms and chest radiate power.

"Dance right. Jab, jab. Now left. Jab, jab," his trainer chanted from the apron of the ring. "C'mon, Champ, show me somethin'. You're coastin'."

There was a final flurry of punches from Johnson before he let out a reverberating whoop and came to the edge of the ring to drape himself over the top rope, where he sucked at the air that so recently he had tried to pummel into submission.

"I'm dry. I'm dry. Why am I so dry?"

"It's the place, man. You're in the desert. Remember?" answered his manager.

"It's the altitude."

This came from the direction of one of the trees. Miguel looked over to see the white woman seated at a table scanning the pages of a book, her face partially hidden by a large-brimmed hat.

"Huh?" Johnson lifted his giant head with what seemed an effort beyond even his legendary strength. "What you say?"

The woman did not bother to look up. "The altitude. Six thousand feet above sea level."

"Well, whatever it is, I don't like it," the Champ snorted. "You know what I need me?"

"What's that, Champ?" asked another of the of the retinue.

"I need me some fruit. Some nice, juicy fruit. That's what. You, boy, come over here."

Miguel realized that Johnson was looking straight at him.

"Yeah, you, boy. Get yourself over here."

Miguel could feel every eye in the backyard on him except for the woman, who was still immersed in her book. Why had he not left when Little Howard had told him to?

"What's your name, son?"

"Miguel."

"Mee-gal?" Johnson sang the name rather than said it.

Miguel nodded.

"Shit, that's a mouthful fo' a dry and thirsty man. How about Midge? You like being called Midge? Well, Midge, I need me some fruit. All kinds of fruit. See that ugly man over there?" Johnson pointed at a large man smoking a cigar, every finger sheathed in a gold ring. "Believe it or not, Midge, that man's name is Bessie. You go to Bessie and get some money and go buy me some fruit. Would you do that now?"

With the presumption that comes from greatness, Johnson turned from Miguel to begin an animated conversation with his manager, confident that his wishes would be instantly accommodated.

Bessie peeled a fiver from a wad of bills and handed it to Miguel.

"Here you go, boy, be quick now. The Champ don't like to wait."

A minute later an out-of-breath Miguel was in the grocery store to fill a paper sack with whatever fruit was available. He found apples, choosing the largest and the reddest. He anguished over some desiccated oranges and blackening bananas before he tossed a few of each in the sack. The peaches were green and hard so he decided against them. Searching for something, anything else that might please the Champ, his eyes fell on the tomatoes. These looked plump and appealing so he grabbed several, paid for his purchases, and was out the door.

A minute after that he was back in the camp. By now Johnson was seated at the table by his wife, mopping his head and torso with one of the towels Miguel had delivered.

"What you got for me, Midge?" The Champ sounded almost childlike in his eagerness to explore the contents of the paper bag. "Let's see, apples. That's good, I like apples. Oranges, kind of puny. And these bananas, I dunno. And what's this? Tomatoes. Midge, what for you bring me tomatoes? I said I wanted fruit."

"It is a fruit."

"Huh?"

"I said," the woman said and finally looked up, "that tomatoes are fruit."

The champion crooned in genuine awe. "Is that right? Why, I never did know that. Well, Midge, I guess you did good."

Miguel held out the change from his purchases.

"No, no, Midge. You keep that. That's yours. You earned it. You taught me something new. Now I know that tomatoes is a fruit."

Johnson laughed and shut his eyes while his spectacularly white teeth chomped down on the tomato. Juice and seeds squirted in all directions and ran down his chin onto his broad expanse of chest.

From that day on, Miguel was a fixture in the Johnson training camp. He ran errands for the Champ and his lieutenants. When unoccupied he sat on a tree stump and watched the best fighter in the world go through his paces. Johnson was sometimes playful in the ring. He pranced around and toyed with his sparring partners. He joked and acted the cut-up for the reporters. Other times Johnson was ferocious, uncommunicative, a punisher of anything that dared stand before him. On those occasions, his face froze in a fearsome scowl that caused those in attendance to fall silent, so that only the grunts that emanated from deep within his belly and the splat of his fists against flesh or a heavy canvas bag punctuated the quiet of the backyard.

By the day of the fight, Miguel was so much a part of the group that he was assigned to tend to the towels in Johnson's corner.

"And don' be handin' the Champ any wet towels. You hear?" the trainer drilled into him.

To the anguish of the town leaders, the expected gate never materialized. At most, three thousand spectators filled the tented arena. Barely a majority of these were actual paying customers, what with the press, the freeloaders with complimentary passes, and a steady stream of crashers who sneaked underneath the tent.

The champion was cheered wildly when he entered the ring. The challenger received polite applause, over which one drunken voice was heard to shout, "Get him, Jim. Get that nigger good." The crowd booed him roundly and then cheered when officers from the sheriff's department escorted the troublemaker out. This, as it turned out, provided some of the better entertainment of the day.

From the opening bell, Flynn showed himself unskilled and overmatched. He ran away as much as he could because when he stood still the Champ hit him. By the fourth round Johnson was openly contemptuous of his opponent. He would stop fighting to speak with his wife or to trade quips with reporters at ringside while Flynn flailed ineffectively at his back and arms. He even managed a wink or two for Miguel.

By the sixth round, Flynn was resorting to head butts.

The crowd hooted. They booed. They wadded up their programs and threw them at Flynn every time he came to his corner. By the eighth round, it was evident that there would be no professional fight of consequence on this day. The audience felt, with justification, that it had been cheated. Frustration washed over them like a heavy layer of sweat. Fights broke out. Chairs went sailing into the ring. In the ninth round, when Flynn tried yet another flurry of head butts, the captain of the state police, there to represent the governor, jumped into the ring, separated the contenders, and stopped the bout. The referee immediately raised Johnson's hand in victory.

The captain was quoted in newspapers across the country the next day: "It was no longer a skillful boxing exhibition, but a test of brute strength and roughbone methods."

Early the following morning, Johnson and his retinue left town $42,000 richer with the guaranteed purse, expense money, and the winnings from side bets that the Champ had placed on himself.

As he climbed into the waiting touring car that would take him to the depot, the Champ saw Miguel off to the side. "Here you go, Midge," he said and flipped a twenty-dollar gold piece high in the air. "If you're smart, you'll get out of this place while you can. There's nothing here. Come on with us. We'll take care of you."

After the Champ rode away and the almost liquid texture of the gold coin threatened to ooze between the fingers of his tightly closed fist, Miguel fought his demons. Should he run after the Champ and jump on the train? Then he remembered the tired, gentle face of Francisquita and trudged slowly home.

It was the only bona fide offer that Miguel would ever have to strike out and find his future away from Las Vegas. But as usual, the timing was wrong.

The licking that the "Fighting Fireman" sustained at the hands of the champion was nothing compared to the financial walloping that Las Vegas took. The promised bonanza from the fight turned into an unmitigated financial disaster. But perhaps all was not yet lost.

The match, filmed and distributed to movie houses across the country, caught the attention of one Romaine Fielding, a flashy and bombastic producer and director of features for the Lubin Film Company. His specialty was westerns, and Las Vegas, with its Old West look and feel and a myriad of natural settings, seemed an ideal location to set up a studio. In August of 1913, Fielding and his troupe

rolled into town with the announced intention of creating a permanent facility to shoot cowboy films. He did manage to film several
movies that summer. But by December, when icy winds and blistering
snow churned to their full vigor, Fielding pulled up stakes and headed
to warmer climes on the Gulf Coast.

Las Vegas was once more devastated. Again, a legendary hero,
one of equal stature to Jack Johnson, came riding to the rescue.

In July of 1915, Tom Mix, the cowboy star, and his actress wife,
Virginia Forde, came to Las Vegas to attend the inaugural Cowboys
Reunion and Rodeo. Mix saw what Fielding had seen before him, an
ideal setting for making western movies. He stayed on and over the
next two years he turned out oaters under such titles as *Never Again*,
Local Color, *The Rancher's Daughter*, and the *Country Drugstore*.
The good times rolled once more in Las Vegas.

Miguel was never able to insinuate himself into the Mix inner circle as he had with Jack Johnson. The movie people, by and large,
were cliquish and self-sufficient and insulated themselves from the
everyday life of the community.

It was at a local saloon on a Saturday evening that Miguel had
his personal encounter with Tom Mix.

The actor was there with some of his buckaroos to celebrate the
wrapping of another picture. Miguel, at fifteen, was there to sweep
the floor, wash glasses, and empty the spittoons.

The film company occupied most of the tables at the back of the
room. Mix had ordered that no glass be empty on that evening and
this kept the saloon keeper and his two brothers-in-law beating a
steady path between the bar and the party.

Into this celebration walked several cowhands from a nearby
ranch. They were ready to spend some money and raise some hell
when they gathered at the front end of the bar and began to drink.

The party at the tables got louder and more rambunctious by the
minute, which caused one of the cowpunchers to cast a baleful look
over his shoulder at them.

"Hey, back there," the young buck finally shouted, "keep it down."

The group quieted for an instant. There were whispers, then tit-
ters, followed by an explosion of laughter, and the volume escalated
once again.

The cowhand turned from the bar to face the noise. "I said keep it down."

"Ah, cool off, mister," someone shouted back from the tables. "Take your keester someplace else if you don't like it."

This was enough for the cowhand. He pushed himself away from the bar, shook off the restraining hands of his companions, and walked to the back.

"You movie picture fellas think you're pretty tough, don't you?"

What the young man did not realize was that although these men were now making their living by pretending to be cowboys, they were real cowboys and pretty tough. They had worked long and hard on ranches in Montana, Wyoming, and Colorado, mostly as wranglers, before being lured by the easy money and high living of Hollywood.

"Easy, son." The voice was low-keyed and languid. "We want no trouble with you. We're just here to relax and have a good time. Why don't you just sit yourself down and have a drink with us? Your friends are welcome too."

What the young man saw was a man of thirty-five, dressed immaculately in doeskin leather frilled at the sleeves and decorated with elaborate patterns of silver studs. The high-crowned, perfectly creased white hat that was the Tom Mix trademark sat squarely on the actor's head.

What the young man did not see behind the frivolity of the costume was a man who had fought, ridden, shot, and roped his way to the top as a ranch hand, a soldier in the Spanish-American War, a featured Wild West Show performer, and only afterward as the most popular film star of the day.

The young man spat on the floor. "What do you know about being a cowboy? Fancy hat. Fancy clothes. Fancy boots. And them guns. Where'd you get 'em? The five and dime?"

The guns were fancy, no doubt about it, both of them, nickel plated and fitted snugly into twin holsters of black, tooled leather. The guns were also real. In fact, shooting was one of the star's specialties during his circuit days. Now he kept up his skills on location, where he took on all challengers and won all matches.

The actor maintained his congenial spirit. "What do you want here, son?"

"I'm here to tell you that you are a bunko."

"And you want me to prove you wrong?"

"Yes sir, I do."

"And just how might I do that?"

The young man slapped at the worn holster at his side. "Let's see what kind of man you really are. You got a gun, I got a gun."

Several from the party stood up and crowded the young man.

Mix raised his voice just a little bit. "Now, now, boys, easy."

The young man bent over the table. "If you can go it alone, that is."

"Boys, you're making the young feller nervous. Just sit down now."

With reluctance, the men complied.

"All right, my young hellraiser. let's think about it for a minute. What's to be gained by all of this? I shoot you and you're dead. You shoot me and, shit, boy, why your own Ma and Pa will sit in the front row at your hanging and lead the cheers. Don't you know that I'm one of the most beloved figures in the United States of America?" This last he said with a disarming irony that sent his companions into convulsive laughter.

The young man's voice cracked. "I don't like to be laughed at."

"They're not laughing at you, son. They're laughing at me, at this, at the silliness we're getting ourselves into."

"Silly to you, maybe."

Mix leaned back in his chair and pushed his hat to the back of his head to dislodge a glossy plume of dark hair that fell across his brow.

"OK, OK Let's settle down now. You want to challenge me to a shoot? I accept your challenge. But, we'll do it my way.

"Son," Mix called across the floor to where Miguel stood, his broom motionless, his mouth wide open.

"Yes, that's right, I'm talking to you. See those glasses over there? Grab yourself six of them and set them up in a nice little row on the bar, right side up."

Miguel looked at the saloon keeper, who gestured to him impatiently to do as he was told.

"Now," Mix continued, "get six of those lemons in that basket there and set them up in the glasses."

Miguel placed a lemon in each of the glasses, where they stood up, plump and glistening like bright yellow electric light bulbs.

"Fine. Now here's what we're going to do," Mix said, turning to the young man. "You are going to empty out your gun at those lemons. Then I'll do the same. Whoever hits the most wins. You win and my friends and I will leave quietly. I win and you and your friends join our party. Fair enough?"

The young man hesitated, not sure if this was quite within the spirit of the challenge he had issued. From behind him, his friends finally spoke up. "Come on, Dooley, do it. It's a fair offer."

By now, the young man's furor had dulled enough that he was beginning to regret the situation he had incited. "Well, I guess it's all right."

The tension that had been building in the room broke apart and dissipated. Everyone began laughing and talking while they cleared tables and chairs away. Someone raised his boot and scraped a line across the floor with the rowel of his spur.

"That about right, Tom? I make it to be twelve or fifteen feet to the bar, give or take a mile."

"Fine with me," answered Mix. "By the way, son," he said and offered the young man his hand, "I'm Tom Mix." The place exploded with laughter.

"Pleased, I'm sure, Mr. Mix. My name's Dooley Rimbert, and I seen all your pictures."

"Well, Dooley Rimbert, you're the challenger so you go first. Take your time, now."

While the young man toed the mark gouged into the floor and prepared himself to shoot, the movie star turned to the saloon keeper. "By the way, señor, don't worry about any damage. I'll pay for all repairs."

"My pleasure, Mr. Mix, my pleasure." The saloon keeper was already calculating the money to be made. He would leave the scars from the competition untouched. "Come see," he would call to passers-by. "Come see the bullet holes made in my bar by the famous Tom Mix."

The young man, nervous and needled mercilessly by his friends, shot six rounds. One nicked the tip of a lemon. Two others splintered the bar. Three buried themselves in the wall behind.

"Good shots, Dooley. You're sure showing that actor fella how a real cowboy shoots," hooted one of his friends.

Then it was Mix's turn. Borrowing some live rounds from one of his companions, he inserted the cartridges into the cylinder of his six-shooter. Then he returned the weapon to its holster and stood squarely to the bar. The long narrow room went completely silent. In a flash the gun cleared leather and barked six times in quick succession. The air was filled with smoke. For an instant a thin curtain of mist hung over the bar before it drifted across the room to bathe those present with the refreshing fragrance of lemon. The six glasses sat undisturbed on the bar, holding shreds of pale yellow pulp and rind.

There were wild cheers and back slapping and Mix finally had to raise his hands to quiet the men. He turned to the young man and winked. "Satisfied, Dooley Rimbert?"

"Yessir, I reckon I am," responded the young man to general cheers.

"Well, I ain't. You've got me het up, boy." Mix turned to Miguel "Set 'em up. Let's see what I can do with my left hand."

Once again, Mix hit all the lemons.

The men began to chant and stomp their feet in rhythm. "Two guns, two guns."

"You heard them, son," Mix told Miguel. "Let's try a dozen."

This time, Mix's aim was not so true. Both guns blazed away but he managed to plug only nine of the lemons. He wanted to try again, but there were no more lemons.

Mix turned to the saloon keeper. "Well, señor, looking at your wall and the holes in your bar courtesy of Dooley here . . ."

"Don't forget the lemons, Tom," a voice shouted at him to renewed laughter.

". . . and two dozen lemons . . ."

"You don't have to pay for three of them," the same voice corrected.

". . . and two dozen lemons," Mix continued, "I'd say that a hundred dollars ought to cover it. Fair enough?"

"Oh, it's fine, Mr. Mix, very fair."

The movie star counted out ten bills and handed them to the saloon keeper.

"And here's something for you, *amiguito*." Mix flipped a coin in a high arc.

When he caught it, Miguel recognized, without looking, the heft and the velvet caress of a twenty-dollar gold piece.

That night after he got home, Miguel handed his mother the thirty-five cents he had earned from the saloon keeper.

"You smell good," Francisquita noted as he kissed her on the cheek.

Miguel headed for the bedroom that he shared with his three brothers. They were already asleep. He slowly worked open a drawer and searched out a sock buried deep under a pile of his clothes. He took the twenty-dollar coin from his pocket, dropped it into the sock, and enjoyed the satisfying clink as it landed in the toe next to another gold piece, the one he had been given by Jack Johnson.

Then he slipped off his shoes, pulled off his trousers and shirt, and slipped underneath the blanket next to his older brother, Joaquín. Before he closed his eyes, he brought his fingers to his nose and breathed in the clean, pungent smell of lemons.

Chapter Eighteen

I had a little bird
And its name was Enza.
I opened the window
And in-flew-Enza.

It was a verse crafted by children on the streets of New York City during the fall of 1918. And the little bird was deadly.

By the time the pandemic called the Spanish Flu had run its eight-month course, some forty million people worldwide were dead. It had taken the Black Death 150 years to wreak the same havoc.

Unless you lived on the tiny island of Tristan de Cunha, a fly speck in the South Atlantic, there was nowhere in the whole wide world you could hide. In one week in October 4,500 people died in Philadelphia and over 3,000 died in Chicago. The disease even managed to insinuate itself into the most inaccessible regions of Alaska to wipe out entire Eskimo villages.

The preferred victims of this pernicious microbe were not the weak among the very young and old. Rather they were the hale and robust in their teens and twenties. The symptoms came on suddenly: weakness, pains that shot through ears, eyes, and head and into the back and abdomen. Lungs filled and saturated with blood and fluid. Death came in a day or two from suffocation, the faces of the stricken a mass of swollen, blackened flesh.

. And there was not a single thing that medical science could do—not save one life, not shorten the duration of the epidemic by one minute. If you got it you either died or survived. It was random and cruel and it disappeared as quickly as it came, leaving behind nothing of itself that could advance medical knowledge by as much as a footnote.

By the time the epidemic reached Las Vegas, New Mexico, in the late summer of 1918, my father, Miguel, now seventeen, had secured steady, full-time employment in the Hidalgo Mercantile Company. His job was mainly behind the scenes, in the warehouse, among the shelves and in the delivery wagon. His cargo consisted of the usual consumer items: ice boxes, furniture, bolts of cloth, farming supplies. When the flu hit, however, Miguel's duties shifted. Now he received and stacked coffins in the store room, showed the stock to bereaved families, and delivered the purchases to the ranches and outlying villages around Las Vegas.

"*¿Cuánto?*" a farmer from the village of San Gerónimo asked and pointed at a simple box with no handles, covered in cheap gray felt.

"Forty dollars," Miguel answered.

The man moved to a casket with a skin of lavender fabric blistered with soft, raised patterns of flocking. "*¿Y ese?*"

"*Es más.* Seventy-five dollars."

The man took his hat off, dangled it at his side, and contemplated his options.

"*Mi hijo.* My youngest. We buried his wife last week."

"*Lo siento mucho.*"

The man returned the hat to his head, the decision made. "I'll talk to Don Benito. *La misa es mañana.* The priest is coming to the village to bury five."

Ten minutes later, Don Benito Hidalgo, fat and prosperous, walked through the door to the warehouse and strolled between the stacks of caskets. Above the elbows the sleeves of his shirt billowed out over silken arm garters. He wore wide, colorful suspenders that pulled his trousers well above his waist and over his neatly pressed shirt. He protected his starched cuffs with two celluloid cones that made his soft, pudgy hands and fingers look as if they had just been squeezed from a pastry tube.

"Miguel," he called, "did you talk to Blas Córdova?"

"Sí, Don Benito.

"Which coffin did he pick?"

"One of those two."

The merchant ran a hand lovingly over the velvety tufts of the lavender casket. "Out of the question. He can't afford this one. He can't even afford the gray one. But we worked something out. Get it out to his place. He'll ride with you. You might as well load up a couple more. You never know. Somebody might stop you to buy one. But don't forget. Strictly cash."

"Sí, Don Benito."

Miguel began to unstack one of the caskets under the watchful eye of his employer.

"Be careful. Be careful. You rip the cloth and you'll put me in the poorhouse."

"Sí, Don Benito."

"That's been a good seller for us. I'll have to order some more. This thing may never end, God help us." By the tone of his voice it was difficult to tell whether the merchant were praying for an end to the scourge or for a continuance of the prosperity he was realizing from the sale of shrouds, paper flowers, crosses, grave markers, rosaries, holy cards, and, of course, coffins.

The trip by horse-drawn wagon to the farm of Blas Córdova took two hours over a dusty, rocky trail incised deeply with a parallel track of ruts. A crow perched on a fence post angrily burrowed its head under its wing and raked its beak through its blue-black body feathers. A prairie dog poked its head out of its ground hole then jumped out and stood bolt upright on a mound of dirt to sniff the wind. A lizard skittered halfway across the road, thought better of it, turned to retreat, and almost lost its tail to the front wheel of the wagon. But no one along the way stopped Miguel to ask the price of his load of cut-rate coffins.

Blas Córdova, his horse tied to the back of the wagon, rode on the seat next to Miguel. He sat straight and with a dignity commensurate with his sad commission. But he did not talk of death. He spoke of the bad summer with no rain. He spoke of his daughter, who now lived in Cheyenne and whom he had not seen for six years. He spoke of the hustle and bustle of Las Vegas with its motor traffic and its faceless commercialism, no place for a simple man of the soil like himself. But he never spoke of his dead son or the daughter-in-law he had buried a week earlier.

Finally they reached a by-lane that met the road square on. This path was less defined. The grass and sunflowers grew high down its center.

"*Aquí*. Turn here," the man directed. "It's only a mile or two that way."

The house where the Córdovas lived was a slapped-together affair of narrow logs chinked with clay mixed with straw. The roof was a slope of scarred and torn oil-paper patched haphazardly with tin from cans flattened out and nailed in place. A stovepipe angled up from a side wall and emitted a thin wisp of smoke redolent with the unmistakable aroma of piñon wood.

Blas Córdova jumped from the wagon and walked halfway to the house. Miguel also climbed down and moved to the back of the wagon where he began to unlace the rope that held the canvas down.

"Wooo," the farmer yodeled, a whimsical sound rendered poignant by its context. "*Ustedes.* Come out. We need some help."

For a moment there was no movement from within. Then a hand pulled back a curtain from the single window under the low porch roof and a face, made indistinct by a thick layer of grime on the glass, looked out.

Blas Córdova gestured irritably at the apparition. "Yes, it's me. Come out here."

He turned back to Miguel. "You'd think they'd never seen a wagon before."

The front door opened and a young man stepped out.

"Papá. It's you."

"Of course it's me. Come here and be of some use. And then take care of the horse."

Between the three of them, they slid out one of the coffins and set it on the ground.

A dog sidled up and began to sniff at the gray box.

Blas Córdova aimed a foot at the animal's flank. "*¡Quítate de aquí!*"

The dog skillfully dodged the kick. Obviously it had much practice at this maneuver. It moved off to the wagon wheel, where it lifted its leg and relieved itself. This bit of business done, it padded across the yard to rummage its nose through a scattering of dried potato peelings and egg shells.

The farmer removed the lid from the box and propped it up against the back of the wagon.

"I'll go get my son ready now," he said to Miguel. "You'd better stay here. There's enough sickness around. There's water for your horse in that barrel over there." Then he added, "Don Benito said you'd take the body to the church for us."

Miguel knew that Blas Córdova had made no such arrangement, else Don Benito would have told him about it. And, more importantly, the shopkeeper would have unquestionably charged something for the service. But out here, Don Benito had no say. So Miguel watered his horse, attached its feed bag, and squatted in the shade of the wagon to wait.

The young man untied his father's horse and led it around the side of the house.

When he returned and opened the door to enter Miguel heard muted voices and soft wailings that slipped across the threshold and spilled out onto the hard, cracked earth in front. Then the door closed and there was silence except for the wind, which had begun to worry a piece of loose roof tin until it flapped and chattered in protest.

Finally, Blas Córdova emerged with his son. They struggled under the weight of a human form wound tightly in a yellowing bed sheet. Miguel stood up and assumed a pose of respect, his hands clasped in front and his head slightly bowed. As gently as possible, the two men placed the corpse in the narrow box. Then they stood back and Blas Córdova made a furtive sign of the cross. His son and Miguel hastened awkwardly to imitate him.

"Bring the lid," the father rasped, barely audible from where Miguel stood.

The son passed the panel to the father, who laid it carefully over the coffin and hooked it shut. Then the three of them hoisted the box up on the wagon and slid it into its slot between its companions.

"Go down the way you came and turn left," Blas Córdova instructed Miguel. "My son and I will follow in a few minutes. If you get to the church before us, just wait. I have to ride to the *mayordomo*'s house for the key to let us in."

Miguel waited for the man and the boy to return to the house. That is when he noticed in the window beyond them the blurred face of a woman. Her mouth was twisted open in anguish, but from where he sat, Miguel could not tell whether any sound issued from it.

Miguel shook the reins and moved the wagon out of the yard. Not fifty feet down the path he heard the voice of Blas Córdova call to him. He turned to see the man coming toward him. In his arms he held a small bundle wrapped in a faded blue coverlet.

"The baby, my dead son's child. He was born just a month ago. We found him just now. *Está muerto también*."

Blas Córdova held up the infant's body as if presenting an offering at an altar.

"For charity's sake, let me put him in the coffin with his father.

He's very small. We don't need another box. Besides," and for the first time, Blas Córdova showed a break in his reserve, "a baby shouldn't have to be buried alone."

Miguel understood. Even as he had walked into Don Benito's establishment to buy a coffin for his son, Blas Córdova had already known that the baby was dead. Miguel also understood that this dirt farmer could not have afforded another casket, even a cheap one made for an infant. Even though Don Benito would insist that every corpse must have its own coffin.

Miguel looked down into the eyes of Blas Córdova. "No, a baby should not be buried alone."

By Miguel's twenty-first year, the family of Francisquita Galván had established itself in its own right within the community. Juanito, the oldest, managed Galván's Grocery and Meat Market for his Uncle Ernesto and saved against the day that he could purchase a share in the business. Labán, the second-oldest, despite pleadings from his mother, took up his father's profession and was a house painter.

"I only paint outside, Mamacita. Not like Papá, who never saw the sun or breathed fresh air."

Joaquín, the only academic among them, had attended night classes at the local Normal school. He received a certificate in bookkeeping and worked behind a teller's cage at the Las Vegas Savings Bank.

María had married the year before. In fact all the children were now married and with families except Miguel.

When he was eighteen, Miguel left Don Benito and the mercantile business to become an apprentice in a printing shop. He quickly tired of having his hands and face always smeared with an indelible coating of ink. He next found employment in a drugstore, where he manned the soda fountain, stocked shelves, and waited on customers. He also filled bottles with colorful tonics and elixirs and doled out tablets and powders into small white folds of waxed paper. For a time he even considered being a pharmacist, until he realized he would have to leave Las Vegas to receive the proper training. So he contented himself with scooping ice cream and living at home with his mother.

The pharmacy was his life until he was twenty-six. That summer he took a trip to California to visit a cousin in Los Angeles. It was the first bona fide vacation he had ever had and when he returned to Las Vegas ten days later it was with the heartfelt resolution never to wander far from home again.

His cousin, Carlitos, two years older than Miguel and a confirmed profligate, had introduced him to the wicked ways of the big city. He made Miguel's stay an excuse for a nonstop binge. Each afternoon he escorted his country cousin into the speakeasies of the L.A. barrios where they remained well past midnight. He was the cause of Miguel's losing his virginity. At least it was assumed by the two of them that it had happened. Miguel could not be sure since he was too drunk to remember the experience. His only recollection was that he handed three dollars to a thin, middle-aged woman with painted face who took him into a back room of the saloon. There he promptly passed out. When he awoke an hour or so later he found himself in a chair with his trousers pulled down around his ankles. His money and his shoes were definitely missing, but he was unsure of the whereabouts of his virtue.

The worst thing that he did on his vacation, however, the stigma that he carried with him for the rest of his life, was to have himself tattooed. He was not drunk but he had already slipped into that liquored-up state that allowed him to be daring. He decided on two tattoos, one for each arm. For the left one, high up on his triceps to hide the scar from his smallpox vaccination, he chose the face of a saucy young flapper, her hair bobbed, her eyes half closed and seductive under long lashes, her mouth a perfect bow. To finish off this canvas the artist dangled a cigarette from the girl's kewpie lips and added a spiral of smoke above her head like a halo. For the inside of his right forearm, Miguel selected the image of Our Lady of Guadalupe with sun rays emanating from her body and a cherub at her feet.

For *mi mamacita*, he rationalized, although he could not imagine Francisquita ever kneeling in front of this patch of painted flesh to say her beads.

His mother never saw the tattoos—neither the Madonna nor the floozy. From the day he left Los Angeles until the day she died, Miguel always wore long-sleeved shirts buttoned tightly at the wrists.

Soon after his return from Gomorrah, Miguel was approached by his brother Juanito.

"Tío Ernesto wants to get out of the grocery business. He says if I don't buy the store he'll sell it to somebody else. But I don't have the money."

"How much do you need?" Miguel asked.

"With what I've already saved, four hundred dollars more for a down payment. He'll settle for a share of the profits until the rest is paid off."

"Four hundred dollars? I can lend you about a hundred."

"I don't want you to lend me anything. I want you to come in as a partner. You can take over the meat market."

"Me? A butcher?"

"Why not? Are you going to work for somebody else for the rest of your life? This is something you can build on. It will be ours. The Galván Brothers Market."

"But I don't have four hundred dollars."

"Talk to Joaquín at the bank. Maybe you can borrow it. Talk to Mamá. Maybe she'll let you use the house for collateral."

"Mamá's house? Are you crazy? It's all she has."

"She'll do it. You know she will. And you can pay off the note in a year or two. I swear it."

So Miguel became a partner in a grocery store at the west end where West National Avenue ran downhill into the plaza. Francisquita did not have to mortgage her home. After a talk with his boss at the bank, Joaquín arranged an unsecured loan of two hundred dollars for his brothers. Although that money combined with Miguel's savings was less than Uncle Ernesto had asked for, the sight of real cash was too much for the avaricious old man.

For better or worse Miguel was now a butcher. It was his last career change.

By the time he was thirty, his never bountiful hair had thinned to where it was hardly worth the attentions of a comb. His eyes squinted through round dark-framed glasses. His shoulders sloped from the weight of beef quarters and from stooping to reach into the meat display case a hundred times a day.

Miguel was still unmarried and his romantic prospects were dwindling daily.

Then one day a young girl of seventeen walked into his store. It was Margarita Juana, daughter of Leopoldo and Tamar Zamora, and Miguel Galván was instantly smitten.

Chapter Nineteen

1929–1930

Hubris.

Leopoldo Zamora had committed it. He had pretended to be what he was not, a French Canadian of all things. His punishment was a fall from the Olympus that was Denver to the nether regions of Las Vegas. His family was not spared his fate.

The house in which they had lived before, the one Tamar had left with giddy optimism three years earlier, was available. It mocked her when she stood once again in its cramped entryway.

Leopoldo found work immediately as a mechanic at the local power and water company. Tamar continued to be unlucky in that she became pregnant one last time at the age of forty-two. It was a difficult pregnancy, and Margarita, who had expected to finish up her high school education, stayed at home to run the household.

After Constancia was born, Margarita looked for any means to get out of the house and out from under the singular joylessness of her mother. She found several openings around town for waitresses. One hotel and two restaurants offered her employment on the spot.

But Leopoldo would have none of it. "It's not for decent girls. The customers are always flirting and making dirty comments."

"And how would you know?" Tamar's question dripped venom.

"¿Qué importa? The point here is that no daughter of mine will wait tables in this town."

Margarita eventually found a clerking job at a dry-goods store in the afternoons. This at least offered twenty or so hours of relief each week, sandwiched between housework and babysitting, always under the stinging scrutiny of her mother.

By not allowing her to work in a restaurant where she would risk exposure to traveling salesmen and other no-accounts, Leopoldo unwittingly opened Margarita up to a different breed of predators, the testosterone-driven young men of Las Vegas.

Margarita's Denver experiences with Dr. and Mrs. Standard had armed her with two assets: a sense of confidence and a sense of style. She was fresh, she was vivacious, she was pretty, she was unattached, and, her pursuers hoped, she was available. During her hours at the dry-goods store the traffic in male shoppers increased significantly. All of them waited to be served by her while the other clerks stood around and backbit.

Margarita's stream of admirers dried up abruptly when Romancito Ortiz came onto the scene.

The family Ortiz was all that the Galván clan, this is to say Miguel's uncles, aspired to. They too could trace their roots back to the conquistadors but, unlike the Galváns, the Ortizes had made the best of their opportunities. From their ranks, over the years, came the judges, the politicians, the men of commerce, and the influence peddlers. They ran the community and had the ear of the powerful and influential in Santa Fe, Albuquerque, and beyond.

The current shining light of the Ortiz clan, Romancito was now carving out his niche in one of his father's most profitable businesses, a highly regarded bootlegging operation. The enterprise was so esteemed throughout the state that its bribes went only to the most distinguished judges and politicos and into the highest echelons of law enforcement.

Romancito, as he was called to distinguish him from his father, Don Román, was born to make women swoon. He was of medium height, lean and muscular with narrow hips and with the tight, suggestive buttocks of a flamenco dancer. His face was the epitome of mestizo comeliness. His hair was sable sleek and his eyebrows, thick and dark, hovered like a hawk's wings over brilliant, bottomless emerald eyes. His skin had the butternut color of warm sand. The nose dipped in a fine curve to generous nostrils and the mouth was full and red, almost feminine. When he smiled there was a boyish crookedness to his two front teeth that made him irresistible to women, old and young.

When Romancito entered the dry-goods store to see for himself this Margarita that all his friends were talking about he was not immediately swept away. He had certainly seen more beautiful women, many of whom he had bedded and abandoned. His considered opinion was that she was not even the prettiest girl in Old Town.

This being settled, he had to admit that she might warrant some attention. Perhaps he was drawn to her because she was the current rage among his friends and he was certain that he, among all of them, could have her for the taking. But there was something more, a certain standoffishness, an inapproachability, that intrigued and challenged him.

On her part, when she saw him standing before her, Margarita was sure that this was the most wondrous creature she had ever seen, eclipsing in his beauty even the actor in *The Rose of Picardy* who had caused her adolescent bosom to tremble.

But then, as their dance of courtship began, and as is the eternal nature of such things, their roles reversed. She feigned disinterest to hide her instant attraction to him, and he countered with bravura to give the impression that he cared more about her than he actually did.

"Hello, I'm Romancito. Who are you?"

"Margarita."

"How long have you been in Vegas?"

"A while."

"Do you live around here?"

"Can I help you with something?"

"What?"

"Do you need something? Do you want to buy something?"

"Are you always so unfriendly?"

"If you don't want anything, I think that lady over there does. Excuse me."

So ended their first meeting. Margarita walked off to wait on a customer who was clicking impatiently through a selection of shapeless house dresses draped on clothes hangers on a pipe rack. Romancito stood where she had left him, confused and angry. He stormed out without acknowledging the flirtatious purrings of the other shop girls.

After the rebuff, Margarita saw Romancito often when he drove around the plaza in an open coupe, always with a female at his side. He honked his horn at people he knew and occasionally flashed his famous smile at the girlfriend *du jour* next to him. But he gave no indication that he even noticed Margarita. However, he let it be known among his friends that she was now off limits to them.

Two weeks later Romancito resumed his advances. "Where can I try these on?"

Margarita was at a table sorting out tangled skeins of embroidery thread and the voice came from behind her.

Romancito was holding up a pair of trousers. "Where can I try these on?" he repeated.

Margarita flushed. "Over there," she stammered and pointed to an alcove.

His "thank you" was crisp and uninvolved.

Margarita went back to the threads but now her hands were trembling and she quickly snared the floss into a mare's nest. More than once she cast a furtive glance toward the dressing room door. When it finally opened she hastily dropped her head to her work and moved her fingers through the tangles with more energy than success.

"I'll take them."

She cleared her throat to control her nervousness. "Just go over to the cashier and she'll wait on you."

"Why can't you help me?"

"Because I'm not a cashier."

He tossed the trousers on the table behind him. "Well then I've changed my mind. I don't want them. What I really need is some thread. Like what you have there." His eyes were serious but there was a hint of mischief around the edges of his mouth.

"Thread?"

"What's the matter? Can't I buy some thread?"

"I guess you can buy anything you want."

"I sew real good."

"How nice."

He began counting on his fingers. "Let's see. I'll take a red one and a blue one and one of those pink ones and your name's Margarita."

He cocked his head to one side and opened his jungle-green eyes wide with welcome. "I'm Romancito."

"I remember your name."

"So, we're properly introduced. Now, can we be friends?"

"That might take a little more time."

"Fine. We need time. When do you get off work?"

"Six."

"I'll drop by for you."

"I have to go straight home."

"I'll drive you."

"I can walk."

"I'll walk with you."

"I don't want to take you away from your sewing."

"At six. I'll walk you home."

Romancito was waiting for Margarita outside the store at closing time. He leaned against the hood of his radiant black chariot, his arms folded in front of him.

"Are you sure you don't want to ride?"

She shook her head.

"Well then, I guess we'll have to walk."

"It's about a mile."

"Well, if you won't ride, there's nothing we can do about that, is there?"

"Suit yourself. You'll just have to come all the way back here for your car."

Romancito did most of the talking. He said nothing of consequence, but his lilting baritone was in itself enough to keep Margarita entertained. When they reached her house, Margarita said goodbye in a rush and ran up the porch into the house.

"Tomorrow," he called after her. Then he stood a few seconds looking at the house before he stuffed his hands in his pockets and walked away. He had gone not a dozen steps before he saw a car heading toward the plaza. He recognized its driver, waved him down, and jumped in.

All of this Margarita observed from behind the curtain of the window in the front room. And she was not the only one spying. She turned and almost bowled Tamar over.

"And who was that?"

"Someone. No one."

Margarita brushed by and walked into the kitchen, where the rest of the family was already well into the supper meal.

Tamar followed her daughter through the door. "Who is he?"

"Just somebody who came into the store to buy some thread." Margarita smiled at her private joke, took a hand basin, and scooped up a bit of warm water from the reservoir by the stove.

"And did you lead him on?"

Margarita fiercely worked a sliver of soap into a weak lather between her fingers. "I didn't lead him on. He just asked if he could walk me home. It doesn't mean anything."

Tamar now attacked Leopoldo. "You hear that? And you were so worried about her working as a waitress. Here she is, bringing strangers home right under your nose."

Leopoldo pushed away his empty plate, picked up his coffee cup in both hands, rested his elbows on the table, and took several sips before finally addressing his daughter.

"What's the boy's name, *hijita*?"

"Romancito. Romancito Ortiz."

"Ortiz? The son of old Román?"

Margarita slipped into a chair at the table and began to serve herself from the pot of green chile stew in front of her. "I think so."

"Well, Tamar, what do you think of that? Our Margarita has hooked the son of the most important man in Las Vegas."

"I haven't hooked anybody. Can't a boy just walk me home without everyone making such a fuss?"

Tamar was more impressed than she would ever admit. The boy came from money. "Well, then why didn't you invite him in, like a decent girl?

Margarita ignored the question.

"Are you ashamed of us?"

Margarita set her jaw and pushed her spoon back and forth in the coagulating grayness of her food. "Of course not."

But of course she was.

Each evening at six o'clock over the next week Margarita found Romancito waiting for her on the sidewalk outside the store. But now, one of his friends drove his car slowly and at a discreet distance behind them and waited to give Romancito a ride back into town.

One afternoon Margarita informed Romancito that she had to stop at the grocery store. "So if you have something else to do."

He cupped her elbow firmly in his hand and escorted her across the plaza and through the door of Galván's Market. "I'm yours. You know that."

Margarita made her way through the store aisles, picking up a can of lard and some potatoes and onions. Romancito trailed behind and poked at the merchandise on the shelves like a bored child. In due course, she arrived at the meat counter.

From behind the meat case, Miguel Galván had seen Margarita come in. He immediately ripped off his blood-spattered apron and put on a clean one. It was closing time, and he had been clearing out the display case to store the meat in the walk-in icebox. He did manage to shove a few trays back into the case and was sliding its window shut as she arrived.

"You just made it."

Margarita smiled. Miguel was one of the few men in Las Vegas who didn't seem to have designs on her. "I just got out of work."

"We have some nice fresh chickens."

"Not tonight. My mamá needs two pounds of hamburger and a chunk of salt pork."

Romancito stepped up. "And watch your thumb on the scale."

Miguel had seen the young man enter the store but did not realize until now that he was with Margarita.

Romancito dismissed Miguel in true patrician fashion. "You have to watch these butchers."

Miguel bristled even as he chuckled feebly. The Ortizes were good customers. No sense starting anything with Romancito. However, he was not happy, not at all. He had been made to look foolish in front of Margarita. Also, the Galván brothers were scrupulously honest in their business. Finally, since Margarita had begun shopping at the store and stolen his heart, not only had Miguel been fair with her, he had been generous to a fault. If she asked for a pound of round steak he gave her a pound and a half. If she wanted a dozen wieners, he counted out fourteen. If she needed six pork chops he wrapped up seven.

Once Tamar realized that they were not paying for these extras, she announced that from now on all their meats were to be purchased at the Galváns'. If the fool wanted to fill their pot because he was mooning over their daughter, let him.

Miguel had contented himself with passing the time of day with Margarita. They talked easily and the girl felt quite comfortable with this earnest little man. She had no inkling of Miguel's feelings. In the normal course of things she would never have found out. Miguel had no knack for romancing. Once he had been on the verge of asking Margarita out. His courage failed him and he ended up slipping an extra slice of liver into her order.

Now that he saw Romancito sweep the bags of groceries into his arms and walk out of the store with Margarita, Miguel could do nothing but gaze ruefully after them. Bad timing.

Out on the sidewalk, Romancito made a stronger case about the car. "Come on now, be sensible. These bags are heavy. What's the harm in riding just this once?"

Once she stepped up on the running board and slid onto the leather seat of his sleek auto, Margarita became, to Romancito's way of thinking, his girl.

The next few weeks of their relationship did nothing to dispel that notion. He picked her up at her house to drive her to work and at the store to return her home. Sometimes he did not take the direct route to her house. Instead he circled around the plaza and drove down Bridge Street across the Gallinas River into New Town for a spin around the university campus. He pushed for longer and longer drives—to the bluffs overlooking the town on the east end, down the Santa Fe highway for two or three miles, or past Margarita's house, by the state hospital, and into the wide, meandering valley at the mouth of the canyon from which the Gallinas flowed.

Soon Romancito tired of their mating game. There were only so many places to drive in and around Las Vegas. He had already spent considerable time and gasoline in courting Margarita with little to show for his investment. While Margarita had allowed him to hold her hand and had even offered her cheek on occasion for a chaste kiss, it was certainly not what he was after. Romancito was a satyr. Many an evening, after he dropped Margarita off, he prowled the town for the women on whom he had always depended to show him a randy good time.

But none of this was any longer enough for him. His obsession was with Margarita. He became less playful, more irritable. He began to tease her in cruel ways.

"How's the princess today?" he might ask, his eyes narrow and belligerent. "What a delicate flower you must think you are."

Margarita was not equipped to respond, nor could she fathom the reason for Romancito's change of attitude. So, the two of them would sit unspeaking in his car until the mood passed and he disarmed her with a joke, an innocent tease, or even a tender word.

Late one evening, after they had been to the pictures, Romancito became sullen, a commonplace condition of late.

"It's late," Margarita noted when they pulled away from the curb.

Romancito's only response was a noncommittal grunt. He made a sharp left turn up Seventh Street, beyond St. Anthony's Hospital and out on the Mora road, on which Margarita had driven her father's truck as a child of twelve. They drove for another mile without talking until Romancito pulled off onto a wide, sloping shoulder. There they sat for a few minutes in strained silence.

"I think you should take me home now," Margarita finally said.

"Don't worry. I just want to sit here for five minutes. Is that all right? I just took you to the movies, for God's sake. Don't you have five minutes to talk to me?"

"Sure we can talk. I'd like that. Did you like the movie? I thought it was very sad."

"Why are you so mean to me?"

"Mean to you?"

Romancito pouted, his favorite ploy of late and one that Margarita was finding more and more tiresome. "You know."

He reached over to play with the tendrils of hair that lay on the nape of her neck. Then his hand slipped down and his fingertips began to nudge and insinuate themselves under the edge of her collar.

Margarita moved away from him. "Don't, Romancito."

"See? See how you are?"

"What do you want from me?"

Romancito had waited a long time for that question. He reached into his jacket pocket and pulled out a thick wafer wrapped in foil.

"Do you know what this is?"

Margarita shook her head.

"No? Of course you don't. You want everyone to think that you're so good. You're nothing but a dumb little *ranchera* from up there." He jabbed his finger into the darkness in front of them where the road to Mora curved into oblivion.

"I know where I'm from."

"Let me show you what I have here, *ranchera*." He tore at the packet savagely and when he had peeled the silver paper completely away, he held out its contents. "Now. You know what this is?"

She looked down at a thick-rimmed circle of rubber across which stretched a diaphanous, milky membrane.

"No? Let me show you."

He held up the index and middle fingers of his left hand and centered the object on their tips. Then, carefully he worked the rim of the object down with his right hand, unfurling a flaccid tube of rubber that eventually sheathed his fingers.

"See that? You know what that's for? It's what a man wears on his *picha* when he sleeps with a woman so they won't have babies."

"Don't talk like this. I don't like it."

Romancito's voice turned gentle and reassuring. "Everything's taken care of. I know you've been worried about that. Now we can prove how much we love each other."

"You'd better take me home."

"No. I've wasted enough time being nice to you."

He took Margarita by her shoulders and forced her to face him. His lips were now tight and curled back over his teeth. His breath was irregular, and his eyes, those deep pools of emerald where she had often lost herself, were shallow puddles of opaque scum. The mask that Romancito now wore was the very same as Porfirio's when he had fondled her many years before. And the slap she now directed at Romancito was just as true as the kick to the knot on Porfirio's knee. When she raked her nails savagely across his cheek, he let her go and screamed in pain and covered his face.

Margarita opened the car door and rolled into a heap on the ground. She was instantly on her feet and running into a field. She wept as she ran and did not stop running even when she heard the engine of Romancito's car roar to life. Its tires spat up gravel, then it bucked onto the highway and careened back toward town.

Unfortunately for Margarita, that was not the end of Romancito.

He let it be known among his friends that he was done with her and she was once again available for their amusement.

"She was all right, I guess. Wild. Look what she did to my face while we were fucking. But I've had better."

The stream of young men into the dry-goods store resumed and escalated in its relentlessness. This time, however, they came to leer, to make suggestive comments, or to invite her out "for a little fun."

On her solitary walks to and from work, passing cars honked at her and their passengers shouted out lewd remarks. One rowdy stood up precariously in a moving vehicle and grabbed at his genitals.

"Oh, Margarita, I love you so much. Meet me tonight in back of the armory. Look what I have for you."

Romancito still prowled the plaza in his car. He still waved at the people he knew and he drove with a different girl at his side every day. But now, rather than ignoring Margarita as he had done earlier, he made a point of catching her eye while he playfully pawed at whoever was sitting with him.

When she was not at home, Margarita's only oasis from the harassment on the streets of Las Vegas was in the grocery store belonging to the Galváns. She and Miguel had so little in common— she a vibrant eighteen-year-old with dreams of travel and romance, he, at thirty, a meat cutter satisfied with the quiet life. Still, they were able to talk and to carve out a middle ground of understanding that accommodated their separate needs for each other.

She tried once to think of Miguel in a serious way. But her imagination failed her. She knew that such a relationship would suffocate her as surely and as completely as did her life with her parents. She still counted on finding a way to leave them all behind to seek out her destiny elsewhere.

Her firm resolve in this notwithstanding, Margarita's friendship with Miguel and her dependence on his stability deepened by the day. Soon it was he who was walking her home, the first time to help her with a load of groceries, thereafter simply to keep her company. It was he who took her out when she could no longer stand to be under the same roof with her mother. They went to church together for evening novenas in prelude to major feasts. They sat in the plaza for band concerts. He took her to the movies and to an occasional dramatic presentation at the college. They went on picnics with his family. She became a welcome guest in Francisquita's house for Sunday dinner.

"Why are you spending so much time with that butcher?" Tamar asked her one day. It was a fresh patch of exposed flesh into which she could jab her acid-laden tongue.

"He's a friend."

"A nobody. Like you. Well, if you marry him at least we'll always have food on the table."

"He's over thirty. Why would I want to marry him? Why would he want to marry me?"

"Well, I don't know much but it seems to me that when a man spends this much time with a woman he has something in mind. Look at Romancito."

And it was Romancito Ortiz who finally forced the issue.

One day before work, Margarita took a walk across the bridge to New Town. She was of a mind to sit and daydream in the sun on the sloping lawn of the university campus. Halfway across the bridge she heard a car pull up behind her.

"Margarita."

No one ever pronounced her name quite the way Romancito did. Every syllable was given its full value, every consonant savored, every vowel caressed. And no voice could affect Margarita with the same power, a tingle that began at the back of her neck and ran down her spine where it forked like an electrical charge into her legs and sparked out through the very tips of her toes.

"Margarita. Please. Get in the car. I have to talk to you."

He was behind the wheel of his open coupe. A lock of hair fell across his forehead; his eyes, those green, green eyes, held nothing now but supplication. The delicious mouth was slightly parted. The tip of the tongue touched the upper lip in expectation. The seat beside him, her seat, was empty.

"Go find one of your friends to ride with you," she heard herself say.

Romancito switched off the ignition. "You know they don't mean anything to me."

Margarita turned to the stone balustrade that ran the length of the bridge and leaned over to watch the turgid stream of water that inched by underneath. "It really doesn't matter."

She heard the car door open and there was Romancito resting his elbows on the warm sandstone beside her.

"But it does matter. What I did that night, the way I tried to hurt you, I don't know what I was thinking. I'm sick about it."

Margarita did not bother to look at him. "You seem pretty healthy to me."

"Please, Margarita."

"What do you want from me, Romancito?"

He opened his hand. "Look, Margarita. Do you know what this is?"

It was another circlet, not of rubber this time but of gold, with a small cluster of diamonds mounted on it. "I want you to marry me."

"Oh, Romancito."

"Think about it, Margarita, all the things you told me you wanted. I can give them to you. We can leave Las Vegas. Go anywhere you want. Like you always talked about."

Yes. Romancito probably could make it all happen. She wouldn't have to wait for her Uncle Delfino any longer. But as she looked at him, she had jagged flashes of that beautiful, earnest face when it was twisted, cruel, and brutish.

"Romancito, I have never felt for anyone how I felt for you."

"I know you love me."

"Not now."

Romancito's voice dropped almost to a whisper but so intense that Margarita imagined that it could be heard the length and breadth of Bridge Street. "I will not ask you again, Margarita. Marry me." There was no respect there, no tenderness. His voice had become a hollow rasp, a threat.

"I'm sorry, Romancito. I truly am."

"Well then, go to hell." He flipped the ring over the parapet, where it caught the light from the noon sun before it tumbled down and sank noiselessly in the swampy water below.

She heard the car door shut and an engine turn over. She saw its shadow creep slowly down the sidewalk, gather speed, and disappear. When Miguel invited Margarita to the weekly Saturday dance and she refused, he pressed her for her reasons. "I've never asked you to a dance before. Why do you say no?"

"I just don't feel like it. I don't like to dance."

"Of course you like to dance. Everybody likes to dance. I don't even know how and I like to dance."

He tapped his feet and made a clumsy attempt at a pirouette that sent him spinning unsteadily off the sidewalk onto the street. This brought a smile to Margarita's lips and Miguel jumped through the breach.

"See, if nothing else, you have to come just to see me make an ass of myself."

"I can't."

"Of course you can. The question is, why won't you?"

Back and forth it went, until, worn down by Miguel's persistence, Margarita confessed. "Romancito Ortiz. He'll be there and I don't want to see him."

"You're not going with Romancito. You're going with me."

"Romancito wouldn't like it if he saw me there."

"Romancito can't have everything his way all the time."

"He might do something crazy."

"He won't do anything. I won't let him. Besides, are you going to spend your entire life worrying about Romancito?"

His logic was unassailable and it fortified her own growing feelings of resentment of the limbo-like existence into which Romancito had forced her.

"All right," she said. The foreboding she kept to herself.

The Rialto Ballroom on a Saturday night was the only place to be if you were young and you lived in Las Vegas. The band was the Rhythm Aces, five local musicians who during the week held down jobs as mechanics, shopkeepers, and a dry cleaner. They had a saxophone sound and played all the current hits—"Charmaine," "'Swonderful," "Makin' Whoopie," "Honeysuckle Rose"—as well as the old standbys and plenty of polkas and Mexican standards.

The attendees were young and wild. Miguel was definitely one of the older and more mature people there. But on that night, with Margarita at his side, he felt as frisky as any of them.

Romancito was also there. However, as the evening wore on and he showed no interest in her, Margarita began to relax. She danced mostly with Miguel but also accepted invitations from other men who were up on the latest steps.

Romancito did not dance at all. He spent his time with a tight little group of friends at a corner by the bandstand. They could be seen making frequent trips into the back room and reappearing minutes later, rowdier and more unsteady by degrees. Only Romancito seemed sober and subdued.

The bandleader gave his best impression of Rudy Valee through a small, glitter-encrusted megaphone. "Thank you, ladies and gentlemen. You've been wonderful. Don't forget next week. More music. More fun. More dancing. More mooning and spooning with your honey. And now, put down your punch glasses and join us for the last dance."

To avoid the rush, Miguel had gone to the cloakroom for Margarita's wrap, so she was left alone to sway to the music. Her mood was mellow, so mellow that she did not notice Romancito making his way toward her through the swirling crowd.

"Where's your butcher boyfriend?" His breath smelled yeasty from the liquor.

Margarita turned away. Romancito pushed his body against her back and bent his head so that she could feel the searing heat of his words in her ear.

"I have a gun. Come with me now or there'll be trouble."

She jerked her head around to look into the blear of his eyes. Her gaze then traveled down to where his hand rested against a hard lump in his jacket pocket. "Romancito, what are you going to do? Shoot me?"

"I'll kill you unless you come with me right now."

"And then what?"

Romancito opened his mouth to answer but before he could Miguel had his hand on the younger man's shoulder.

"Leave her alone, Romancito."

Romancito shook off the hand and took an unsteady step back.

"He's drunk," Margarita said. "He says he has a gun in his pocket."

"Is that right, Romancito? What do you want to carry a gun for?

You're not running booze from Mexico right now."

Romancito lunged at Miguel, his fist headed in a sluggish arc for Miguel's jaw.

"*¡Chinga tu madre!*"

Miguel's looks had always been deceiving. At five foot nine inches and 130 pounds, with his owlish spectacles and thinning hair, his strength was well disguised. Timid and innocuous as he appeared, he had been annealed from his boyhood in a furnace of adversity. His will was iron. And after years of grueling physical labor, the last five of them hefting countless sides of beef, his arms and shoulders were a network of tensile steel.

Romancito's blow whistled harmlessly past Miguel's head and his momentum sent him toppling forward. Miguel caught him from behind and pinned his arms to his body like a steel hoop encircling barrel staves.

Romancito tried to rip himself from the embrace but Miguel only squeezed harder. Romancito began to kick and squirm and curse. Miguel allowed the kicks to bounce off his shins with unflappable disregard. Then Romancito began to scream, not in anger but in pain and growing panic. Then his breath shortened so that he could no longer scream. Miguel squeezed some more and Romancito simultaneously evacuated his stomach and his bladder.

Then, just before Romancito blacked out, Miguel bent his head and whispered quietly into his ear, "Never mention my mother again. Never."

He let go and Romancito slipped to the dance floor into the muck of his own vomit and urine.

When Margarita left the church after Mass the next day, Miguel was waiting for her. He took her by the arm and pulled her aside. "Come with me." Then he escorted her around the side of the church and through the door of the right transept into the sacristy. Father Alfredo looked up from putting away the last of his vestments.

"Hello, Miguel. How's your mother?"

"She's doing fine, thank you, Father. Do you know Margarita Zamora?"

"I've seen her at Mass, but we've never spoken, have we, child?"

"No, Father."

"You look like a man with something on his mind, Miguel."

"Father, we want to get married. Right away."

Margarita stared open-mouthed at Miguel.

The priest hoisted his eyebrows to full mast.

"It's a long story," Miguel continued, "but there's been some trouble and the best way out of it is for Margarita to marry me."

The priest's right eyebrow shot up even higher. "Trouble?"

"No, no, Father. It's not what you think. Not at all. It's about her safety. She needs me to protect her. The best way to do that is to marry her."

The priest made a calming motion with his hand. "Miguel, Miguel. This all sounds very peculiar to me. What does the young lady have to say? What do you think, my child? Are you in some sort of danger?"

"I . . . I don't know, Father."

"Father, believe me," Miguel said. "It's the only way."

"Well, even if that's true, I just can't marry you like that. Do I look like a justice of the peace? These things take time. The Church has rules. There are banns to be published, inquiries to be made, instructions to be given. You need time to think it over."

"But we can't wait."

The priest was unaccustomed to being challenged by a member of his flock. "Of course you can. And you shall. Come see me tomorrow and we can talk about it."

By the time they left the sacristy, Margarita had regained her tongue and she was in a blistering rage. "What are you thinking? I can't marry you!"

"You have to."

"I don't have to do anything."

They were now standing in the forest of gravestones that flanked the church. Miguel pointed at one of the monuments. "Sit down. I have something to tell you."

"I don't want to sit down."

"Well then I will, and we'll stay here until you're ready to listen." He sat on the gray marble and patted the space next to him. "Please, Margarita, it's important."

She looked down at him and huffed, but sat down. "All right. What's so important?"

"Someone came to my home this morning, a man sent by Don Román Ortiz."

"Romancito's father?"

"He wanted to talk to me."

"About last night? But that wasn't your fault. He was drunk. There are witnesses."

"Don Román doesn't care about that."

"So what did he want to talk to you about?"

"You."

"What about me?"

"He said that Romancito is getting harder and harder to control. He's sending him to Mexico tomorrow. He'll be gone a week."

"Well, that's good."

"Let me finish. The old man knows his son. When Romancito gets back he won't leave things alone."

"But there's nothing to leave alone. We're through with each other. I told him that."

"Don Román said that Romancito is threatening to do harm to you and your family. Maybe get your father fired. Or worse."

"But what can I do?"

"Don Román suggested a quick way out, and I think he's right. You have to be married by the time Romancito gets back from Mexico."

"But this is crazy. All of you are crazy."

"The only crazy one, Margarita, is Romancito."

Miguel took a breath and plunged deeper into his argument. "I love you, Margarita. Surely you know that. I will be a good husband for you. I don't have much but it's yours. Maybe you don't feel the same way about me but I know you feel something. I swear I will take care of you. Please try to see. It's the only way."

Margarita was trapped, betrayed by her own fates. Hopeless and helpless.

Miguel stood up and held out his hand. "Come on. Let's go talk with my brother Joaquín. He's smart. Maybe he can see some way out of this."

Miguel had not been completely forthright with Margarita. In fact, he had been downright disingenuous. For, while it was true that Don Román Ortiz had summoned him for an early morning conversation, it had not gone quite as he described it. Romancito had made no threats on Margarita's family. By the time he was carried home he was too drunk for anything but bed. Don Román, however, had made threats . . . not against the Zamoras but against the Galváns.

"How are you, Miguel Galván?" The old man was a paragon of Old World courtesy as he escorted Miguel into the formal dining room of his home.

"I am well, Don Román. And yourself?"

"What can I say? I'm an old man and I have a young devil for a son. God laughs at me every day."

"Many would say that God smiles on you every day, Don Román."

"What? All this?" The old man dismissed the surroundings with an impatient wave of his hand. "*Es mierda*. But sit down at my table, please. Can I offer you something? Coffee? A light collation?"

"No, thank you, Don Román. I am keeping the Communion fast. My mother is expecting me at 10:30 Mass."

"Ah, yes, your mother. I cannot think of a person I admire more. What she did with her family. Quite marvelous. No thanks to those vulturous uncles of yours."

"Yes, Don Román."

"Miguel, forgive me for coming so quickly to my point. Who is this girl?"

"Girl, Don Román?"

"You know who I mean."

"Margarita Zamora?"

"That's just a name. Who *is* she?"

"Just a girl."

"But she's not just a girl. She's the girl that my son offered marriage or death not eight hours ago."

"That was just the liquor talking."

"Oh yes, I agree. The liquor creates the talk but it does not," and the old man repeated himself, "it does not create the cause for him to say it. Let me be clear about this, Miguel Galván. I do not want my son to marry Margarita Zamora. And I do not want him to kill her. In either case he ruins his life. I will not have it. Do you understand me?"

"Yes, Don Román."

"How old are you? Twenty-nine? Thirty?"

"Thirty."

"Well, don't make the mistake I made. I didn't marry until I was thirty-six. Now I'm too old to horsewhip my son when he needs it."

"I think you could if you wanted to, Don Román."

"Perhaps. Yes. But, getting back to this girl. Do you want her?"

"I admire her greatly."

"The hell with admiration. Do you ache for her? *Hombre*, do you want her?"

Miguel stared at his hands folded on the table.

"Yes, Don Román. Yes, I want her."

"Then, by God, take her. Get her out of my son's life."

"But how?"

"I don't care how. Beat her. Frighten her. Tell her that I'll beat her and her whole family too. Tell her that I'll ruin them all. Tell her that she's not good enough for my son. Tell her anything. Just marry her."

"She's a very stubborn girl."

"Well, that must change. Why? Because, Miguel Galván, if she doesn't marry you, it is you who have a problem. Not from my son. From me. I know your bank. I know your creditors. I could buy up all your notes tomorrow. And then what would you and your brother do if I called in the debt?"

"I do not fear you, Don Román."

The old man's eyes bored into Miguel. "Ah, but you must. Remember, I am not my son. I am not a drunkard you can squeeze the piss and vomit out of."

Don Román reached into the wide pocket of his velvet dressing gown. From it he removed a brown envelope, which he slid across the polished mahogany where it bumped against the tips of Miguel's outspread fingers.

"Here. Call it a wedding present."

Miguel felt anger. He clutched the envelope and rose, determined to hurl the insult back in the old man's face. Then he stopped and considered. The old man was absolutely right in sensing that he would do almost anything to have Margarita. And, for better or worse, Don Román was offering himself as a powerful ally in achieving this goal.

He fanned open the contents of the envelope on the table. "Five hundred dollars. Too generous for a wedding gift. An amount suitable for a bribe, perhaps. But I thank you on behalf of Margarita and myself for this." He picked up a hundred-dollar note. "You have been most kind."

With a courtly bow, Miguel left.

"Yes," said Joaquín, the bank teller. "I see the point. Marriage is the only solution."

By now, Margarita was worn down. Fears for her family and desperation over her own situation had so hobbled her that she no longer had the will to resist.

"But," Joaquín continued in his analytical fashion, "you can't wait. It must be done today. Romancito doesn't leave town until tomorrow. That gives him plenty of time for mischief if he chooses."

"That's what I think too, but Father Alfredo won't hear of it," replied Miguel.

"We can change his mind."

"But how? He said that there are rules. The Church."

"Aha. I'll tell you about Church rules. Something the Church definitely forbids."

"What?"

"You, my brother, are forbidden to live in sin. You are forbidden marriage outside the Church."

Miguel threw his hands up. "Well, I know that."

"And that's exactly what you're going to do."

"What?"

"It's simple. You're going to be married by the judge."

"*Es un pecado.*"

"Exactly. A sin you must commit to get what you want. Listen to me. First we talk to the county clerk. Ignacio Garduño owes me a favor. We'll make him open up the courthouse and issue a marriage license. Then we'll talk to Judge Armenta. He was one of Papá's best friends and he hates the priest. He'll marry you."

"But we can't do that. I don't want to be excommunicated. Besides, Mamacita would kill me!"

"Hear me out, brother dear. Once we have you married by the law, we'll take a walk over to Father Alfredo's. He'll be furious, of course, but he can't let you live in sin, can he? He'll have to marry you in the Church. No banns, no inquiries, no instructions."

For a moment, Miguel sat in awe. Then he stood up and hugged his brother with almost the same force as when he had mauled Romancito.

"Let go, you fool," gasped Joaquín, "you're breaking my ribs."

And, no surprise to Joaquín, his plan went flawlessly.

The county clerk who owed the favor issued the license. The judge who had loved Miguel's father and hated the priest married the couple. And the priest, who was indeed furious, blessed the union.

Early the next morning, Miguel rose quietly and left his room in the house of his mother to dress in the kitchen so as not to disturb his bride.

Margarita's eyes were closed but she was not asleep, had not been all night. She heard the front door close when her husband left the house for work. She heard his steps recede down the sidewalk and meld into the morning sounds of barking dogs and crowing cocks.

And Margarita continued to lie in her marriage bed.

She was wed to a man she barely knew, much less loved. What had become of her dreams? What about her unwavering belief that one day she would be somebody? In Margarita's world, so replete with separation, this farewell to her hopes was the most wrenching of all.

She turned her face to the pillow and shook and sobbed for a long time. Then, slowly, she came to grips with her reality. From this moment on she was the wife of a butcher.

Nothing less. Nothing more.

Chapter Twenty

1930–1935

Every morning, Miguel was out the door at dawn to open the store for the daily deliveries. Every night he was home at seven for his supper. This was his routine week in and week out, six days out of seven. The energy he had expended during his courtship of Margarita was evaporated and unrenewable.

"We're married," he explained to her. "We don't need dances and parties. It's time to stay home and start raising a family."

Miguel also insisted that she quit her job at the dry-goods store. "I can support us."

Her life in the house of her mother-in-law, Francisquita Galván, was as undemanding as the old woman could make it. Margarita learned to cook the foods that Miguel liked. She helped with the housework, cleaning, and laundry, but with only two adults and herself to care for, the work consumed almost no time. Thus she found herself with little to do for the greater part of each day. She took long walks, sometimes alone, sometimes with her mother-in-law. They visited the sick, bringing hot soup and warm comfort. They went to church to arrange for Masses for the deceased or to light candles for the living. Francisquita gave her an embroidery frame and they sat for long hours discussing stitches, patterns, threads, and colors. On Sundays after Mass the newlyweds and the old woman joined the rest of the family for dinner, a movable feast where Francisquita's children ate, talked, and fortified themselves to face another week of unchanging routine.

It was not enough to satisfy. Then, even the delicious temptation to dream of what might have been with Romancito Ortiz was denied her when the young man turned up dead in his apartment hideaway. An enraged husband, whose wife was experiencing the very attentions that Margarita only dared imagine in her bed next to a snoring Miguel, had knifed Romancito in the heart. And any fantasy she may have harbored for escaping her fate—back to Denver, to the

California that Miguel detested, anywhere away from Las Vegas—was smothered two months after her marriage when she became pregnant.

Miguel was ecstatic. The sisters-in-law were a gaggle of clucks and giggles. The brothers were all over Miguel with backslaps, knowing winks, and elbows to the ribs. Francisquita became more solicitous than ever and forbade her strenuous work. This made Margarita's days stretch out even longer. It was all almost enough for her to yearn for the chaos of her father's house.

When my oldest brother was born they called him Miguelito. He was beautiful, and while his delivery was easy, his first breaths were not.

"Here is your baby, Margarita," the nun announced, her achingly white, severely starched habit fairly crackling as she passed over the bundle to the new mother.

"We're not very happy about his color. Nursing him should perk him up."

Once the nun was gone, Margarita lay stiffly with the infant tucked in her arm. She had held her share of babies. Tamar dropped them in her lap with regularity and her instincts for mothering were good. But now she was so depressed, so immersed in a feeling of helpless ensnarement, that she could not find it in herself to draw the child to her bosom.

But the infant would not be denied. It began to move and to make low clicking noises with its waxy bow lips. At last she unbuttoned the top of her nightgown and exposed one of her small, tender breasts. It was nothing close to the splendid brown bounty that Tina's mother had presented to her toddler son in the pueblo at Picurís. She adjusted the crook of her arm to position the child's mouth against her. The infant moved its head from side to side, found the nipple, and began to suck contentedly.

"Now there are two of us," Margarita whispered to the child. "What are we ever going to do?"

Thus it was that the mother bonded with her infant, as cellmates, as allies, perhaps eventually as escapees.

Miguelito's color did not improve over the next twenty-four hours.

His lips and the tips of his fingers and toes were now an even deeper shade of blue and purple.

After careful examination the doctor met with Margarita and Miguel. He was not known for beating around the bush. "I'm afraid the news isn't good. Your baby has a septal defect in his heart. He was born with it. There's a leakage of blood because the holes in the partitions between the heart chambers are not closing properly. Some of the blood on one side of the heart is not mixing with oxygenated blood. This causes a loss of color under the skin and at the extremities. You might have heard the term *blue baby*? Your son is a blue baby."

Margarita and Miguel understood little of what the doctor said. But they knew what mattered. Miguelito's heart was not sound.

Margarita tried to sift through the doctor's words. "What can you do?"

"Well, surgery is out of the question. We just don't know enough. Especially in the newborn. Sometimes nature takes care of it and finishes its work after the baby is out of the womb. There's nothing to be done right now. Just wait. And maybe pray for a miracle."

The doctor believed in only one kind of miracle in cases like this—death. It would offer closure. There would be time for other babies.

When the doctor left them, Miguel cried with his wife, kissed her, and went back to work. Shortly thereafter, the nun came in with Miguelito for his feeding. Margarita took the baby in her arms and lost her control in sobs.

"Now, now, Margarita. These things have a way of working out. And besides, there's always prayer. That can be the best medicine of all, you know."

"Will you pray with me, Sister?"

"Of course I will. In fact, all the sisters will. Have you heard of the Little Flower?"

"No, Sister."

"She was a French nun, Ste. Thérèse of Lisieux. A Carmelite. She died when she was barely twenty-four, about your age. The poor dear was always very sickly, but she never complained. The Holy Father just canonized her about five years ago. Anyway, since she's such a new saint, she's still anxious to please, don't you think? Everyone who turns to her seems to have their prayers answered. It's amazing. Why don't we ask her to help your baby?"

"Oh yes, Sister. Please, let's pray to her."

A sudden grimness crept into the nun's face and she drew back. "There's only one thing. A nasty little habit she has. Who could imagine it in so gentle a soul? When she grants a petition she always manages to take something in return. Does that frighten you?"

"No, Sister. If she helps my baby, I'll give her anything she asks."

"Are you sure, now? Are you quite sure?"

"Yes. Yes, I am."

And so prayers spiraled upward from the chapel of the nuns at St. Anthony's Hospital and from the mouth of Margarita while she sat with her child by the window of her hospital room.

By week's end, Miguelito had improved dramatically, so much so that the doctor once again convened a meeting with the baby's parents. Again, his words were unvarnished, to the point.

"Your baby seems fine now. I've never seen so remarkable a recovery. You are lucky. That's all I can say. If you'd like, you can take him home tomorrow."

What the doctor could not admit was that he had, in all likelihood, misdiagnosed the problem. There could be no other explanation since, as already noted, he did not believe in miracles.

But the nuns were under no such constraint.

"How else to explain it?" the same nun said to Margarita.

"I will pray to Ste. Thérèse always," Margarita vowed to her. "She is my baby's special saint."

Eighteen months later, Margarita and Miguel had another baby, a second son, who was named Luis. This time the birth was not so easy as he had not been expected for another month. Miguel and Francisquita had left early that morning for Santa Fe to represent the family at the funeral of a great-uncle. Margarita, because she was so far along and had not been feeling very well, stayed at home. Her sister-in-law, María, came by.

"Just get some rest," she said. "I'll take Miguelito off your hands."

The pains began at midmorning and by the afternoon they were white-hot rods that bore into every cavity of her lower body. She sat heavily in a chair for she could neither stand nor lie down without the sensation that she would faint. Finally, she realized that the pain was not abating and that she must find help. She struggled to her feet and made toward the front door. After four or five halting steps she could feel the darkness springing up around her, a whirling, stygian cylinder that enveloped her and sent her to the floor. When she finally came to it was early evening. She did not have the strength to stand so she crawled to the front door, out on the porch, and onto the sidewalk, where she again slipped into unconsciousness.

A neighbor found her there and with help from a passing motorist took her to the hospital.

"You are a very lucky young woman," the doctor informed her. "You could easily have bled to death. As it is, your baby is fine, a little blue but nothing serious. None of the problems you had with Miguelito. You're going to need a lot of rest after this one. And don't even think about breast feeding. This one is a bottle baby."

She was in and out of wakefulness for a full three days, unsure whether the images that formed and dispersed around her were real or snatches of illusion. There were Miguel, Francisquita, Leopoldo, and Tamar. There were nuns in white and black. There were aides in blue. And intermingled with these visits were those by Tía Adela, Doña Prisca, and even Don José Argüello, the woodcarver. In time, the mists cleared and she could distinguish the two mounds that her feet made under the sheets at the far end of the bed. She could taste the flatness of the tepid water that was carefully tipped into her mouth from a glass held by an aide. Finally, she was strong enough and alert enough to receive her new baby.

The nun handed the baby to Margarita along with a bottle of formula. "He's a hungry one, all right."

Margarita lay with little Luis, listening to the sounds he made as he sucked at the rubber nipple. She looked out the window. She looked at the flower arrangement on her bedside stand. She watched the ever-dropping level of milk in the inverted bottle as though she had been hypnotized. But she could not look at the child. Finally, when the baby had begun to suck in more air than milk, she pulled the nipple from his protesting mouth and examined his face. Here was no Miguelito, no angel with a crown of pink-gold ringlets and the Dutch blue eyes of his grandpa Leopoldo. Even as newborns go, Luis was homely, his face broad and his features flat and coarse, his head long and ungraceful, very definitely Tamar's grandchild.

She would grow to love him. But this child would be no soulmate. From Miguelito's birth he had been her ally, her coconspirator as she fantasized over their escape from her butcher's-wife prison. The child that she now held would be an iron ball that she would have to drag behind her. Flight, even the thought of it, was now impossible. With the coming of Luis, any thought of deliverance died.

In Las Vegas, New Mexico, the Great Depression was a redundancy. Once the railroad shops were gone and most of the banks were closed in the early twenties, the market crash of 1929 was a mere formality. In fact, in one way, the people of Las Vegas had the advantage over their fellow Americans, since they already had a leg up on misery.

Ironically, Leopoldo was one of few who benefited from the collapse. The company that had bought out his lumbering operation in the mountains beyond Guadalupita went bankrupt. The local bank now held the timber rights and all the equipment in receivership. When the bank president mentioned to Miguel's brother Joaquín, the teller, that they were looking for someone to keep the mill running while they considered their options, he thought immediately of Margarita's father. Leopoldo jumped at the offer. Tamar was apoplectic but it was too late. Her husband had already quit his job with the utilities company. The Zamoras—the husband and wife, the two oldest sons, Eugenio and Gerónimo, and the two youngest, Elisandro and Constancia—loaded up and took to the road. Agapita, the middle daughter, had been farmed out the year before to a cousin in Taos.

"Leave Alfonso here for some schooling," Margarita urged her father. "Eugenio and Gerónimo are old enough to help out at the mill but Alfonso is too young. At least let him finish the eighth grade." At least give him a chance, was what she wanted to say. Maybe he'll make better use of his opportunities than I did.

Leopoldo fought the idea but Tamar jumped at the prospect of relieving herself of one more of her children. So Alfonso stayed behind and moved into the dwindling space of Francisquita's house.

Even as Joaquín was making arrangements for Leopoldo to take over the sawmill he was informed that his hours at the bank would increase with no reflection in his paycheck.

"We're letting two employees go," his boss explained. "I'll probably be spending some time in the teller's cage myself."

It was at this time that the Galván family fortunes and misfortunes converged.

While Miguel built up the store's reputation for having the best meat market in town, while he put in fourteen hours a day, six days a week, stocking and cleaning, butchering and selling, his partner, Juanito, was letting the business slip slowly through their fingers. Juanito bought too much inventory. He allowed himself to buy from suppliers who flattered him then charged him top dollar. He opened up credit accounts for friends and acquaintances who had no means nor intention of paying. While Miguel had stoked the boiler, painted the decks, and polished the brass, his brother had allowed their tiny ship of commerce to run aground.

One Saturday evening after closing the grocery store, Juanito called Miguel into his office, actually a small alcove leading into the stock room. As usual with Juanito, every surface of the scarred roll-top desk was buried in clutter. On top of it all, and the only article that seemed to be deliberately in place, was a ledger opened to the entries for the current month.

"I don't think we can keep the store open," Juanito declared. "We owe everybody and everybody owes us."

Miguel leaned heavily against the doorway. "*¿Pero por qué?* We have lots of customers. We have full shelves and a full meat case and people are always coming in to buy things."

"But they don't pay. Don't you see? No one has money to pay. Look here."

Juanito started running down the columns of numbers.

After several minutes of hearing his brother drone on, Miguel reached over and slammed the book shut. "Stop it. You come with me."

"Where are you going?"

"To Joaquín. To someone who knows about such things."

Joaquín's eyes followed his thin finger as it inched down the rows of figures. "This is not good."

Miguel and Juanito sat silently and watched.

"Not good at all." He straightened up from the book and removed his glasses to rub the bridge of his nose.

"I could have told you that," Juanito said.

Joaquín turned a page of the book. "And what, my brother, do you intend to do about this mess?"

"What *can* we do? Shut the store. Maybe I'll go into house painting with Labán. He says he can use the help. I can start with him next week if I want."

Miguel gaped at Juanito. This was betrayal.

"Why do you look at me like that?" Juanito shot back.

"You knew all along what was happening and you didn't say anything to me? What were you waiting for? Making sure you had another job first?"

Juanito jumped up from the table and stuck his finger in Miguel's face. "And what's your problem? You had a place to work for six years because of me."

Miguel stood and brushed his brother's hand away. "I already had a job. I'd probably be managing the drugstore by now, maybe even with a chance to own some of it. But then you came with all your big talk and promises."

Joaquín tamped at the air with open hands. "Sit down, both of you, and stop shouting. There are people living on the other side of this wall. Do you want everybody to know our business?"

Miguel slumped into his chair. Juanito turned his back in disgust and strode to the window to look out into the backyard.

"Now then," Joaquín continued. "It's easy enough to say you're going to close the store. It's not so easy to do it. You have debts to pay. Taxes are due. You have to get rid of inventory and fixtures. Sometimes it's harder to close a business than to keep it running."

In his rage against Juanito, Miguel had consumed the last of his reserves. His shoulders sagged. "Do you have any ideas, Joaquín? Anything?"

"There's only one way that I can see. First, Juanito, you're out. Talk to Labán tomorrow and get on with your life. You've lost the business and that's all there is to it."

Juanito shrugged his shoulders in indifference.

"Second, starting now, Miguel, I am your new partner. I'm practically on notice at the bank. It's just a matter of time.

Miguel opened his mouth to commiserate, but Joaquín cut him off with a wave of his hand.

"I've already settled the whole thing in my mind. I'll work at the bank until they let me go. The rest of the time I'll work at the store, mainly on the business end of things. Miguel, you'll have to run the store by yourself for a while."

"I will, I promise you. Whatever it takes. I'll even sleep there if I have to."

"I'll talk to the suppliers. See what we can work out. They don't want us to go out of business. What good does that do them? And starting Monday, it's cash and carry. I don't know how much we can collect from the outstanding accounts but something is better than nothing. Even ten cents on the dollar. And then it's one day at a time. Buy a quart of milk for a nickel and sell it for a dime. Cash. Always cash."

Miguel was actually getting excited. There was reason for hope.

Nor had Joaquín's words been lost on Juanito. He had turned from the window while Joaquín was detailing his plan and he was now listening intently. Finally he cleared his throat. "Of course," he said, "I do have a considerable investment in the store. I just can't walk away and leave everything, you know."

Joaquín turned to him and smiled sourly. He closed the book and held it out to his brother. "Fine, Juanito, don't walk away. In fact, here you are. Go ahead. Take it."

"Don't get me wrong," Juanito stammered. "I think your plan is excellent and I certainly don't want to stand in the way. But," and his voice slipped up an octave, "I think I deserve something."

"Yes, you do, and here it is. Over two thousand dollars in debts. Over a thousand dollars in uncollectibles. Over four hundred in taxes. You want what you deserve? Here. It's all yours."

Joaquín laid the ledger carefully on the floor and slid it across the linoleum with a sweep of his hand. It stopped when it bumped against the toe of Juanito's shoe.

"Be reasonable, Joaquín. I need something."

"All right, here's the offer. Fifteen dollars a week in free groceries for a year. That should help you out while you get started with

Labán. And for that you sign a paper giving up all claim to the store. That's the best you can hope for, and more than you're entitled to."

Juanito signed the papers. Perhaps the settlement was not of the same biblical proportions as Esau's selling out to Jacob for a bowl of lentil stew. However, in the modest setting of Las Vegas, New Mexico, Juanito sold what might pass in those parts as his birthright for fifteen dollars a week in free groceries for a year.

The store was making money within three months after Joaquín instituted his regime. It was a turnaround that surprised even him. He decided, however, not to share the good news with Miguel. At first he did not want to raise false hopes. But then, recognizing his leverage as long as Miguel thought they were in trouble, he kept the news of their steady progress to himself. Long after the store was reasonably solvent, Joaquín maintained the fiction that they were still one late payment away from being closed down. And, Miguel, so totally involved in the daily running of the store, so trusting, never thought to question his brother.

In time, Joaquín was able to convince himself that, indeed, Miguel had every reason to regard him as a savior. For this reason he felt justified in taking more from the store for his own pocket than he permitted Miguel to have. He also stopped remembering that, without Miguel, who was its heart and soul, there would have been no store at all.

When, after six months, he and his wife bought a house and moved out of their duplex, Joaquín explained to Miguel that he had been saving for years.

Miguel was happy for him.

Margarita was nowhere near as generous. "How is it that you do all the work and Joaquín has the money to buy a house?"

"Because he made money at the bank and saved it."

"Then why is Marigold always telling me how little he earns?"

"Marigold doesn't understand these things. Joaquín is a very smart man and doesn't tell her everything, you know. He's good with money."

"It's money he's making on your back. You're not his partner, you're his slave."

Miguel was shocked at Margarita's mutinous outburst and for one of the few times in their entire marriage he lost his temper with her. "Joaquín saved the store. How can you be so ungrateful? Without him we wouldn't have anything. Now that's the last word on the subject."

But it wasn't. Margarita would not permit it. She resented the bondage into which Miguel had sold them. She refused to be beholden to Joaquín for every extra dime he gave them. She seethed when Marigold came over to talk about the electric refrigerator or the washing machine Joaquín had surprised her with. It was a constant aggravation to her the way they were treated like poor relations. She grew tired of hearing from Miguel and Marigold how wonderful Joaquín was, how smart he was, how selfless he was, how hard he worked for them all.

As for Joaquín, he stayed as clear of Margarita as possible. He knew that she had not been buffaloed like her husband. So he made sure that Miguel always stood as a buffer between them.

Miguel did not care about any of this so long as he had his store. Galván's Grocery and Meat Market had become his passion. It took on the trappings of a real person for him, one whose deathbed he had attended, whose miraculous recovery he had witnessed, and whose continuing health he embraced. *La Tienda*. You could almost hear the italics when he said the words. The store was something he grew to cherish almost as much as his own family. He went so far as to give it a place of prominence in his daily prayers. Every night before he went to bed and every Sunday at Mass he prayed in no particular order for Margarita, Francisquita, Miguelito, Luis, and *La Tienda*.

For all of Joaquín's business savvy, he had a flaw. This fact was brought to his attention in chilling fashion one morning while he manned his teller cage at the bank.

"Joaquín," the bank manager informed him, "the examiners will be in next Wednesday. Make sure you're available in case they have any questions."

There had never been any questions before. Joaquín was a slave to detail and his books were meticulous. More than once, the visiting inspectors had complimented him on his work. They even suggested that he apply for a job with the state banking commission.

But now there would be questions.

Flush with his success in righting the fortunes of the grocery store, Joaquín became practically flamboyant at the bank. The fact that he was on borrowed time made it all the easier for him to assume a somewhat cavalier attitude with the bank's money. If he promised Marigold a trip to Santa Fe over the weekend for dinner and some shopping, he thought nothing of pocketing thirty or forty dollars from his till before he left the bank on Friday. The next week he would juggle books and move monies around until he was able to dip into the cash box at the store to erase the shortage.

What's the harm? They didn't pay him enough. He was working like a dog for them and they showed no loyalty toward him.

His larceny was also abetted by the fact that no one at the bank knew more about the books than he. This made him more willing to take risks. Sometimes weeks would go by before he replaced the money he had taken. Instead, he worked the books with his usual flair, deriving almost sexual pleasure from his flirtation with discovery and disaster.

But now the bank examiners were coming.

How much was he short? He would have to stay late that night and figure it all out. Now there was nothing for it but to check his figures, raid the cash box at the store, and get the money back to the bank by Tuesday next at the latest.

"Staying late, Joaquín?" His boss, hat and coat in hand, stopped at the counter on his way out the door.

"Just a couple of things I want to recheck. You know how those examiners are."

"Well, don't stay too long. It's the weekend, after all."

When Joaquín was finally alone he began his review of the books. At several steps along the way he found himself stumped by his own cleverness. He had to think long and hard about the chronology of his transfers, the amounts he had moved around, the winding paths he had taken to hide the shortages.

When he was finally finished and studied his worksheet he was stunned. There was a sudden, uncomfortable looseness in his sphincter, a clamminess in his hands. He was presently showing a debit of eight hundred and forty-seven dollars and sixty-three cents. This was no longer borrowing. It was a bona fide embezzlement.

Why had he been so careless, so arrogant, so stupid? How could he come up with over eight hundred dollars by the next week? He reshelved the books, turned off the lights, locked the door, and trudged home, disconsolate and very much afraid.

By nature, Joaquín was not a thief, present evidence to the contrary. What had happened? His heady success with the revival of the store and his growing resentment toward the bank were only incidental to the real reason he had strayed. His ultimate fall from grace could be placed directly at the long, narrow feet of his wife, Marigold.

The Las Vegas of the thirties operated under a peculiar set of standards, a malaise that hung on well into the sixties. To wit, it was better to be Anglo than Hispanic. Anglos, or so went the conventional wisdom, were smarter, better looking, cleaner, more industrious, and more virtuous. It was even considered flattering among some Hispanics to be mistaken for Anglo. In fact, the ultimate compliment one could pay to the proud parents of a Hispanic baby was to say, "*¡Qué bonito!* It looks like an *americano.*"

Joaquín had met her at the bank when she came to cash a check, her stipend from serving as a live-in companion to one of the widowed dowagers who peopled the rows of Victorian houses on Seventh Street in New Town. She was from Oklahoma. Her father had been a dirt farmer, one of the early casualties of the Dust Bowl. She was on her way to California but her money only got her as far as Las Vegas.

Joaquín declared himself the luckiest man on earth on the day she agreed to marry him. Perception can be bliss. Reality is sometimes not so kind.

Marigold might be blue-eyed and blond but to the gringos across the river she was no more and no less than what she was, an Okie. So, as it turned out, Marigold was not Joaquín's entree into polite Anglo society, but rather he was hers into the more tolerant Hispanic community of Old Town.

The word for Marigold was rawboned. There was no softness whatsoever about her. Her entire skeleton seemed to be lurking just beneath the surface of her epidermis waiting to burst through. On every part of her body where there was a protuberance of something bony—from her forehead to her cheeks, the bridge of her nose, and her chin; from her clavicles to her shoulders, scapulae, elbows, wrists, knuckles, and finger joints; from her sternum to her rib cage, hip bones, coccyx, knees, ankles, and toes—there were vivid splotches of red where the hardness pushed through, contrasting with the blue-tinged pallor of her skin. Her hair was the color of dull straw. Her eyes were pastel blue, shallow and teary.

But she was Anglo.

Along with her physical liabilities Marigold was also of a decidedly prickly bent. She complained. She nagged. She badgered. She never tired of reminding Joaquín that he had practically shanghaied her off the train.

"And for what? To keep me here in this godforsaken place? As soon as I find the money I'll be on the first train out."

Her constant threat was Joaquín's constant fear.

That is why his brothers, Miguel and Juanito, did not matter. Only Marigold meant anything.

"We have the store now. Things are going to change," he promised her.

"We'll see."

And things did change. There was a new home with new furnishings. She had clothes. They took trips. But, of course, it was never enough.

"When are we going to get a car? Why do I have to walk or take a taxi every time I want to go someplace? What good is a store if we still have to live like this?" She had started to say, "live like Miguel and Margarita," but decided that was a bit presumptuous even for her.

So Joaquín took more than he should from the store and cooked his books at the bank. And now, because of his obsession with Marigold, he owed the better part of eight hundred and fifty dollars.

The next day, Saturday, Joaquín spent his time in his cubicle at the store, running figures and calculating assets and ready resources. The store had about two hundred dollars in cash. They would probably realize another three hundred in sales between today and Tuesday. Still not enough. If he sold the refrigerator, the diamond ring, and the wristwatch he had just bought for Marigold, he could get another two hundred dollars. Marigold would be a fury to live with but better to dwell in her hell than the one that surely awaited him in a federal prison.

But he was still one hundred and fifty dollars short.

That evening, after they had closed the store, Joaquín summoned Miguel to his office. It was eerily reminiscent of the meeting that Juanito had convened in this very spot so many months before. The same fateful ledger lay open on the desk.

"We've got a problem. Things have not been going as well as I might have led you to believe."

Once again Miguel felt himself go limp and leaned heavily against the door frame.

"What do you mean?"

"I've tried to keep up with our bills and pay us both a salary but it's just not working. Here, look at this." Joaquín began a declamation of the esoterica of the ledger.

Again, and Joaquín was counting on this, Miguel understood little of what he was hearing. This time, however, since it was Joaquín, the all-knowing Joaquín, and not Juanito who was doing the explaining, he did not interrupt. His hope was that his brother would not only define the problem but also propose the solution.

"And so there it is. We owe over eight hundred dollars that we have to come up with by Tuesday. We'll have about five hundred from the store. I'm willing to sell my refrigerator and some of Marigold's jewelry. My question to you is, what can you do to help? We need a hundred and fifty dollars from you to stay in business."

"I don't know."

Joaquín hid his guilt with anger. "You can't always leave it up to me, you know. It's time for you to take some responsibility."

That night Miguel's prayers did not include Margarita, Miguelito, Luis, and Francisquita. He prayed only for the store. The same was true the next morning at Mass. *La Tienda.*

Later he excused himself from the customary family gathering.

"I have to go talk to some friends," was the only explanation he would give. He was not lying. From these friends, five in all, he was able to borrow eighty dollars by the end of the day.

That night, after the children and Francisquita were in bed, he sat Margarita down and unburdened himself. "I have eighty dollars that I borrowed today. I told my friends I'd pay them back when I could. The money that I gave you on Friday for bills, how much do you have left?"

Margarita had been listening to Miguel in silence. His question opened the floodgates. "What is Joaquín doing to us? First he treats you like a slave and now he expects you to give him back·the little money he throws at you?"

"Margarita. Please. Not now. He's done as much as he can. He's already sold some of his own things . . ."

"Things he bought with your money."

"Seventy dollars. I have to find seventy dollars more."

So this is what it was to be married to a butcher's wife. She went to the cupboard, drew out some money from underneath a large bowl, and laid the bills out in front of Miguel.

"Here. Twenty-five dollars. Fifteen dollars I owe the doctor for Miguelito. Ten dollars I was going to use for some shoes for the boys. That's all I have."

Miguel raised his head, smiled wanly, and patted her hand. Then he left the room. Moments later he was back, carrying an old, worn sock. He took it by the toe and shook it. Out tumbled two twenty-dollar gold pieces, making their distinctive ring as they fell together to the table top. They were the coins given him by Jack Johnson and Tom Mix. Even Margarita, from whom he hid nothing, had never known about them.

On Tuesday evening, after everyone had left the bank, Joaquín made his surreptitious deposit. The next day the examiners came. When they were done they had no questions for Joaquín. As usual they praised him for the fine way he kept his books. After the auditors left, Joaquín's boss also congratulated him, but tempered his enthusiasm with regrets that they would be letting him go at month's end.

Miguel was more grateful than ever to his brother, who had once more saved the day. Marigold did not speak to Joaquín for a good two weeks and only then when he presented a plan to her by which she could redeem the goods he had sold from under her sharp, red nose. Margarita kept her peace, but Joaquín, more than ever, avoided being alone with her.

In time, everything settled down. Marigold got her jewelry and refrigerator back and a new radio for her pains. Miguelito's doctor bill was eventually paid. The boys made do for a while longer with their old shoes.

But the two gold pieces were gone forever.

241

Chapter Twenty-One

A year after the incident at the bank, when the store was once again on its feet, and after much lobbying by Margarita, Miguel moved his family out of his mother's home and into a street-level apartment on the corner of the plaza almost diagonal from *La Tienda*. Alfonso stayed on with Francisquita.

Naturally, my mother would have preferred a house of her own such as Marigold had, but at least this was a step in the right direction. She now set about the task of creating her own household. The apartment was already furnished, so she concentrated her efforts on painting rooms, lining cupboards and drawers with bright cheerful shelf paper, sewing curtains, and hanging pictures cut carefully from old calendars.

The boys were three and two now, and she spent many hours with them in the grassy inner area of the plaza. She sat under the same cottonwood tree that had shaded her as a girl while she waited for her father to unload his truck at the lumberyard. She no longer distracted herself with reveries of glass globes and porcelain castles blanketed with imitation snow. Now her eyes were those of a she-bear watching over her cubs. Luis was still clumsy on his feet and preferred to squat next to his mother to play with the dirt between the exposed roots of the tree. Miguelito was another matter altogether. He was agile and curious about everything, particularly if it tested the invisible cord that secured him to his mother.

"Don't go too far, Miguelito," Margarita constantly called.

Invariably he did, and his mother would have to gather up a grunting Luis and follow after her eldest. The chase was on. He laughed and stayed just out of reach. She tried to be angry but the sight of him, all giggle and tease and so thoroughly a joy, was too infectious and soon she was laughing along with him. Their game ended only when he allowed his attention to wander to something else. When his mother approached him he was already onto the new thing, appropriately solemn or silly as the situation dictated.

"Look, Mamá, look. There in the tree. A bird. What's it doing?"

Margarita followed his finger to the low limb of a maple tree where a feisty, dark-eyed junco pecked at the bark.

"He's looking for bugs to eat."

The boy wrinkled his nose. "Bugs. I couldn't eat bugs."

"If you were a bird, you could."

"And then I could fly, too, couldn't I?"

"Yes, you could fly, too."

"And I'd go far, far away."

"And leave me behind?"

"But if I was a bird then you'd be a bird too, Mamá," he noted brightly after a frowning moment of deep thought. "We could fly away together."

It was during one of these visits into the park that Margarita collided head on with her past. She had been there about an hour and was just gathering up the boys to walk across the street to Galván's Grocery.

A pickup truck pulled up not ten feet from them. The door on the cab read *New Mexico State Hospital*. In the open truck bed huddled a group of women. They all looked alike. Slack-mouthed, blank faces. Dull blue smocks, hair cut in straight, savage horizontal strokes high up the backs of their heads.

The driver and an attendant jumped from the truck and went around to the back and released the tailgate with a crash. "All right, ladies. Stay together. No wandering off."

Slowly, the passengers began to alight. There was no talking, no complaints, no sounds of excitement at the prospect of taking a stroll through the park. Their every effort was concentrated on the task of getting from the truck bed to the pavement.

"Who are those people?" Miguelito asked his mother.

"They're from the hospital."

"Are they sick?"

"In a way."

"Why aren't they in bed?"

"Because they're not that kind of sick. Now don't ask any more questions. It's not polite to talk about people."

"Is that little girl sick, too?"

Up to this point, Margarita had avoided looking directly at the women. But the mention of a child among the patients piqued her curiosity and she looked over to the group, now a tightly bunched flock on the sidewalk.

"There are no little girls at this hospital," she began, and then stopped.

It was immediately obvious whom Miguel was talking about. To one side of the group was a tiny woman, well under five feet and weighing no more than seventy or eighty pounds. She turned her face toward them just as Margarita saw her.

It was the Indian bondservant, Nasha.

The years had left few marks on Nasha. Her hair was not as black as it once had been, but her skin was still smooth and unlined and she stood as straight and strong as ever. Only as Margarita approached did she notice Nasha's eyes. Those once black and lustrous almonds were now yellow, mucous coated, and unblinking.

"Nasha."

Nasha raised her head at the sound, smiled, and gently placed her small, brown hand on Margarita's cheek.

"Margarita. *Angelita*."

Even after more than a dozen years, during which Margarita had grown into womanhood, married, and twice become a mother, Nasha, responding only to her inner vision, had recognized her little angel immediately.

Margarita freed her hand from Miguelito's grasp and brought it up to cover that of the Indian. Then wordlessly she moved Nasha's caressing fingers from her cheek to her mouth to kiss them and tasted her own tears.

The night in the decaying house in Guadalupita when Doña Prisca had beaten her mercilessly, Nasha stumbled outside into the darkness. But she did not go far. Barely able to walk, she found refuge in an elevated wooden shed used to store sacks of feed grain.

Early the next morning, through a gap between the door and its frame, Nasha witnessed an unholy procession of two walking to a barren depression by an arroyo. She heard Filiberto's shovel break through the packed earth and the dull thuds of adobe-hard dirt landing to one side. She saw Doña Prisca set a bundle into the shallow hole. She saw Filiberto refill it. She heard Doña Prisca's unheeded plea for prayers. She waited until she heard the door to the kitchen slam shut. Then she slithered down the wooden steps of the shed, worked her way slowly into the arroyo, and circled back. With her hand, she raked across the mound of the newly turned grave. She pulled some of the dirt to her, cupped it in her hands, sprinkled some of it on the top of her head, and fiercely rubbed the rest over her face. Then she sat back on her heels and began to rock and to sing.

> "*Hati pam'one*, Precious little blossom,
> *Tcakwil 'a'eye*, Come to me.
> *'Amaxutcetci*, Let me hold you."

After many minutes she crawled up and out onto flat ground. The arroyo now cut between her and the house. She covered her flight by creeping from tree to boulder to bush until the dark hulk of the hacienda was swallowed up in the low-hanging morning mist.

She walked across the mountains for three days, sustained by the roots and succulents she knew so well.

On the evening of the third day she stumbled into the village of Rodarte. There a kindly old woman gave her something to eat and drink and permitted her to sleep on her porch.

The next morning, before her benefactress was up, Nasha was on the road again toward the rising sun. At midday, while she squatted alongside the road under the sparse shade of a spindly piñon tree, she heard the unmistakable sound of iron-rimmed wagon wheels biting into the hard pack of the road.

A man braked to a stop next to her. "Where are you going?"

Nasha lifted her arm wearily and pointed down the road.

"Are you Picurís?"

At the mention of the pueblo that had disowned her when she was a mere five years old, Nasha shook her head vehemently.

"Taos?"

She recalled the cruelty of the two Taos women who had made life so unbearable for her in the house of Doña Prisca and shook her head again.

"San Juan?"

It was apparent that the man would not let it rest until Nasha admitted to a pueblo. She knew nothing about San Juan but it sounded as good as any. She nodded slowly.

"Well, I'm only going as far as Peñasco but if you want a ride you can come with me."

By the time they reached the village of Peñasco the farmer, relentless in his probing, had deduced that his passenger had no actual destination. She was rootless, with no pueblo to claim, no family to go to.

"You might as well stay with us," he said when he pulled in front of his house. "My wife can use the help. You'll have food, clothes on your back, and a place to sleep."

The offer turned into three years of hell. The farmer's wife starved and beat Nasha and made her sleep in a crawl space underneath the kitchen.

When she could stand it no longer, Nasha ran away. This time, unlike her pell-mell flight from Guadalupita, she prepared herself. For weeks she stored away bits and pieces of venison jerky she trimmed carefully from the main store hanging in the dispensa. She also kept back a dress that the farmer's wife had given her to let out. When she was ready, on a night when there was no moon, she crawled from underneath the kitchen floor and scurried away, always eastward.

By morning she reached the gorge that pinched the Río Grande into a muddy ribbon that snaked down from the Taos plateau. The river directed her downstream to the valley below, eventually to the outskirts of Española. There she found a secluded cove to bathe and change her clothes. Now, as presentable as she could make herself, she climbed up to the road, which was the town's main street.

Drawn by the smell of baking bread, she soon found herself at a bakery shop, where she knocked tentatively on the back door. When a man in a white apron and cap answered Nasha held out a five-cent piece, a coin that had fallen between the floorboards into the crawl space that had been her Peñasco prison. "*Una torta de pan, por favor, señor.*"

The man disappeared behind the door. In a moment he was back with a loaf of bread. "*Toma.* Baked yesterday. But it's perfectly good. Keep your nickel."

Nasha was not used to kindness from anyone, particularly men.

She broke off one end of the loaf, sat down by the door, and began to chew slowly.

"What is your pueblo?" the baker asked.

She remembered what had happened to her the last time she had been lured into such a conversation. Now, rather than risk an answer, she stood, shook the crumbs from her skirt, and began to walk away.

"Do you know how to make bread?" the baker called after her.

The pueblos up and down the Río Grande were noted for the breads baked in their beehive-shaped hornos, and the baker had just that week lost his Indian helper.

Nasha brushed a stray hank of hair from her face before nodding.

"I might be able to use you."

Within an hour of her arrival in Española, Nasha was employed in the first real job she had ever held. For four years she toiled for the bread she ate, for hand-me-downs, and for a living space in the attic above the shop.

But then the hard times hit Española and the bakery faced fore-closure.

"What will we do with Nasha?" the baker asked his wife.

"Why should we worry about her? We have troubles enough."

But the baker was a good Catholic and he fretted about his duty toward the Indian. When times got better, as they always did, would God forget about him and his wife because they did not take care of Nasha?

So the next time he had to drive the thirty miles into Santa Fe he took Nasha aside. "Pack up your clothes and take one of these loaves of bread. You're going with me."

Two hours later they were in the Santa Fe Plaza.

They drove slowly by the rows of Indians selling their wares under the portal of the Palace of the Governors. "There. Maybe your own people can help you now. God knows I've done my part."

With that he stopped the truck and motioned Nasha to get out. His Christian duty done, he drove away to leave her with her small bundle in the middle of the street. He did not look back, already self-congratulatory for his charity to a fellow human being, an Indian at that. God would surely not forget this kindness.

There was, of course, no reason for the Indians in the Santa Fe

Plaza to have the slightest interest in Nasha. On her part she, who had never lived among her own, felt no kinship. She sat on the curb and ate her bread. Then, realizing that there was nothing for her here, she walked a block east on Palace Avenue and slipped through a wrought-iron gate into a quiet retreat of footpaths winding through trees, lilac bushes, rose arbors, and gladioli beds. There she found a bench, lay down with her head on her bundle, and promptly went to sleep.

She awakened to the sudden coolness of the evening, sat up, and appraised her surroundings. She saw that she was actually in a large courtyard. Behind her loomed the massive stone fortress that was the Cathedral of St. Francis. In front of her rose a two-story territorial-style building turned at a ninety-degree angle to form an L.

Just then, a door opened and a nun stepped out onto the wooden veranda to shake out a dust mop.

Nasha knew little about nuns. But she did know that they were women dedicated to helping others. The thought of being left alone to survive the night in the alien environment of the biggest town she had ever seen was enough for her. Her well-honed mistrust of strangers notwithstanding, she approached the nun on the porch.

By sheer happenstance, or by the grace that God was already beginning to shower on the baker's good deed, Nasha had ventured into the rear *cercado* of St. Vincent's Hospital. The nuns who oper-ated the hospital were the Sisters of Charity, and true to their name, they immediately took in the Indian. They offered her a bath, found her clean clothes, fed her, and gave her a bed. It was the first night that Nasha had slept between sheets in the eight years since she had lived with Adela and Delfino Arellanes.

She stayed at the hospital for a month and earned her keep in the kitchen and the laundry. Then, after much inquiry among staff, patients, and visitors, the nuns found a permanent position for her as a charwoman at the state capitol.

For the next three years Nasha worked for the State of New Mexico. She mopped and polished floors, dusted furnishings, and scoured rest rooms. She made enough money to rent a one-room lodging on Don Gaspar Street for ten dollars a week and had enough left over to fill her other needs. It was as good a life as she could imagine for herself. Her work hours were regulated and, away from her job, she had a place that was her own and the freedom and leisure time to do as she pleased.

But Nasha was not meant for a life of ease. In her third year of independence and gainful employment, her world came crashing down yet again.

She was cleaning a stall in one of the women's rest rooms. No one had thought to alert her that the handyman had been through not ten minutes before to dump scoopfuls of granulated lye into all the drains.

Slow-running and overflowing toilets had led to words between the janitor and his boss. So it was that his mood was foul that morning when he made his rounds and it was with particular malice that he heaped measure upon measure of the caustic crystals into each offending receptacle. The one at which Nasha was now kneeling to clean had been more balky than the rest so the man had given it a quadruple dose of the chemical.

She scrubbed the bowl with her usual vigor and when she was done she pushed down on the flush lever.

Whatever witch's brew had been simmering unseen in the trap of the waste pipe, the churning of the water from the toilet bowl was all the provocation it needed. An instant after Nasha had flushed the commode her face was blasted by a belching plume of concentrated lye solution. Some of the mixture rushed up her nose and into her mouth. But the worst assault was to her eyes.

When the doctor removed the bandages several weeks later he found that her eyes were burned and scarred beyond reclamation. Nasha's world had turned into a smear of lights and shadows.

"What do we do with Nasha?" asked the maintenance supervisor. "She can't work anymore. She has no family."

"Send her to Las Vegas," one of his crew suggested.

"What's in Las Vegas?"

"The state hospital."

"But that's for crazy people."

The subordinate shrugged his shoulders. "What else can you do with a blind Indian?"

Nasha was delivered to the New Mexico State Hospital in Las Vegas. They cut her hair. They issued her a smock. They placed her in an open ward with other women who were considered no threat to themselves or to others. There, since she never complained and no one could tell whether behind the gelatinous bulbs that had been her eyes she wore the same blank stare as the other inmates, she fit in quite well.

She had been there just a year when her angel, Margarita, found her in the park.

The discovery of Nasha in residence not a mile and a half from the Old Town plaza opened a new and disturbing chapter in Margarita's life.

She spoke with the supervisor in charge of Nasha's ward and arranged for the Indian to spend time with her one or two afternoons each week.

For Nasha, the time spent with Margarita away from the hospital was therapeutic. For Margarita, it had just the opposite effect. It led her into dark moods of resentment and self-pity. Over the last four years, with two sons and a husband to care for, she had learned to live more and more for the day and less and less in the nettling thickets of her disappointments. But with Nasha back in the picture, she allowed herself to remember and to regret opportunities lost.

Their talk was nearly always about their days as protégé and guardian spirit. Together they reviewed the pages of their history in Mora with Don Delfino and Doña Adela Arellanes. The seasons were their bookmark. The mere mention of spring, for instance, opened up conversation about cleaning and planting, or visits by the damas of the community to the Arellanes parlor for the recitation of the rosary followed by tea and sugar buns. Say *summer* and they talked about picnics by the Mora River and long walks along rocky ridges above the town looking for wild strawberries. Talk of fall filled their nostrils with the smell of drying herbs and of corn steaming in the horno. Winter evoked memories of sitting around the kitchen stove to sew and gossip or to wrap themselves in a down-filled comforter to sit on the front porch and watch the snow fall gently across the valley.

It was enough to unearth within Margarita a long-interred cache of bitterness. Miguel noticed the change in her almost immediately. She was more distant, less patient with him and their situation. She began to complain with renewed rancor about their life compared to that of Joaquín and Marigold.

Miguel tried to lighten her spirits but it was an unfamiliar role for him.

One evening he brought out a brown paper package tied neatly in string. "Look what I have for you."

She opened it without comment and pulled out a bright red dress of stiff, sheeny taffeta with a scooped neck and a heavy brocade of small, tightly stitched roses across the bodice.

"Who gave you this?"

"I bought it. For you. I saw it in the window at the mercantile and I thought how pretty you would look in it."

She did not even bother to lift the dress out of its wrapping. "We can't afford it."

"I've taken care of it."

But Margarita was not done. "What's it for? Where am I supposed to wear it? To go to the park with the boys?"

"I thought you could wear it for special occasions."

"Well, we don't have any special occasions so you might as well take it back."

"But I want you to have it."

"I don't want it." And she stormed out of the room, leaving him to stare, dejected and rejected, at the husk of shimmering cloth in which he had thought she would find delight.

Miguel had no way of knowing that nothing he could do would please her, short of turning the clock back and allowing her to take a path that would never converge with his.

Using Nasha as the doorkeeper to her past became Margarita's obsession. Once she had settled the children down for a nap or in some quiet game so that she and Nasha could talk, the first words out of her mouth were invariably, "Remember when. . . ."

Often, Nasha would have no recollection of an event.

Then Margarita would badger her with an onslaught of detail. "How could you forget that?"

"I'm old now, Margarita. Sometimes it's hard to think back so far. But if you say that's how it was, I'm sure you are right.

The morning came when Margarita called the hospital and was told that Nasha was not available for a visit that day. When pressed, the woman on the other end of the line would only say that the rules had been changed.

Dr. Farrell Porter was unfulfilled.

He had been graduated close to the bottom of his class from medical school at the University of Indiana in Bloomington. His residency at the Methodist hospital in Gary was equally undistinguished. When he was done with his training he moved on to St. Louis to open up an office as a general practitioner. There he quickly discovered that he had no talent for the healing arts. Looking about for ways to salvage a medical degree that had cost his father dearly, he settled on psychiatry. It was a field where he felt he would not be pressed for results. Armed with a letter of recommendation from a family friend who was also a prominent contributor to the University of Michigan, Dr. Porter entered that institution's School of Psychiatry. Once again he graced the rear of his graduating class.

With his new degree handsomely framed, the doctor looked about for a place to hang it. He decided that his best bet was to go to a part of the country where none of his classmates would stake a claim. It was not long after that he found his niche as Assistant Director of Psychiatry at the New Mexico State Hospital in Las Vegas.

Here his talents blossomed, not as a healer of minds, but as a politician. He set his sights on befriending all the right people by finagling invitations to every smart salon in Santa Fe. So it was that, eight uninspired years later, when the chief administrator of the hospital dropped dead, Dr. Porter was in a position to move up. He drove to the capital and, with help from several patrons, he made a strong case for himself, first as interim director, later as the permanent appointee.

The dazzle of his self-promotion blinded Dr. Porter altogether to the fact that he was at best an incompetent administrator, and he soon became restless and dissatisfied. If he could head up this hospital, why could he not do the same in more congenial surroundings, say Chicago, Atlanta, or even California? But of course, to orchestrate such a move he would have to do something noteworthy enough to merit attention beyond the boundaries of New Mexico. In this he was stumped.

William Handley provided the answer. Mr. Handley was a salesman for a pharmaceutical company that had recently developed a series of experimental drugs for use on mental patients.

"We have approval for their use in test studies, Dr. Porter. But so far most hospitals are a little too conservative to give us a chance.

However, the results from Europe and South America are impressive. Any hospital in the States that agrees to use our products would put itself on the map. Guaranteed."

Dr. Porter had no interest in putting the New Mexico State Hospital on the map. The whole idea was to put himself somewhere far from Las Vegas. Mr. Handley's proposal could do that very thing. If the drugs proved a breakthrough therapy, the pharmaceutical company would make sure his name was ballyhooed. He could already envision articles about him in the medical journals, or even better, *Reader's Digest* or *The Saturday Evening Post*. And, of course, there would be the lecture circuit to consider before he settled down in some posh office.

And what if the drugs were less than advertised? Who would ever know beyond the walls of the hospital? It was a chance he was willing to take.

"What do you need from me?"

"Twenty patients would be ideal. But if you can't manage that, I'm sure the company would settle for ten."

"Twenty you need and twenty you shall have."

A week later, Dr. Porter received a letter of confirmation and a formal agreement from the drug company. The writer informed him that two representatives would be in Las Vegas within the month to set up the protocol.

"It would be preferable," the letter continued, "that the subjects for the program be selected by then. Appreciating your busy schedule, we would presume to urge you to begin your screening process immediately according to the enclosed parameters."

Dr. Porter glanced at the list of criteria. What he read caused him to shake his head and grunt with amusement at the demands of a research laboratory half a continent away. On the spot, he composed his own list. It contained but one item—whomever he could get.

He called in the supervisors from the different wards and gave them his instructions.

"We have the opportunity to do some good here. I need twenty people. These things can be touchy. It would be best to select patients who have no strong family ties. Transients. Anyone who's been abandoned to our care. You know what I'm looking for."

If anyone fit this single criterion, it would be a ward of the state. It would be Nasha.

And so Nasha became Subject #16, female, mid-fifties, diagnosed as antisocial, non-communicative, and probably suffering with complications from clinical melancholia. Her regimen, as set up by the two people who had arrived from the East to manage the program, was convulsive shock treatment. This would be accomplished through an aggressive use of the drug pentylenetetrazol.

The therapy came to Nasha courtesy of Ludwig von Meduna of Budapest. Dr. Meduna had noticed a marked improvement in those of his schizophrenic patients whom he subjected to artificially induced epileptic convulsions. Break the electrical patterns of diseased brain activity through repeated chemical shocks and you jolt the patient right back into reality, went the theory. Unfortunately, none of Dr. Meduna's notes spoke to the effects of this therapy on a healthy brain. The clinicians who strapped Nasha down, injected her, observed her convulsions, and meticulously charted her post-therapy catatonia were equally ignorant about what they were doing to her. All they knew was that once they began the therapy nothing must interfere with its course.

This is why, when Margarita made her usual telephone call to the hospital to arrange for a visit from Nasha, they informed her that the rules were changed. Nasha could no longer leave the grounds.

It would not have mattered anyway. Nasha was now in a deep and unrelieved state of drug-induced dysphoria. Thanks to Dr. Porter, Nasha at last qualified as a bona fide mental patient.

When Margarita was finally able visit her, Nasha was six days into the treatment. She sat in a dayroom while the sun from the window blasted mercilessly across her unflinching face.

Margarita touched her arm and spoke her name and the Indian raised her head and smiled as she had always done. But she said nothing, knew nothing of her visitor, and the smile, the only defense left her, remained frozen in place for the entire visit.

"Save yourself the trouble of coming up anymore," the nurse advised Margarita on her way out. "I'm not sure what that new medicine is supposed to do but . . . well, see for yourself."

The nurse moved off to stop a patient who was striking her head rhythmically against a pillar in the center of the room.

Without Nasha as a sounding board, Margarita's memories of her childhood moled underground once again. This time, however, they tunneled directly into her dreams.

At first, the dreams were nothing more than impressions with no linkage or logic. The stove in Tía Adela's kitchen crackling angrily with the pitch-sotted kindling in its belly. A huge crystal punch bowl in which she found herself submerged in sweet, red liquid and slid down its slippery sides each time she tried to escape. A charred rooster that pecked at her little-girl legs.

Then the images began to weave themselves into a cohesive fabric. Walks with Nasha through fields where she learned the names of towering, alien plants. A serio-comic interlude in Delfino's store where she tried on every pair of shoes in stock while her uncooperative feet grew longer and longer between each fitting, all to the consternation of Tía Adela.

Finally she had a dream of Tina, her childhood friend from the pueblo of Picurís.

They were both dressed in white, part of a procession of similarly clad girls, different only in that the others wore impenetrable veils over their faces. Four of the girls carried a pallet on their shoulders, on which rode a cottonwood carving of Santa Rita. The rest carried a single, green-stalked calla lily. Everyone wore shoes except Margarita, who was painfully aware of the hot sand that burned the soles of her feet. They walked solemnly behind the statue, two by two, toward a high tower on the crest of a hill. A bell in the tower tolled a relentless note of melancholy. When they reached the tower, Margarita turned to Tina to ask why they were there but her friend was gone. The other girls suddenly broke ranks and joined hands to encircle the statue. Then they began to move faster and faster until the white of their dresses became a seamless blur, a swirling, gauze-like curtain that suddenly shot upward like a billow of angry smoke to engulf the girls in a giant, undulating cone of silken threads. The spongy cocoon quivered for a moment and then began to tear downward from its tapered top. The shimmering white skin opened up and began to stretch itself out languidly into the shape of a gigantic calla lily. In its center, in place of a pistil, was the statue of Santa Rita, its face replaced by Tina's. She was beautiful, radiant, and unblemished except for her eyes. These were now the yellowish, mucous-laden, sightless eyes of Nasha.

For the entire next day, Margarita could not get the dream out of her mind. Was it the memory of her lost friend, Tina, or was it the overwhelming whiteness of the scene and the way it swirled and unfolded before her that haunted her? There was something about the dream that resurrected long-ago feelings of foreboding.

The next night she had no dreams but when she awoke it was with the clear memory of a dream from her childhood. A river and a white winding sheet that twisted in the swirling currents until it shaped itself into the person of Nasha. And Tina had died. How alike the two Indians had been. Now she dreamt of Tina. Did this bode ill for Nasha?

Miguel had already left for work. Margarita dressed herself hurriedly, awoke the boys, and walked quickly with them across the early morning emptiness of the park to the grocery store.

Miguel was startled to see her with the children complaining and still in their pajamas.

"What's the matter? Is something wrong?"

"No."

Margarita picked up the phone by the front counter. "This is Margarita Galván," she said after the operator made the connection to Nasha's ward.

The voice on the other end was curt, testy. "Why are you phoning so early? This is our busiest time of the day."

"I'm sorry. I'm just calling about Nasha."

"What about her?"

"Is she all right?"

"She still isn't allowed to leave the hospital."

"Just tell me, please. Is she all right?"

"Yes. She's fine."

"Are you sure?"

"I'm looking at her right now. She's sitting in a chair having her hair combed."

"Thank you. I'm sorry to be such a bother."

Margarita slowly hung up the telephone and, drained of the panic that had energized her, she leaned against the countertop for support.

Miguel, who had squatted to wrap both his sons in his arms, looked up. "¿*Qué pasa?*"

"It's nothing. I was just hoping I could see Nasha today. And milk," she added quickly, "I came for milk for the boys' breakfast."

Miguel laughed. "Milk? I brought some home last night."

"Oh. I forgot."

Somewhere about eleven that morning, Margarita heard the wail of the ambulance that passed by the apartment and around the circle of the plaza. She thought nothing of it. It was something that happened with regularity since the plaza was the hub for all traffic in Old Town.

What was not a regular occurrence was the appearance of Miguel early that afternoon at the front door.

"Did you forget something?" Margarita asked.

"No," he said and looked at the floor. "I just heard some news. Not good news. There's been an accident by the tracks down by the river."

"Nasha."

"She wandered off. The train didn't even stop after it hit her."

Margarita put away her childhood and her feckless quest for entry into storybook castles. She also willed herself to have no more dreams.

In this she succeeded for another year.

Chapter Twenty-Two

1936–1938

She lay uncovered on her bed, quite alone. Every door and window seemed to be open for she could feel a wind whipping at her nightgown and she could hear the banging of doors and the flapping of curtains. She rose and found her way into a dark hallway. The bottoms of her feet burned with each step as if she were walking on hot sand.

The passage seemed to stretch out forever. The wind blew stronger now. It pushed her ahead of itself. With one final gust, it collided with the blackness. There was a loud crash and the darkness succumbed to a long rectangle of pale light, a doorway in her own house. She walked through to the normalcy of her kitchen. The only movement in the room was from the lacy curtains hanging across the window by the sink. The window was cracked open and an icy breeze whistled in, dropped to the linoleum floor, and scurried to her feet, where it split into twin serpents that wrapped around her ankles and slithered up her legs. She shuddered from the shock and rushed to the window to push it shut. When she turned back to the room everything seemed as she had left it the night before. The pot was on the stove waiting to be filled for morning coffee. A broom and dustpan leaned against the side of the icebox. The canned goods on the open wall shelves by the sink were stacked neatly next to pots, pans, and dishes. Four chairs were pushed up against the small table, which sat squarely in the middle of the room. Then she noticed that there was, after all, something different about her kitchen. On the table was the white cloth she had spread out after the previous evening's supper. However, it no longer lay flat and unwrinkled. Someone or something had gathered it up into a loose, elongated bundle. She pulled out one of the chairs and sat down. Her hands on her lap, she studied the wrinkled whiteness of the bundle. Finally, she reached out for one corner of the cloth and carefully pulled it to herself. The wrapping had a familiar heft. Like an infant in a blanket. She picked it up, cradled it in her arms, and began to slowly rock back and forth. Then she began to sing a lullaby. It was clear to her that if she stopped what she was doing the order of her universe would be irreversibly disturbed. And so she kept rocking, cradling the bundle and singing to it.

It was a year later, almost to the day of Nasha's accident, that Margarita Juana had this, her third and final premonitory dream.

After the death of Nasha under the ponderous, grinding metal of the freight train, Margarita took firm grip of her situation. She resigned herself to the fact that the past was gone, never to be reclaimed. She reluctantly accepted the present and made plans for the future, a future that now rested squarely on her two sons.

Luis, she surmised, would grow up to be a good, industrious, plodding man like his father. There was certainly nothing wrong with that. Miguel had always been a good and loving husband. Luis could do worse than to turn out like his father.

But Miguelito? Ah, yes, Miguelito.

Margarita's first son was, and she could think of no other word for him, a marvel. His hair, which had started out as a reddish gold, had ripened quickly into a lustrous, wavy auburn that framed the oval of his face. The nose was straight and strong. The mouth was somewhat thin but it was saved from weakness by a slight upturn at the corners in eternal anticipation of some new delight. However, it was the eyes and the sable strokes of the brows above them that made the boy's appearance truly riveting. The eyes were green, a matched pair of emeralds set in orbs of white porcelain. They were, in fact, the eyes of her first love, Romancito. She knew this could not be. Their intimacies had never gone beyond clumsy embraces and tight-lipped kisses. Still, in spite of her reasonings, she wondered if somehow his breath, that sweet breath, had confounded nature. Had it entered her mouth to slip down her windpipe past her lungs and heart and into her belly? Had it searched the hidden recesses of her body until it found her fallopian tubes? Once there, had his breath brushed softly

against her ovaries to leave its mark? It was an impossibility. Still,
Miguelito's eyes were not hers, not Miguel's. They were indisputably
Romancito's. But, where in her lover's moody glower she had seen
arrogance, in Miguelito there was self-confidence. Where Romancito
projected cynicism, she saw in her son innocent curiosity. Where
there had been cruelty here was only boyish mischief. And that preda-
tory cunning of Romancito's was in Miguelito transformed into a
voracious intelligence. No, these were not Romancito's eyes. Save for
their color they belonged unquestionably to her marvel, Miguelito.

By the time Miguelito was four and Luis three they had settled into
their sibling roles. Miguelito was the leader, the instigator of all they
did, the good and the not so good. When they found a bird with a broken wing in the backyard it was Miguelito who scooped it up and ran
with it into the house, to hand it to his mother for care. When a pair
of scissors was left unattended on the arm of a parlor chair it was
Miguelito who sat Luis down on the front stoop and cut his hair off in
uneven clumps that left him looking like a half-plucked chicken. When
word came from Denver that Tío Delfino had died, it was Miguelito
who climbed up on his mother's lap to hug and kiss her and to tell her
about the angels who were taking care of her uncle by now.

It was Tuesday, the first day of October, 1936. Magistrate Pacunio R.
Baca was holding court in his office on the north side of the plaza.
The two rooms were in a half-block building that he owned, a long,
rambling, one-story edifice that squatted like a footstool for the
dowager that was the Plaza Hotel.

It was at the far end of this little compound that Miguel and
Margarita lived with their two sons.

El Juez, as he was called by all, was as self-made a man as there
was in Las Vegas. He had not gone past the fifth grade. An only child,
he had been forced into peonage on his father's small ranch in the
Rociada Valley. When Pacunio was sixteen his father and mother had
died within hours of each other of the influenza. The county seized
the ranch and its livestock and equipment for back taxes. Pacunio
gathered what he could in a gunnysack and walked the twenty-two
miles to Las Vegas. There he sold his mother's silver-backed brush

and comb, the only things left from her dowry, and bought shoeshine equipment. With these he set up shop in a corner of the county court-house, a redstone building across the street from the parish church of Our Lady of Sorrows. Here he daubed, polished, and buffed dusty shoes and boots and listened to the politicians and lawyers talk amongst themselves and with their constituents and clients. Within two weeks he expanded his business to include a wooden orange crate on which he displayed and sold chewing gum, tobacco paper, pencils, and small writing tablets. In six months he had a permanent stand. In a year he had two, one at each entrance, and he had hired a near blind vet-eran from the Great War to help him. Three years later he owned four other kiosks, one in the post office and three others in public buildings in New Town. He earned enough to buy a house, fix it up, and sell it to buy two more. Within a decade he had acquired considerable prop-erty on both sides of the river, most of it in apartments.

He was now a successful merchant and a landlord, enough for most men but not for him. He had money but no prestige. Exposure to the law as practiced in the San Miguel County Courthouse had ignited a spark in him that smoldered into an obsession. He knew that he would not need a law degree to be a justice of the peace or a magistrate. He knew of several men now in office who had no more education than he. Their paths to power had been cleared through patronage and politics. Pacunio Baca was supremely confident that he could do the same. His only shortcoming, as he saw it, was his lack of facility with English. Not that this seemed to have held back others, but he felt that with a working knowledge of the Anglos' lan-guage he would have a leg up on winning over some of the New Town electorate. And so he set himself to learning English.

He began with a primary reader and soon graduated to the more complex works of Horatio Alger. Now here were characters and sto-ries with which he could identify. There was *Andy Grant's Pluck*, *Joe's Luck*, *Paul the Peddler*, *Phil the Fiddler*, and, his favorite of all, *Tom the Bootblack*, all of them poor boys like himself who succeeded in classic rags-to-riches fashion.

As much as he loved these books, his enduring passion was the comics. While writers such as Hemingway, F. Scott Fitzgerald, and assorted members of the Algonquin Round Table vied for the mind of the country, it was the comics that had a firm grip on its heart and

soul. Where else could the hoi polloi better come to grips with its humdrum existence than in the simply drawn panels that dealt with the day-to-day of the common man? There were *Toots and Casper*, *The Gumps*, *Moon Mullins*, *Tillie the Toiler*. There was *Little Orphan Annie*, whose adventures and travails shrank their own to manageable proportions. And there were *Krazy Kat* and *Felix*, who tweaked the nose of convention, thus offering a vent for life's frustrations. All of these characters created a mirror in which the lower classes could laugh at themselves and learn to cope with life's daily grind.

Although Pacunio Baca could not personally relate to any of these characters, he did appreciate what he could learn from them, both the Anglos' language and the ethos from which it sprang. So convinced was he that the comics could teach him all he needed to know that he made of habit of memorizing balloons of dialogue to use in conversation. Soon he was spouting phrases like "but of course, m'dear," "what can I do for you, my good man?" and "what a sorry state of affairs." He peppered his speech with the onomatopoeia of the comics, pronouncing the sometimes unpronounceable hieroglyphics as faithfully to their spelling as possible. At the least provocation he would let out with expressions like "yikes" and "harrumph." When he was confounded he would say "whew." When disgusted, "ptooie." Once, when a mouse scurried across the floor of his courtroom he was actually heard to squeal "eek!" By the time he was elected magistrate, a foregone conclusion once he set his mind to it, he spoke a slightly off-kilter if surprisingly literate brand of English. The Anglos laughed at him behind his back yet voted for him as the least of all evils, since they were in the minority when it came to countywide elections. The Hispanics also laughed at him, but not so cruelly, and not for his affectation but for his self-delusion.

Immediately after the election he had a sign painted for display in the front window of his plaza office. It read, "Magistrate Pacunio R. Baca. Please knock before entering." Inside, there was a shelf behind his desk on which he kept bound volumes of the county's statutes. However, by and large he practiced the law of common sense. The couples the priest refused to marry he obliged. He was practically Solomonic in finding between parties in civil disputes. He knew which drunk to jail and which to send home. He understood which man he could fine to the limit and which he would let off with a reprimand or a few hours of community service. In time he became one of the fairest and canniest judges that San Miguel County ever elevated to the bench.

On the Tuesday that began that year's October, Judge Baca was in session. He had just finished bringing a judgment against a woman who claimed to have been cheated by a seamstress with a dress that did not fit.

"M'dear," he declared, "the fact that the dress does not fit you today does not mean that it was measured improperly on the day it was fitted. Heavens to Betsy, we both know why that is so, don't we?"

The woman dropped her eyes and her cheeks reddened. For she knew that the judge knew that she was now pregnant. Had she not won a paternity case just a week ago in these very chambers, a case that now obliged a married man to give her fifteen dollars a month until that time that the price for her virtue had been met?

Before the next case was brought in, the judge heard the call of nature.

"Offissa," he addressed the deputy in attendance, using the word he had picked up from Krazy Kat, who was always in some trouble with Offissa Pupp, "I will be back in a jiffy." It turned out to be a very long jiffy.

Although his apartment building had piped-in water for all the units, indoor toilets were not included in the amenities. Instead, in the fenced-in courtyard that ran along the entire rear of the building were three majestic outhouses painted a forest green. These retreats sat up on a low platform to keep their patrons high and dry in rain and snow.

The judge took a roll of tissue from his back window and ambled out into the courtyard. There he stopped for a moment to appraise with satisfaction the small grape arbor growing next to the back porch. The harvest had been good that year. What wine he would have! And the jellies and jams. It was time to prune back the vines and get ready for winter.

He walked to the outhouse while he undid his robe and noted with satisfaction that the end stall, his favorite, was unoccupied. He

came up short when he saw Miguelito and Luis playing on the platform, recovered, and smiled at them with unctuous goodwill.

"Oh, no, no, boys. This is no place to play. Phew! You don't want to be around here. Be good little critters and go inside to your mother."

Miguelito looked up at him with those green eyes and returned the smile. "Come on, Luis," he said.

The judge nodded his approval. "Good boys."

What he had not seen in those eyes of Miguelito was the glint of mischief in the making that Margarita had learned long ago to interpret and to watch for.

The judge proceeded to enter his second-favorite chamber, where he sat down on his second-favorite bench. When he was comfortably situated he began to hum loudly, a grunting version of "Smoke Gets In Your Eyes." He was at that moment a very happy man, grateful for who he was.

Once the door on the privy slammed shut, Miguelito launched his quickly crafted plan.

"Shhh, Luis."

Miguelito led his brother back onto the platform and gestured for him to go down on all fours by the door of the end commode. Then he carefully stepped up on Luis's back, which put him at eye level with an outside bolt, used to keep the door from swinging in the wind when the stall was unoccupied. Ever so slowly he drew the iron into its staple.

When they were both safely down off the platform, Miguelito cupped his hands along both sides of his mouth and spoke loudly to the door.

"Juez Baca?"

"Yes?" came the muffled response.

"We're going in now. My mama needs us."

"Yes, yes. Go, go," the judge answered. "I told you not to play around here."

"Goodbye, Juez Baca."

"Goodbye, lad. Goodbye. Don't be a bother now."

Five minutes later, the judge was ready to reconvene his court. He pushed on the door. And then he pushed harder. His suspicions growing, he leaned over to look through the space between the door and its frame. His worst fears were confirmed. He could just make out the bolt spanning the crack and resting firmly in place.

"Boys, are you out there? Open the door now. Be good, why don't you?"

There was no answer. Cursing softly, he patted his pockets for his penknife. Perhaps he could work the bolt back from the inside. But then he remembered that the knife was in the pocket of the coat he had removed to put on his robe.

"Hallo! Yoo-hoo!" he shouted. "Can anyone hear me?"

He waited for a few minutes in the vague hope that his deputy would come looking for him.

Another look through the quarter-moon cutout on the door told him that the courtyard was completely empty.

His earlier restraint now breached its limits and he began to bang on the door. He kicked at it. He forgot the niceties of his comic-strip English and began to bellow and to swear in Spanish.

"What is that?" Margarita asked from her kitchen, where she had just served milk and cookies to her sons.

Miguelito's eyes were wide and innocent over the rim of the glass. "What, Mamá?"

"That noise."

By this time the judge was taking a breather from his rantings.

"I don't hear anything," Miguelito could say truthfully and winked at Luis.

But just then the judge chose to take up his shouting and banging with renewed vigor.

When Margarita finally rescued him, the judge's face was a mass of reddish splotches.

"M'dear," he sputtered. "M'dear," he started again. Finally it was all too much for him. "*Esos malcriados van a cayer en la pinta. Lo juro*," he managed before he stomped back to his office and slammed the door behind him.

Margarita was unsure why such a childish prank should land her sons in the penitentiary, but she would have to have a little talk with them. However, it would have to wait until she could keep a straight face.

It was, as mentioned before, October 1, 1936. It was the feast of The Little Flower.

Later that afternoon, when Thérèse of Lisieux came to settle her long-standing account with Margarita Juana, she tried to be as gentle as possible. As gentle, that is, as her taking of Miguelito would allow.

The impact from the motor car on the boy was not much, really little more than a nudge, but the vehicle was very large and very heavy and the child was very small. The fall was not much to speak of either. Miguelito had taken much harder falls while playing in the park across the street. It was how he fell that made the difference here. His head struck the edge of the raised curb at just the right angle and with just the right force to fracture his skull and instantly kill his brain. Thérèse made sure that he felt no pain; she was a gentle soul, after all. But a bargain was a bargain and when Margarita had prayed to her four years earlier to save her son she had well understood that she must eventually face a day of reckoning.

Margarita was relegating the boys to the sofa in the front room when her brother Alfonso dropped by on his way from school to Doña Francisquita's.

"How is my *suegrita*?" Margarita inquired after her mother-in-law.

"Fine."

"I'm making tortillas for supper. Wait and you can take some to her."

Margarita went to the shelf and pulled down a mixing bowl. Then she gathered up a canister of flour, a carton of salt, and a can of lard.

"Oh, I forgot. I don't have any baking powder. Can you run to the store for me?"

From the front room, a bored Miguelito was following the conversation. "Can I go?"

"You are going nowhere," his mother answered. "Not until you march yourself over to the judge's office after court to apologize."

"Let them go with me," Alfonso said. "We'll be back in five minutes."

By this time, Miguelito was at the kitchen door. "Please, Mamá. Please. I promise we'll go see the judge when we get back." Miguelito gave her the look he knew she could seldom resist and, as usual, his eyes performed their magic on his mother.

"All right. But as soon as you get b ack we're going over there, you understand? And watch out for cars."

Down off the curb, Alfonso took Luis's hand. "Now we look both ways. All clear? OK, let's go."

At that instant, Miguelito saw what Alfonso hadn't. In the front car of the two they were walking between sat Judge Baca. This had the makings of a confrontation the boy preferred to delay as long as possible. Where could he hide? While his uncle and brother proceeded across the street, he squatted down behind the car's rear bumper.

The judge had been sitting in his car for a good ten minutes. He had returned to his courtroom in a most foul mood after his misadventure in the commode. Neither plaintiffs nor defendants had a chance. Every complaint was met with a loud "pshaw." He interrupted every claim and counterclaim with an exhalation of "tsk tsk." The slightest hesitation from a witness elicited an "ahem." Finally, after a few distracted attempts to mete out justice, he ordered the deputy to clear the room.

"Court is closed for the day," he said sourly and banged down his gavel.

Even after he was alone to doff his robe and put on his coat and hat he fumed. Such a state of affairs! He harrumphed loudly as he locked up his office. The indignity of it! He muttered to himself all the way to his car. The disgrace. It was only after he had sat there for some time that he was able to regain some of his composure. Boys, after all, will be boys.

When he turned on the ignition and slowly let out the clutch he did not notice that the car was still in reverse from when he had so carefully parked it this morning. He expected to ease forward into the street. Instead the car lurched backward. He felt a bump, not a large one, but enough to return him instantly to his foul mood.

"Egads. What now?"

He glanced to his left and saw Alfonso running toward him from the park across the street. Luis dragged behind.

One of those naughty boys. The judge heard Alfonso shout at him but he could not understand the words. Now out of his car, he walked back to see what all the commotion was about. Surely the bump had not caused that much damage.

"Goodness gracious, such a fuss," he said.

Then he saw Alfonso kneeling in the gutter, propping Miguelito up by the shoulders. A small bead of blood was making its way down the child's cheek from his ear.

"*¡Dios mío!*" the judge cried. "I didn't see him. I swear I didn't see him."

Alfonso did not answer. He picked up Miguelito and ran into the apartment. Luis, wide eyed and uncomprehending, had begun to cry and stood abandoned on the sidewalk.

Margarita was at the sink when Alfonso rushed into the kitchen and placed Miguelito gently on the table. "A car, a car," was all he could say, but considering every parent's waking dread, it was enough.

Margarita began to rub her son's chest in a circular motion with her still wet hands. "Miguelito. Where does it hurt you? Miguelito, wake up. Go get the doctor," she cried to Alfonso. "Next door. The doctor."

Alfonso sprinted out of the apartment and kitty-corner across the intersection to the doctor's office. He did not even notice Magistrate Pacunio Baca, who was now seated on the curb, his head bowed and shaking as he repeated over and over again, "*Dios mío. Dios mío.*"

By the time Alfonso was back in the apartment with the doctor, Margarita was applying wet compresses to Miguelito's head.

The doctor pulled her gently aside and sat her down in one of the chairs by the table.

"Let me look at him. Just sit there now."

He lifted the child's eyelids, but the green eyes were rolled back in his head to shroud their already fading luster. He took the child's limp hand and felt for a pulse. He inserted the black rubber stubs of a stethoscope into his ears and placed the small silver funnel on the child's chest.

Finally, he looked up at Margarita. "Is Miguel at the store?"

Margarita nodded dumbly.

The doctor turned to Alfonso. "Go fetch him. Tell him to come home right now." Then he turned back to Margarita. After a slight pause he said simply, "I'm sorry. I am truly sorry."

Sorry for what? What was there to be sorry for? Doctors were not supposed to be sorry for anything. They were supposed to mend and heal but were not allowed to be sorry. She looked at her son as she had done so often, lingering over him while he slept. He looked no different to her now.

The doctor took both edges of the white tablecloth and drew them slowly over the boy. "I'm sorry," he said again.

Why does he keep saying that? She leaned over the table and brought Miguelito into her arms. Settling heavily back into the chair she pushed her son's head into her bosom. She mustn't look at him. She mustn't turn down the cloth and look at him. She began to rock and to croon, knowing that when she stopped nothing would be the same again.

A month later Magistrate Pacunio Baca resigned his judgeship and left town. He paid the back taxes on his father's homestead and returned to the Rociada Valley. Every month from then on he met an agent at a designated spot on the road leading into Las Vegas to collect the money from his kiosks and rental properties and to give the man his instructions. Then he would drive up through Mora to Taos, where he deposited the money in the bank. He never set foot in Las Vegas again.

Margarita did not go to Miguelito's funeral Mass and burial. In fact, it was not until they buried Leopoldo, her father, some twenty years later that she stepped into the cemetery that had already held her marvel of a son for two decades. While the others prayed for Leopoldo she could only think of her arms and how much they ached.

About six months after the accident, and then only at the urging of the priest, the doctor, her family, and her friends, she allowed her husband to impregnate her again.

"Luis needs a brother," they had argued.

"You need something to fill your life again."

"You need another baby."

Of course, none of them could understand that she had no more needs. Since there was nothing she could change, she preferred to leave things as they were. But perhaps they were right. She did not know. Did not have enough interest to form an opinion. Perhaps it would help. She did not think so. But Miguel and Luis seemed to be getting on with their lives. Perhaps she should also. In the final disposition of things she did not so much accede to the copulation as just let it happen.

Nine months later, she had another son. I was born.

Chapter Twenty-Three

When I was born, the doctor called me a miracle baby.

Already with her fill of miracles, Margarita exploded at the doctor when he said it and told him to be quiet and to leave her alone.

The nuns and the rest of the staff at the hospital attributed these postpartum histrionics to the fact that they had to remove Margarita's womb shortly after my birth.

"Hormones," they whispered to each other outside of her room.

When I came home eight days after my birth, Margarita remained behind to recuperate from her ordeal.

"We shouldn't wait to baptize the baby," Miguel said to her.

"Whatever you want," Margarita said.

"Do you have a name?"

She turned her face to the wall. "Let the *padrinos* choose."

This was not an unusual proposition given that godparents in northern New Mexico often named their godchildren, a practice intended to accentuate the spiritual bond between them.

My godmother was to be Miguel's sister, María. She was a simple soul. When asked to stand in at the baptism and to choose a name for me, she strained her brain to its limits before she proudly announced her intentions to her husband.

"We will call the baby Miguel."

"Miguel? Are you sure?" he asked.

"Of course I'm sure. It's his father's name and, since he is taking poor Miguelito's place, it's quite proper."

He did not argue with her. He never did.

And so, after my baptism, which my father did not attend, choosing rather to be with Margarita at the hospital when the godparents came to present me to them, Aunt Mary walked into the sickroom with me. Her husband followed behind with a shopping bag filled with diapers, powders, oils, clothing, and bottles of formula.

Proudly she recited the formula she had so struggled to memorize the night before. "Miguel and Margarita Galván, I give you your son, now a child of God and our sacred responsibility as his *padrinos*. His name is Miguel." Then she gushed with pride at her cleverness, "You can call him Miguelito."

Not another Miguelito. Margarita couldn't listen to this. She wouldn't have it. She turned her head to the wall and cried for two days, which delayed her discharge from the hospital by another week.

She never called me Miguelito. In time, to distinguish me from my father, the family called me Miguel Chiquito and him Miguel Grande. But, in the inexorable Anglicization of Las Vegas, this was corrupted to Little Mike and Big Mike.

Years later, at the reception after my return from Rome as a priest, my *madrina*, Aunt Mary, gushed at me, "Can I call you Father Miguelito?"

I smiled and thought what a simple soul she was. I did not appreciate that her naming of me twenty-five years before had been more astute than I could ever envision.

Every August the National Guard, direct descendant of earlier citizen armies, came to Camp Luna, just north of Las Vegas, for its annual exercises. In 1940, the New Mexico National Guard's 111th Cavalry replaced their horses with artillery pieces and became the Army National Guard 200th Coast Artillery.

That same year, Alfonso finished high school. Too educated to return to the sawmill and too uneducated to attend the local Highlands University, Alfonso looked around for something to do. Jobs were still scarce. The Depression was reluctant to let loose its grip on Las Vegas even after the programs of FDR had America moving again.

Thursday, the first day of August, found Alfonso under a tree on the sidewalk directly in front of the main entrance to the state hospital. There might be some work for him at the hospital farm. He plucked and sucked grass and waited for the word.

Down the road, to the south, a military convoy came into view and motored slowly in his direction. By the time it reached him he was standing and staring open mouthed at the parade passing in review. Olive-brown vehicles pulled caissons or two-wheeled artillery pieces, their barrels pointing backward and capped with hoods of gray canvas. There were staff cars and behind them more trucks than

Alfonso had ever seen, open bedded with lattice fencing on the sides, crammed full of uniformed men. The soldiers were in high spirits, laughing and shouting. Some jumped off the backs of the trucks to run alongside and shake the hands of the people who had poured out of the hospital to cheer them on. Alfonso shook several of these hands, hard gripping and vigorous. A soldier or two even patted him on the shoulder. This made him feel important and somehow a part of them.

"Alfonso!"

Two of his friends were waving frantically at him from the back of one of the trucks.

He broke into a trot and was at the truck and being hauled aboard before he realized what was happening.

"We're going to the camp to look around," one of his friends screamed into his ear over the rattle and roar. "They said we could."

"I have a job at the hospital."

"You can always find work," the friend lied transparently, "but you can't always ride in a real army truck."

This was true. And anyway, they'd only pay him fifty cents for the whole afternoon. So he stayed with his friends and took up the waving and shouting with everyone else on the truck. It felt good and he was very happy about where he was.

The rest of the day he and his friends toured the camp, helped to unload trucks, and met many of the soldiers. They spoke at length with a sergeant who couldn't say enough good about life as a guardsman.

That evening, Alfonso burst into Margarita's kitchen.

The Galváns were now renting a house away from the plaza, Margarita being unable to stay at the apartment with its memories of Miguelito. Even now, four years later, the sight of her brother still disquieted her. She had never blamed him for Miguelito's death. Neither had she ever forgiven him.

Alfonso waved a piece of paper at Margarita's nose. "You have to help me with this."

"What is it?"

"It's so I can join the National Guard. I talked to them. They want me."

"Why do you want to do that?"

"Because it's something to do."

"If you want something to do why don't you look for a regular job?"

"But they pay. Fifteen dollars a month for a buck private. That's what I'll be," he added proudly. "And you get an extra dollar a night for drills every weekend. And I can work the rest of the time during the day. Except August when we train full time over at Camp Luna for ten days."

Alfonso was eighteen going on nineteen so it was not a question of needing Margarita's signature to join. And, it was true, she thought ruefully and not for the first time, there was nothing to do in Las Vegas. So she sat down with him and helped him with his application.

Early the next morning Alfonso was at the camp to seek out the sergeant he had spoken with the day before. By that afternoon he had been sworn in. He was now Private Alfonso Zamora of the New Mexico National Guard, 200th Coast Artillery, 2nd Battalion, Battery H.

For the Japanese it began in earnest with Manchuria, which they took as the first building block in their Asian empire. It was 1931. Chinese resistance was spirited but ultimately ineffective. For six years Japan built up the region. Manchuria became a two-hundred-thousand-square-mile military base, at once a bulwark against the Soviet Union and a substantial foothold in Northern China.

In 1938 Japan finally let the rest of the world in on its intentions to establish a New Order in East Asia. This meant the unification of Japan, Korea, Manchuko, Inner Mongolia, and China into a homogeneous political, military, and economic entity. Its key ingredient was lockstep nationalism. Shortly after, the Japanese widened their plans to include something they called a "coprosperity sphere." The entire Pacific was now up for grabs.

In the Philippines, General Douglas MacArthur, retired from the army for four years, was serving as military advisor to the newly created Commonwealth. There were repeated assurances to Washington by the Japanese that their intentions in the Pacific were benign and limited. MacArthur, however, could read the signs. He had his commission reactivated and became overseer of Far East activities. One of his first requests was for American troops on which he could rely while the Filipinos organized their defenses.

Rumors were flying across the undulating mesa of Camp Luna that August of 1940. Something was brewing but no one knew what. To begin with, the length of the training had been doubled. This led to considerable grumbling among the men. Teachers had to get back to their schools to prepare for classes. Ranch hands were expected for the fall roundup. Employers had to be notified. End-of-summer plans with families flew out the window.

The bitching was grand.

"What the hell is going on?"

"England."

"Again? We already bailed them out once."

None thought of the Far East.

For his part, Alfonso groused as much as anyone. After all, he was now one of them. But secretly he found no reason for dissatisfaction. He enjoyed the discipline, the drills, the camaraderie. And the uniform made him look mature and dashing. By the simple act of putting it on his self-esteem rose by several notches, so that he began to disassociate himself from the ravenous pack of young men who ranged across Las Vegas in pursuit of work.

When the Guard broke camp late that summer and its members dispersed to their real lives, Alfonso maintained his new persona. He felt estranged from his pals. The days stretched out agonizingly for him while he waited for the weekends. It was only then that he truly came to life. On Saturdays he was always the first one at the armory to wait for the door to open. On the steps in his laundered and pressed fatigues he could only hope that passersby noticed him. And so it went for him throughout that fall and into winter. All the while he endured the taunts from his friends that he was a "weekend warrior." He was beginning to dream of glory.

Two days before Christmas he burst into Margarita's kitchen once again. "We're being federalized."

Margarita had no idea what that meant. Perhaps, she thought, it had something to do with the WPA, the CCC, the NRA, the PWA, the CWA, the AAA, or one of the others in a string of alphabet programs that FDR had initiated as part of his New Deal. By now everyone knew that salvation for the country lay somewhere in a thicket of federal acronyms.

"My unit. We're going to be part of the regular army."

"That's nice," said Margarita, unsure of an appropriate response.

"Don't you see? I'm not going to be a civilian anymore. I'll be a full-time soldier. We're going to Fort Bliss after the New Year. I'm getting out of Las Vegas."

This Margarita understood. Getting out of Las Vegas. Alfonso, whom she had practically raised, whose diapers she had changed and whose constantly running nose she had wiped, was escaping. She felt a wave of intense envy sweep over her like a dry, life-sucking wind.

"That's nice," she repeated and immediately regretted her self-absorption. "Where is Fort Bliss?"

"El Paso. We're going there to train, and then we'll ship out."

"Will you be doing anything dangerous?"

"Nah. All the troubles are in Europe. We're going the other way. To Alaska or someplace. Maybe somewhere in the Pacific Ocean." He said this last in a hushed tone as if uttering a magical incantation.

Margarita had read about the Pacific. Blue waters, white sands, and palm trees. Island paradises where you could pluck exotic fruits off the trees and wade knee deep in warm ocean currents gentle enough to soothe yet strong enough to wash away distasteful memories.

She hugged her brother. It was the first time she had touched him since the death of Miguelito. "Well then, if you're not going anywhere that's dangerous, I'm happy for you."

The 200th was officially mobilized on the sixth of January, 1941. On the fourteenth, Alfonso said his goodbyes and hitched a ride to Albuquerque with some of his buddies. There they boarded a special train for Fort Bliss. In El Paso the original 750 guardsmen were joined by other enlistees to swell their numbers to a war-strength regiment of 1,800 men in two battalions.

The next eight months were the most rigorous Alfonso had ever experienced. It was all different now. The drills were more intense. There was less joking and horsing around, fewer demonstrations of high spirits. Men whom he had known and socialized with in Las Vegas were now his superiors. No more Robertos, Miguels, and Joes. Now they were Corporal López, Sergeant Jiménez, and Lieutenant Harper.

He began to miss things.

Dear Margarita:

We went to Juárez last week. They don't know how to make chile. It doesn't taste like yours. The tortillas are made out of corn. Can you send me some thick socks? My boots are giving me blisters.

Your brother, Alfonso

It was not that he was a stranger to blisters. He had never owned a pair of shoes that didn't require breaking in. It was just that back in Las Vegas he knew he could go home and soak his feet in a tub filled with warm water to which Francisquita had added a capful of mineral oil or Epsom salts. Now, exhausted, he fell into his cot at the end of the day unwilling to face the pain of removing his socks, their fibers fused into the rawness that covered the balls and heels of his feet.

Some things he did not, could not write Margarita about. There were the fights, for instance. Someone from Santa Fe or Española would besmirch the good name of the lads from Las Vegas and old animosities would boil to the surface. Or a gringo would make some remark about the Mexicans, those across the border and those, by association, in the battalion. Sides would form. Eyes were blackened and noses bloodied in barracks-clearing free-for-alls. But somehow, magically, from all of this discord, a bond stronger than steel was forged among the men of the 200th. They developed a self-identity, an esprit de corps. By the time they were battle-hardened soldiers in the Philippines they were referred to by other units as "those damn New Mexicans, thick as fleas on a Filipino dog." It was a bond that would eventually save many of their lives.

There was also more to Juárez than Alfonso's experience with Mexican chile. He learned to drink and he got drunk. And he learned of other forbidden pleasures that could be had across the border for two American dollars or fifteen Mexican pesos.

His first encounter with the señoritas of Juárez was spotty. It was a Friday evening and he was sitting with some of his comrades in a packed cantina just on the other side of the Río Grande. At the bar stood a row of women, already bored with what promised to be another long night. Periodically one would peel off and walk up to one of the tables. She began with a few stale remarks that flattered the manhood of her audience. Soon she was sitting on a soldier's lap and taking drinks from his bottle of beer. It was only a matter of time before she was leading him across the room by the hand. Then they would line up in front of a closed door, solemn as penitents waiting to enter the confessional box. Every five or ten minutes the door opened and a soldier emerged, sometimes blushing, sometimes grinning while his lady companion adjusted some part of her dress before returning to the bar to wait her turn again. Then everyone moved up a place in the line.

Alfonso sat in considerable discomfort. He wanted to leave. Didn't dare. When some of the women approached his table and reached for his hand he pulled it back and shook his head. They shrugged or sneered or laughed and took the hand of another to lead that soldier to the end of the line by the door.

Since the age of puberty, Alfonso had lived the life of a monk in the house of the saintly Francisquita. His virginity, however, was not the reason for his reluctance to taste the fruit from this most forbidden of trees. To be blunt about it, the women were not attractive. Some were old, some were older. Some were fat. Most were pockmarked or scarred with acne. Some showed gaps from missing teeth when they smiled. One of them flashed two upper canines sheathed in gold, garish quotation marks for the loud obscenities that spewed from her mouth. None of the women held the slightest appeal for Alfonso, with their caked-on makeup that streaked at their necks, their cheap-smelling perfume, their outrageous speech, and their brassy attitude.

He realized, however, that with regard to his virtue, he was on borrowed time. If only he could overcome his revulsion before he was dragged into his manhood.

"Here you go, Alfonso. This one's got eyes only for you. And look at those globes on her!"

He finally gave in because he was drunk enough to lose both his inhibitions and his fastidiousness. He was drunk enough to think that the woman who finally took his hand and led him away was prettier, cleaner, and younger than the rest.

While they waited in line she complained about her feet.

"*Estos zapatos altos son un castigo de Dios,*" she whined and leaned against him to remove a high-heeled shoe so she could rub her foot against a meaty calf.

He could certainly relate to sore feet. He broke into a lengthy dissertation about army boots. So intent was he on his recounting of his blisters that he did not notice her eyes glaze over, nor the beads of perspiration that had built up among the dark mustache hairs over her upper lip, nor her hand that dropped casually to scratch her crotch through the sheen of her grease-spattered, kelly-green organdy dress.

They had reached the front of the line. The door opened, and a tall cowpoke from Roswell burst out with a whoop and a holler and rushed back to his table. "Unbelievable," he shouted again and again to his companions.

"*Venga.*" Alfonso's woman pulled him through the door and closed it.

The room was a twelve-by-twelve windowless square. Along one of the walls stretched an army cot, its canvas sagging, faded, and stained. It was very much like the cot into which Alfonso eased himself every night, sore and exhausted. They had been warned about the Mexicans around the camp, about their skill in pilfering anything that wasn't bolted down. But how could you sneak an army cot past the gate? Forgotten for the moment was that he had not been brought into the room to critique its decor.

The woman walked over to a sink anchored to the wall, turned on the tap, and began to fill a glazed pottery basin with water. When she was done she dropped a piece of soap into it, reached over to a pile of folded cloths and took one. Armed with these she came across the room to him.

"*Ándale,*" she said impatiently and pointed at his crotch. "*Los pantalones. Desabróchalos.*"

Embarrassed both by her brazenness and by his own lack of experience, Alfonso fumbled with his belt and fly and lowered his trousers to mid-thigh.

"*También los calzoncillos,*" she ordered.

"*Sí, señorita,*" he answered as if to a commanding officer, and pushed his drawers down.

She knelt before him and he looked away. He was feeling enough shame for the both of them. He stared at a fly-specked lightbulb that glowed harshly on a frayed wire that snaked into the ceiling. Transfixed on the light, he waited. Was he supposed to do something? Why hadn't he asked someone?

He heard the comforting sound of water sloshing around and looked down at the woman lathering up the cloth. She wrung it out, raised it to his genitals, and began to wipe him.

At her touch and without even the benefit of a full erection he ejaculated into the soapy rag.

The woman showed no reaction. This happened so many times with boys deciding to be men. When his spasms were over she wiped the head of his penis. Then she stood up, went over to the sink, dumped the water, rinsed the basin, and stood it on its end to drain. She replaced the soap on a cracked saucer, threw the cloth into a wicker basket, came back to him, and held out her hand.

"Two dollars," she said in perfect English.

Alfonso reached for his wallet and felt only the smoothness of his left buttock.

The woman rolled her eyes, folded her arms across her ample bosom, and tapped her foot impatiently on the tile floor.

He hauled up his trousers with great difficulty. His drawers bunched and rolled painfully across his privates. With his legs spread to hold up his britches, he fished for his wallet, pulled out two dollars, and handed them to her.

"Okey dokey," she said and walked to the door.

Still clutching at his unbuttoned, unbelted trousers, Alfonso waddled out behind her, a debutante being introduced. The first thing he saw were his companions. They were pointing at him, laughing and pounding each other on the back. Then one of them began a chant that the others immediately picked up.

"Al-fon-so! Al-fon-so!"

Unsure, he stood there for a moment. Then remembering the lanky ranch hand who had exited the room just before him, he raised both arms high in the air and gave out a lusty whoop.

His trousers dropped to his knees like a stone.

On August 16, Washington informed General MacArthur that reinforcements were on the way. The next day the 200th had its orders.

August 18, 1941
Dear Margarita,

We got our orders. We are going to San Francisco to take a boat somewhere. Our train will be leaving El Paso on August 31. Can you come and see me? Can you bring me some more socks? How are Big Mike, Little Mike, and Luis? How is Doña Francisquita? I hope you can come. I hope you get this letter in time.

> *Your brother,*
> *Alfonso*

Margarita received the letter two days before the 31st. She immediately rushed down to the train station to buy a ticket to Albuquerque. From there she hoped to catch a bus for the 280-mile trip into El Paso.

"Sorry, ma'am, there are no seats left," the ticket agent informed her.

"But I have to see my brother. He's in the army and they're sending him very far away for a long, long time."

The man knew all about it. The railroad had already informed everyone up and down the line about possible reroutings and schedule changes to accommodate the movement of the troops out of El Paso. The trains would be heading north for a short jog into New Mexico before they turned due west to the coast.

The ticket master dipped his head toward her through the small window and looked both to his left and to his right, although they were completely alone in the station. "I really shouldn't do this, but if you show up tomorrow morning with a ticket, I guess they can't very well tell you to go home, can they?

He stopped between stampings of the ticket. "And if you happen to run into a Private Darryl Holbert, tell him his Uncle Henry says hello and to be careful."

Margarita rose at three o'clock the next morning. First she mixed, rolled out, and griddled a batch of tortillas. While they cooled on a clean cotton dish towel she dressed herself and packed a small suitcase. Just before she left the house she wrapped the tortillas tightly in waxed paper and cheese cloth and stowed them in the bag along with six pairs of woolen socks and a handful of Hershey bars that Miguel had brought from the store. Then she kissed her sleeping family goodbye and was gone.

Miguel, who did not drive, had fully intended for his brother and business partner, Joaquín, to drive Margarita to the railroad station. As usual, nothing between the brother and sister-in-law was ever that simple, not with their history of mutual wariness. Joaquín had learned early on that he could not control Margarita, he could only contain her by controlling her husband. This he tried to do at every opportunity. It had nothing to do with malice. In fact he rather liked Margarita for her youthful spirit and recognized her as his intellectual equal, one whose company, under different circumstances, he would have certainly sought. His need for control sprang solely from guilt. Having cheated his brother more than once, he could not risk discovery by allowing Miguel and his wife any sense of independence from his influence.

"It's a waste of time and money just to see Alfonso for a half hour. Why doesn't she just phone him?" Joaquín hissed into his brother's ear while Miguel tried to wait on a customer at the meat counter.

When Miguel told him that the money was taken care of and that Margarita was adamant about the trip, Joaquín walked away in a sulk. Perhaps he could not sabotage her plans but there were certainly other ways to complicate matters to show that he was still in charge.

When he came back from delivering groceries that afternoon, he informed Miguel that the panel truck was acting up.

"I'd better get it over to the garage right away. We need it for deliveries tomorrow."

For Miguel, to whom *La Tienda* was everything, this made consummate good sense, except that he also knew that the truck was always balky, always in need of some attention. "Can't it wait?"

"Of course it can," Joaquín shot back. "Everything can wait. But if we lose customers because we can't make deliveries don't come crying to me."

When Miguel informed Margarita of the problem she responded, "That's fine. I'll walk. I did it this morning and I can do it again tomorrow."

"Maybe Joaquín can borrow Marigold's car," Miguel suggested.

"I'll walk."

The next morning, the two-mile walk across the river and through the deserted heart of New Town took her about half an hour.

When the train arrived she boarded immediately. Unchallenged, she edged her way down the aisle of a crowded car and found a space to stand next to the water cooler.

She looked out the window at the gathering light to the east until she heard the conductor yell his "All aboard."

With the sound of escaping steam, the train lurched and began to move slowly out of the station. The train gathered speed and put Las Vegas behind it. Margarita gauged its speed. How far could the train take her? She calculated the contents of her bag. How long could the provisions sustain her? She had to shake her head vigorously to rid her brain of such foolishness. Then, to distract herself further, she unwrapped one of the tortillas, broke off a section of chocolate bar, and had her breakfast. When she was finished, she sat down on the floor by her bag and eventually nodded off to sleep.

Margarita did not know the time that Alfonso's train would pull into the station. She was in El Paso a day early but her only contact with her brother had been a letter that was now nearly two weeks old. He might have tried to write her again with a change of plans. Perhaps he had already come and gone.

"No, ma'am," the ticket agent advised her, "no troop trains from Fort Bliss yet."

"No, ma'am," he answered to another of her questions. "No way of telling. The army does what it does when it does it. From what I've heard, it'll be sometime tonight or tomorrow."

Margarita staked out a bench in one corner of the depot. With the announcement of every arrival, she grabbed her bag and hurried to the platform. Trains came and went, disgorging and taking on passengers. None of them carried troops. She spent some of her time walking the long brick veranda that flanked the several lines of parallel track. Occasionally, she stopped to look at the jewelry of silver, turquoise, and vermilion coral displayed on blankets by Indian peddlers who sat dispassionately on the cement platform. They were not as plentiful as they had been in Albuquerque, and here they had to compete with Mexicans up from Juárez with their leather goods, black and green onyx chess pieces, and tinwork. Canny about who was a buyer and who was just a browser, most of them did not even bother to look up as Margarita examined their wares. One, figuring that nothing could be lost during the lull between trains, held up a necklace and bracelet to her.

"Ten dollars. Very nice. Very pretty."

Margarita smiled and moved on.

Always she returned to her bench, where she paged through a discarded day-old paper, read Watchtower tracts from a stack at the end of the bench, or napped. Not knowing how long she would have to wait, she rationed out the little money she had brought with her. She bought a bowl of soup and a cup of coffee for supper but mostly she relied on the contents of her bag for a corner of a tortilla or a square of chocolate. These she washed down with tepid water from the public fountain.

It was not until late the next afternoon that the train from Fort Bliss finally pulled in. Its arrival went unannounced. With sudden thunder the doors banged open and a flood of soldiers cascaded into the terminal, laughing and shouting and heading for rest rooms and the restaurant.

She stood on the bench that had been her home for the past twenty-four hours and looked over the mass of bobbing heads. How would she ever find Alfonso? What would he look like? Would she even recognize him? She had her doubts as the men surged by her. They were all so alike in their uniforms. Perhaps she had even looked right at him and not realized it.

"Margarita."

She turned in the direction of the voice and saw her brother fighting his way through the crowd. Of course she could recognize him! It was still Alfonso. He had changed. He was bigger, more filled out. But it was still Alfonso. What actually surprised her was how young he looked. It was probably his shaven head, which made his ears stick out, but there was also a startled innocence about the eyes that made her think of him when he was a boy.

"The train is running late," were his first words when he finally reached her. "We'll only be here for twenty minutes."

Twenty minutes. Too long for hellos and goodbyes and too short for anything else.

"Would you like something to drink?" she asked.

"Yeah, sure."

Margarita pointed toward the cafe. "Over there. But I don't know if we can get in."

"Come on." He scooped up her bag and cut a wake through the crowd for his sister to follow.

In quick order they had elbowed their way through the double doors of the cafe and up to the counter. Alfonso pushed her in front of him so that she was squeezed between two soldiers on swivel stools.

A waitress moved a dirty rag in circles across the countertop, leaving dull streaks of scummy wetness behind. "What's your pleasure?"

"A Coke," Alfonso shouted over the noise of the crowd.

"One Coke. And what about you, honey?"

"A cup of coffee, please."

"Just poured the last of it," the waitress said, "and it'll be ten minutes at least before we have a fresh pot."

The soldier seated at the stool next to them turned to Margarita. It was the cowboy from Roswell who had preceded Alfonso into the whores' room the night he lost his boyhood. "Here you go, ma'am. Take mine. It's done been saucered and blowed. But I ain't taken from it yet."

Margarita started to protest but the soldier was already guiding her to the stool.

"Please, ma'am, take it. I want you to have it."

Margarita reached for her coin purse.

"No, ma'am, it's all right. Lord knows when I'll have the chance to buy a drink for a pretty lady again." He saluted and pushed his way into the crowd behind them.

"What a nice man," Margarita said to Alfonso after she was seated and he was wedged in beside her at the counter. "Do you know him?"

"Oh," said Alfonso a little too offhandedly, "I've seen him around."

They watched while the waitress placed the green glass bottle of Coca-Cola on the counter and bull's-eyed its mouth with a sipping straw. "That'll be a dime when you're ready."

Margarita waited for the woman to move down the counter. "You look good." She leaned into the side of his cheek to be heard.

"You too."

"Where are you going?"

"Somewhere. At least we don't think it's Alaska."

"You can write to us, can't you?"

He nodded.

"Are you happy? Is this what you want?"

He nodded again but she was quick to notice a wariness in his eyes. He flipped a nickel and a dime on the counter.

"Let's get out of here."

The noise in the eatery had reached deafening proportions, and she understood what he was trying to say to her only when he pointed to the door and made a wiggling motion with his hand.

Back in the main terminal, they looked for a quiet spot but even there the din that bounced off the high ceiling overwhelmed.

"Outside," he shouted at her.

The platform was just as crowded but at least here the sound was dissipating upward into the blistering Texas sky. There were soldiers everywhere, and with them were clinging groups of parents, wives, children, and sweethearts.

"I put your name down in case something happens."

"I thought you said you weren't going anywhere dangerous."

"I'll be OK. It's just something they make you do. It doesn't mean anything."

"Well, just be careful."

"Me? Don't worry. I ain't no hero." He parroted a phrase he had heard often during the last two weeks. In his heart of hearts, however, he thought he might welcome the opportunity.

Just as Margarita opened her mouth to answer, a soldier walked by with a whistle clamped between his teeth. He blew on it just as he passed them and up and down the platform and in the terminal the signal was taken up and repeated by other soldiers with other whistles.

"I'd better go," Alfonso said. "I don't want to lose my seat."

"Here," Margarita said and shoved a rolled-up five-dollar bill into his hand.

"What's that?" He opened his hand and laughed. "What do I need money for? They give me food and clothes and a place to sleep. And, don't forget, I make fifteen dollars a month."

"But it's all right. I brought it for you."

"Keep it. Buy something for the boys. I'm OK."

"If you're sure." She took back the bill from him. "I brought you some things." She cracked open the suitcase. "Here are the socks. And I made you some tortillas. I hope they're not too stale. And Miguel sent you some candy bars from the store."

She was talking rapidly now and found it a labor to catch her breath.

Alfonso kept his eyes downcast, squarely on the gifts. "Thanks. This is great. Tell Mamá and Daddy I love them and I'll write as soon as I can."

Margarita took her brother's face in her hands and forced him to look at her. "I won't tell you to hurry home. How lucky you are."

"Yeah. It should be great."

"If the ocean is as beautiful as in the pictures, maybe I could sneak on the train with you."

Alfonso had not heard her attempt at a joke. He pulled his face away from her hands and looked nervously toward the train and the file of soldiers starting to board it.

She patted his cheek. "Go."

He ran from her, butted the front of the line, amid shouts of protest from the other soldiers, and hopped onto the train. He was gone, and he had not looked back.

The Second Battalion departed Angel Island in San Francisco Bay aboard the *USS President Coolidge* on September 9.

Six thousand miles later they steamed into Manila Bay.

Chapter Twenty-Four

We're the battling bastards of Bataan,
No Mamá, no Papá, no Uncle Sam;
No aunts, no uncles, no cousins, no nieces;
No pills, no planes, no artillery pieces.
And nobody gives a damn.
Nobody gives a damn.

We never heard that song in Las Vegas, New Mexico.

All we heard was that the Japanese had overrun the Philippines and that Alfonso was lost to the family somewhere in the jungle.

On good days, my mother hoped for the best. Perhaps Alfonso had been one of the lucky ones who had managed to escape and join one of the Filipino guerrilla bands hiding in the mountains. On bad days, which were most of them, she knew that he was dead or a prisoner who soon would be.

When Margarita told her parents that he was missing in action, Leopoldo cried. Tamar was stoic. Then they got on with their lives. Leopoldo had never been busier or more prosperous with lumber suddenly at a premium. Tamar perceived no actual difference in her day-to-day life with Alfonso gone, whether dead or lost. Her drudgery at the sawmill was unaltered. Her arthritis was always worse. Since it seemed to make no difference one way or another, she chose not to think of Alfonso any more.

The Galváns, along with the rest of Las Vegas, settled in for war on the home front.

Las Vegas had its blackout drills. The sirens, those used to summon the volunteer fire department, blasted across the peaceful evening. Lights went out, window shades were drawn, and families huddled around flickering candles to play cards or dominoes or to tell stories. Outside, the air-raid wardens in their white helmets and armbands patrolled their assigned blocks, whistles at the ready should an illegal chink of light be visible through a window or should they catch the bouncing headlights of someone trying to sneak home.

Uncle Juanito, my father's erstwhile partner, now a house painter, was one of these wardens, and he wore his helmet and armband with great solemnity. One night after the all-clear had been sounded he dropped over to our house for a cup of coffee.

I pointed at the whistle dangling from a shoestring around his neck. "What's that?"

He blew it so loudly that I had to cover my ears. After wiping the mouthpiece on his sleeve, he turned it toward me. "Blow. But only once. It's not a toy for children."

Which, of course, it was, since he had picked it up just a week before at the five-and-dime.

I was delighted with the sound I was able to produce. "Can I play with it?"

"No," he responded, now quite serious. "I need it to help us win the war."

But the whistle still intrigued me. I pointed at some raised lettering on the small, round barrel. "What does that say?"

"Let me see." He held the whistle as far away from his eyes as the stretch of the shoestring around his neck would allow. "Made in Japan," he read slowly, then dropped the whistle so that it bounced against his chest. "But I bought it at Newberry's. I didn't know. What will I do?"

"A whistle is a whistle," noted my father, stifling a grin. "It didn't sound Japanese when you blew it."

The crisis was settled only after Miguel took a file to the brass lettering and scraped it into illegibility.

I looked at the filings sprinkled across the tablecloth and I was horrified. There was something Japanese in our house. Was there no place we could hide? Then I remembered that I had actually had the whistle in my mouth.

I began to cry and no one knew why.

Whenever my mother left the house in those days she always checked her purse to make sure that she carried the family's book of ration stamps.

"You never can tell," she said to me, "when you might run into some shoes or sugar."

Each month some three billion postage-size stamps passed hands across the country, from the government to consumers, to retailers, to wholesalers, to manufacturers, and back to the government. Every man, woman, and child was entitled to two ration books monthly. One had forty-eight blue stamps for canned goods. The other book held sixty-four stamps for meat, fish, fats, and dairy products. Of course, having the stamps was no guarantee that you could obtain the products. Finding the store that carried the item you needed was the game.

"Where did you get the pound of sugar?" my father asked my mother one day. "We haven't had sugar at the store for a week."

"Safeway."

Safeway! If there existed a more odious word in the English language, my father had yet to hear it. Better that he had been told that Margarita had spread her legs at high noon in the plaza for the emperor of Japan in exchange for the sugar than to hear that she had actually walked into Safeway and stood in line for it.

"You went into Safeway?" How could my father tolerate such treason under his very roof?

"No," my mother answered sweetly. "When they heard that Miguel Galván's wife was standing out in the parking lot they brought it out to me."

"What will people say?"

My mother carefully measured out half a spoonful of sugar into Luis's and my oatmeal. "I don't know. Why don't you ask Marigold? Or your sister, María. Or your mother. They were all standing in line with me."

Second only to Safeway, my father held the words *black market* most in contempt.

"Conrad's Market is selling under-the-counter bacon," he might say in tones usually reserved for talking about *los volteados*, those Hispanic turncoats who had abandoned the Holy Mother Church for the Baptists or the Jehovah's Witnesses.

Although, as children, we cared little about the scarcity of such grown-up items as coffee, we were very much put out that we were now being denied the pleasures of bubble gum. It had something to do, we were told, with chicle, the prime ingredient of all chewing gum. Chicle came from trees in South America, and ships that would normally bring it to our shores had been diverted for more important uses. So when we heard that the man at the barber shop was selling bubble gum for five cents apiece, Luis and I turned criminals twice over. First we stole a dime from our mother's purse, then we spent it in the black market.

With our ill-gotten purchases in hand, we ran home. First there was the careful untwisting of the ends of the paper wrapping. With trembling hands we took the perfect little drums of pink from their wrappers. Next we licked the powdery residue off the paper. Then we lifted the gum to our noses to inhale its singular aroma. Finally we popped the tiny pink pillows into our mouths and began to chew. This batch was hard and stale but we didn't care. It was bubble gum. We worked it with our teeth for a while until our jaws ached with the effort. Now the moment of truth. We shaped the gum around our tongues, sucked in extra breath and blew.

My father caught us in mid blow.

"Where did you get that?"

Luis and I looked at each other.

"I asked you where you got it."

Luis let me speak for both of us.

"The barber shop."

"Black market." My father spat out the words with such vehemence that I felt the gum harden into a chalky lump in my mouth. Then he held out a hand and we spat our contraband into it.

"Don't you know there's a war going on?"

He had often proclaimed that the people who said, "Don't you know there's a war going on?" were just looking for an excuse to deliver shoddy products and sloppy service. I did not dare remind him of his inconsistency at this moment.

Alfonso was not the only one of their children that Leopoldo and Tamar would sacrifice to the war. Their two oldest sons had been 4-F'd, Eugenio for ludicrously flat feet and Gerónimo for chronic asthma. But Agapita, Margarita's younger sister, also heard the call of her country. Her acceptance had nothing to do with patriotism.

By 1943, a full third of America's work force was female. This included those working in the private sector, everything from auto mechanics to hearse drivers, as well as those directly involved in war-related industries.

Agapita had not had an easy time of it. She had married at seventeen. Her husband was a roustabout whom she followed from oil field to oil field, where he worked, got drunk, shot dice, lost all his money, fought, and was fired. By the time they got to Nevada, where he found work in an open-pit copper mine, their marriage had failed and she was pregnant.

After a quickie Reno divorce, she returned to New Mexico and moved in with her parents at the sawmill. There she was exposed to German measles through her baby sister, Constancia. Seven months later she delivered herself of a son, Hector, born with seal flippers for arms. Back in Las Vegas, she took a small apartment, left the baby with Margarita, and learned the seamstress's trade.

"I'm going to Oakland," she announced to her sister one day. "They're hiring at the factories that sew for the army. It's better than anything I can find around here."

Margarita, never one to discourage anyone willing to make the break with Las Vegas, made no argument.

Julio Coca did. "But I love you," he told Agapita, "and I won't let you go."

Agapita laughed in his face. "Don't talk crazy. I never told you to get serious. It was all fun."

"You'd better not go if you know what's good for you. That's all I have to say."

She told him to go home.

A week later Agapita left for California.

"You can start whenever you want," the woman behind the desk at the uniform factory told her.

"As soon as I can find a place to stay."

"Good luck on that. Of course, you are Mexican. Most people don't want to live in the Mexican section of town. You're chances are better there."

Agapita ignored the slur but heeded the suggestion. By day's end

she had found a unit in a duplex where the landlady occupied the
other. For a reasonable price, the woman agreed to sit with five-year-
old Hector during the day. Agapita wrote home:

> Dear Margarita,
> I found a job! I'm sewing dress uniforms for officers in
> the Army. Very nice material. If it wasn't such an ugly color
> I'd steal some and send it to you. Oakland is a crazy town.
> There are lot's of cute sailors but I'm too tired after work to
> do anything about it. No fun cuz there's no place to spend the
> mun (???). Hector also takes a lot of my time so I'm really out
> of circulation.
> Tell Eugenio and Gerónimo that if they want to get out
> of the sawmill and make some real money they should come
> here. There's jobs for everybody.
> Say hi to Mom and Dad.
> I miss you all.
> Agapita

Leopoldo would hear none of it. "We're making enough money
here. Why go to California?"

Before Eugenio could complain that he and Gerónimo were seeing none of this prosperity, Leopoldo switched on the giant saw and
rolled a log onto the trestle for cutting.

That Friday, after Eugenio had delivered the weekly load of lumber to the lumberyard, he walked into one of the bars on Bridge
Street for a beer.

"Eugenio! Come have a drink with me." It was Julio Coca calling to him from the far end of the bar.

After Eugenio had drunk two more beers than he had intended,
all at Julio's expense, the conversation came around to Agapita.

"How's she doing?" asked Julio.

"Fine. Making lots of money."

"We're thinking of getting married."

"She never said nothing."

"Mujeres. You know how they are."

Eugenio didn't so he let the comment slide.

"By the way, I lost her address. Do you know it?"

Eugenio produced Agapita's letter, which he was still carrying in his pocket to return to Margarita before he left town.

Two weeks later Agapita turned up the sidewalk to her home and saw Julio Coca sitting on the top step of her porch.

"Surprise."

"What are you doing here?"

"I've come to Oakland to visit you. Aren't you happy to see me?"

"We settled all this in Las Vegas."

"I know. I know. But we can still be friends. *¿Qué no?*"

"I don't have time for friends. I have a son to take care of. Go away."

She tried to maneuver past him but Julio put up a hand to the porch post to block her.

"Hey, is that the thanks I get for coming all this way, especially since it might be the last time?"

"What do you mean?"

"Actually, I'm here because I've joined the navy," he lied. "We're shipping out tomorrow. I just didn't want to be alone on my last night in the States."

Agapita was disarmed by this announcement. She was also thinking that it had been a long time between breaks from the routine. And Julio knew how to have a good time, she gave him that. "What did you have in mind?"

"Oh, I don't know. Maybe a movie. A little dancing. Nothing much. I have to be back at the barracks by eleven. For an old friend? How about it?"

"All right then. But I can't stay out late. I have to work tomorrow."

"I'll pick you up at six."

"Seven. I need to get ready and feed Hector and take him over to my landlady's."

"Six-thirty?"

Agapita shook her head in resignation and laughed for the first time. "Six-thirty."

Julio was at her door fifteen minutes early.

"I couldn't wait," he said and pushed his way by her and into the apartment.

Agapita closed her bathrobe at the throat. "I'm still not ready."

Julio took a seat on the small settee by the front window. "That's OK. I'll just sit here and stay out of your way."

"Well, let me take Hector next door and then I'll finish dressing."

By the time Agapita was back from delivering her son, Julio was in the kitchen.

"What are you doing?" she asked, her aggravation returning.

"Ice," he said and continued to chip away at the block in the top section of the icebox. "I thought we might have a little drink."

"And I thought we were going out."

"Why go out? There's so little time. We've got everything we need here. I brought some whiskey. You've got a radio. We can dance a little, drink a little. A little of this and a little of that."

"I knew this was going to happen. I think you'd better leave."

Julio stopped chipping at the ice block and turned squarely to face her. "What's the matter, Agapita? Are you too busy being a little *puta* for all the sailors in town? Didn't you save something for an old sweetheart?"

"Get out, or I'll get somebody to throw you out!"

She turned to the door and heard him say, "Not again, Agapita, not ever again," just before he plunged the ice pick into her back.

When the landlady had not heard from Agapita by midnight and saw that the lights were on next door with the radio blaring, she went over. There she found two bodies.

According to the coroner's report, Agapita had died of multiple stab wounds.

"I stopped counting after thirty," he told the detective in charge of the investigation.

Julio Coca slit his wrists and drank a tumbler full of lye. He languished for two days before he died.

Agapita's funeral in Mora was sparsely attended. The shortage of tires and gasoline made travel difficult for some. Others used it as an excuse for not being part of the biggest scandal to rock the family within anyone's memory.

One of the tabloids in Oakland, brought home by Leopoldo when he went to claim his daughter's body, said it all. "Lovers' Tryst

Goes Bad!" screamed the headline. Below it was a photograph of a detective in a fedora hat. His fingers, protected by a handkerchief, dangled the ice pick by its handle. Superimposed in one corner of the photograph was an intertwined pair of oval frames. In them was an artist's sketch of Agapita and Julio, drawn from photographs a morgue attendant had been bribed to take.

"I don't know why she ever went to California," Tamar remarked to a cousin who stayed with her after the funeral. "Leaving home never went well for her. Look at Nevada. Well, at least we found someone who wants Hector. They need a child and he needs a mother and father. We're lucky someone would have him with those arms of his."

And those were her last words on the subject of her daughter Agapita.

When Margarita returned home from her sister's funeral in Mora there was an official-looking envelope waiting for her. Inside was a bent and soiled postcard. On it was a printed form that someone had filled out on a typewriter.

> **IMPERIAL JAPANESE ARMY**
> 1. I AM INTERNED AT (left blank)
> 2. MY HEALTH IS . . . EXCELLENT; FAIR; POOR.
> 3. I AM . . . INJURED; SICK IN HOSPITAL;
>   UNDER TREATMENT
> 4. I AM . . . IMPROVING; NOT IMPROVING; BETTER
> 5. PLEASE SEE THAT (left blank) IS TAKEN CARE OF.
> 6. RE: FAMILY: (left blank)
> 7. PLEASE GIVE MY REGARDS TO Mom and Dad

When the 200th arrived in the Philippines in 1942 they were 1,800 strong. Cowboys. Artisans. Lawyers. Teachers. Miners. Merchants. Husbands. Fathers. Men. Boys.

Only half of these saw New Mexico again.

By the grace of God and with the unflagging support of his brothers in arms, Alfonso was one of them.

Would she know him?

Margarita stood on the platform of the train depot in Las Vegas on a cool, cloudless September day in 1945. The train had arrived on schedule and she watched the conductor swing from the door of one of the cars and put down a portable step.

A soldier stepped into the daylight. Momentarily blinded by the sun's reflection off the silver skin of the car, Margarita could not see. Then the soldier stepped down into the shadows and she smiled. Of course she would know him. It was Alfonso, her brother. Thin? Of course. Older? Yes. But she also noticed that he had not lost that familiar look of startled innocence.

They embraced, and as he held her close he whispered in her ear, "I don't ever want to leave home again."

Part Three

Michael

Chapter Twenty-Five

I am Margarita Zamora Galván.

Sometimes, mostly at night when I lie beside my husband, Miguel the butcher, I take stock of myself. *Margarita-No-Cuenta.*

I call myself no-account not so much from self-pity as in regret for opportunities lost. I now content myself with enjoying small triumphs dotted across a desert of insignificance—as is only proper for a woman of my station.

1950–1955

So what happened after I met my brother Alfonso on the platform of the train depot in Las Vegas, New Mexico, on his return from four years in a Japanese prisoner-of-war camp?

Many people died. Among others, my dear mother-in-law, Francisquita Galván; Magistrate Baca, who broke my heart when he broke my son, Miguelito; and Soledea, the princess bride.

My younger, son, Michael, was ordained a priest and left in disgrace seven years later. And Miguel and I bought our first car, a Chevrolet Bel Air.

As with everything that involved money, the store, and my brother-in-law Joaquín, the purchase of the car was not a simple thing.

Joaquín had not learned anything from his close shave with the law while embezzling bank funds. He insisted that all major purchases and expenses by either family be paid for through the store.

"Tax purposes," he explained. "We can hide a lot of our income."

When I heard this from Miguel, I had to laugh. "What income?"

The brothers showed as little personal wealth as possible. The store owned a panel truck, which they used to deliver groceries. And for all the good it did Miguel and me, the store also owned, on paper at least, Joaquín's home and a Plymouth coupe, which he purchased for his wife, the angular Anglo Marigold.

"She's always sick," Joaquín explained to Miguel, and through him to me. "She needs a way to get to the doctor. And God forbid she should have an emergency. We'll see about a car for you next year. If business is better." It never was, according to his reading of the account books.

Of course, I was having none of it, but Miguel warned me repeatedly not to disturb the delicate balance between the two brothers. "We need the store. We don't need a car. Don't go and make Joaquín mad. He's still talking about maybe finding other work. Then where would we be?"

Joaquín had at least agreed to pay for our elder son's high school education at an all-boys Christian Brothers academy in Amarillo, Texas. He was quick to point out, however, that since he and Marigold had not been blessed with children, this gave Miguel and me a real head start in using the store's small reserves.

"Here's the check for the first three months' tuition," Miguel said to me one day in late August before what was to be Luis's sophomore year at the school.

I took the $630-dollar check, folded it with great care by matching up the four corners, and slipped it into the pocket of my apron. As best I could, I hid from my husband the twist to the edges of my mouth while I served him his supper.

For, you see, there was a family secret, one that only Luis and I knew about, and he had been sworn to silence. He would not be returning to Amarillo that fall. He had not done well in his freshmen year, the director of the school had informed us in a letter. I did not share this news with my husband.

After Miguel left for work the next morning, I put on my best, went to the bank, stood at the high marble table, endorsed the tuition check, deposited it into the family checking account, walked across the bridge to New Town and into the Chevrolet dealership, opened up the checkbook, and made the down-payment on the Bel Air.

Afterward, I went to the Woolworth counter for a club sandwich and a fountain Coke, shopped at the J. C. Penney's for some undershirts for Miguel, recrossed the bridge into Old Town, walked up Bridge Street, crossed the park, and entered the door of Galván's Grocery.

It was that quiet time after the rush of the noon hour and Joaquín was at the front counter immersed in the latest issue of *Grocery Sales and Promotions Monthly*.

I plopped down a packet of papers in front of him and waited. "What's this?"

"The papers for the store's new car."

"What new car?"

"The one I just bought with Luis's tuition money. We've decided that Amarillo's not a good place for him."

"But you can't use that money to buy a car."

"Well, it's too late to tell me that now. The money's spent. Look at the papers."

The papers, when Joaquín spread them open, told the story. Owner: Galván's Grocery. Acting Agent: Margarita Galván, Second Vice-President.

I tried not to sound too nasty. "Marigold is still First Vice-President, isn't she?"

Then I went to the back of the store to the meat department, where Miguel was standing. He had heard it all but chose to stay behind the barricade of his butcher block. His eyes were as popped out and white as the joints of the soup bones he was trimming.

I placed the keys to the car on the milky enamel top of the meat case. "Here, find a way to get it home. It's blue with a cream top. You'll like it."

I did not even bother to stop when I walked by Joaquín on my way out the door. "The payments are thirty-two dollars a month. They said I was really good at driving a bargain."

And I was gone.

And that's how we got our first car.

The summer of 1955 was not a good one for me. My father, Leopoldo, died in early June at the age of sixty-six.

It was not sudden. Like many alcoholics he had stretched out his wasting away over a number of years, during which his liver slowly lost the cells it needed to, as the doctor said, "metabolize the ethanol which he consumed in all forms."

He liked bourbon the most, and he would go to great lengths to obtain it. He and my mother were now living in retirement in Las Vegas, where they played that game shared by addicts and their caretakers everywhere.

When Leopoldo ran out of his stash of hooch, hidden in an old boot or in the toolshed behind the house, he would get in his truck and drive to the plaza and down Bridge Street. This short block had at least six saloons with such pretty names as The Palms Garden and La Mariposa. At each Leopoldo was known and served. A few good snorts and a bottle in a brown paper bag and he was back home in half an hour.

Tamar would go through his trousers at night and remove his wallet and keys. This did no good whatsoever since Leopoldo had long before hid a duplicate set of keys beneath a loose piece of flagstone by the side of the house. Having no wallet was not a problem either since his truck carried a bottomless chest of tools that were as good as gold to the saloon keepers, who conducted a profitable side business as pawnbrokers. In Las Vegas, if you were shopping for an authentic piece of Indian silver, you didn't go to the jewelry store, you went to one of the bars.

Tamar next asked one of the neighbors to remove the distributor cap from the truck. This did no good since Leopoldo had several extras in the toolshed. Tamar had a padlock put on the shed. Leopoldo had already guessed ahead and had taken the caps to a closet at the top of the stairs of their rented house that Tamar could not climb because of her arthritis. The truck, however, stopped being a problem when Leopoldo ran it headlong into a tree and punctured the radiator. Then he backed up the vehicle and drove it until he burned out the engine.

No quitter, my father took to the road on foot and walked the painful mile into town for his daily bottle. With no truck, there were no tools to barter with. But he was able to set up a running tab at two of his favorite cantinas by showing them that his signature was still good and the bank would cover his bill.

Then Tamar took away his shoes, one pair at a time, until he was left in his stocking feet to pad back and forth in the house like an old badger. But Leopoldo still had a few cards up his sleeve.

One day Tamar phoned me to say that Leopoldo had walked away again, "in bare feet," she supposed.

I was used to this kind of call. I often had to fetch my father, and I knew all of his favorite bars. Indeed, when I entered the very first saloon on my list, there he was at the bar, entertaining a fellow drunkard with talk about government regulations and how hard it was for small operators to make a profit from timber cut on National Forest lands. And he had not walked into town barefoot. On his feet I saw a pair of salmon-colored satin mules with oversized pompoms. I recognized them as the slippers I had given my mother for her birthday three weeks before.

When Leopoldo was delivered back to his warden, Tamar made a bundle of his shirts and trousers and gave them to me. "If we need to go someplace, you can bring over a set of his clothes. He might wear my slippers into town but I don't think he'll put on one of my dresses."

Tamar was right. Leopoldo was finally grounded. The point was hers but not the game.

One day, when Tamar felt a sudden taste for some custard, she brought out a large mixing bowl, some eggs, milk, and sugar and set them on the kitchen table. When she opened the cabinet where she kept the spices and took down the brown bottle of vanilla extract, she found it empty. A check of the other bottles of flavorings on the shelf showed that they were also drained.

As it turned out, nothing in the house with even a hint of alcohol had escaped Leopoldo's hankerings. In one day in the bathroom, he polished off some hair tonic as an eye opener. The aftershave lotion proved a satisfying afternoon treat. The rubbing alcohol and liniment for Tamar's aching joints gave him several after-dinner drinks. And for a nightcap? What else? A bottle of *Evening in Paris* cologne.

When Leopoldo and I sat down in the doctor's office, the old man was already eyeing the tall glass column of alcohol, which held a variety of stainless-steel medical instruments. He licked his lips. I could have just strangled him.

We were there because Dr. Mercer invited us in, at my request, for a little chat. On the desk was a stack of photos in vivid color of livers in various conditions.

"Leopoldo," the doctor began, "you're killing yourself."

"I know, I know," my father answered. He looked out the window. Probably he was trying to visualize all that liquor out there and he unable to get any of it.

"Here, let me show you what I mean." The doctor pushed the photographs across the desk so that they lay right under my father's nose. "Now see this? That's what a healthy liver looks like."

"Where did it come from?" Leopoldo asked after thinking about it for a moment.

"What?"

"The liver. Who did it belong to?"

"Well, I don't really know."

"A dead person?"

"Yes, I think it would be safe to say that. This liver would have to be from a cadaver."

"So, it's a healthy liver from a dead person who died of something else?"

"Yes, I guess it is." The doctor was unsure where he was being led.

My father leaned back and the haze once again dropped over his eyes to cover that twinkle that I knew so well but had not seen in so long. I knew what he was up to. Fluster people and get away in the confusion. It had always worked for him before. But not this time. I would sit on him if that's what it took for him to listen to reason.

"Anyway, that's not important." The doctor did not sound too happy with the interruption. "What is important is to compare it with an unhealthy liver."

Dr. Mercer took the picture on the top of the stack and moved it to the side to show another photo.

"This is what happens when the body takes in more alcohol than the liver can handle. First you start to kill off healthy cells, and when you do that the liver starts to retain fluids it would ordinarily process. Then the liver gets inflamed and it swells. See how big that looks compared to the other liver I showed you?"

Leopoldo nodded but I knew he could no longer remember what had been said about the other liver.

"Now then, the body tries to make more cells but it can't. All it can do is produce tough fibrous stuff, like dried-up orange pulp. You see what I mean?" He took a desiccated orange half from the side drawer of his desk and placed it next to the photo.

Leopoldo stared at the orange and licked his lips once again. What was he thinking? Oranges. Orange juice. Orange juice and vodka?

Dr. Mercer took the photo of the enlarged liver and moved it to the side. The picture beneath was of a distorted, knobby-skinned mass of tissue that looked like a football that somebody had taken all the air out of.

"See what happens then? The fibers make the liver hard and bumpy. We call it a hobnail liver since the bumps look like nail heads."

The doctor put a fat finger on the photograph and began to tap across it, hitting node after node. "See how hard that is?"

Leopoldo looked at the desktop with a lumberman's eye. "Walnut. Good wood."

"And when this happens," the doctor continued, now refusing to be sucked in by Leopoldo's nonsense, "the liver stops working. And when that happens, you die."

The doctor leaned back. All in all, aside from stumbling on that bit about the healthy liver from the dead person, I thought that his talk had gone pretty well. From the smile on his face, it seemed that the doctor thought so too.

I spoke up. "So, Daddy, is that what you want? To die?"

Leopoldo raised a shaky hand to scratch his head. He obviously needed time to come up with an answer that would satisfy everyone. His gesture drew attention to the red, finely drawn, spidery network across his scalp, like very delicate embroidery stitches over white linen. His drinking had ruptured many capillaries, and the evidence extended down from the top of his bald head to his pale, Dutch face, across his cheeks and nose, onto his neck and underneath his shirt to widen and spread like a river delta across his trunk to his belly, buttocks, and legs. I had seen all this on many an occasion when I had to undress him for bed or bath.

"Is it?" I repeated when he did not answer. "Is that what you want?" I stabbed at the air above the photograph of the hobnail liver. "To carry that around in you?"

The doctor took up the cause again. "Leopoldo, I'm telling you this now. Unless you stop drinking, you'll be dead in six months."

Six months? So long to wait? I could see the questions in the squint of his eyes and the tilt of his head. He was so very, very tired of it all. Ten years of pain after the two-ton pillar of pine rolled on his leg and pinned him. Ten years of hobbling on one good leg. Reduced to sitting at the saw while others drove the horses up the trails to retrieve the giant logs of ponderosa. Ten years of shrieking saw blades, his face a perpetual mask of sawdust. The forced retirement. The weaning from the morphine when the pharmacist would no longer refill his prescription. The drink. And now, six months more, the doctor said.

The doctor was off by two. It took only four more months to kill Leopoldo.

Chapter Twenty-Six

1955

Shortly after my father's death, our son Michael told us that he wished to study for the priesthood. Miguel was delighted. I, to my own surprise, said nothing one way or the other.

Later I went up and hugged Michael. "I've thought it over. How wonderful! Imagine—my son, a priest. A very important thing. You'll be able to go places and see things. No family to hold you down. And I won't have to share you with another woman."

I don't know why I said this last. I certainly did not feel it. Just something to bring the conversation to an end.

Michael was not a strong boy—healthy enough, I suppose, but wobbly in his spirit. My fault. I had both babied and mothered him. What could I do? I did not want to lose another one. He was my second Miguelito, after all. So I protected him from everything, including the realities of life. And the priesthood seemed a safe enough place to hide him from whatever could hurt him.

What I could not discount, as well, was the pleasure I was starting to feel. A priest. A man of importance. Somebody. A pillar of the community like my Uncle Delfino, el juez. Much more than what any of us—Miguel, myself, our brothers and sisters—had accomplished. What more could I ask for Michael?

What more could I dare ask for myself?

Chapter Twenty-Seven

1966

On a bright, early spring day in 1966, I, Margarita Juana Galván, buried my mother, Tamar, in Las Vegas, New Mexico. I mean that I was the chief mourner while my son, Father Michael, conducted her funeral.

As the eldest, I sat with my husband, Miguel, the sole occupants of the front pew. Behind us were the rest of Tamar's children—the four sons, Eugenio, Gerónimo, Alfonso, and Elisandro, and the only other surviving daughter, Constancia. Missing were the children who were already gone, two at birth, and Agapita, a rejected lover's murder victim. Tamar's husband, Leopoldo, had died eleven years earlier.

I could tell that my eyes were wet but not swollen. I had not cried nearly enough for that. Even the few tears I dabbed were not so much from grief over the death of my mother as from regret that my mother's death could cause so few tears.

I had never much liked her. Few did. Tamar had not been blessed with a loving personality, and she had not aged well. She was blunt and standoffish, an old woman people tended to avoid.

Greet her with a pleasant *good morning* and you left yourself open to some comment about your appearance.

"You don't look good. Too fat," or "That dress just doesn't fit you. You should wear something more your age."

Go further and ask about her health, and you risked the good name of your children.

"What are they doing in there? What are they trying to break now? Why don't you teach them better?"

No remark was too offhand or innocent to elude her acid tongue. She was at her happiest when she could drill you with her little yellow eyes and slice at you with her razor tongue.

To my knowledge she had no close friends. To my recollection, I had never seen her hug or kiss anyone, man, woman, or child—ever.

Tamar's funeral took place in the days before the New Mass, when we would have sent her on her way with guitars and bongo drums.

Instead, my son recited the traditional Latin poem of the dead, the *Dies Irae*, and God called Tamar to judgment amid black and purple mourning colors and a sad Gregorian chant badly sung and accompanied on a wheezing organ. Then it was off to the cemetery.

The funeral procession uncoiled into a long snake of cars, pickups, and panel trucks headed by a black-and-chrome hearse and two limousines that carried the immediate family. The caravan made its way out of the town and into a countryside of squat hills dotted with sagebrush, prairie grass, and stunted pine trees. To the left, a trailer court nestled up to an open field covered with discarded automobiles in various stages of being taken apart. The sun bounced off a pile of silver hubcaps and into our eyes as we passed by. Finally, we turned onto an unpaved road, rattled over a rusty cattle guard made from ten-foot lengths of rusting railroad tracks, and entered the *camposanto*.

A *camposanto*, a blessed field, is not a park for the living to enjoy, and it is nothing like the cemeteries I've seen in movies and magazines. There are no manicured lawns under perpetual care. There are no maintenance covenants here, or rules that control native creativity. It is a place for the dead and fulfills its purpose to perfection. It is not a disgracefully neglected piece of land, as I've heard some people say, but a personalized memorial to the individuals who lie buried here.

The hearse stopped on a stretch of hard, rut-scarred mud a few yards from a freshly dug grave. A mound of dirt and the area around it were covered with worn green sections of carpeting. The motorcade, which had stretched out for nearly a half mile while in transit, now compressed like an old sofa spring to a more modest size as each vehicle pulled up to kiss the bumper of the one in front of it.

People piled out of the cars and the slamming of doors reverberated across the camposanto, dead, hollow thuds relieved only by a cough, a snort, a laugh, a shuffling of feet through weeds and adobe dust.

We picked our way through patches of nettles and briars that, like souls looking for one last prayer, reached out to grab us. We passed through a strange garden of wire frames, wreaths, and crosses, stuck into the ground on spindly legs. They held onto faded remnants of crepe-paper pink carnations, white lilies, red roses, and green leaves. Some of the graves were marked by lidless Mason jars that had once held fresh flowers, but were now only receptacles for twigs and dried sediment that coated their insides with a chalky, tan film.

A friend of the family delivered the eulogy. The address was mercifully short and dwelt on Tamar's fifty-year struggle with arthritis that eventually twisted her into a knot of dried-up flesh and swollen, dislocated joints. She seldom complained, the speaker said, but accepted her situation with resignation. This was true. My mother could not tolerate pity and had been strangely attached to her affliction, certainly the most loyal companion she ever had.

She had been a saint, a Job, a model of patient suffering for those around her, continued the eulogist. This was not true. No one present thought that Tamar was a model for anything. You just didn't talk about her in those terms. In fact, mostly you didn't talk about her at all. Unless she were present in the room with you, you tended not even to think about her.

Afterward, on signal from the funeral director, we approached the grave and stooped down for handfuls of dirt to toss into the void. It was quite orderly, solemn and dignified. Small, soft clods of dirt gently kissed the bronze lid, slid off its smooth, metallic skin, and pattered like raindrops into the pine liner.

This ritual was suddenly shattered by a jarring clang. One of Tamar's great-grandchildren, a wiry five-year-old, had armed himself with a baseball-sized piece of rock-hard clay and flung it with all his might at the casket. The boy's father was instantly on him and jerked him to one side by one of his scrawny arms. We walked back to our cars to the rhythmic clap of several smacks being applied to a small, bony backside. I expected screams and wails but heard only denial.

"What?" he screamed. "I didn't!"

Back at our house people streamed in to plant kisses, exchange embraces, and shake hands. Those with food moved on to deposit aluminum-foil-covered platters and bowls on all available surfaces. There were turkey and ham, whacked generously into fat, uneven slices. There were bowls of prepared salads; rainbow concoctions of grated carrots with raisins in sweet mayonnaise; and lime, orange, and cherry gelatin molds holding suspended bits of fruit cocktail and secret caches of cottage cheese. There were steaming bowls of pinto beans with chunks of salt pork floating on top. There were julienne green beans studded with slivered almonds and French-fried onion slivers from the can. Tureens of mashed potatoes whipped to tiny peaks. Casseroles of chopped creamed squash mixed with corn kernels and laced with thin strips of green chile that made the unwary weep. And, of course, there was the red chile, fiery stews of bite-sized cubes of pork and beef or ragouts of ground meat for scooping with pieces of tortilla.

People ate and talked and children ran in and out of doors to amuse themselves with those endless games of chasing and being chased. The talk was as expected. Everyone tried to dredge up any pleasant memory they might have of Tamar. What emerged was a litany of her pettiness and ill temper. The best that could be said for her was that she had indeed suffered a lot of physical pain and self-imposed loneliness.

The consensus of the afternoon was that Tamar's main accomplishment in life was that she had outlived her brothers and sisters. For her, this had probably been enough. For all her failures in life, set against the successes she so begrudged her siblings, she alone had met life's greatest challenge. She had died last.

All of Tamar's sisters and brothers had lived well. All of them had large ranches with considerable herds of cattle or thriving businesses in the city. But none of them, not one, had died in bed.

A brother, Donaciano, was killed while chopping down a tree. The tree, dead for many years, had stood as an eyesore at the edge of his property from the day he and his bride had moved in. Ten years later he finally decided, after the constant naggings of his wife had worn him down, that it was time to bring the old tree down.

"We'll have a picnic," his triumphant wife declared.

So there they sat, his wife and four children, in comfort on a large blanket with a pail of cool spring water and a freshly laundered cotton flour sack that yielded some cold chicken wrapped in cheese cloth, a jar of pickled beets, some bread, and, treat of treats, a watermelon.

The day was sunny, the air was festive, and Donaciano's labors were mighty. The tree had petrified into an iron-hard pillar that mocked his puny ax strokes. Two of the bolder children came close to watch and make a game of dodging the few chips of wood that flew off his ax blade.

His wife chattered away about the trip they would be making to Albuquerque in a few weeks to visit her parents. She took the green globe of melon and with a sure hand and a wide kitchen knife hacked it neatly in two. With a few more strokes it lay in sections.

"Take a rest. Come have some melon. See how red and sweet it is," went her call to her sweating husband.

As he walked to his wife, thinking that perhaps, after all, the tree didn't look so bad where it stood, there was a loud crack. A gust of wind suddenly uprooted the tree, which, unknown to Donaciano, had been ready to topple from its own weight for some time. How majestically it came down. How squarely it fell on him. A splintered branch went through his back and neatly skewered his heart.

Tamar's sister Emilia had been shot to death by her son-in-law, who claimed he thought he was firing on an intruder in the dark of night. She was on her way back from the outhouse, grumbling that her soon-to-be assassin had forgotten her as usual when he passed out the chamber pots that evening. She had noticed the slight but said nothing. She preferred to walk outside in the cold so that she would have something to complain about to her daughter the next morning over coffee.

No one in the family really believed the son-in-law's story about what he saw and heard that would cause him to fire his gun blindly out the window. But nothing could be proved and nothing was ever openly said.

The youngest brother, Pacunio, also died of a gunshot wound—self-inflicted, the authorities determined. It was another of those curious accidents that were stuffed into a family closet already bursting with skeletons. As his wife told it, he had been drinking heavily. They argued, and while he struggled to pull a revolver from a gunnysack to shoot her he had accidentally discharged the weapon into one of his own eyesockets. Strangely, the gunnysack had no bullet hole nor any traces of powder burn. His wife offered no further explanation and none was sought.

Another sister, Elisea, was gored to death by an angry bull when she tried to save time by crossing a field on her way to church.

Rachel, Tamar's youngest sister, drowned in the Great Salt Lake. She was afraid of water but her friends assured her that she could not sink. Unfortunately, her bathing garment ballooned and she floated face down for many minutes before anyone noticed her.

For the better part of the afternoon my son Michael succeeded in avoiding me and I him. I attended to the needs of our guests and he found a spot to lean against a car in our driveway to welcome or say goodbye to the sympathizers who came to kiss our cheeks and eat our food.

Neither he nor I wanted to renew a conversation that had ended so badly about a week before.

"I just need a change of scenery," he had told me.

"Again?"

It was his third assignment to a new parish for the year.

"The archbishop sends me where they need me." He sounded defensive.

I knew he was lying just as surely as I had come to believe all the rumors that had drifted into Las Vegas over the past two years from the places where Michael had been stationed.

The drinking. The hospitals. The moves.

Finally, he sought me out.

"I've got to go now. Sorry about Grandma." His hug was not that of a man but of a child in fear.

"Already? We didn't even get to visit."

"I'll call you."

"From where?"

"Albuquerque."

I pulled away to look into his eyes.

"What?" he asked. "I've got my letter of assignment. Want to see it?"

"No, I don't want to see it." I heard an edge to my voice that I had not used since Michael was still a boy living in my house.

"Well, OK, then I guess I'd better get going."

"I guess."

Now there were real tears in my eyes. I had feared for his career and I had feared for his health. These were nothing to the fear I now felt for his soul.

By the time he got on the highway for Albuquerque, it was almost dark.

Part Four

MARGARITA JUANA AND MIGUEL

Chapter Twenty-Eight

1969–1970

The Israelites laid the towns [of the Moabites] in ruins, and each man threw a stone into all the best fields to fill them up, and they blocked every well-spring and felled every sound tree.

—2 Kings 3:25

One day I drove up State Road 518 into Mora and took a right turn at the mill where Doña Adela Arellanes had brought her grains for grinding. The gigantic wheel sat off its axle, quite scuttled. The water channel was now clogged with weeds and small bushes. I drove up toward Guadalupita, thinking of the many trips I had taken this way as a boy to visit my grandparents, Leopoldo and Tamar.

Over a rise in the road I saw a field. There were sad clumps of grass growing between protrusions of stones, large and small. A single strand of rusted barbed wire sagged between weather-grayed fence posts. These all leaned in the same direction, urging me to pass by rather than stop to annoy them.

And I remembered the story my mother told me about this place. I even used the story in a practice sermon for a homiletics class when I was in the seminary.

The professor had passed out slips of paper with different scriptural quotations typed out on them.

"Five minutes, gentlemen. No longer. No shorter," he said. "And I'd like to see a little theology from you. Considering the money they're paying for your education, your bishops would probably appreciate that."

A week later I stood before my peers and the professor and this is the sermon I delivered.

"My text is from the Old Testament, the Second Book of Kings, Chapter Three, Verse Twenty-five. 'The Israelites laid the towns of the Moabites in ruins, and each man threw a stone into all the best fields to fill them up, and they blocked every well-spring and felled every sound tree.'

"I have seen a field like these. It sits between two round hills on the road that goes from the town of Mora to the village of Guadalupita in my home state of New Mexico. It is known locally as El Llanito de Consuelo.

"The land was never good for much. It was too far from the river to irrigate and too full of locoweed and sagebrush for grazing. But for some reason this useless piece of real estate was very important to two families. It sat between their properties and each laid claim to it by right of grant from the Spanish Crown. They had been back and forth in the courts over its ownership for generations. The boundary lines of the field were supposed to be clearly marked by boulders at each corner but there was a dispute as to which boulders were the true ones. It became a question of family pride on both sides to gain exclusive rights to the property. No one ever asked what they would do with it once they got it.

"The field eventually became a thorn of division in the sides of everyone who lived in the valley. 'You must choose between us,' the two feuding families declared to their neighbors.

"Through the years the quarrel boiled over and subsided many times. Words would be spoken, fists would fly, knives would be pulled out, the sheriff would be called in, peace would be restored. And then the anger would simmer underground until something would happen to bring it belching to the surface.

"It was during one of the quiet times that the daughter of one of the families was to be married. Her name was Consuelo.

"Everyone who claimed allegiance to Consuelo's family attended the ceremony at the church. After the wedding, the guests retired to the reception. For reasons that could only be attributed to spite and stupidity, the patriarch of the clan decided to hold the party under a huge canvas tent in the middle of the disputed field.

"There was music, there was dancing, and of course there was drinking. Everyone was having a great time. Everyone, that is, except the other family and their friends. While one side was enjoying the party the other side gathered in town to do some drinking of its own. It wasn't long before they decided that they would have to do something about this insult to their honor. So they mounted horses and buckboards and headed for the field.

"It was not easy to hide their noisy, dust-raising charge. By the time they reached the field the other family was waiting for them at the fence. There were angry words. Someone pushed. Someone shoved. Someone threw a rock and someone else threw one back. Soon they were all throwing things, cursing, and swinging fists and fence posts at each other. Then there was a gunshot. It was never determined who fired it. The only sure thing was that the bullet struck the bride, Consuelo, and passed through her heart to kill her instantly.

"The next day, Consuelo was buried on the spot where she fell. That very night her family returned with wagonloads of boulders, which they scattered everywhere. Now the field was more useless than ever. And it is still that way today. Nothing can grow there. There is nothing of value there. Even the stone that marked Consuelo's grave is lost among the hundreds of others that dot the landscape.

"Christ has told us that our hearts are fields in which He wants to sow the seed of His Gospel. The tender young shoots will wither and die if we do not clear our hearts of the stones we have placed there. Every self-centered, arrogant, or mean-spirited act we perform is just one more life-smothering stone that we have hauled in and discarded. One day, if we are not careful, our hearts will be good for nothing more than to bury our own best intentions."

After the class, the professor handed me a crisply folded paper on which he had written his critique of my talk.

M. Galván
Homiletics
2/9/63
Presentation: You keep shifting your feet.
Try to maintain better eye contact.
Work on your enunciation.
Grade: B-

Content: Read your exegesis texts, Mr. G. The quotation you were given deals with the mandate to the Chosen People to banish evil from their midst so that the Kingdom of Yahweh could be established. That's why they got rid of the Moabites by destroying their fields. The text has nothing to

do with your quaint little story. You don't know enough to take such liberties with holy scripture.
Grade: C-

Of course, he was right. The Israelites and Moabites had nothing to do with Consuelo, her gravesite, or even me.

In my thirty-second year, my seventh as a priest, I, Michael Galván, stopped praying. I no longer prayed for anyone or for anything, not even for myself.

Of course, if I didn't pray, what good was I? I was ordained to pray. I was even paid to pray. But by now my priesthood had literally become a lip service.

"I baptize you . . ."

"I absolve you . . ."

"This is my body . . . this is my blood . . ."

"I pronounce you . . ."

"I anoint you . . ."

"I commend your soul . . ."

These were the formulae I continued to recite over infants, penitents, bread and chalice, bridal couples, the sick, the dead. But there was no part of me behind the talk. Whatever good my words brought to the faithful of the parish was strictly up to God.

Call it burnout. Call it laziness. Call it a loss of confidence in my ability to function. Call it what you want. The reasons for my defection are immaterial to this narrative. What it came down to was that I didn't want to be a priest anymore.

This presented a problem. *Thou art a priest forever.* I could no more undo my Orders than I could undo my baptism. I could turn my back on them but I could not shuck them off like some old coat.

So I decided to turn my back.

I did the minimum. The rest was patchwork. If I felt like being in the office, I sat, with no personal involvement, and handled the problems brought across my desk.

"Father, all me and my wife do anymore is argue and scream at each other."

"Go to a marriage counselor."

"Father, my husband beats me."

"Talk to a lawyer."

"Father, our son is taking drugs."

"See a doctor."

Sound advice. Admirable advice. But my motives were not pure. My only objective was to get rid of these people as quickly as possible.

The beauty of my situation was that, as long as I didn't prance naked on the high altar of the cathedral, no one could tell whether I was a good priest or not. Plumbers are held accountable for leaky faucets. If a farmer doesn't grow things he's out of business. Even a shoe salesman must worry about correct fits. But a priest? Where is the accountability? People don't return babies and say that your last baptism didn't take. No one spits out the Host and claims you performed a faulty consecration Mass. As long as you go through the motions, it's all taken care of for you. If the sacraments are administered, however perfunctorily, God sees to it that grace is imparted, souls are saved. It's the perfect job. Any functionary can do it. Even half sober.

But I couldn't fool everyone. The housekeeper and the parish secretary knew that I was just going through the motions. Time and again they covered up for me.

"Father is not feeling well today."

"Father can't make it for the meeting. Something came up."

My mother was an unwitting beneficiary of this cache of deceit. After all, it was because of me that she rode on the crest of celebrity for almost a decade. Her own dreams of ascendancy had been crushed twice: in the dark, drafty sacristy of Our Lady of Sorrows Church when she became the wife of Miguel, the butcher, and when the back bumper of Magistrate Pacunio Baca's car had dashed Miguelito against an unyielding curb. From the moment of my ordination she had basked in the sun of my success. I was the one to make the leap from Las Vegas. I was revered and respected. I had even met the pope. I was the vicar to Margarita's dreams.

I can't tell you when the drinking started. I do not mean the beer after golf or the scotch at clerical functions.

Somewhere along the way I began to drink alone. I would

sequester myself in my room of an afternoon and have a beer or two while I watched TV or read a trashy novel. I got into the habit of scotch and soda before dinner with quick hits of whiskey so that the liquor and the mixer would come out even at the bottom of the glass. Genteel nightcaps were but a preamble to the moment when I started taking the bottle into my room with me at bedtime.

My bedside alarm was always set for 5:45, enough time to shower, shave, and open up the church for 6:30 Mass. In earlier, more virtuous days, my internal clock snapped my eyes open well before the alarm went off. The drinking changed that.

Now every morning I was jarred into semiconsciousness by the jangle of the clock. I groped for it blindly, shut it off, fell back, and tried to focus on the swirling ceiling above me. It was what I had to do next that most filled me with dread. I knew I must eventually push my legs to the side of the bed until my feet could feel the floor. Then I would endure the fruits of my wantonness, the throbbing head, the churning stomach. The sweats. Worst of all, I would now have to confront the reality of the previous night.

The barometer of my conscience sat next to the clock on the nightstand. The level of liquor in the bottle told all.

And then the trembling would start and would not stop. It stayed with me while I tried to shave, while I fumbled with the buttons of my clothes and cassock, while I walked stiff-legged to the church, and while I struggled to fit the key into the sacristy lock. Out on the altar, my folded hands trembled as I tried to pray. They quivered uncontrollably as I spread my arms in the traditional greeting of the Mass, *The Lord be with you.* They shook when I held them up during the Eucharistic prayer. They only calmed down when I took the wine at Communion.

Take this, all of you, and drink.

All too eagerly, I rushed to obey. I brought the chalice to my lips and drained it. It was my Lord. And He was my first drink of the day.

My ultimate undoing started with the death of a prominent parishioner. The rosary was scheduled at the mortuary. The mayor would be there, as would the vicar general of the archdiocese and various monsignori and priests who had been beneficiaries of the family's favors throughout the years. Everyone showed up.

Except me.

I started drinking early that day, and by evening I was passed out on the couch in the living room. The parish receptionist left at five, but not before shaking my shoulder to remind me that I had to be at the mortuary by seven. The housekeeper left an hour later after telling the back of my head that she had left my dinner in the oven. I stirred at six-thirty and tried to sit up but the room was spinning so wildly that I dropped back. Just a few minutes more. Just enough time so my head could clear.

When I walked out of the church after Mass the next morning and started across the street I noticed an unfamiliar car parked in front of the rectory.

The voice called to me just as I turned up the sidewalk to the house. "Michael."

It was the vicar general, the bishop's strong right hand.

"Monsignor Domínguez. What brings you out at this hour?"

"I'm delivering the eulogy at the funeral today."

The funeral. The mortuary. What had happened with the rosary? Had I been there? I could not remember.

"But the funeral's not until ten."

"I know. I thought we could have a cup of coffee."

"Sure. You should have come in. I never lock."

He walked by me into the house. "We missed you at the rosary last night."

So, I had not gone.

In the kitchen, I wrestled with the innards of the coffee maker.

"We came over and knocked on all the doors and shouted at the windows, but nothing," the vicar said.

I misfired several times before lining up the center hole of the coffee basket with its metal tube.

"It didn't look like anyone was home. I was worried about you. That's why I came over early this morning. I poked my head in the church and was relieved to see you saying Mass."

"I must apologize, Monsignor, to you and to the family. I don't know what happened. I wasn't feeling very well yesterday so I took something. Very strong stuff. The doctor prescribed it the last time I had the flu. It must have knocked me for a loop. How embarrassing."

He eyed me. "Well, just as long as you're all right."

"Oh, yes. Fit as a fiddle. I'm fine, really. Probably just that twenty-four-hour bug that's going around."

"The family was not happy."

"I'll talk to them right after the funeral."

"Why don't you let me handle the service. Go back to bed."

I made too much noise as I banged around the cupboard for some cups. "I'm fine. Really I am."

"Please, Father. You must obey me in this."

There were several other times after the incident with the funeral when my drinking betrayed me. Nothing catastrophic. Missed meetings. Late for Mass by fifteen or twenty minutes. Times when I left the rectory for my day off and failed to return until late the next day.

And then I really screwed up.

My first recollection of that night was a powerful beam of light prying open my eyelids.

"Father?"

"Who are you?"

"I'm Officer Leyba. Are you OK?"

"Of course I'm OK. And will you get that damned light out of my face?"

I tried to push open the door to get out of the car. I couldn't budge it.

"What the hell?"

"You can't get out this way, Father. It's blocked. Try the other side."

With some effort, I slid across the front seat. He was already waiting for me there, bent low to open the door.

"Watch your head, Father."

"What? What's wrong with my head?"

"Nothing. But the roof of the carport came down on your car."

The officer pointed his light and in the wide sweep of its cone I could see that my car was pancaked neatly under the collapsed roof of the carport.

"What's going on here?"

"You took out the supports. Are you hurt?" He shone the light back on me and made me wince.

"I said I was OK."

"Let me drive you to the hospital."

"I'm not going anywhere." I turned to walk away, stumbled on a piece of corrugated vinyl roofing, and fell to the ground.

The officer reached down to take hold of my arm. "I think you'd better come with me, Father."

"Let go of me!" I whipped my arm wildly across his face with enough force to send him reeling backward.

My little act of defiance took me not to a nice, sanitary emergency room, but to a holding cell at the district police station.

Then the phone calls began. The sergeant called his captain. The captain called the chief. The chief called the assistant district attorney. The assistant district attorney called the chancellor. The chancellor called the lawyer for the archdiocese.

While everyone was talking to everyone I found an iron cot, embraced the comfort of its naked springs, and fell asleep.

Returning from a poker party in the next parish I had almost made it home. However, when I turned into my street I jumped the curb and knocked over a street sign. I continued on through my neighbor's newly seeded lawn, crashed through his fence, ripped off the rear bumper of his car, landed back on the street, and veered into the alley behind the rectory. There I took out the back fence of yet another neighbor before finally turning into my driveway. Then auto met carport. And I had finished off my evening by assaulting a police officer while resisting arrest.

The whole thing was kept hush-hush. The lawyer for the diocese accepted all sorts of conditions for my release and got me to the hospital. The admitting doctor's notations on my chart were cryptic. "Blackouts. Cause unknown."

Another cover-up.

The archbishop, of course, was well aware of the cause. Somehow I had to convince him otherwise when I stood at his desk three days later.

"I must have fallen asleep behind the wheel. I haven't been feeling well. The medicine. I shouldn't have taken it just before I climbed into the car."

The archbishop formed a peak with his hands and placed the tips of his fingers just under his lower lip. "Father, Father, Father. I've talked at length with our lawyer. He saw your condition at the police station."

"He exaggerated."

"He barely kept you out of jail."

"I could have handled it."

"No, Father Galván, I don't think so. This isn't the first I've heard of your little problem."

"There is no problem, Your Excellency. Things will be just fine."

He handed me a white sheet of paper. "I'm afraid I can't wait for that, Father."

"What's this?"

"Your letter of reassignment. I'm sending you to St. Clement's."

"Where's Father Cook going?"

"You will be going there as an associate. You will work under Father Cook. I've already talked with him. He understands your situation."

I had lost my parish.

I recalled instantly those of my fellow clergy who had suffered the same fate. They were now shadow-priests who went stoop-shouldered from assignment to assignment in constant recycle throughout the diocese. And now I was one of them.

The letter of reassignment fluttered so violently in my hands that I had to set it down on the desk.

"I need time."

"Of course," the archbishop said. "Go back to your parish. Say your goodbyes. I will expect you out of there before Sunday."

"I'm not sure I can do this."

"It's not your choice, Father. Take a little time off if you want. How long has it been since you spent a few days with your dear parents?"

"I'll let you know." I turned to leave without being dismissed.

"You forgot your letter, Father."

"I already know what it says."

"Father Cook will be keeping me posted on your progress."

"Yes, I'm sure he will."

My goodbye reception in the St. Cajetan parish hall was a thrown-together affair. The ladies of the Altar and Rosary Society served punch and cookies. The men from the Usher's League moved the line of well-wishers by me.

I left most of my belongings behind. No treasures here. Books I

had never read, a black-and-white TV, my golf clubs and shoes, a
fielder's mitt, a tennis trophy, some fishing gear. The rest I piled into
my car with its dented roof and drove away.

Father Cook was not happy to see me.

"Oh, you're early. The archbishop said not to expect you until
the end of the month. I don't even have a room ready for you."

"I just wanted to drop off a few things. I'm on my way to see my
folks."

"Well, I suppose we can find some place for them."

"Fine," I said, the equal parts of anger and envy welling up in me
against him and all others in good standing anywhere, "and in case I
don't show up, you have my permission to burn it all."

I was certain that this would trigger Father Cook's first posting to
the bishop concerning my progress under his watch.

I now turned my attention to Margarita and Miguel. What lie
would I tell them?

"I've been working too hard and it finally caught up with me. The
archbishop wants me to take it easy for a while. He promised me a
parish in Santa Fe by the end of the year."

If they bought my story it was only because they wanted to.

"I'm glad you're home, *hijito*," my father said to me, patted my
back, and went back to the store, his port in any storm.

Margarita said nothing at all except to ask me what I wanted for
supper.

I unloaded my car the next morning, bringing in what was left of
my worldly goods. I knew I would be traveling light from now on.

"It's just a couple of boxes I don't want to lug around until I'm
settled," I explained to my mother, who was kneeling in a flowerbed
in the front yard.

She stabbed the trowel into the dirt with the ferocity of a ditch
digger.

"Make some room in the basement."

The basement was actually just a small room for the furnace and
the water heater. Up high on one wall there was an opening to the
crawl space, which ran under the rest of the house. I hoisted up a carton and began to slide it into the hole. Halfway in I met an obstacle.

"Damn it."

It was one of those overnight cases with a carrying handle. It had once been a light blue but now it was covered with dust, and lines of dirt had etched themselves into the textured grain of its imitation leather.

I snapped the lid open and pushed it back until a metal bracket locked in place. Then I stared, unsure of what I was looking at.

On top was a neatly folded pair of child's overalls, pale gray with white vertical pinstripes. I began to dig and found a pair of wire-rimmed spectacles with one cracked lens, a wrinkled playing card, a tin FDR campaign button, a rubber wheel from some kind of toy, and a wooden top, its belly scratched and splintery, its metal fulcrum pin worn to a nub. Underneath it all was a flat cardboard container the size of a book. Embossed in green in one corner were the words *Prestige Studios*. I undid the flap at one end and tilted the box. A hinged, gilded double frame for photographs slid into my hand. On the left side, encased in a cardboard matte, was a picture of my brother, Luis. He must have been three or four at the time. The frame on the right had a similar matte but no photograph.

By the time I came back upstairs my mother was at the kitchen table sorting a pile of pinto beans into a metal colander.

I sat and placed the case between us. "Look what I found."

She stared at it for what seemed a lifetime before she spoke. "I forgot it was down there."

"Family secrets?"

"Just things I saved."

I held up the overalls by their straps so that they hung down limply like the skin of a small creature. "Luis?"

"Miguelito. He was wearing them when he was hurt. The rest of those things are what he had in his pockets."

I held up the open picture frame. "And this? There's Luis but the other side is blank. Was it Miguelito?"

She gave undue attention to the beans as she spread them across the expanse of the table with the flat of her hand. "No. It was another picture."

"Whose?"

She looked at me for a moment, her eyes a silent plea for mercy. Then she saw that there would be none.

"A week before the accident, a photographer came to town. He set up shop at the Plaza Hotel and left advertisements in doors all over town. He was offering a special, two pictures for the price of one. I can't remember how much it was but it must not have been very much because we didn't have a lot of money. Anyway, I decided to have the boys' pictures taken. So I dressed them up in their Easter outfits and took them over.

"He told me that they were the most handsome boys he had ever seen. I knew he was just saying that about Luis to make me feel good. But I could tell that he saw something special in Miguelito. The way he spent so much time with him, getting the lights just right, running back and forth from the camera to fix Miguelito's collar or to brush the hair from his forehead. Things like that. He told me that I would get the pictures in about a month. Then Miguelito got hurt and I forgot about everything."

We sat in silence while she finished sorting the beans and emptied them into the colander. Finally she spoke again.

"And sure enough, after about a month the package came. I didn't even unwrap it. I put it in a drawer and tried to forget about it. When I finally unwrapped it there was a note from the photographer. It's probably still in the box."

I shook the container and a yellowed piece of paper fell out.

Dear Mrs. Galván (I read to myself),

Enclosed is the work which I did for you. I'm afraid I have some bad news. The photograph of one of your sons did not come out. I don't know what happened. This is the first time something like this has happened to me. There seems to be a cloud across the negative which I could not correct. Since I promised you two photos for the price of one I have taken the liberty of sending you a much nicer frame than the one you paid for. I hope this makes up in some way for the camera's malfunction.

Sincerely,
R. Cobley

I put down the note. "Too bad."

My mother scooped the beans back into the colander, went to the sink, and began to run water over them. "On the right, where Miguelito's picture should have been, there was another picture. I guess it came from the factory. The photographer just left it so the frame wouldn't look so bare. It was a picture of St. Thérèse, the Little Flower. I took it out and burned it, may God forgive me."

Then Margarita told me everything. She talked about her three dreams, the one with the river when Tina died, the one with the calla lily that foreshadowed Nasha's accident, and the one with the white tablecloth and its unspeakable secret. She told me about Miguelito's heart problems at birth and how the nun had advised her, warned her of the Little Flower's potent powers of intervention. She told me how she had all but forgotten her bargain with the gentle Carmelite until that first day of October four years later when Miguelito was killed. She told me about my name and how I came to be called Michael rather than Miguelito.

"How could there ever be another Miguelito? I think God made a mistake. I don't think He meant things to turn out this way."

Then she looked at me, not unkindly but with a certain objectivity that I could only accept in humility. "I thought maybe, if it wasn't to be Miguelito who made us proud, it might be you. I guess God made another mistake."

I lasted with Father Cook for two months.

The chancellor handed me the new letter of assignment while I was packing my suitcase in the hospital room where I had spent a week drying out.

"Father Cook was more than patient with you, Michael. But he just could not have you running drunk through the rectory while he was trying to conduct parish business."

I worked to generate some saliva so I could talk. I was trembling so furiously that I had to cross my arms and clamp my hands under my armpits to steady them. "I understand. The doctor says it's nothing physical. I've just got to straighten out my brain. I know I can do that."

"The archbishop is counting on it. We're moving you out of Albuquerque to Socorro. You'll be with Father Haskell."

"Yes, I know Father Haskell well. I served Mass for him when I was a kid. He's a good man."

From Socorro I was reassigned to Roswell, then Tucumcari. and finally Los Alamos. Each time I tried to be useful when I was sober, and I raised hell when I wasn't. Each time it ended badly, with me back in some hospital.

After my last screw-up, the chancellor was back in the hospital room with me on my release. He had seen me pack my bag so often that I almost asked him to do it for me, since I was making such a bad job of it.

"Where to now, Monsignor? I don't think we've tried the north yet. Taos? Arroyo Seco? Costilla?"

"The archbishop wants to see you. Would this afternoon be convenient?"

"Sure. I don't have any place else to go."

Apparently that was not quite true.

The archbishop shook his head as he shook my hand. "Michael, Michael, Michael. What to do, what to do?"

"I don't know what to say, Archbishop. I thought this time I had it licked."

"Like the time before, Father? And the time before that?" He pointed me to a chair.

"Just give me another chance, Excellency."

"Michael, where can I send you? You've burned many bridges. Many priests have stuck their necks out for you, including me. Yet you continue to abuse this trust."

"Perhaps another diocese? Somewhere that I can make a new start."

"And in conscience would you have me do that to a fellow bishop?"

"I think a change of scenery would do me a lot of good."

"I agree. Only I was thinking of Jémez."

And thus I was informed that I had hit bottom.

Jémez. A group of mountains in the Nacimiento Range. An Indian pueblo. A town.

But for the clergy, Jémez meant something much different. In the high country north of Albuquerque was a place where bishops sent priests—alcoholics, pedophiles, homosexuals, thieves, philanderers, gamblers—when there was no place else to send them. It was a sanitarium, or better still, a confinement.

"Just a couple of months," the archbishop assured me. "Enough time, I should hope, for you to think things through. And then we'll see."

The director pushed open the door of the room that was to be mine. "Here we go. Make yourself comfortable. Vespers are in the chapel at 5:00. Obligatory."

He started to walk out the door and then stopped. "Oh, and Father, may I have the keys to your car? We might have to move it during the night and I would hate to bother you."

I tossed him the keys. "How about my shoelaces?"

"I beg your pardon?"

"Skip it. Bad joke."

He quietly shut the door behind him.

After checking to see if I had been locked in—I hadn't—I sat on the bed next to the open suitcase. My Roman collar lay on top of my clothes. The bag, once jammed with my possessions, now had room to spare. I had left part of myself behind at every parish I'd been in.

"We hope you will take serious stock of yourself during your stay at Jémez," the archbishop had said to me. "With God's grace we can all learn from bad situations."

And what would I learn here that I did not already know? That I had failed miserably? That I was unfit for the priesthood? Suddenly I had to laugh out loud. I remembered someone else once counseling me to learn from a bad situation. It was Pope John XXIII.

It happened during my seminary days at the North American College in Rome. The West Point for priests, it was called. Anyone ordained from here had to be a bishop or at least a monsignor by the age of fifty or be considered a failure. Pope John was making a state visit to us, his *homage* to the Church in the United States.

The central corridor of the building was equipped with two elevators, which climbed the six stories from the courtyard to the penthouse. I was assigned to operate one of these elevators on the morning of the pope's visit.

On the great day, and only a few minutes behind schedule, I found myself face to face with Good Pope John.

Behind him, ecclesiastics in red, purple, or black were talking and gesticulating. Amid the genial confusion the pope entered my elevator, followed closely by two bishops. Just then, some Vatican factotum in velvet knickers rushed forward. Whether he had detected some breach in protocol or he was merely acting on the lackey's primeval need to insinuate, rearrange, and rescript, it was hard to tell. His voice, high pitched and strident as any Latin teacher running through declensions, sliced through the hubbub to freeze all parties in their tracks. Embarrassed, the two bishops hopped obediently out of the elevator. The pontiff turned in the smallish cubicle and brushed me away from the control panel. Before he could step out, the doors slid closed. The last I saw of his entourage was a view of its collegiate mouth dropping.

I lunged forward, neatly sidestepping the pope's belly, hit the panel with my open hand, and depressed every button on the board. We would now be ascending the entire six floors one stop at a time, me and the vicar of Christ.

One of us managed to remain calm.

"*Va bene,*" the pope said. "*Allora, cosa faranno?*"

What they did was to run like hell up the stairs next to the elevator. We could hear them shouting while their patent leather shoes rapped sharply against the marble steps.

When the door opened on the *primo*, then the second floor, the pope tried to step out. What to do? Get him back to the ground floor. That seemed the best plan. I certainly could not abandon him in an empty corridor.

"*Non ancora, Santita,*" I advised him.

They finally caught up with us on the fourth floor. A hard-breathing Swiss Guard in plainclothes rammed his arm into the car as the door was closing and pushed me aside. Then he ordered me to leave, barking at me in a guttural Italian that betrayed his Swissness.

"*No, no,*" the pope said as he laid a hand on my arm. "*Sta bene.*"

When we finally got back to the ground floor and just before I was plucked away by the absolutely apoplectic vice-rector of the college, Pope John patted me on the cheek. "There must be something we can learn from this. When you decide what, let me know."

Now I sat on a small bed, confined and abandoned.

So what could I learn from this? What had almost eight years in the priesthood taught me that would be of use to me now?

I placed my Roman collar on the pillow at the head of the bed. Then I fished into a corner of the suitcase and found my extra set of keys.

When I walked out the front door I was relieved to see that they had not yet found an excuse to impound my car.

It was getting on about vespers when I turned onto the highway from the gravel road, picked up speed, and headed toward the just-beginning-to-twinkle lights of Albuquerque.

And so it was done.

I had separated myself from everyone and everything—from my priesthood, from my Church, from New Mexico, from Margarita Juana.

In 1971, while waiting on a customer, my Uncle Joaquín, my father's business partner for two generations, died of a massive stroke, dead before he hit the oiled floor of the store.

Luis resigned his position as a teacher of history at the local high school and took over the store's management. To my father's amazement, considering it was a threat he had lived under for forty years, the business did not collapse without Joaquín.

That same year I made a formal request to Rome to be relieved of my priestly duties. Had I done this when the Church was still the Church of my youth I would have been subjected to months, perhaps years of paper shuffling and endless scrutinies and even then my chances for lancination would have been slim. But, in all the confusion after the Second Vatican Council, when so much of this kind of thing was going on, my thin stack of documents was rubber stamped and in the return mail before the priest at the appropriate desk within the Roman Curia had taken his second cup of espresso for the day.

After my flight into the Jémez twilight, I eventually looked to Denver to fulfill my promise. This city did considerably better by me than it had by my mother when she was young and so full of hope.

I went back to school to learn the writer's trade and made my living thereafter as a freelancer scripting ad copy for TV and radio and writing industrial and educational videos.

I did not stop drinking immediately and found myself in the hospital to dry out every six to eight months. After each incident, I vowed to reform. It was during one of these stays that I met a woman, a nurse who helped care for me. I fell in love with her.

Hopeful of gaining her respect and affection, I decided to face my demons. So I joined AA.

After a year of sobriety, I called up my nurse, who eventually became my wife. We had two children.

With the help of my wife, I became a good son. We made the six-hour drive from Denver to Las Vegas every six weeks or so. Eventually, Margarita accepted my defection, due for the most part, I suspect, to the gentleness and love that my wife showed her. About me, Margarita always seemed to manifest a studied indifference. She never asked me what I did, how I did it, or how happy it made me. I really don't think she cared.

Chapter Twenty-Nine

1984

In 1980, my mother began at last to live in her dreams, or at least in a nightmare chamber with walls of tightly intermeshing threads, nerves held together and plastered over by a starchy binder. It was the year she began to show advancing memory loss and a fractious dislocation from reality. It was the year she began to die. She was sixty-seven years old. We calculated that her death occurred when she was seventy-five, when she slipped entirely away from us, no longer responding to any words nor forming any of her own. We buried her when the doctor said we could, when she was seventy-nine and her heart finally got the message that there was nothing left of her that was worth keeping alive.

Such is the course of Alzheimer's. To watch a person linger from it is to see a personality stripped away, layer by layer, until there is nothing left of that creature except a flayed-to-the-bone psyche, a skeleton of chalky white coral.

It was during one of our visits in the eighth year of my defrocking and the sixth of my marriage that we began to notice an insidious difference in Margarita Juana.

She would be talking to us, lose her train of thought in the middle of a sentence, grapple for a concept, a memory, or even a simple word, and finally exclaim, "Isn't that funny. I used to know that."

We would find small articles, ashtrays, eggbeaters, lids to saucepans, in odd places—under the bed, in the refrigerator, in the washing machine.

When we asked her about it she always answered, "I have no idea."

My father's ready response was, "She just wants to keep things out of reach of the kids."

Finally on one of these visits, we came face to face with the devil that was slowly claiming possession of my mother and for whom there was no exorcism. Even my dormant priestly powers, to be used in emergencies only, were useless.

We had gone to bed after an evening of watching Margarita pace from room to room like a house pet, its latent instincts tuned to an ancient call from the dark outside. Nothing we could do or say would get her to sit down and relax with us.

My father explained her behavior away. "She's nervous about the leak in the roof. She and me. We're getting old and old people do things like that. You'll see."

My wife finally talked her into taking a warm bath. She toweled her, rubbed her with sweet-smelling talcum, and put her to bed.

It was sometime during the night when I felt a hand shaking my shoulder.

I sputtered to wakefulness, sure that I had been snoring and angry that my wife expected me to do something about it.

Then I heard a soft moan. My wife turned on the bedside light and we both sat up.

There in a corner of the room, in a padded wing chair that she herself had upholstered, huddled Margarita Juana. Her legs were drawn up underneath her and her arms were wrapped tightly around her upper body. She looked no bigger than my seven-year-old daughter. I could see the whites of her eyes completely encircling her pupils. Her look darted from the window to the door to the bed where we lay, my wife and I.

"Can I stay here?" she asked. "I'll be quiet."

"What is it, Mom? Aren't you feeling well?"

"Those men," she said. "They're looking at me through all the windows. And they won't go away."

The next morning, my father cried. He admitted to us that this sort of thing had been going on for months. The pacing. The constant pacing. The paranoia. She never slept. He seldom could.

When the professionals talk about Alzheimer's they talk about a thirty-six-hour day. That's how long each day seems to last for those with the condition and for those living with them. The hours go on and on. Each minute stretches with slow, agonizing elasticity until it is difficult to remember its beginning or see its end. It is as if the earth has expanded, gotten fat and lazy, and slowed its spin to an almost imperceptible quiver.

This was the clock by which my mother's brain now told time.

And my father, who would not let go of her hand, was pulled with her into this snail-paced vortex of bloated seconds, minutes, and hours.

"I don't mind," he insisted. "Luis takes care of the store, so I can spend more time here with her. I take naps while I'm watching the TV. I don't mind, not for my *reina*."

And his queen would demand even more of her only remaining subject before she was finally done with him.

Six weeks later, we were back in Las Vegas for a funeral.

My brother, Luis, was dead. A heart attack at the age of fifty-one. My mother had lost her second son but this time, mercifully, she was not present for the grieving. By now "those men" were gone. Perhaps the thicket of the tangled nerve fibers in her head had gotten too dense for them to cut through, or the plaque had so thickly cal-cimined the windows of her soul that they could no longer peer in. Whatever the reason, they had moved on to press their faces against other panes of glass, to set other people to pacing and to wringing their hands through the night.

Now Margarita had only smiles for everyone, mysterious, small, upward curvings of her mouth while she conversed and conspired innocently with the friendlier phantoms that now peopled her brain.

"How nice," she would say. "How pretty. Oh, yes."

And the mourners for my brother and sympathy givers who passed her chair in her living room in her dream house smiled back. They made it a point to tell us how peaceful she looked and how much she seemed to understand what they said to her.

When the last of them was gone with empty, encrusted casseroles and foil-wrapped turkey carcasses and ham bones, I announced that I was going to take my mother for a walk. "Maybe I'll drive her down to the park. Walk around the plaza for a bit. Get her nice and tired so we can all have a good night's sleep."

We stood under a cottonwood in the plaza. It was the same tree that Margarita had sat under as a girl. The same where she waited for her father to finish his business at the lumberyard so she could take the money from him to keep until she turned it over to Tamar. It was the tree she had sat under as Luis played on her lap and she watched her marvelous Miguelito run across the grass and laugh at how splendid life was and he was.

It was late spring, and the old cottonwood was just creaking open its pods to let the whiteness fly. Down came the wispy tufts around and on us. They stuck to our hair and our eyelashes.

"Oh, look. It's snowing." Margarita held out a hand to catch some of the cotton.

I stared at her. She had not articulated a thought in weeks and I had not seen such a clarity and confidence in her eyes in years.

"And look at the beautiful castle," she said and pointed to the duchess on the square that is the Plaza Hotel.

Margarita Juana had finally found her way back to the home of the old hunchback Don Florencio and his blind wife Doña Clara and into that crystal globe with its enchanted winterscape and its fairy-tale castle.

She should have known all along. Here and only here would she find the answer to her dreams.

"Walk with me, Miguelito," she said.

She took my hand and kicked, like a playful little girl, at the cotton tufts swirling around us.

"Walk with me through the snow."

1990

We closed *La Tienda* after Luis died. Now Miguel Galván could devote his full time to his reina.

When we visited them, my father and I would sit in the living room watching cable TV. He preferred the boxing matches. Margarita Juana, long past awareness, sat in a wheelchair by my father's Strato-lounger, her head lolled to one side, a terry-cloth bib scrunched underneath her chin.

"Your mother looks good, doesn't she, *hijito*?"

"Yes, Dad."

"I love her so much."

"I know you do. You've been a good husband."

"You like to watch the boxing?"

"Yes, Dad."

"She does too. She laughs when someone gets knocked down."

The bell rang, announcing the beginning of a new round, and the boxers squared off. After three more bloody or bloodless minutes, I really wasn't paying attention, the conversation picked up again.

"That was a good round."

"Yes, Dad."

"He's a good little fighter, the one in green. He makes the sign of the cross before every round. I like to see that. It's nice."

"He's Mexican, Dad. They all do that."

"I hope your mother dies first, but not for a long time."

"Yes, Dad."

"But if I die first, promise me you won't send her to a nursing home."

"Yes, Dad."

I lied. I had to.

Even as the all-too-familiar group of mourners filled the house after my father's funeral I was on the phone making the arrangements.

While I waited for the administrator of the nursing facility to ring up some figures I looked over to where Margarita sat.

She was in her wheelchair. Her sparse hair, earlier slicked back with a comb dipped in water, had dried, and wisps of it were waving back and forth with the movement of people walking by her. The angles of her skull caught the light from the window and shone with a ghostly glisten. Her teeth, those few that still remained, jutted over her bottom lip. She looked, sitting there in her wheelchair with her hanks of hair and the rictus across her mouth, like the wooden carving of that skeletal crone on the *carreta de muerte*.

After Margarita's death in the nursing home eighteen months later, when all the mourners had left, I told my wife that I was going for a drive.

We had buried my father with enough space between him and Miguelito for my mother. She would have wanted to lie next to her marvelous son, and Miguel would be content as long as he was somewhere close to her.

I took a shovel from the trunk of the car, dug a hole between Miguelito and Margarita, and buried the overnight case filled with those relics that my mother had never known what to do with.

New Mexico is a state of mind that still holds sway with a cozy fatalism. It is a prison so subtle that few try to escape.

And the santos, those saints carved from cottonwood, look on. Their eyes are unblinking, black and deep.

Careful.

If you stare too long into those eyes they might swallow you up and you might fall into nothingness.

Then again, you might float through to the promise beyond, far from here, this land of unfulfilled dreams.

Only the cottonwood saints know for sure.

Acknowledgments

Cottonwood Saints is a work of fiction. It is based on forty hand-written pages of reminiscences which my mother, Margaret Ortega Guerin, committed to a spiral notebook. Without her memories there would be no book. Should anyone take umbrage over a character or a set of events, I accept full responsibility. I can only say that I assumed the novelist's prerogative of exaggeration, fabrication and manipulation for the sole purpose of a good story.

I used many sources to set the historical context of the book. May I particularly recommend Howard Bryan's *Wildest of the Wild West* to anyone interested in a rip-roaring visit to Las Vegas, New Mexico, a town that, in its heyday, made Dodge and Tombstone look like Sunday school picnics.

This book took about eight years to write, mainly because it was done in fits and starts while I learned the skills and discipline that a novel demands. Along the way I had a great deal of help. Thanks are due to:

Rex and Sharon Brown, who read two very shaky opening chapters and saw something.

Robin Cerwonka, who sloshed through six hundred pages of an early draft and didn't lose her enthusiasm.

Toni Lopopolo, who practically grabbed me by the scruff of the neck and showed me the difference between a writer and a hack.

The librarians at the Park Hill Library in Denver, who allowed me squatter's rights at a table by a window for over two years while I wrote, researched and pestered them for arcane books - how to drive a Model T Ford comes to mind.

Beth Hadas, my editor at the University of New Mexico Press, who oversaw my ordeal of cutting over 100,000 words from a bloated manuscript and then patiently and skillfully helped me hone what was left into something publishable.

But most of all, I thank my wife, Rita. As often as I tossed the project into a desk drawer with the vow of never touching it again, she was there to bring it back to life. And she's a pretty good editor/reader in the bargain.

Thanks also to my children, Philip and Rebecca. From the beginning, there was no doubt in their minds that I could do it. I hope that I have met their expectations.

I thank Joe Berninger who declared the book a masterpiece. No matter that he happened to be my newly acquired son-in-law.

And a special thought for dear Katra.

Lastly, thanks to my grandson, Luke. Just because.